Lucy Ayrton has an MA in Crea̶ University, and is a novelist and p̶ novel, *One More Chance*, the story̶ imprisonment and addiction, wa̶ Dialogue Books and was a finalist in ̶ wrote and performed two full-length spoken word shows at the Edinburgh Festival, which were respectively turned into a poetry pamphlet and a radio play. She also competed as a national finalist at the UK Poetry Slam. Lucy is a lecturer at Oxford University.

'Brilliant.' – *Daily Mail*

'This moving story of grief and loneliness is beautifully told and the characters are so vivid and memorable, I couldn't stop thinking of them.' – *Good Housekeeping*

'Tingling with the tension of complex family dynamics and friendship, and the swell of secrets, this is a richly resonant novel of our time.' – *LoveReading*

'A riveting read.' – *i News*

'A vivid and affecting journey into the heart of Jenny, the main character, but also the heart of a community, and the heart of a family. A moving exploration of self, family, and what it means to be truly "home", this novel will grab your heart and never let go.' – Suzette Mayr, author of *The Sleeping Car Porter*

'An elegant, assured novel about family, friendships, secrets and the push-pull of home ... A poignant story of the earth opening up under your feet and what is revealed as things fall apart.' – Priscilla Morris, author of *Black Butterflies*

'A finely-drawn and relatable tale of family and friendship, and how our past shapes who we become. I thoroughly enjoyed this story, with its artful writing and beautifully-crafted setting. A writer to watch!' – Laurie Petrou, author of *Stargazer*

'A moving depiction of grief and isolation told in beautiful prose. The characters are so well-drawn and memorable – I can't stop thinking about them!' – Angela Chadwick, author of *XX*

Also by Lucy Ayrton

One More Chance

THINGS WE LOSE IN WAVES

LUCY AYRTON

RENE
GADE

RENEGADE BOOKS

First published in Great Britain in 2023 by Dialogue Books
This paperback edition published in 2024 by Renegade Books

10 9 8 7 6 5 4 3 2 1

A CIP catalogue record for this book is available from the British Library.

Paperback ISBN 978-0-349-70189-9

Typeset in Berling by M Rules
Printed and bound in Great Britain by Clays Ltd, Elcograf S.p.A

Papers used by Renegade Books are from well-managed forests
and other responsible sources.

MIX
Paper | Supporting
responsible forestry
FSC® C104740

Renegade Books
An imprint of Dialogue
Carmelite House
50 Victoria Embankment
London EC4Y 0DZ

The authorised representative
in the EEA is
Hachette Ireland
8 Castlecourt Centre
Dublin 15, D15 XTP3, Ireland
(email: info@hbgi.ie)

www.dialoguebooks.co.uk

Dialogue, part of Little, Brown Book Group Limited,
an Hachette UK company.

For Mum and Dad and Yorkshire – still my home.

High on the storm-torn coast of Iceland
February Sixty-Eight
Ross Cleveland out of Hull lay hiding
With anxious eyes her skipper waits

Gale force twelve and the black ice building
Blinding snow and the radar gone
On the cruel rocks of Ísafjörður
She'll be thrown before the dawn

from *Harry Eddom*
by Bill Meek

CORRASION

Spring 2020

Jenny had been staring blankly out of the window of Chris's cab. The stretches of grass, the squat grey houses, the sharp drop down to the sea. She wasn't expecting to see this landscape again until summer, at least. Christmas, if she was honest. She hadn't been coming back a lot, but there wasn't time to feel guilty about that now. There were things to do.

This coastline was as familiar to her as anything else in life, and much more so than the shine and hard lines of London. She barely even registered it, eyes skating over the white dots of caravans, the looming hulk of the ruined hotel, the brown crumble of the cliffs, until she saw the road.

'Stop!'

It used to be a road. Now there was just a jutting of pipes and wires into air where there should be solid land. Where she was sure there used to be solid land.

He didn't look round, but Jenny could practically hear Chris rolling his eyes.

'What?'

And he was heading straight for it. Not checking his speed, not showing any indication that his plan was to do anything other than drive straight off the cliff.

Jenny let herself picture it – the full force of forward thrust, the moment of weightlessness, of soaring, gliding, before the fall. Smash and crush onto the beach below. It happened to the caravans, sometimes, and you never got used to the shock of seeing them down there, their insides spilled and churned by the force of the impact.

She swallowed.

'Nothing.'

He swerved right without indicating, and they lurched down the coastal road – which, now she'd had a chance to think, she remembered was the main way into the village now – that he'd taken her down when she came home for Christmas. This road was far too close to the shoreline for comfort, but it undeniably existed.

'You not seen a wrecked road before?'

Jenny chewed her lip beneath her face mask. Chris wasn't wearing one, and he'd given her a proper dirty look when she'd got in the back of his cab. She'd tried to tell herself that it was just because he didn't recognise her with the mask, but of course he did. Like it or not, they'd never not know each other.

'It's further back, isn't it?'

Surely there'd been more road last time she'd lived here. Surely it hadn't just stopped like that.

'It's a metre a year.'

Jenny rolled her eyes. A level geography and being driven around by Chris Blower. It was like sixth form all over again. 'Yeah. I know.'

'So how long have you been away? Fifteen years, right? Fifteen metres. It in't rocket science.'

Jenny sighed. 'Yeah, yeah. All right.'

There'd been a time when she would never have sighed at Chris. She simply wouldn't have dared. For all of her teenage years, she'd lived in fear of a cutting word or a hard look from him. It seemed laughable now, but there was a time when him calling her a geek could have ruined a whole term for her.

Such a lovely idea, that that was the worst thing that could possibly happen.

He caught her eye in the rear-view mirror. 'I aren't about to drive you off the cliff, you know,' he said, voice soft for once.

And the two of them looked at each other. Except they didn't. They were both just looking at the mirror.

'Yeah. I know,' she said. But she wondered. 'Cheers. Just on the left here.'

He curled his lip at her. Like she was eleven again and had committed some crime against his idea of what being cool might mean.

'Yeah. I know.'

Jenny unbuckled her seat belt before the car had stopped moving. She had spent the twenty-minute trip frowning at her phone and not talking to him, trying hard to project the impression that it was because she had a series of important work emails to attend to, rather than that she simply didn't want to. Chris had not felt the need to make up any kind of excuse as to why he didn't want to talk to Jenny.

He pulled up and cut the engine dead. Flicking his eyes to her in the rear-view mirror, he said, 'You want me to get your bags out, then?'

She'd let him put her bags in the back when he'd picked her up in Driffield. She'd packed in a hurry, back in London, and way, way too much. Clothes for all seasons, fifteen books, hair straighteners. A ridiculous amount. She'd wanted to be prepared. She wasn't sure for what.

'I . . . No. I'll do it.'

He hadn't used hand sanitiser once, in the entire trip. Which was a stupid thought, she knew. If there was any germ spreading going on, it was almost certain that she was bringing the virus up from London, not that she'd catch it here. They were saying they might shut London down, or even the whole country, even the pubs. They were saying not to travel unless it was necessary. They said a lot of things. This was necessary.

With an effort, Jenny pulled her bags out of the boot and set them down on the pavement. Her bigger bag hit the ground with an accusing thunk. Like she was going to finally read *White Teeth* now, when she'd owned it for ten years and not even opened the cover.

Chris craned his head out of the window.

'What you got in there? Rocks?'

Jenny very nearly rolled her eyes. Nearly.

'Haha. Yeah. Books.'

She was done now, with this small talk, with this endless journey, with this endless week of sad administration and frantic news refreshes when she was meant to be working. They hadn't locked her down, and she was here. Now all she wanted was a cup of tea, made far too weak, the way she'd liked it when she was a teenager, and a spot on the sofa. *Pointless* would be on. A blissful end to thinking.

'Not tins?'

Jenny reached for her smaller bag, the one with her chargers and laptops and expensive toiletries she'd be sad to see stolen. There'd been so much space on the way up she'd put it on the seat next to her. Normally she couldn't guarantee that even she'd get to sit down on the train, today her bag had had its pick.

'What?'

Chris jerked his head towards her parents' house. Her mother's house. She had to remember. 'Everyone knows she's got food stockpiled,' Chris said. His voice had a note of real anger to it, not just his usual sarky patter. He was really upset. 'Mountains of cans. She's well known for it. Makes sure she's all right, does our Alison.'

'No she doesn't,' Jenny said automatically. But how would she know? It might be true. She hadn't checked the cupboards. And she wouldn't. Over these next few days, she'd be being kind to her mother, and helping to sort things, and minding her business.

'Course she does. Everyone knows. Has done for years.'

He was glaring at the house, like he wanted to set it on fire.

Jenny felt a throb of defensiveness and irritation, and something else. Worry. Was Chris struggling for food? Was Si?

'Why?' she said.

He turned his glare on her. 'I suppose the shops never run out of anything in London. You don't need to plan. Just get yourself a Deliveroo and get on with your life, don't you? Everything all right there.'

She blinked. Well. Yes. That was true.

'You run out of food? Like, often?'

She couldn't help herself from sounding awkward as she asked it. Once, she'd asked Alex why she didn't pay for her lunch. Chris had slammed his fist into the wall by her head and shouted at her so loud, the whole lunch room had turned around and hot tears had rolled down her face and onto the baked potato that she always paid for, her dad making sure to give her enough for lunch and a little something at break time every day. She didn't know she was meant to ignore Alex not paying, that was all. She hadn't meant anything by it.

This felt like that.

'Wouldn't expect you to understand.'

She found herself prickling. They were both grown-ups now, weren't they? And it wasn't like she was having an easy year. 'Well, it's all of us now. Empty shelves in London too.'

His face didn't change. He'd always understood how to intimidate people, Chris, even when he was a little boy. Stillness and movement, unpredictable. Building the tension and catching you by surprise. When he spoke his voice was hard as flint.

'I see the news.'

But Jenny was too old for Chris's bullshit now. She wasn't in sixth form and she knew all the tricks.

'Well. Cheers anyway,' she said, making sure her voice didn't sound as if she was remotely thankful.

She reached into her purse and pulled out a couple of twenty-pound notes, pleased with herself that she'd remembered to go to a cashpoint, that no one here accepted cards ever, as if you'd travelled back in time twenty years as well as two hundred miles north.

Chris raised an eyebrow at her and she immediately felt like she'd done something wrong. He was always like this when he was on shift. Even he couldn't bring himself to be outright rude to a paying customer, so he got really sarky and passive aggressive instead. She'd forgotten.

'That's thirteen pounds, love.'

She tried to smile, but she was still wearing the mask and she wouldn't have been at all surprised if it hadn't reached her eyes. She handed over a note and he started a laborious count of pound coins. Jenny imagined all the different hands that'd been on them. All the germs.

'Keep the change,' she said, and he did it again, that eyebrow lift that made her feel like somehow she was in trouble, like she was thirteen again and she stood accused, as she always had been, of the crime of being uncool.

'Serious?'

Jenny shrugged.

'Cheers,' he said, in a way that still wasn't entirely friendly. He'd be on the phone to Si and Alex as soon as he pulled out of her parents' – no, just her mum's now, she had to remember – driveway. Well, let them talk. She wasn't going to see them anyway, except for the funeral, and that was different. A time apart, not real life. She'd be going back to her real life soon.

'See ya,' she said, flatly, and she slipped her mask off. The world smelled of salt and seaweed rather than the musty ghost of her own breath that was all she could smell inside it.

'Eh up. Jenny.'

She turned around, braced for another little jab. Some humiliation dredged up from school, perhaps, or something about her clothes. Everyone always had opinions on her clothes, up here. She was always wearing too much, or not enough. She never seemed to get it right.

'Sorry about your dad.'

Jenny blinked. She hadn't cried all day. She'd been busy.

It had been a blessing. It'd be good to at least get into her mum's house before she did.

'Thanks,' she said, but she was talking to empty air. He'd already roared away.

She picked up the bags again and turned to her mother's front door. It opened before she could get out her key.

On the short walk over to her late father's pub, Jenny let herself dawdle and look up. Ravenspurn was built on two levels – below, one pub, a Co-op and a raggedy collection of charity shops and shut-up fish and chip bars and tourist kiosks, with a grubby promenade dividing them from the sea like it was holding the buildings back. Above, there were the cliffs, with the caravan park and the hotel ruins and no houses anymore, not that anyone lived in at least. The face of the old hotel still stood high on the edge of the cliff, poised as if about to jump. Jenny didn't know how many years it had been since the hotel closed its doors. How close had the cliff edge got before the owners had given up and got out? The grounds, at least, must have crumbled away, taking outbuildings and tennis courts down with them, smashing to the beach below. Surely they hadn't waited until the actual rooms collapsed. Jenny pictured guests still in there, the ground disintegrating beneath them, what was once solid land sliding away, leaving only insubstantial air. Maybe. Round here, people didn't let go of anything without a fight.

Now, the hotel was just a front wall, standing improbably straight against the dark grey sky. It had been closed and decaying for a long time, but unlike the railway station and the grand cafe down on the beach, it hadn't been knocked down and replaced with cheap housing that nobody wanted; it wasn't safe to build up there. All the big institutions of the once-grand seaside resort of Ravenspurn were lost for ever now.

As to the rest – it was hard for Jenny to tell. The shops and the ice-cream stands had an abandoned, dusty sort of look about them, but then the summer season hadn't started yet. March had always been a month of waiting, here – until the sea and the air heated up, the village always seemed to be holding its breath.

The same as everywhere else, this year.

Jenny made her way across the lower part of the village, the part that was beach level, safe from crumble and tilt. She had two heavy carrier bags in one hand, and in the other hand, the keys. Her dad's keys – or at least, they had been. Her mother plodded beside her, staring at the floor. She didn't look up to the old hotel. Had Jenny looked up when she still lived here? Surely she had. But did she marvel at the sights in London, or did she just trudge about her life? Surely she looked up sometimes. A coffee on the Embankment with Ben, a run through the park with Priya. Surely she appreciated life more than her mother did. Sometimes, at least?

But when she got to the door of The Railway, her dad's old pub, Jenny didn't let herself hesitate for a moment. She had her mother to think of, as well as herself, and there was no point in making it hurt more. She turned the key and pushed.

Jenny took a deep breath in. Salt and smoke and spilt beer and memories, all layered on top of each other so that you couldn't quite tell what was now and what was then and what really happened and what you maybe just dreamed of. Her dad's old pub, a part of her childhood and a part of her, was still the same as it ever was. As if he was going to walk right in from the back office and have a go at her for not having the till on yet. As if Alex and Si were going to roll in, eighteen again and still in her life, still the biggest part of her life, and light up fags and cackle and grin.

It was just ghosts, though.

'Here. This'll do.'

Her mother stomped in after her. Alison did not stop to breathe in the smell of Lambert and Butler mixed with sea air – the smell of her late husband, Ted. She was not a sentimental woman. She walked straight over to the biggest table, the one by the corner window that Chris Blower always got to sit in when he was out, and dropped the carrier bags of funeral food she was carrying onto it. They hit with a rustle and thump. Horribly final.

'I don't know why you insisted on having it here.'

Jenny smiled brightly, the fakeness of it aching in her cheeks. She tried to look happy to be here, in this bar so painfully full of her father that it throbbed with him. 'It was his favourite place. The place everyone knew him.'

That was true, at least. And that was the point of this, wasn't it? Dad. What he would have wanted. One last thing she could do.

Jenny put her own handful of carriers down. A tinfoil-wrapped bundle of sandwiches rolled out of one of the bags and onto the table. Jenny saw that there were still the odd few flecks of fag ash there. This was odd, partly because Jenny had told Uncle Pete to pay Alex a bit extra to do a proper deep clean the day before, and partly because smoking had been banned in pubs for nearly fifteen years now.

Alison didn't notice. She was scowling around the bar. 'Dingy, this pub. I was always telling him.'

The bags had made deep red welts across Jenny's palms. She held up a hand, examining it. It didn't hurt. She couldn't feel it at all.

'It's where people will want to come to say goodbye,' she said, and she busied herself setting the food they'd brought with them out on the bar. They wouldn't be taking any money tonight; her dad would have died of shame. He probably wouldn't have liked that no one would be pulling pints and all there'd be would be bottles, but it was that or make Si and Alex work, which hadn't seemed fair, and would also have meant that she'd have had to phone Si and Alex.

Alison sniffed. She wasn't helping with the food. 'He was here enough.'

Jenny ignored her. She'd always tried to stay out of her mum's spats with her dad when he was alive, and she certainly wasn't going to get drawn into them now he was dead. Of course he spent a lot of time in here. It was his business, as well as the only pub in the village. Everyone did, apart from Alison, who'd never liked it, despite it paying for her house and her food and her extensive collection of pale pink blouses.

'Well, we won't have to worry about running out of booze, at least.' She smiled and gestured to the boxes of bottles behind the bar. Boxes and boxes and boxes, far too many, surely. But Jenny had wanted to make him proud, and anyway, they were from the wholesaler. She'd checked the quote twice; it had cost less than drinks for twenty for her thirtieth. Enough to get the whole village pissed.

It was, genuinely, what he would have wanted.

'I still think we should have had it up at the old caravan park hall.'

Jenny rolled her eyes behind Alison's back. Her uncle Pete owned the caravan park, which was a grand name for a smattering of grubby mobile homes plus a creaking old hall perched on the top of a crumbling cliff. Like the hotel, they were perpetually in danger of being disintegrated into the sea if there was a particularly bad storm, but unlike the hotel, they were moveable. Each one had been taken apart and put back together time and time again, the caravans retreating from the edge like they were frightened of it. And why not? Everyone else was, even though, as far as Jenny knew, there'd never been a death.

Such a stupid place to build a village.

'Dad hated the caravan park.'

Which he had, and so did Jenny. That cramped little hall was absolutely the wrong place to go to remember a man who'd always seemed so big. When Jenny thought of her father, the spirit and presence of him, he was huge. She thought of him on the beach, striding his way across the sand on long legs, eyes always up looking for someone to talk to, or driving around in his beaten-up old Volvo, shout-singing along to the radio no matter how much she and her mother begged him to stop. Most of all, Jenny thought of him in this pub, propped up at the end of the bar, chatting easily to his regulars but always with an ear out to tell you what the change was or if you'd missed a pint of lager off the order. Jenny couldn't even remember him ever going up to the caravan park, which was his brother's domain. He'd never had an easy relationship with Pete, and besides, he'd always been terribly afraid of heights.

Alison gave her a look that Jenny had hated since childhood. A silly-little-girl look. 'How would you know?'

Jenny bit down on her lip and all the things she shouldn't say pushed at the back of her throat. *I knew him better than you did I might not have been here a lot but at least I talked to him at least I liked him at least I loved him not like you.* But she was here to help. All she allowed herself was, 'Have you heard from Uncle Pete today?'

Her mother's lips pursed, and for a second, a look of understanding flashed between the two women, because as a family they agreed about Pete. He was Ted's younger brother, and the kind of man who made enemies easily. *Could start a fight in an empty room, that one,* was what Ted used to say, and he was one of the few people who'd ever had time for Pete. Probably the only one, since Kevin died.

'No. I've left a message.'

And Jenny thought her mother's eyes looked damp, and she felt like a total shit for it. She was meant to be here to help, wasn't she? That was the point. To make her mum feel better, and to sort things out. That was what she did.

'It doesn't matter. We can do it on our own. Can't we, Mum?'

And she looked over to Alison. Maybe their eyes would meet and they'd share a wry smile and, now that Dad wasn't there, it would feel like they were a team, the two of them. But her mother was frowning at the carrier bags, half empty now, their sandwich-guts spilled all over the bar.

'I don't think this is enough sandwiches, you know. There aren't many meat ones. They're all cheese.'

'Right.'

Alison sniffed. 'We need to put on a proper spread. I always thought you'd grow out of that vegetarian nonsense.'

Jenny closed her eyes briefly and swallowed, hard. She'd had to force herself to make as many as she had. Cold slices of ham, wet and obscenely pink, slimy on her fingers and dead dead dead.

'I'll make some more.'

Alison nodded and, to Jenny's horror, her lip trembled and she gasped out a sob. The sound was so unfamiliar that for a moment she thought her mother might be about to throw up. Jenny wasn't sure she'd ever seen her mother crying before.

But she was here to help. She sprang over to Alison and laid a hand on top of her mother's, gentle as if she was trying to catch a wild blackbird. 'Hey, Mum, it's okay. We'll get through it together. It's just a hard day, okay? Just one hard day.'

That was what Gail always said to her. She'd tuck her under a bright blanket on the knackered sofa of the flat Gail and Ben shared and make her tea, with sugar, even though Jenny kept telling her she didn't take it, and tell her the same stories about her parents' lives back in Ghana, which always had the same message: anyone can get through one hard day. Things always, *always*, get better. Was it weird that she was upset that her boyfriend's mum couldn't be at her dad's funeral? Not that she wouldn't have come if Jenny had asked. And Ben himself had asked a hundred times, over and over again.

Jenny forced her hand to keep up its gentle pat-pat. It wasn't that she was ashamed of where she came from. She'd tell anyone who asked her, of course she would. But the idea of Chris, or, more likely, Uncle Pete, making some crack about woke millennials or southern fairies or – and she wouldn't put it past either of them – a racist comment to Ben – or Gail, Jesus – made her feel hollow with exhaustion. She just couldn't deal with that, not along with everything else. So Ben wasn't here, and neither was Gail, and there was no one to comfort Jenny, because in this side of her life, that was what her dad always did.

Dad.

Alison gave her a watery smile, dabbing at the underneath of her eyes with a tissue. It came away stained with concealer and eyeliner and tears. 'Thanks, pet.'

Jenny smiled back. Maybe this could be the new start that they needed. Out of this horrible thing, maybe something good could come. Maybe.

Alison gave Jenny's hand a decisive squeeze, and then let go as if it was something dead. 'Well. You'll get to see your friends again. That'll be something.'

Jenny forced herself to breathe in for the count of four and keep her eyes trained on the beige shine of a piece of pastry as she smiled and nodded. It had been fifteen years. Could she still call them her friends? Had they even ever been friends, or were they just people whose lives were so closely entwined with her own that to separate them out had felt like losing a part of herself? It was perfectly possible, of course, to be close to a person without ever really liking them much at all.

But you have to try, she supposed. You have to try.

Jenny set out the last of the plates. It had been comforting, in a way, busying herself with trays and tea towels and the various trappings of throwing a respectable wake. There was a hidden language to the preparations of a funeral, one that

Jenny had never had to give a thought to until, suddenly, she did. No thoughts to anything else for weeks now: the endless administration of death had shocked her. A relentless slog of forms and phone calls and decisions that were treated as the most important thing in the world but that you realised, wide-eyed at your laptop at midnight with a shout of laughter you had to stifle to avoid waking your housemates, were utterly meaningless: mahogany or pine effect on the coffin, what kind of handles. Who even cares, he'll still be gone, won't he? We're going to burn it anyway. Burn him. There's no decision you can make that will bring him back, that will give you another Sunday evening with him, watching *Death in Paradise* and working your way quietly through a bottle of cheap red each, his heavy reassuring presence radiating comfort from the knackered armchair he always refused to replace. So what was the point of any of it?

The two of them stared at the plate of sausage rolls, sitting in the middle of the greying meat-and-bread-and-pastry funeral spread. That was the last piece of food. The last task to keep them busy and normal before they had to walk into the tiny church, with everyone looking at them, and sit on a hard flat pew and stare at a box that they'd say contained a man, but couldn't possibly. Not Ted Fletcher, with his belly and his arms and the shout of his laugh and his life. Alison looked about her, face pinched and creased.

'Well. That's that done.'

Jenny heaved a sigh. The air in the pub didn't smell so much of Dad anymore. She'd got used to it, and now it was just normal fag ash and stale beer.

'Yes.'

'We should go then. Get ourselves ready.'

'That's right.'

But neither of them moved. Not for a long time.

Jenny had barely heard the service, and now it was nearly over. The whole time, all she'd been able to do was stare straight ahead at the coffin (mahogany effect, brass handles) and think about how, sooner and sooner, she'd have to stand up and deliver a eulogy. The idea of it filled her head, and only 'Bread of Heaven' had been rousing enough to cut through. A final goodbye and then he'd really be gone, and she'd be the one to say it. She would have liked to have shrugged the responsibility off – to luxuriate in her sorrow, sit quiet and tearful on the front row as if she was still a child. But she was his only child, and Alison had said that she couldn't stand to do it. She had barely said a word since they'd left the pub, sitting stiff-lipped and dry-eyed in the pew beside Jenny, looking tired and old in her severe black dress. It turned out the pastels really did suit her. So there was no one else to remember him except for her, and in a way, that felt right. There shouldn't be.

Bread of heaven,

Bread of heaven ...

The church was fullish. When Jenny had first walked in, she'd been disappointed to see it not packed, but as she looked around, working out the gaps, she realised she knew why most of the ones she'd expected to see weren't there. Old Mr Harris, dead. Kelly, moved away. Tim Ford the butcher, dead. Hannah, moved away. Alex's Auntie Jean, dead. Alex's mum, never expected to turn up. Si's kid sisters, moved away. Si's mum, unaccounted for. But she was pretty much the only one.

Feed me now and ever more . . .

Jenny snuck a look at her notes. What she'd written seemed meaningless now. She was sure that it had made more sense when she was looking it over the night before. It had been just another comforting task, then. Another thing to tick off the list and be done. Now, it was a real thing. Sitting in this church she'd been coming to since childhood, the grandest building for miles around now the hotel was ruined. She could almost believe that Ted would be able to hear her.

Feed me now and ever more.

The hymn finally ended. The vicar, who Jenny had never seen before, shuffled papers together. He was obviously nervous in front of the congregation, not his usual. This vicar had been driven in from Driffield. It used to be old Reverend Dennis, who would come into the primary school and tell them Bible stories every Thursday and glare sternly at them for giggling during any rude-sounding bits of hymns (*I was cold, I was NAKED*, they'd shout, gleeful and shrill from their benches at the back, the king and queens of their tiny school). But Reverend Dennis was dead and gone now, just like Dad, and he'd never been replaced.

'And now we will welcome Ted's beloved only daughter, Jennifer.'

Jenny felt her mother stiffen beside her at that. She'd always hated anyone calling her Jennifer; she'd phoned the school about it three times before they'd stopped. It seemed a funny thing to get upset about on a day like today, but then Alison was very good at getting upset about minutiae. Maybe it was to protect her from the bigger things, or maybe everyone in the village was right about Alison. Maybe Alison was just uptight.

Jenny walked up to the lectern. The air was thick with dust motes and memories. Harvest festivals, with their tins of beans all stacked up around the altar, and the Christmas she'd been Mary in the school nativity, riding solemnly down the aisle on Si's back – he'd been the donkey. Alex had been Gabriel. She'd had more lines than Jenny, but she'd still thrown a tantrum about not playing the lead. That was what growing up with Alex had been like.

Now she was the one doing it. Caught up in little details, just like Mum.

Focus, Jenny. Do it right.

She took a deep breath. Wood polish and candle wax. She hadn't been up here before. It was never her who did the readings at school. She didn't like getting up in front of every-one, so it had always been Alex, even though they were just as good at reading as each other. It was funny, Alison always said, that Jenny was the one who ended up being a lawyer, when it was always Alex who was the loudest. As if Jenny's job was like a barrister on TV, swishing about and shouting. But Jenny wouldn't say anything, of course. She never really wanted to talk about her other, London life, when she was here. She didn't like her worlds to mix.

Jenny looked back at her mother, hoping for . . . something. Some word or look, or maybe just an encouraging smile. A *you can do it, pet*, sent psychically through the dusty air. But

Alison wouldn't meet her eye. Jenny bit her lip. *Come on, Mum. Please.* Of course her mother was upset, and of course she could show it however she wanted, by withdrawing and acting numb, if that was what she needed to do, but it still hurt. Couldn't she offer some little word, some scrap of love, to help get her through? But she couldn't. She never did.

Jenny turned back to the front, to the rows and rows of eyes staring up at her expectantly. She allowed herself a blink, a swallow. It was just like in a meeting, wasn't it? Just words. And this would be easy, wouldn't it? Surely she knew her dad better than anyone.

'Um. Hello, everyone.'

Jenny winced at the way her voice sounded, bounced back to her from around the church. Ridiculously plummy, like a TV character, or someone taking the piss. Some people kept their accents after they moved to London, wore them like a badge, but not her. She regretted that, now. It would have been nice to sound like Dad. But arriving in London, eighteen and unsure of herself, she'd just wanted to fit in.

She took another breath. *Come on. Focus.* The church looked back at her, the buildings and the faces in it familiar but altered, like the kind of dream you'd hesitate to call a nightmare but wasn't far off.

Jenny looked down at the sheet of paper in her hands, but this time she couldn't even read the words, they just swam in front of her eyes. It wasn't going to work. Jenny scrunched the paper into a messy ball, and started speaking.

'When I was a little girl, Dad always used to tell me this story. It was about these two lovers ...'

The words echoed around the church. Was it inappropriate,

to say that word in a place like this? *I was cold, I was NAKED.* But that's what he'd always said: lovers. When she was a teenager, it had made her snort every time, but when she'd been too little to know that it meant sex, she'd loved the word. Lovers. That was what she wanted – to be loved. That was all anyone wanted.

'And one day, an evil witch cast a spell on them. She hated to see them so happy together, so she turned the man into a stone, and the woman into a bird.'

She let the sound decay. It was fine. Just a little speech. She could have easily done them when she was a child, and she could do them now. She'd known these people since she was a tiny little girl.

'And the two lovers were terribly sad. Because even though the bird could stand with her scaly feet on the stone and feel him beneath her, and the stone could feel the weight of the bird perched on his back, the stone-man and the bird-woman could never be together. They lived completely different lives.'

As she said that, she caught Alex's eye and the connection ran through her like a shock. Alex, still with her heavy make-up and her tight clothes, looking like she'd stepped out of 2004. Jenny hadn't been expecting her to be sitting so close to the front.

She licked her lips, and went on.

'But for one day a year, the enchantment broke, and the stone turned back into a man and the bird turned back into a woman. And they could laugh and talk and be together again. And that one day would tide them over for the rest of the year.'

Jenny squeezed her eyes shut. It had been more than once

a year, that she'd made it back from London. Almost every year, it had been more than that. She may have only come for one night at a time, and she may have never gone over to the pub with him like he'd wanted, but she hadn't just abandoned her mum and dad. She'd been there a bit.

'One day, after a hundred and one years had passed, and the witch had seen how they came back together, time and time again, she relented. The stone-man and the bird-woman had proven to her that their love was true, and so she turned them back into themselves and they were reunited. Because time passes and things change, but people don't. Love doesn't. And as long as you hold on, and stay true, then things will always work out in the end, no matter how bad they look at the time.'

Jenny looked up along the pews. There was an awkward pause. She wasn't sure what she'd expected. Applause? Her uncle Pete, skulking at the back and still in his work clothes, looked at his watch. Pete looked like Ted anyway, but that gesture, checking the time, made it seem just for a moment as if her father were alive again.

Jenny swallowed, and gripped the ball of paper that used to be her notes.

'I don't know why I remember that story so well. I don't know why Dad told it to me so many times, or why I always asked him to tell it again and again. But Ted was like that, wasn't he? He was charming. Magnetic. He knew how to talk so that people would listen. And that's how we'll all remember him, isn't it? Talking.'

There was a ripple of laughter at that.

Jenny allowed herself a small smile. That was something

that she'd learned from him, something that he'd shown her. No one could tell a joke like her dad.

'And I know I'm not the only person here that loved him. I know I won't be the only one who'll miss him. He was my dad, but he was like a dad to the whole village in a way.'

Alex wiped her eyes, a thick trail of black eyeliner smearing under her fingers. Jenny was surprised. But then, Alex had been working for her dad for donkey's years now – since she and Alex were both eighteen. And her dad was a decent man. They would have been friendly – friends, even, as strange as it was to think of it. Alex and her dad had probably known each other much better than she and Alex had.

And as Alex placed her hand back in her lap, now streaked with eyeliner goop, she tilted her head and Jenny noticed a glint at her throat. A little gold gleam, the brightest thing in the dreary church.

Jenny narrowed her eyes. Surely not. Surely even Alex wouldn't have the nerve to wear that necklace today.

But then, was there anything Alex didn't have the nerve to do? Jenny shouldn't even be surprised.

She slapped on a fake smile and hated how much it reminded her of the one her mother wore for parents' evenings and going into The Railway. Jenny hoped she didn't look like her, and then felt disloyal.

She glanced over at Alison, but she didn't look up. She was just staring resolutely at the front, as if she was some back-row mourner who barely knew the deceased but wanted to be polite and get a couple of free drinks out of it.

He'd been her fucking husband.

*

Jenny wished Ben was here. She wished that she'd let him, or that he'd come anyway, perhaps, brushing her objections aside, *I'm your boyfriend, aren't I? I'm coming to your dad's funeral, and that's that.* Who was she going to tell this to, now?

Jenny looked beyond her mother and out to the crowd, or what there was of it.

'He'd have been pleased to see every one of you here. He loved this village, and he loved the people in it.'

Si caught her eye and gave her an encouraging little smile.

A shock of familiarity ran through her. She couldn't have seen Si for more than ten years now, but a little gesture from him still meant as much as it had when she was seventeen.

'I love you, Dad. Goodbye.'

There was an approving murmur from around the church and Jenny waited to feel relieved. They hardest part was done, now, wasn't it? From now on, it was all plain sailing – the handshakes and curling sandwiches and one more night in her teenage bedroom and then back to London, and normal.

But as she walked back down to take her seat by her mother, who did not smile at her the way Ted would have done, who did not take her hand and squeeze it in two big warm paws, Jenny didn't feel the sense of a burden lifting that she'd expected. All she felt was hollow, and absolutely alone.

Coming out of the cellar, Jenny held the crate of bottles carefully away from her dress. The cardboard was dusty, with sticky patches from a leaked bottle of lime cordial all over the top. Jenny always forgot how filthy things got in a working pub, and this was a stupid dress to wear.

She kicked the door shut and snatched a breath as the latch scratched a deep red welt down her arm. Everything was dusty or sharp or damp or somehow out to ruin Jenny's date-night dress, the one that Ben had said she looked hot in, back in the days they used to pretend they weren't seeking each other out at every Friday night drinks, both of them drifting away from their own departments to sit next to each other, squashed up thigh to thigh, much closer than the tables warranted, back before they were officially going out. It wasn't a dress to be hauling boxes around in. But the whole village seemed to have come back to the pub with them, working their way steadily through drink after drink, smashing bottles together, each round of 'to Ted!' getting louder. They'd already run through more drink than she thought she'd need for the whole night.

It was what he would have wanted, at least.

She reached out a foot and kicked open the door to the main bar. A little dog sat in front of her, greying and thinner than the last time she'd seen him, sure, but unmistakably him.

'Barney?'

The dog tilted his head to the side, questioning, like he always had, and gave her a stiff little tail wag. But Alex's Auntie Jean was dead, she was sure of it. And this little dog would surely be long gone – he wasn't even really a puppy when she'd known him fifteen years ago.

She slid the box of beer onto the back ledge of the bar and reached out a hand. The little dog tottered over to her on shaky, stubby legs and reached out a hot tongue.

Jenny smiled. In a pub full of ghosts, Jean's was a friendly one, at least.

And for a moment, she even thought that she could hear her voice.

'You asked her about this place yet?'

But there was something a little off. That wasn't Jean, not quite. The accent was exactly the same, but Jean had always sounded like she was smiling.

Jenny looked over and there, perched on bar stools just a few feet away, were Alex and her mother, Karen. Jenny was hidden by one of the pub's many little walls – the place was a warren, especially when you were drunk – but they were close. She could hear them perfectly.

'No, Mum.'

Karen hadn't been at the funeral, and Jenny hadn't expected her to be. She hadn't expected her to be at the wake either, but here she was. Jenny craned around the corner to see her. She was wearing a bright red dress and lipstick to match and she was clutching her wine glass tight tight tight.

Jenny narrowed her eyes. Who was 'her'? Were they talking about Alison? What was there to ask?

'You'd best get a move on.'

Karen swallowed at least half of the glass of wine she was holding, and Jenny frowned. She'd only bought six bottles to top up the pub's stock. It'd better be enough. She'd never hear the end of it if they ran out of anything today, and besides, it'd be embarrassing. She'd been manager here, once upon a time. She shouldn't be fucking up a stock order.

'I'm not going to.'

Karen pursed her lips in a gesture so like Jenny's own mother, she felt like rubbing her eyes. 'Chris won't lend you again. He said it was a one-time thing.'

Alex downed the end of her can of cider and crunched it in a claw-like hand. She immediately cracked open another one. Had she just been holding it, in her other hand? Jesus.

'It's not the day for it, all right?' Alex said. Jenny felt a rush of gratitude. At least someone was paying their respects to her dad properly. She must have been right earlier. Alex and Ted must have been friends. 'It's a shit enough wake as it is without me starting something.'

Maybe not.

Karen snorted in approval and the two women gulped at their drinks and glared at the rest of the guests, as similar to each other as they'd ever looked.

'You've put on weight,' Karen said, conversationally.

Jenny tried to lean round further to see if she'd been right about the necklace she'd seen in the church. She couldn't see.

'Have I? Since last Saturday?'

Alex sounded bored. It seemed like a conversation they'd had many times before – a dance as well-worn as the one Jenny had with her own mother about making her own sandwiches for lunch. Shop-bought ones were so expensive and full of salt, she knew, she knew.

'I'm only saying because I care, you know. He'll leave you.'

Alex let out a contemptuous little snort, and Jenny privately agreed. Si wouldn't ever leave anyone. He'd cheat on them perhaps, he'd behave so badly that they'd leave him, certainly, but he'd never be the one to pull the trigger. He wasn't that kind of man.

He hadn't been, anyway. Who knew, now?

'Shut up, Mum.'

Karen tipped the glass of wine high into her mouth even though it was long empty.

'Don't you tell me to shut up.'

Just then, the dog barked. Jenny started back, as shocked as if she'd been burned. Alex whipped her head around and caught Jenny's eye and, for a moment, the two women just stared at each other. And Jenny couldn't read her. Was she angry? Amused? Surely she knew that Jenny had been spying.

But what was there to do except for brazen it out? What was there ever? Jenny plastered on her funeral smile and stepped out into the main bar. When she spoke, her voice sounded high and posh and fast and all wrong.

'Alex, Karen. Thank you so much for coming.'

Alex smiled back, her grin as brittle and fake as the one Jenny was wearing. She was wearing some kind of necklace, definitely, a delicate gold chain that easily could be the right one, but the pendant had slipped under the neckline of her jumper. It was impossible to tell.

'You all right, Jenny? There's something on your dress.'

Jenny looked down. There was a thick stripe of sticky grey

along her hip where she'd been leaning on the door frame. For a sharp moment, she felt like crying.

'Oh. Yeah.'

Karen didn't acknowledge her at all. She turned to Alex. 'I'm off for a fag. You coming?'

Alex sighed and flipped her ponytail, the same way she had since year seven. 'I quit.'

Karen cackled and pulled a pouch of Golden Virginia out from a battered old clutch bag. She staggered down from the bar stool, the way Jenny had seen people slide off them a hundred times. They were too high, really, for drunks.

'Yeah, yeah. That's what you always say.'

Alex watched Karen wobble out of the pub through narrowed eyes.

'I quit five years ago. Daft old bat always forgets.'

And for a second, Alex looked almost nervous. For the first time, it occurred to Jenny that Alex might be trying to impress her.

'My mum always forgets I'm vegetarian.'

Alex rolled her eyes, but in a friendly way. Like they were on the same side again. She raised her drink and said, 'Always reminds me of him, cider does. It'd have been better draught, though. He wasn't one for tins.'

Jenny felt her jaw clench.

'Yeah. I know.'

There was a long, pulsing silence. Alex drank, and Jenny wished she had a drink in her hand. It hadn't seemed right. She felt like she was still on duty. Maybe later Mum would want to split a bottle of wine with her and go through some old photos. Even though she'd gone straight to her room after the washing-up was done last night, saying she was tired, but then not turning her bedroom light off until way, way after Jenny had gone to bed. Even though they didn't really have old photos, not as a family, and Jenny's own collection didn't start until she was old enough to spend her pocket money on disposable cameras, one for every summer, full to the brim of shots of Si and Alex and moody seascapes. She had more photos of them than she did of her parents, and more of her parents than she did of herself.

'You could have phoned, you know. I'd have worked for free. For him.'

Jenny looked over to Alex, surprised. Her mouth was a hard-pressed line, but Jenny could tell that she meant it. Alex never said anything she didn't mean.

Or rather, she hadn't. Jenny kept forgetting.

'I wanted you to have the night off. To come to the wake properly. You know.'

Alex nodded and gave her a real smile. So quick you might have missed it, but definitely there. 'Cheers.'

There was another silence. Jenny reached back through the bar and pulled a cider out of the sink, swimming with cans and ice. Maybe just one. Maybe she shouldn't be working either. As she cracked it open, the dog came trotting around the corner and popped up on his hind legs, whining and pawing at Alex.

'Eh up, Barney. Come on then, you silly sod.'

Alex reached down and scooped him onto her lap. Barney wriggled in pleasure, his whole back end swaying along with his tail as she lovingly ruffled his fur.

'Is he yours?' Jenny asked, even though she'd never seen

a dog who looked more like he belonged to someone. Alex looked different with the terrier in her lap. Something about her shoulders, and her back. She looked less worried, somehow.

'He is now.'

It was somehow ridiculous, the idea that Alex was old enough to have a dog. But, of course, it was different round here, to London. Jenny could never have a dog, with her hours and her house share. She hadn't really stopped to think about whether or not she wanted one, before.

'I was sorry to hear about Jean.'

Alex's mouth hardened at the corners, which made her look like Jean for a second. Older. 'Yeah. Me too.'

There was an awkward silence. Jean had been more than an aunt to Alex, Jenny knew that. She was the one Jenny could remember at the school gate coming to get Alex, the one who'd always taken her somewhere at the weekend. Jenny took a nervous swallow of her drink. Maybe she should have come back up for Jean's funeral. She nodded at the little dog.

'I thought I was seeing things.'

Alex stroked Barney's ears. The rest of his little body was covered in greying, wiry hair, but his ears still looked soft and velvety, puppy-smooth. Her mouth relaxed back into her own again, and even the dog smiled.

'He's seventeen now. Senile little git.'

It was funny, the way people slagged off their dogs as a sign of affection. And their friends, here. The amount of old men with moist eyes who'd told her gruffly that her dad was a daft old bastard, today. He'd been well loved.

'He's still lovely,' Jenny said.

And again, Alex smiled up at her, a proper smile, like she was seven again and she'd beaten everyone in the playground in a race, which she always did. Then she looked down and kept on stroking the dog's ears.

Jenny took a deep drink of her cider and tasted sugar and rot. She should circulate, really. That was what you did, wasn't it?

'Is your boyfriend here?' Alex craned her neck around, as if he was going to pop up suddenly from behind the bar.

'No.'

Jenny thought of Ben, and his smile and the way he could always make her laugh, no matter how much of a mood she was in. But she'd see him in a few days. The wobble in the church aside, she was glad he wasn't here. This day was hard enough without having to look after him as well as her mother. He wouldn't get this weird, brash, windswept place, and they wouldn't get him.

Alex tilted her head, absolutely unashamed of being nosy. Jenny had forgotten that. In Ravenspurn, you just asked people stuff, if you wanted to know. It was kind of refreshing.

'Why not?'

Because she'd told him not to, was the reason he wasn't there. She'd told him again and again, making up excuse after excuse why he couldn't come up, same as she did with every visit. The train ride's too long, it's too expensive, you have to work, there isn't room. She'd had to come up with even more of them than usual this time.

'He had to work. He wanted to. I'll bring him next time.'

Alex stared back at her, expressionless, and Jenny suddenly

remembered that for years and years she'd believed that Alex could always tell when she was lying. And maybe she could. There'd been a time when they knew each other better than anyone else in the world. But that was in the past now.

'Right,' Alex said, still looking at her, slow and steady, but Jenny made herself treat Alex like she was anyone else. Because she was just a woman, wasn't she? There was nothing so special about her, not really. She gave her a smile. You could just ask people, up here, if you wanted to know stuff.

'Is Si all right? You two okay?'

Alex shrugged, and for the first time today, she looked uncomfortable. 'You know what Si's like. He's always happy. And I can't complain.'

Jenny leaned in so that no one else could hear. She knew what he could be like. She really knew. And despite how long it'd been since they'd spoken, Alex was a part of her past, permanent and immovable. And she'd turned up to her dad's funeral, and she'd looked upset. She was her oldest friend, Jenny supposed.

'You can. If you like.'

And it seemed like maybe Alex might tell her something. And maybe then she could ask something back, maybe about the necklace, or maybe just about how things had been these last few years, working with her dad and living a life that Jenny always thought about. Every bad day at work, she thought about what it might be like if she hadn't left. An alternate life lived in parallel to hers, but it wasn't unknowable. There was someone living it right now.

'I'm glad it's at his pub,' Alex said suddenly. Had she always been that abrupt?

Jenny relaxed back to lean against the bar. She didn't want to circulate. She wanted to hear about what was wrong with living with Si.

'Yeah. I said—'

'Your pub. I should say.'

The idea hit her like a missed step. Jenny stared at Alex.

'What?'

It wasn't that she didn't understand. It was that it hadn't occurred to her for a moment.

'It'll be your pub now,' Alex said, her face and voice both flat. 'Congratulations.'

Jenny chewed her bottom lip. A habit she'd carefully trained herself out of in her early twenties. For the most part. 'Thanks.'

Barney whined and looked up at Alex with big, liquid eyes. She sighed, drank the last drops of her cider, and slid off the bar stool.

'I'd better take him out. He needs a piss every five minutes. Poor little bugger.'

She set him gently on the floor by her feet.

'Nice to see you,' Jenny said, and to her surprise, she meant it.

Alex gave her a tight nod, then stared around the pub: the gas lights, still working, glowing gently on the walls, the nicotine-stained ceiling, the bar, polished to a high shine by generations of elbows.

'Look after it for him, yeah?'

And she was gone.

That night, Jenny dreamed of her father's pub. Not as it had been in the present, full of the bent-over bodies of men Jenny was sure used to be tall, but as it had been back when she was eighteen and that bar, and the beach that lay in front of it and the soaring cliffs above, were Jenny's whole world. And in the dream Barney was barely more than a puppy and Si was there, half pissed already and laughing, and Alex was propping up the bar with that old cheeky look about her, not tired, not sad, not paying her respects. And her dad was there, of course, checking the time on his watch and announcing that that'd do for the day and pulling them pints and alive alive alive.

Jenny snapped awake. There was a figure above her, looming in the darkness. Jenny felt like she could feel the ghost of fingers against her cheek, as if someone had been pressing into her, feeling her flesh as she slept.

'What the fuck?'

This was surely still a dream. One of those horrible, disorienting dreams-within-a-dream. She tensed a fist, then dug her fingers deep into the palm of her hand and it hurt, but she didn't wake up. That almost always worked for her. Didn't people say that when you couldn't wake yourself up from a dream that meant that you were dead? Or perhaps that was when you died in a dream? Not that anyone could ever know. But this certainly felt more real than any nightmare that Jenny had ever had before: the softness of the mattress underneath her and the nails in her palm and the whistle of wind through the trees outside.

'You were making a noise.'

The figure moved, and the light from the hall hit a fuzzy pink dressing gown and the edge of a pair of glasses, never worn in the daytime.

Jenny swallowed down the scream that had been building up in her throat. It was just her mother.

'Mum. You scared me.'

Jenny gasped air into her lungs, forcing herself to breathe. In. Out. Count them. She was abuzz with adrenaline, and she couldn't shake the thought that she was still trapped in a dreamland – that this was just a trick, very realistic, to make her relax, let her guard down, so that this nightmare version of Alison could . . . what, though?

Jenny rubbed at her eyes, paying attention to the way that the fingers felt on her skin. Real. She was real.

'You were making a noise,' Alison said again, huffy this time. She hovered, so close to the bed she was almost sitting on it.

'What kind of noise?'

Jenny wanted Alison to move. She couldn't say anything though, could she? This was her mother. It was her house.

'Were you having a bad dream?'

Jenny clutched the duvet up to her chest and wished that she was still asleep, or still back in London, perhaps. That Dad was still alive. She'd have been able to tell Ted to back up a bit. He wouldn't take offence; he'd just shrug and move back. But she couldn't do that with her mother. They'd never been as close.

'Maybe,' she said.

Alison heaved a deep sigh, as if Jenny had somehow disappointed her again. She finally, blessedly, moved back to the door.

'Well, it's over now. Go back to sleep.'

And, as she left, Jenny felt her heart rate drop back to normal. She didn't go back to sleep, though. It was only when she saw dawn peeking through the thin pink curtains that she finally relaxed enough to slip back into unconsciousness. This time, she didn't dream.

Jenny banged the front door shut behind her and turned her collar up to the wind. It wasn't that she was in a bad mood, exactly. She was glad to have been able to come home, to help with the funeral, to sort her mum out. She was grateful. She was fine.

She stopped and crossed the main road carefully, looking right and left and right again, on a kind of muscle memory. More careful than she'd ever be in Hackney, despite the fact that she'd been competently crossing roads for over thirty years now, despite the fact there was never any traffic here at the best of times, despite the fact that she hadn't seen a car since Chris had dropped her off in one. And she'd see him again when she got picked up in three hours, and then she'd be away. She still had a twenty-pound note in her purse waiting for him. In the four days she'd been here, there hadn't been anything to spend it on.

Jenny stared up the cliff path, and then to the sky. Menacing grey, with lighter cloud scudding past in the wind, moving fast. She wouldn't go up there, this trip. It was almost a shame. She usually made a point of scaling the cliff path, as treacherous as it was, and as steep. The path, plus picking your way through Pete's depressing caravan park, was worth it for a trip to the hotel ruins. From up at the ruined hotel, the village below looked small and inconsequential, and the bigger towns – Bridlington, Withernsea, Flamborough – were reduced to smudges on the horizon. It was easy to imagine that nothing really mattered, or even existed, except for you and the sky and the sea. That high up, you could almost believe you could fly.

The closer it got to the time when Jenny would be leaving, the more conflicted she felt about it. On the one hand, the sadness was crushing. Jenny's limbs felt heavy with it – every movement was an effort. And despite her best efforts, she couldn't get her mother to thaw to her. No matter how hard Jenny tried, they were never going to sit on the sofa together, feet both tucked under the same blanket, while Jenny did her knitting and half watched some TV programme that her mother was narrating for her. That wasn't her mother, however much she wanted it. That was Gail. On the other hand, this pause in life had been weirdly glorious. No London, no tubes, no constant checking of the news, no daily meetings about conveyancing and hand sanitiser. She'd needed the break. She still needed the break.

She turned onto the street with the Co-op and closed her eyes against the wind for a second. It was refreshing, though. A blast of sea salt to the face was a nice change from breathing in the same central-heated and Yankee-Candle-scented air of her mother's house day in and day out.

It didn't matter. Only a few more hours, and she'd be gone. This one last task, of topping up the cans of tuna and sweetcorn and buying a jar of mayonnaise – not squeezy, a proper glass jar – and then her duty to Dad would be done.

Jenny walked into the Co-op, which was newly familiar to her now. She'd had to 'just nip out' for her mum at least seven times over the last few days – Alison seemed to live

in fear of running out of anything, and anyway, it was something that Jenny could do to help. And get out of the house,
if she was honest. The shop used to be a Spar, and never
the kind of place where you could reliably buy the kind of
mayonnaise you wanted, or even brand-name ketchup, but
things had changed in Ravenspurn since Jenny had left. You
could even get oat milk now.

She still hadn't checked the cupboards.

'You still here?'

Karen was standing by the till, glaring daggers at Jenny.
Alex was behind it, working as usual, her forehead ruffled in
a thick scowl. That was how Jenny felt about seeing Karen
too, but she forced a thin smile.

'That's right.'

She didn't want to get into it. She tried to estimate the
distance between them. Three metres – maybe four? She
took a step back anyway.

'Hmm.' Karen pressed her lips together, her mouth a red
slash across her face. The brightness of the lipstick made the
tracksuit bottoms she was wearing seem even grubbier.

Jenny walked through the shop, picking up cans. Her
mum had specified amounts that seemed ridiculous to
Jenny – six of everything – but maybe she didn't eat a lot
of variety. Jenny had been cooking for them both, and her
mother had been peering, suspicious, at anything she made,
pecking at it, asking and asking what was in it until she knew
every ingredient, down to the last grind of pepper.

She found the mayonnaise. It was the last jar. Looking
around, Jenny registered that there were a lot of gaps on
the shelves. People must have been panic buying, just like

London. Jenny frowned. This wasn't panic buying though, was it? It couldn't be. It was just what her mum wanted. More cans than Jenny would buy herself, but only a couple of things.

Jenny chucked the jar in her basket. This was stupid. She'd be home soon. This place was getting to her. She walked up to the till and the two women fell silent as she approached. Jenny felt a familiar prickle of discomfort.

No. That was silly. She smiled and put the basket down. She tried to think of something to say to Alex. Absolutely nothing came to mind.

'Cheers,' was all she came up with.

The three of them stood in silence while Alex bleeped through the tuna. Jenny looked forward to lovely, anonymous London; she knew the people who worked in the corner shop by sight, but she didn't know their names and they didn't know hers and she only had to talk to them if she wanted to. Bliss.

Karen was looking uncomfortable.

'I'm sorry I didn't go to the ceremony,' she barked out, then looked down at the floor again.

Jenny smiled, disarmed. She hadn't expected that, from Karen. She hadn't expected her at the funeral. She and Ted hadn't been friends. It had been nice to see how much he meant to people, round here. That was something to hold on to.

'Oh. Um. That's okay. It was nice to see you at the wake.'

To her surprise, Karen glowered at her. She looked deeply offended, and like she was looking for something to kick. 'Nice to see you there, as well.'

Jenny had to stop herself chewing her lip. 'What do you mean?'

Karen curled her lip. Jenny was reminded of another dog – not Barney. The one Pete used to keep, years ago, that had to be put down because it bit him once too many times to be covered up. 'My Alex has been more like a daughter to him than you have, these last few years.'

At the sound of her name, Alex looked up from Jenny's cans.

'Mum. Fuck off. Leave her alone.'

It was at Alex defending her that Jenny really thought she might cry. No, though. Not here.

'What? I'm just saying, aren't I? I'm only saying. Did you even come back for Christmas last year? I don't recall seeing you around.'

The blood was pumping around Jenny's brain, making it hard to concentrate. She knew that she should just walk off. What good could possibly come of this? And she wasn't meant to be hanging around chatting in shops anyway, was she? Her hands twitched for sanitiser. But she stood, cheeks burning. One last task. Then she could go.

Alex looked at her, and then to Karen.

'You going to buy that, or you going to stand around all day slagging off my customers?'

Karen looked down at the single tin of beans she was holding. 'I ain't got it. You'll have to lend me.'

Alex rolled her eyes and, for a moment, she looked like Ted. That's just how he used to look when he was kicking out a regular who'd hung around taking the piss for too long.

'Fine. Get out.'

Karen tottered off to the door with her tin of beans and paused in the doorway.

Jenny stood. She held herself still and tried hard not to throw up or punch her.

'Bye, dearie,' Karen said, voice heavy with sarcasm, and she left.

Alex flipped her red ponytail over one shoulder. Her roots were starting to come through – grey, Jenny noticed with a jolt, not brown.

'Stupid old cow. What's she coming to the shop for anyway if she doesn't have the money? She knows she can just get me to pick her up whatever she wants.'

Jenny felt shaky with adrenaline. She'd never liked Karen, and she'd privately thought she was a shit mum to Alex, but they'd never argued before. But then, she'd been a child.

'What was that about?'

Alex shook her head, dismissive. 'Ignore her.'

Still shaken, Jenny nodded. She took the mayonnaise and shoved it into a carrier bag. Alex bleeped the last can through and regarded Jenny, head tilted.

'You're staying, then?'

Jenny frowned. 'What? No, I'm going this afternoon.'

Alex raised her eyebrows. 'You allowed? Is your work one of those essential services? I didn't think you were that kind of lawyer.'

Jenny stopped, a tin of dead fish still in her hand. 'I'm not. What?'

Alex raised her eyebrows. She looked almost amused. 'Have you not seen the news today?'

'No, there's no reception at Mum's. No Wi-Fi.'

She felt stupid again. Not in on the joke. She remembered now, that apart from that last summer, Alex had often had jokes that she wasn't allowed in on. That was what being around her had felt like, most of the time. Like something was being kept from you.

'You want to have a look. Maybe call your boss. There's going to be a lockdown. You might have to stay here.'

Lockdown. Jenny swallowed the word like it was a stone. 'What?'

Alex slid a paper over to her.

LOCKED DOWN!

PM: Brits banged up in houses

Police fines for gathering in groups

Stay home unless absolutely necessary

Jenny blinked. Surely not. They'd been saying for weeks they were going to do this, and they hadn't. They'd got through the funeral without a lockdown. That's as far as Jenny had let herself think – until the funeral. Now it was past, she was in a new stage of time. She hadn't quite realised that things could still happen.

'That's a tabloid, though.'

Alex rolled her eyes. 'It was just the closest. They all say it.' She shoved another paper over.

Johnson: National emergency declared. Stay at home.

Jenny swallowed. And again.

'Fuck.'

Alex shrugged. She looked distinctly unbothered.

'Fuck, indeed.'

Jenny couldn't stop looking at the paper. She had to talk to Ben, to Darren, to Priya. To Alison as well, she supposed.

'Sorry. I have to ... Sorry.'

Jenny gestured to the cans and packets on the till and turned to leave, head spinning. Where could she go to get reception? Would the far end of the beach be okay, or would she have to go all the way up to the old hotel?

Alex nodded to the food on the counter. She did it in such a way that, once again, Jenny felt like she'd got something wrong. 'I'd get them, if I were you. Everyone knows what your mum's like about her cans.'

This, again. Jenny didn't know what her mum was like about cans. It seemed like she didn't know much at all. She looked at the spread of food, obscene-seeming now. But her mum had asked. And if there really was a lockdown ... Jenny scooped the tins up as fast as she could, and hurried out and away.

'Have you seen the fucking news?'

Jenny was still out of breath. She hadn't been able to get reception on the beach. She'd had to come all the way up the cliff path, skidding and gasping the last third of it, cans clunking in her bag and swinging like sharp pendulums against her legs. This place.

'Yeah. I know. I tried to call you. How was the funeral?'

Ben sounded as calm and assured as he ever did. Just the sound of his voice made her heart rate drop back down a little.

Jenny eyed up a knackered old bench, so tilted and worn it looked like it was about to slide into the sea.

'Yeah, it was ... Yeah.'

She couldn't find the words. Maybe because this wasn't a conversation for a phone. This was a conversation for a real person, one you could see and smell and touch, and have a shared bottle of wine and a hug at the end. She'd wait to tell him. She'd see him soon enough. Surely she would. Surely she wouldn't have to stay.

'You haven't been answering your messages,' he said.

Jenny found a mist-damp patch of grass instead and sat down on that. She could still see the sea, from the ground. She stretched out her aching legs. She'd come to the ruins of the old hotel. Apparently still the only place with guaranteed phone signal in Ravenspurn, and the best view for miles. Dropping rock and far-flung sea.

'There's no reception here. No reception anywhere, I couldn't ...' Jenny pressed her hand to her face, trying to push her thoughts back in, contain them. 'How the fuck am I meant to get home now?'

There was a sound of fabric rubbing against fabric. Jenny was suddenly bothered by the fact she couldn't picture where he was. Was that him pulling a coat on? Where was he going? It was too early for him to be going for lunch, surely.

'I dunno. I think the trains are still running. Then a taxi. With the windows down, I guess? But I'm not sure if you're meant to.'

Not meant to? Jenny stared out to sea, trying to push down the panic, the voice that was telling her to run for it, swim for it, even, just get out, get out, get away from here. She hadn't been home for this long since she'd been eighteen.

'But I have to get back. I have to go to work.'

There was a pause.

'Jenny, have you not seen your emails?'

She didn't like the tone of his voice. He almost never called her Jenny.

She was on compassionate leave, wasn't she? She didn't have to look at her emails.

'I said, there's no reception.'

'We've all been furloughed.'

A seagull landed on the old mantel of the hotel's front doors – grand double doors, rich mahogany in their day, now ghostly white with the salt. It was amazing it got so far up.

'What the fuck is a furlough?'

Jenny felt a prickle on her neck. As if she was being watched. She craned her head around, but she could see no one. The wind would snatch her words away long before she could be overheard, anyway. She needed to find a way to calm down.

'You don't need to come in to work. Not for the three weeks this is on.'

Three weeks. Jenny stared out at the sea and counted her breaths, four in, four out. From here the water was all she could see. As if Ravenspurn, and the other towns on this coast, simply didn't exist. It was only her and the ruin.

'You're not at work?'

Not a coat. Of course. *House arrest.* It must have been him shifting on the sofa, or turning over in bed. She still wanted to be able to picture him, exactly where he was, what he was wearing. Would it be weird to ask? Her old life felt like it was sliding away, like every time she tried to reach out for a piece of reality, it slipped between her fingers and was gone.

'No.' Ben sounded a little alarmed, now. 'You really haven't seen any of this before today?'

'It was my dad's funeral, Ben. I've been busy.'

She hated it when she used that tone. Snappy and high and sarcastic. It made her sound like Mum.

'Okay,' he said. He sounded gentle, deliberately so. Jenny squeezed her eyes shut. She hated feeling like she was a problem he needed to solve. 'I know.'

Jenny took a deep breath, and let it slide out of her mouth, like they did in yoga. She could deal with this. She'd dealt with worse than this. She made sure her voice sounded normal again when she said, 'What am I going to do then? Cooped up with Priya and Adam. They'll kill each other.'

'You don't want to just stay where you are? It might be easier.'

Ben sounded tentative. Like she was unreasonable, like she was going to fly off the handle and shout at him. But Jenny was always incredibly reasonable. It was something she prided herself on. She forced herself to smile, so it sounded like she was joking.

'Then me and Mum will kill each other.'

There was a pause. Jenny stared up at her seagull. She hadn't sounded convincing.

'Well, if you want to come back to London, maybe you should stay with me and my mum.'

Jenny sat up. For the first time since she had left the shop, she felt real again.

'Seriously?'

'Well, we've got the room. It might be a nicer way to spend the next couple of weeks. We could finally watch *Get Out*.'

Jenny smiled. That was meant to be their first date. Three years ago, Ben had told her that he had no one to go with, it wasn't his mates' kind of thing, and was she free that night? They'd talked so much in the cinema bar that they were a bottle of wine deep, and the film was nearly over, by the time they realised they'd missed it. It was a great film, apparently. Ben was better.

She let herself imagine. A taxi ride, two trains, a tube, a bus, and then presenting herself at their door. That veggie stew she liked and a big glass of red wine, and sleeping in Ben's bed, which was bigger than hers, and comfier, and softer, and had him in it. She slept better there than she did in Hackney, and much, much better than she did here. And she hadn't been round for ages, because Gail was worried about the virus – one of the doctors she worked with had told her to watch out because of an old heart condition she had.

Jenny bit her lip. Fuck it.

'But your mum. Her heart condition. I couldn't live with myself if . . .'

There was a long pause. Suddenly, all Jenny wanted was to be told that she was wrong. That it didn't matter, that Ben wanted her there so much that he thought she should risk it, that it wasn't that bad, that it was all going to be okay.

'Yeah. No, you're right. Her heart condition.'

Jenny sighed. Back to Hackney, then.

'The rates are through the roof round here, Jen. They're low where you are. You'd be safer there.'

She squeezed her eyes shut.

'From a virus, maybe. Not from chucking myself off the cliff.'

He laughed on the other end of the line, and she smiled.

'Don't you think your mum would like the company, though?'

'Not from me.'

There was a pause, and Jenny could imagine Ben pulling his reasonable face. She hated it when he used his reasonable face.

'She's still your mum. She's grieving. Give her a break.'

Jenny stared up as the seagulls wheeled above her.

'I don't know. I mean, you're right. Obviously. Twat.'

She could hear him smiling and it made her heart throb for home. His home, really, but she was allowed to share sometimes. It was the best she'd got.

'You've been promising me you'd finish that scarf for months. There's still a couple of months of cold left. I need it.'

Jenny stood up and stretched. She peered over the edge. The village was much the same as she'd left it – boring and grey. And safe, she supposed.

'Yeah. Well. I have been saying I wanted more time for telly and crafts.'

Maybe it would be nice not to have to fight Priya and Adam for sofa space. If she wasn't going to Ben's and she wasn't going to work, and she wasn't going to bars . . . Fuck. He was obviously right. It was what a good daughter would do, wasn't it? It was obvious.

'We could still watch the film. You know. On WhatsApp.'

Jenny picked up a stone and flung it off the edge of the cliff. It was surprisingly satisfying. The moment when the inertia of the throw gave out and gravity took over. She couldn't hear it land, but she could imagine. *Thunk*.

'There's no reception.'

'Oh. Right.'

There was a silence. Far, far below her, Jenny saw a figure making its way along the beach. She was too far away to tell if it was Chris or Si. They looked pretty similar from a distance.

'It's only three weeks.'

It was meant to only be four days. That was the amount of time that Jenny had steeled herself to bear.

'Yeah. I suppose.'

'It might be nice to have a break? Slow down a bit.'

She could hear him cajoling her. Like she was a child. And she was acting like a child, she knew. Nothing like your childhood bedroom to send you back in time.

She forced herself to smile, to get rid of the sulky note in her voice.

'Yes. You're right. I could probably do with it.'

Maybe it was for the best she didn't have constant access to messaging him. Maybe she'd say something childish, or selfish, something like the teenager she'd been. This way, before she talked to him, she could prepare. It was for the best.

Oh god. She really was staying, then. Three whole weeks, with just her mum and the seagulls and the sea.

'You take care of yourself, yeah? You're important.'

It was what they said instead of I love you at the end of phone calls and dates. It made her smile, normally. Not today. Today, she'd quite like to be loved. To have a lover.

'You're important too,' she said.

And even though she knew she should hurry back down to her mum, to tell her the news, to tell her she was staying, she stayed for a moment and watched as the birds wheeled around above her, shrieking angrily at the empty sky.

'Where were you?'

Alison didn't sound particularly interested in the answer. A magazine lay open in front of her, a headline screaming up in stark red – NAN WARNED ME OF CHEATING HUBBY ... BUT SHE'D BEEN DEAD FIVE YEARS! Alison loved those magazines, but they made Jenny's head hurt. Stories about brutal murders nestled up with word searches and pictures of people's grandkids, like it was perfectly normal. The kind of thing a serial killer would read.

'Have you seen the news?'

Alison looked almost affronted. 'I had it on earlier. I always have it on at lunchtime.'

Jenny blinked. The day must not feel so much like an emergency, for her.

'So did you see it? The lockdown.'

Alison raised her eyebrows at Jenny. 'I told your dad that this would happen. I told him back in January. I said.'

She didn't look upset, or scared. She almost seemed pleased.

Jenny swallowed down a lump in her throat. Had everyone seen this coming except her?

'Ben says we won't be back at work for another three weeks. So I'd just be taking a load of trains and tubes for no reason. It's all over the place in London. That's what they're saying.'

Southwark and Westminster, especially. Jenny's offices

were in Southwark. But there was no point in thinking about it. Not now.

'I told your dad, we should stock up. I said we should have got some more toilet rolls. He wouldn't let me.'

Alison pursed her lips and glanced towards the downstairs toilet. Upstairs, Jenny knew that there were three unopened twelve-packs clogging up the airing cupboard, making it impossible to get to the towels without hauling them all out.

'We've got plenty.'

Alison ignored her. 'Maybe you could nip out for me. Before you go. Just to top up.'

Jenny briefly closed her eyes. She felt as if she were going mad.

'I'm not sure if I'm going to go. I think I should stay here.'

'Oh.'

Perfectly neutral. No emotion at all. Why was there never any emotion there? Surely Alison was scared. Surely everyone was. Jenny smiled at her, reassuring. Perhaps this was just a hard outer shell that Jenny could break through. She smiled and sat down next to her mother on the sofa. It sagged alarmingly beneath her. They'd had this suite since she was a little girl.

'I could look after you. You'll need someone to do the shopping. You shouldn't be going to shops if I can, you're more vulnerable.'

Alison flicked a page of her magazine. There was a picture of a grim-faced woman wielding a hairbrush under the headline CUTE NEW FELLA STOLE MY HAIR AS I SLEPT.

'I said to him that this time it'd go global. He said I was making a fuss over nothing. But now look.'

On impulse, Jenny reached out and took her mother's hand. She squeezed, but it lay on Alison's lap, cool and unresponsive. 'Mum, do you want me to stay?'

Alison didn't look at her. She stood up, shrugging Jenny's hand away. She needed to lean on the arm of the sofa now, to stand up. Jenny was sure she hadn't had to do that at Christmas.

'Let's get you a cup of tea, if you're staying.'

Jenny followed her mother into the kitchen and sat at the kitchen table as her mother fussed around with tea and cups and plates for biscuits that neither of them would eat. A familiar ritual.

'Remember, I got you oat milk,' Jenny said.

'Oh yes, I know. Don't worry, I won't drink it.'

Chris's words were still nagging at her, and Alex's. Jenny hadn't seen in the larder. She'd bought all the ingredients for meals. It had seemed mean to take anything from her mother, especially while she seemed worried about food. She'd assumed she hadn't had chickpeas, anyway. But now it felt hard to let go. She surely wouldn't stockpile food. Only wankers stockpiled food, the kind of people who bought the *Sun* and thought foreigners should go back to where they came from. Her mum wasn't like that, was she?

Jenny had to know. It was a simple question. Did she trust Chris or her mum? Obviously her mum. So what was the harm in checking? Just a quick look. No harm at all.

'Can I help?'

She walked over to the larder without waiting for an answer. Her mother, visibly rattled, walked over and put a hand on the door. 'What are you doing?'

She must know what people said about her. In a village this size, it was impossible to avoid gossip, even if it was about you. Especially if it was about you. There was a type of person that took deep joy in telling people the spiky, secret things that other people thought of them, and Ravenspurn was full to the brim of that type of person.

'Looking for biscuits.'

The two women looked at each other. Alison's arm and the skin around her mouth both stretched.

'I can get you biscuits.'

Jenny held tight to the doorknob.

'Why? Do you not want me looking in the pantry?'

'No,' Alison met her eye, unflinching. 'You can look where you like.'

Jenny shoved the door open and stared at the neat rows of beans and soup and the bags of pasta. It was well stocked, sure. But was it a stockpile? Jenny didn't have any more food than she could cram in a single cupboard, at home, but that's because she only had a single cupboard. If she had a whole larder, would she fill it? Probably. Choosing at random, she counted up tins of beans and came to twelve. There were seven bags of pasta. Was that normal?

'What's the matter?' her mother said, her voice perfectly neutral, giving nothing away. Dad had always been the expressive one. Enough emotion for both of them. 'Can't you find the ones you like?'

'No. Just choosing, that's all.'

She picked out one of five packets of chocolate Hobnobs and closed the door.

'You always liked those,' her mother said.

They were one of the few foods that Jenny liked as much now as when she was ten years old.

'Yes.'

She took the plate from her mother and started arranging biscuits on it. Neat concentric rings, far more than they'd eat, but it was how her mother liked them. She set them down on the table, exactly halfway between the two of them, in the place the plate always sat.

'I thought I'd stay,' Jenny said, studiedly casual. Ben had already rejected a suggestion of moving in together. She wasn't sure she could take another one from her own mother.

'Oh yes?'

Alison was not eating the biscuits. She never did.

'I don't have to,' Jenny said.

Alison wrapped bony fingers around her cup of tea. The cup was patterned with pale pink flowers. Jenny used to love pink. She'd always tried to do what was expected of her, back when she was a little girl.

'It's still your home. I never changed your room. I didn't touch it.'

'I know,' Jenny said. The room was pink, too, the shelves and drawers still full of soft toys and dried-up gel pens. It was like a shrine to 1999 up there. 'Do you want me to stay?'

Alison stared at her and, for a moment, the women made eye contact. Jenny felt unaccountably nervous. It was just her mother, wasn't it?

'Do you want to stay?'

Time stretched. And why not? There was nowhere to go.

'I want to know what you want.'

Alison was the first to look away. Jenny felt a rush of triumph, which she knew was pathetic, but there it was.

'Oh, you know me, love. I'll be happy with anything.'

This was an outright lie. Alison was never happy with anything. Just because you didn't shout about things didn't mean you were happy about them. There was more than one way to express displeasure.

'I'll stay then.'

Alison took a sip of tea. The sip sounded unnaturally loud in the quiet of the kitchen. Alison didn't like to have background music on.

'If that's what you want.'

'It'll only be a couple of weeks. Then it'll go back to normal.'

Jenny took a sip of her own tea. Too weak and too hot and made with skimmed milk, because Alison had forgotten about the oat milk, actually, so it tasted thin and insubstantial. Her mother smiled, and Jenny told herself firmly that it was nice to be home.

'Well. We'll see.'

She stared at the plate of biscuits. Concentric circles, made of circles, closing themselves in.

'I'd better go and unpack,' Jenny said. She needed a reason to leave the kitchen, and the conversation, which were both starting to feel, as they had so many times before, like a trap.

No matter how many times Jenny walked the beach, she couldn't help but notice the air. The constant thrum of anxiety, so much a part of her life that she was barely aware of it, about pollution, about the summers getting hotter and the bushfires on the news and about how we all kept on getting on planes and driving cars and just ignoring it – this past week, it had all suddenly and blessedly ceased. There were no planes and no cars and there was only one thing to worry about and everything felt simple again. In Ravenspurn, there was nothing to do except walk on the beach, and on the beach there was just the sea and sun and open sky and you could smell the space of the place on the wind.

She hadn't said it to anyone. She didn't want them to tear the idea down. But was it possible that with a little bit of a break, the world might heal itself? Nature fought back fast.

Maybe she was kidding herself. She needed something nice, after Dad.

As if it had heard her, a seagull swooped overhead, calling out, harsh and loud. Jenny stopped to watch it, white wings cutting their way across the grey. She stood until she felt foolish, staring at a bird, and pressed on. It was hard to stop behaving as if you had somewhere to be.

Today, Jenny was doing her usual loop. Five minutes through the street that led to the sea, smiling at Mr Todd, who went out with his dog at the same time she did, and Mrs

Baker, who liked to pop to the shops every day and insisted to Alison that was allowed as it was still buying essentials; as long as she got her pint of milk along with a paper and her scratch card, it was fine. She seemed to drink a lot of milk. Then Jenny would be by the sea, and she'd always pause for a moment to take in the great wide stretch of it, a different colour each day, ready to be noted and filed away as a point of small talk with her mother. The ruins of the old hotel would loom high up above, looking down on the village, making Jenny feel tiny, like they had since she really was small. Then she'd walk past her dad's old pub and along the promenade with its mainly closed-up shops, like knocked-out teeth in the smile of the street, and then she'd step out onto the sand and she was at the best bit.

She scanned the horizon with her eyes, taking in the end-less flat grey stretch of the sea. When they were kids, she and Alex and Si used to play pirates. Jenny hadn't enjoyed it as much as they both seemed to. Like all of Alex's games, pirates involved getting soaking wet and covered in sand and usually beaten up in some small way that wasn't signifi-cant enough to complain about and have an adult take you seriously, but would still stay with you and sting for days, reminding you of the little injury and the injustice that went along with it. But one of the things that Jenny really had enjoyed was playing lookout. If you scanned the horizon for long enough, you were bound to see some pirates heaving into view in the end, flashing knives and black sails and treasure. It was inevitable. And Jenny had liked that. The waiting and the watching and the sureness that something exciting would happen.

She was still staring at the horizon and thinking about pirates when they both appeared. As if she'd summoned them from the past, or they'd been what she'd been looking out for all along. Already close enough for there to be absolutely no option to pretend she hadn't seen them. She forced a smile and stopped in front of them. Two metres away. How close did she normally stand to people?

'Um. Hi,' Jenny said. It was hard to shake the idea that she might have summoned them.

'All right, Jenny!' Si said, smiling at her like a golden retriever. 'I thought we'd bump into you. Chris said you'd cancelled on him. I told him you'd probably just found someone to drive you back to Donny that weren't a complete prick, but he was having none of it, he said you'd stayed.'

Alex rolled her eyes. 'Course she stayed.'

'Well, yep. God's own county, in't it? Of course she stayed if she dun't have to go to work for the best part of a month.'

Jenny smiled blandly and tried not to react to the idea of staying here for a month. She was trying to take it one day at a time. A month was too overwhelming.

Alex scowled out to sea. 'Hmm. Some of us do still have to go to work.'

Si grinned again. Jenny had forgotten quite how much he smiled. Always happy, always joking. She'd never met anyone since who took so much raw joy in life.

'We can't all be key workers, pet. Me and Jenny here are on easy street. That's what you get for not being essential.'

'Well,' Jenny said, and couldn't think of anything to add. She didn't want to complain. She was grateful not to be working in a shop at the moment, of course she was.

Alex ignored her. 'Jenny's probably got her furlough payments sorted. Not just dossing around the flat doing fuck all, bringing no money in.'

Si pulled the same face he always had when anyone mentioned responsibilities, back when he was at school. 'I've asked Pete, an't I?'

Alex's scowl deepened. She jerked her head up over her shoulder and towards the cliff, and the caravan park, and Pete. As a village, Ravenspurn was not fond of Pete, but Alex hated him in a sharp, pointed way, and had done for as long as Jenny could remember. Something about a push, or a grab, or something. Grudges went back a long time around here. 'But you know he'll do nothing about it. He can't even turn his computer on without you going up to help. No way he'll sort the forms out.'

Si shrugged and grinned. 'Can't do more than that. It's illegal.'

Jenny looked up to the caravan park. 'He hasn't sorted your furlough form out?'

Alex laughed, loud and brittle. 'You surprised?'

Jenny shrugged. From what she'd heard, Ted had been doing the lion's share of Pete's admin for years now. It was no excuse. 'Pete's acting manager. He has an obligation.'

Si scratched the back of his neck, his T-shirt sleeve riding up just enough to show a flash of armpit hair. It was hot for March, but not T-shirt hot.

'Aye, well, maybe. It'd be nice to have the cash, I reckon.'

And Alex pulled a face that made Jenny half expect she was going to lamp him. She certainly would have, when she was a teenager. Times had changed, though. She really was quieter now, less aggressive, which was a low bar, but still. 'Oh, you'll hear it from her. I've told you till you're blue in the face, Simon Blower, but the second Jenny says—'

Si held his hands up in front of him, in mock surrender to Alex. Jenny noticed absently that it would be very annoying to get that kind of response when you were only trying to get your partner to sort their finances out. And she remembered now – going out with Si had been so much fun, but only ever that. Never anything serious, and if something heavy ever did come up, he'd find some reason to slip away.

'Well, she's a lawyer, in't she? Aren't you? She knows about stuff like that. She's not thick like us.'

Jenny blinked. It used to be her and Si who were the thick ones. Alex had always left them both for dust, with Si falling behind and not giving a fuck and Jenny working her arse off to get her B+. But she was a lawyer now, yes. She'd kept working her arse off. She'd kept getting B+s. She glanced over to Alex, expecting her to look murderous, but, worse, her face was completely blank. She only used to do that when she was properly upset.

Si carried on, oblivious. 'So, yeah, all right. I'll have a crack.'

'Where's Barney?'

Jenny only asked to change the subject. But now she thought about it, it was weird to go on your daily walk and not take the dog.

Alex shrugged. 'Can't handle a big walk. Legs are knackered, bless him. I'll take him out later.'

Si smirked. 'You'll carry him about, you mean.'

Alex gave him a playful smack on the arm. 'It's not his fault his legs are fucked. He still needs to get a bit of fresh air.'

It was funny to see her so defensive about Barney. Jenny would never have had Alex down to grow up into one of those women who had a little dog she carried around and got mushy about.

'Yeah, he's on furlough from being a dog.'

And a shadow crossed her face like a storm cloud, so obvious even Si noticed.

'What the fuck have I said now?'

She shook her head. 'It's not you. It just pisses me off.'

Si sighed, pretend-patient.

'What does?' Jenny asked. She felt sorry for Alex. Si wasn't as fun when you had something serious you wanted to say.

'Dun't matter.'

The wind whipped along the barren stretch of the beach, fluttering Si's T-shirt. But he just stood, solid as ever. He never had felt the cold. A lump came to Jenny's throat.

'Go on.'

Alex squinted, weighing her up.

'The idea is that people get paid more because they work harder, in't it? But that falls down when no one's working. Why are you getting more money for sitting on your arse than Si is?'

Jenny opened her mouth and then closed it.

'Because she's got a better arse than me?' Si said.

'Fuck off, mate.'

Si shrugged. 'Well, I don't care about people getting more than me. They always are, aren't they? I'd be happy to be getting anything.'

Alex glowered out to sea. 'You're always happy. Dun't make it right.'

He grinned and slung an arm around her shoulders. 'You got a better idea then, Jeremy Corbyn?'

Alex didn't shrug the arm away, but her face was clay-cold.

'Yeah. Universal basic income. But no one's listening to my ideas, are they?'

'You should stand,' Jenny said. She was desperate, suddenly, for Alex to say something cocky. To be a bit more like she used to be. And she'd be great at politics, surely. Charm and lived experience. That was what people wanted, wasn't it? Outside London anyway. 'Be a councillor and work your way up.'

She got a withering look in response.

'You need a degree to be an MP, Jenny. Even in backwaters like this.'

Jenny felt her face flush bright red. The blushing was concerning. She didn't do that kind of thing any more. All the careful work she'd done, building a new self away from here, one where she could be successful, and liked. It was upsetting how easily it could all be unpicked.

'I'd best …' And then it came to her. She had a perfect excuse to not talk to anyone she didn't want to. For the next three weeks, at least. 'I don't think we're meant to be chatting. But take care, yeah? Let me know if you have any trouble with Pete.'

Alex rolled her eyes and she and Si smirked at each other, on the same team again. It was obvious that they were one of those couples who fought like they watched TV or drank tea. Nothing meant by it at all. She and Ben weren't like that. They never argued.

'Might be easier to let you know if there's a miracle and we don't have trouble with Pete.'

Jenny looked up to the clifftop caravan park. Her father had given her a lecture, that first day she'd been made bar manager. His voice rang in her ears. *You've got to remember, it's not just ordering people about, when you're the boss. You've got a responsibility.*

'Look, do you want me to talk to him?'

Alex looked suspicious, but also heart-twistingly hopeful.

'You don't have to do that.'

Jenny shrugged, awkward. She did though, didn't she? She did really.

'But I can do.'

Si shook his head decisively, his jaw clenched. 'I can't let you.'

'Why not?' And it was obvious, suddenly, that she'd get no credit from Alex for making the offer. That Alex had been waiting for her to say it since it had come up. 'It's her uncle.'

Si pressed his lips into a hard line, the same way Jenny had seen her dad do when her mum offered to take the bins out. 'Even so, but.'

Alex raised her eyebrows. 'It is her pub.'

'It's not,' Jenny said, automatically, and Alex skewered her with a gaze.

'It's going to be.'

And Jenny knew that she was right, and that she should have done a better job of looking out for Si, and that Alex thought that too. Jenny wasn't sure how she could have thought that Alex was any less assertive than she had been when she was seventeen. She'd grown up, that was all. She'd become a lot more subtle.

Pete opened the hall's kitchen door and didn't say hello. Jenny wasn't sure he'd ever said hello to her in her life, or anyone else. He always just started talking.

'Haven't had many visitors up here for a while,' he said, not looking at her, studiously hanging up a tea towel. That counted as friendly, for him. 'You'd best come in.'

The towel was faded and greying but impeccably clean and neatly pressed. Clearly Pete was still hiring in a cleaning lady – he would never have such high standards himself. But who could it be, now that Jean was dead? The population of Ravenspurn was getting older, creeping towards retirement age, while the young ones left, scattering to Leeds or Hull or even Driffield – anywhere that wasn't here. Except for Alex and Si, of course. This place would bury those two.

Jenny remembered the hall's kitchen from Brownies, with its beaten-up steel tea urn and its bottles of squash and plastic beakers. Were there still malted milk biscuits in the cupboards? Jenny didn't check. Instead, she followed him through the main hall, which was somehow worse than she remembered. The ceiling was patched with yellow puddles of leaked-through damp and the whole place smelled of generations of sweaty football socks and old pork pies. The corners of the room were stacked high with chairs and tables – enough for hundreds, thousands, it seemed like, more than anybody could possibly want, more than lived in the village. They crowded their way into the meagre floor-space and gave the room a cramped air and a feeling of only being half-used, like a school hall in the summer holidays, or an ice-cream stand in winter. Waiting.

She shivered. She shouldn't have come in.

'We can go back outside if you like,' she said.

Jenny would have much preferred to go outside. Outside smelled of sea and clean and safe. The hall smelled of damp and socks, the same as it always did, but underneath it, a hint of menace. *Germs germs germs*. Could they have got to Pete? It was possible. She'd only come with one mask, and she'd worn it and worn it until the ear loop snapped, and you couldn't get more, in Ravenspurn, and when she'd asked Alex to order some in, she'd laughed and asked Jenny if she'd heard of the shortages and if it might not be hard enough just to keep them in milk and bread? She hadn't asked again.

'No,' he said, face blank and arms crossed over his belly. He stalked over to his office in the corner and disappeared in.

Jenny followed Pete through the door and into the poky little storage room he used for an office, so the chairs and tables just had to sit out in the hall. The walls of the office were cracked and grey, and like most places where you can see the sea, the room smelled overwhelmingly of damp. Jenny shifted, uneasy. He certainly wasn't two metres away.

Pete threw himself into a chair and scowled up at Jenny, the way she'd seen him scowl at Dad a hundred hundred times. A little brother kind of a scowl.

Jenny hovered awkwardly by the desk, trying not to breathe in or out too much.

'Have you seen the news?' he said. 'They've got the police out harassing people just for being outside. Fucking nuts.'

Pete settled himself back in his chair and scowled out of the tiny window. The chair was the one expensive thing in the whole caravan park. Every other piece of furniture in the entire place looked like it had been bought in the nineties, and second-hand at that, but Pete's chair was glossy leather and as plump as him.

'I know.'

Pete was still looking out of the window. Jenny followed his gaze. A seagull landed on one of the nearby caravans, the tip of its beak shocking red.

'They'll be busting down that door any minute. You wait and see.'

He leaned back in his desk chair, head nearly brushing the mildewed wall.

'We're okay,' Jenny said. She was talking to herself, more than him. Trying to convince herself. She was right, though. She'd checked the website again and again. 'It's all legal if it's work.'

Pete shrugged, as if to say he didn't give a shit what was legal or not, which was not a surprising viewpoint from him.

'What work do you want to do, then? Pub's shut, isn't it? The caravan park too. All shut. Fucking government.'

'I want you to sign the furlough papers for Si.'

She pulled the sheaf of papers from her handbag and laid them in front of him. He didn't even look down. It had taken the printer in her dad's office a whole morning to laboriously chunter them out, but there was no way Pete would have done it himself.

'You do it,' he said.

Jenny took in a deep breath of damp and tried to be professional.

'I'm not the legal owner.'

He shrugged. 'Nor me neither.'

Jenny bit back a sigh. You had to be patient, with Pete, or you got nowhere.

'But you're acting manager. You're the one he named.'

He was still looking out of the window. Pointed, this time, his mouth a hard line, like he was avoiding looking at her more than he was choosing to look out.

'It's going to go to you, though. Obviously it is. Even though it was me he wanted to manage it when he was ill.'

Jenny swallowed, nervous. She hadn't realised Pete would give a shit. He'd never seemed ambitious, happy to run his park as long as it brought in enough for the bills and a few beers on the weekend. She hadn't known he'd wanted the pub. It had been his father's, once, she supposed. But he wasn't generally a sentimental man.

'I don't know.'

He glared at her. 'Have you not seen the will?'

She kept her face blank. Now wasn't the time to be smart with him. There was a lockdown on – no she hadn't seen the will. No need to be stuck up about it, though. 'No.'

Pete sniffed, deep and rich. 'It'll be you. He always wanted you to take over that place.'

Jenny shrugged. He was probably right.

'I don't know about that. I'm just here about the form.'

He was still glowering. It was easy to imagine him as a child, like this, sulking and pouting. He must have been such a pain in the arse to have as a little brother. It was enough to make Jenny grateful she was an only child.

'I'm the one who's run his own business for umpteen years,' he said. 'What are you going to do with a place like that?'

'I don't know who the pub's going to, Pete. I don't know anything about it. But Si needs this signing to get his furlough money.'

Jenny's voice came out harsh and posh and aggressive, bouncing around in the tiny office.

Pete shrugged, unbothered. Jenny supposed that if you went through your life being Pete, you got used to people shouting at you.

'I'm not paying that fucking space cadet to sit on his bum and not work. I don't give a fuck about some pandemic. He can stick it up his arse.'

She rolled her eyes. Pete was so full of shit. He was fonder of Si than he was of anyone — had been since he was a little kid. 'It's not you paying him. It comes straight from the government. All you've got to do is sign.'

Pete stared down at the forms. The very presence of them seemed to make him uncomfortable, as if it was a spider squatting there on his desk rather than a few bits of paper.

'It bloody won't be though, will it? All these government things, council things. You have to make an account, fucking password full of numbers and pound signs, spending hours on the computer sweating over it. I haven't the time.'

Jenny resisted the impulse to ask him exactly what else he was doing with his time.

'I've printed it all out. All you have to do is sign, so Si can get his furlough money.'

He stared at the forms suspiciously. 'You don't see me getting any fucking furlough money.'

Jenny dug her nails into the palms of her hands. She kept her voice level as she said, 'You get separate as a business owner. I can help you with that. But you've got to sign this for Si.'

Pete gave her an unpleasant little smile. 'Why do you care? Still carry a torch for him, do you?'

Jenny ignored that extremely impertinent question and fixed him with a hard stare. Surely even Pete had a little shame.

'Dad would have done it.'

Pete picked a pen up and put it down again.

'He would have done a lot of things.'

Jenny thought of Si. Her dad really would have wanted to look after him. Anyone would. Si had that kind of air about him – he was an innocent. Sweet and loving, and perhaps, you'd maybe admit to someone who knew him as well as you did, who loved him like you did, a tiny bit thick. He needed a hand, and some fucking cash to pay his rent while the pub was shut.

'Didn't you tell Kevin you'd look after Si?'

Pete glowered at her. 'Fucking low blow.'

She shrugged and didn't look away, and wouldn't let him either. 'It's just the truth.'

Much to her surprise, he smiled. Ted's smile, like it always was.

'You always were a clever one, our Jenny.'

Our Jenny? She was pretty certain he'd never called her our Jenny before. She had no idea how to answer, so she said nothing, and it seemed to be the right decision, because he picked the pen back up.

'No one was surprised, you know. When you left.'

Jenny grimaced to herself. She'd heard this before. People loved telling her. They always seemed to think they were the first.

'What, because I'm a stuck-up cow? And I think I'm too good for this place?'

But he wasn't laughing.

'Because you are too good for this place. You had the spark. You were always going to get out.'

Jenny felt her teeth on her bottom lip before she could stop herself.

'Alex was the one with the spark. I was just ordinary.'

Pete shrugged and let the chair tilt him upright. He was so tall they were almost level, even though she was still standing up.

'Alex is still here.'

Pete picked up the papers and licked his finger, riffling through the sheets.

'Do I do a form for her?'

Jenny shook her head. She really wanted to use her hand sanitiser. So funny how quickly that had become a habit. She wasn't sure she'd ever owned a bottle of hand sanitiser before last month. Now it felt as necessary as brushing her teeth. The Co-op didn't stock that either, though. She'd nearly run out, and the wait time online was two months. Useless. By then they'd all have gone back to happily eating on buses and touching each other and going to work and living again. 'No. It's a second job, it doesn't qualify.'

'Poor cow.' He was looking out of his tiny window at the grey waves beyond the line of caravans. 'There's another storm coming, you know?'

Jenny followed his gaze. It was blustery, sure, but there was more blue than grey in the sky, and more white than either of them. It was a perfectly normal day.

'Yeah?'

Pete scowled out at the horizon.

'Yeah. I can feel it.'

'It didn't say on the news.'

Pete snorted. He clearly held the concept of the news in some contempt. 'I can feel it. Besides, there's always another storm coming.'

'I suppose so,' Jenny said. It was undeniably true, in a broader sense. But it wasn't like Pete to be philosophical.

'This village gets buffeted, over and over again, storms and seas and a recession, and another one, and another one, and another one, and now this. Every time we fight to get back to where we were and we never quite make it. It always ends up a little bit worse than it was.'

And Jenny had never heard it laid out like that. But that was exactly it. Every time she came back here, year on year, it was just a little bit worse. That was why she hated coming home.

One of the reasons.

'I'm sorry.'

He got out of his chair and, in one quick movement, he was across the room and beside her and holding her hand tight in his, the germs of his skin on her skin and his breath in her face and his fingers tight around her wrist.

'I'm glad you got out. Don't go sticking around here for too long again. I'll look after Ali for you. Honest.'

She could feel her heart pounding and her breath coming fast, rabbit-like, but she'd trained for years to never show she was afraid. Not just at work, but every night bus and bad date that she'd wished herself out of. She could hide it. She'd be fine.

'He was my brother,' Pete said. His fingers loosened and Jenny felt her breathing slow. Forced it to. 'He was my best mate.'

And for the first time that day, Jenny felt properly close to tears. Because she could tell that Pete was serious – he meant it that Ted had been his closest friend. But Ted had never got on with his brother. He'd tolerated him at best. Maybe that was the kindest anyone had been to Pete, a sort of grudging acceptance.

'I know.'

'I kept his secrets. He kept mine. Our whole lives, you know? It's a long time.'

The fight was gone from his voice. He looked so much like Dad when he wasn't scowling.

And he dropped her hand and he finally signed the papers.

Jenny sat on the floor of her mother's bedroom, surrounded by cardboard boxes. She opened the one in front of her to find a nest of flat caps and scarves. She tilted it to show her mother the contents.

'What about this one?'

Alison looked over and pursed her lips as if the hats had offended her. She turned away to a bag of pyjamas and dressing gowns.

'I don't know. Put it in the maybe pile.'

Alison's back was turned, so Jenny allowed herself to roll her eyes. There was barely anything that wasn't in the maybe pile. A couple of files of old accounts from the pub and some of Alison's clothes that had been sorted into the wrong box were in the no pile, and Jenny's GCSE and A level certificates (wrong box, again) were in the yes pile. Everything of Ted's was a maybe. Not one thing or the other. This was a pointless task.

She opened another one.

'Books.'

But she had insisted. Her mother kept saying that she had to go through the boxes, that she was too busy to do anything else, that she simply must.

'Maybe pile.'

And finally Jenny had been desperate enough to ask to

join her, rather than spending another night alone on the sofa, picking up her phone and then remembering she wasn't reachable, again and again and again.

'Right.'

It was an activity, at least, that she was doing with her mother. It was helping. It was something. And besides, the walk only filled up an hour a day.

She opened another box.

'Hey. What's this?'

Inside was a nest of wool. She picked up a hat – bright red, a simple pattern, but nicely made. And a scarf, uneven and tapering off to one end with dropped stitches. They smelled of dust and Old Spice.

Alison looked over her shoulder.

'You should know. You made them.'

Jenny turned the scarf over in her hands. She had made it, she remembered now. Year six, this one. A Christmas present for Dad. She'd spent weeks on it, labouring over a couple of lines a night in front of *Fun House*.

'For Dad?'

She still remembered the feeling of finishing it on Christmas Eve. She hadn't thought she'd be able to.

'That's right.'

Jenny picked up scarf after glove after hat. Birthday and Christmas presents for her father, going back years. She rummaged through to the bottom and found a thin strip of garter stitch made up in cheap pink acrylic. The first thing she'd ever finished. A 'tie' for him.

'He kept them. Even the shit ones.'

Her mum eyed the box and cracked a rare real smile. She

reached out and stroked the red hat. 'Of course he did. He'd never throw away something that you made him.'

Jenny felt tears pricking at the back of her eyes.

'I didn't know.'

Alison reached over, folded the flaps of the box back up and put it silently next to Jenny's certificates. Yes pile. Without a word, she went back to flipping through a box of old ties.

Jenny smiled to herself and reached for another box. This one was different – the rest of them were old crisp boxes from the pub, scrawled on in Sharpie with her dad's untidy hand. Not that the labels helped, at all – all he ever wrote on them was 'loft stuff'. But this box was a pale yellow one, sturdier than the rest, and with a proper lid, rather than just flaps that folded down. This was a box that had been bought, not found, to put something important in. Jenny started to lift the lid—

'Not that one!'

Alison dived across the room, snatching up the box. She pulled and, for a moment, Jenny was so shocked she clung on, and the two of them tussled over it.

'Let go!'

Alison shouted it, shrieked, almost, and Jenny forced her hands to obey. Her mother staggered back a step or two and clutched at the box, her arms caging round it. The two women stared at each other, separated by a bed and a box and more than thirty years.

'Okay, fine.'

Alison glared at her, the smile just a memory now. 'This one's private. Don't go snooping in it. Understand?'

And Jenny felt really and truly told off. Even though she knew rationally she'd done nothing wrong. But then, she hadn't really when she was a child, had she? It didn't matter; she'd still get told off or frozen out when something upset Alison, no matter what had caused it.

She sighed. 'Look, I'm going to take a break. Let's do the rest of this some other time. *Pointless* is on. Okay?'

And she forced herself to stand up, to walk calmly out of the room, and to put the kettle on.

The only way to get past it, when her mum was like this, was to pretend that nothing had happened. In a few hours, or a few days, Alison would join in, would drop the silent treatment, and they'd never mention it again, and then it'd be kind of true that it hadn't happened. If you don't remember something, maybe it's almost the same as it not existing in the first place.

'I'm making a tea,' she shouted up the stairs. 'Do you want one?'

There was a silence. Jenny almost gave up on getting a response.

Then, 'All right.'

The kettle boiled and Jenny brooded. What was in the box? Letters from an old lover? Something Alison had done, years ago, now hushed up? Everything Jenny could think of seemed so unlikely.

She made tea for both of them, much weaker than she would in London and called up the stairs again.

'It's in the kitchen.'

And since she was in the hall anyway, she went over to the tote bag she'd brought with her from London. Her big headphones, and knitting – a standard travelling kit. She took the knitting with her, clicked on the TV and settled down on the sofa. On screen, contestants stood far too close together and laughed into each others faces. A window into the past.

Jenny answered the questions in her head and thought about Gail and Ben. She wished she was back in London, talking out loud and bickering about the answers. She wound the wool around her fingers, smooth and squashy and comforting, and finished the row she'd abandoned when they had pulled into Driffield two weeks ago.

'Thanks for the tea.'

She had to stop herself from jumping. Her mother had appeared, ghostlike, in the doorway from the hall.

'You're welcome,' Jenny said, and started on the next row. As she did, she noticed that she'd missed a stitch. She briefly thought about unpicking it, but Gail had always told her not to try to knit a perfect piece. *It'll drive you mad if you're aiming for flawlessness, and anyway, it's not symmetry we find beautiful, it's just a tiny little bit off of symmetry.*

It was okay, sometimes, not to be perfect.

Alison perched on the far edge of the sofa.

'Have you decided what you're going to do about the pub?'

Of course she had. She was going to sell it, wasn't she? How could she do anything else. Obviously she was selling it.

'Nah. Still thinking.'

Her mother sipped her tea and her shoulders dropped, just a little. She turned to stare at the screen.

'Well, I haven't changed your room.'

A contestant was crying, but Jenny hadn't been concentrating. She couldn't tell whether they were happy or sad.

'What?'

Alison's eyes flickered to Jenny, and then back again. Was she nervous? What about? It couldn't be Jenny, could it? This was the wrong way around.

'I just mean. If you want it. Still your home.'

Jenny looked, long and hard, at her mother, and then down at her weak tea and her knitting. Was this as much a home as anywhere?

Maybe.

'Thanks,' she said.

They watched the rest of the episode without a word.

'So it didn't wake you up? You're sure?'

Jenny shook her head and ploughed on up the cliff path. Her mother had been talking about the storm all morning. Talking about the weather was a sure sign that they'd run out of things to say to each other, and Jenny could tell that Alison was hamming it up to make conversation.

'Well, fancy that. I would have thought it would wake you up. I would have put money on it!'

She'd agreed to come and survey the damage anyway. Like Alison, she had run out of things to talk about.

'No. I slept really well.'

Which was true, in a way. Jenny had stayed up for four hours after her mother had gone to bed the night before, self-medicating with old romcoms on VHS and the end of a bottle of whisky. It must have been open at least five years – her dad liked to spin spirits out. When was the last time he'd had a glass of it? Was it at Christmas, or maybe his birthday? Or just a random day he'd found particularly hard? Had he used alcohol to celebrate – to mark the tiny triumphs of his life? Or had he used it, as Jenny did, to soften the edges of the bad days, to smooth them down until the spikes were worn away and it was finally possible to sleep?

Now she'd never know.

Jenny herself had been drinking every night since lockdown

started. If she didn't, she found that she woke up, almost exactly at 1 a.m., with a start and an unshakeable feeling that she was being watched.

Alison tutted. 'Well, you're a better sleeper than me. I barely caught a wink.'

Jenny nodded and paused while her mother caught up the few yards she was trailing behind her. She was surprised she had to keep remembering to slow down for her mother, despite the hangover. Jenny walked this cliff path every day now, and her legs had got used to it fast. Her eyes fell on a small tree by the path. It had completely blown over, exposing roots so shallow it seemed incredible it had ever been able to cling on in the first place.

'I hope it didn't cause too much damage,' her mother said, panting a little.

Jenny looked back down to the lower level of the village, already so far below that it looked toy-like. Unreal.

'It won't have.'

She longed for London. Not the geography of it, so much. She still wasn't bored of the way the cliff dropped into the sea, which rose to meet the sky, the stark drama and the sweep of the place. Ravenspurn made the rest of the world seem so flat. But the emptiness of it was starting to make her itch. She could feel thoughts swirling around inside her, faster and faster, every little thing waiting to be picked over again and again. It was too quiet. She needed to get back to the noise.

But London was quiet too now. People kept sharing pictures, Trafalgar Square and Oxford Street all screamingly empty under the bright spring sunshine. Only ghosts and photographers in the city these days. Who knew when it would go back to something vaguely resembling normal? Not her. She was only watching the headlines of the news, and even then, only half-watching, catching it out of the corner of her eye, standing in the kitchen while her mother watched it in the living room. She didn't want to see, but it was too humiliating to keep finding things out through Alex, and it wasn't the kind of thing she wanted to ask Ben about. They were too precious, the snatched half-hour chats she had with him up the cliff. The one time a day she felt normal; she couldn't bear to let the dread in.

Her mother stopped and Jenny reluctantly came to a halt.

'Can you hear voices?'

Jenny worked hard to keep her face neutral. Why would there be voices? It had just been a bit of rain. It hadn't even woken her up. She turned and continued her plodding up the endless steps of the path.

'No, Mum.'

All she could hear was the wind. Really. But when they got to the top of the cliffs, nosing out into the exposed air, it seemed like the whole of the village was there. Jenny noted absently that it was just like her father's funeral.

She turned to her mother, suddenly seven again. 'What happened?'

Her mother didn't answer. Grim-faced, she walked over to the group. The definitely illegal group.

Jenny hung back, staring at the gaggle of people, taking in the scene and trying to work out what had changed. There was something subtly wrong. She couldn't quite put her finger on it. It went beyond being people together in person, and the altered-yet-familiar faces of the people who used to be the whole of her community, and who she hadn't really thought about in years.

Her eyes kept combing, combing, until it clicked.

There weren't enough caravans.

Jenny went and peered over the edge of the cliff, staring down at the beach below.

Pete came up beside her, shook his head and said, 'Fucking mess, that is.'

And it was a fucking mess.

One of the caravans had slid down the cliff. It hadn't fallen cleanly, but looked like it had skidded reluctantly down, smashing and scattering debris as it went. It had ended up on a sheltered little cove that lay beyond Ravenspurn's main beach. The ruined caravan seemed to almost fill the whole space of the smaller bay. Splintered kitchen workshops and walls had exploded all over the sand. A sofa bed hinged sadly apart in the middle of a pile of rubble, and Jenny could see a fridge and a cooker as well, dented and bashed in. Might they explode? She supposed there wouldn't be anyone down there to hurt, even if they did. Everyone in the village was already on the top of the cliff.

'Get back, Jenny,' Alison said, but no one paid attention.

Pete went on. He was much more animated than usual. Pete was the kind of man who loved a bit of bad news. 'First fucking storm of the year, and there's one gone already. It'll only get worse, mind.'

Si was staring down at the beach, grim-faced and ashen.

'Pack it in, Pete,' he said. He was the only one who could

talk to Pete like that without getting his head chewed off. Pete had been Si's dad's best mate before he died, and Si and Chris still got special allowances on account of it.

Pete didn't pack it in, though.

'It's the fucking council. They put up the sea walls around what they think's worth protecting, and the waves come for me instead.'

Jenny rolled her eyes.

'The sea hasn't got it in for you, Pete.'

And there was a silence. Jenny looked around at all the faces staring back, so familiar and yet all much older than they were in her mind, all subtly changed. She got the feeling she'd made some kind of deep faux pas.

It was Alex who spoke first, of course.

'He's right, though. You can't stop the sea taking the land, you can only push the problem down the coast. If Brid didn't have sea walls, we'd be losing land at half the rate.'

Jenny blinked. She looked along the coast, but it was too grey to see Bridlington today, and even if she could, it's not like she could examine the walls from here.

'Seriously?' How could the council let another town steal their land?

Alex smiled a tight, fake little smile. 'You're the one with A level geography, you look it up. I just live here.'

Jenny felt her cheeks flush. Along with lip chewing, blushing was something she'd managed to leave behind in her early twenties. But Alex had always been able to make her feel stupid with just a quick word. Anyone would think it was Jenny who'd failed everything and not got into uni.

But it would be very churlish to bring that up. Instead,

she said, 'But that's awful. They can't just pass the buck like that. Isn't there something you can do?'

'Jenny, get back.' This time, Alison put a hand on her arm and pulled her away. Jenny let herself be dragged like a child.

Pete gave Jenny a withering look. 'We're more bothered about the caravan at the moment, lass.'

Alison walked her back, too close to the rest of the group, surely only a metre or less from old Bill Jones, if that, then dropped her arm like it was something dead.

'That's right.' Alex's mum, still in her dressing gown and with a look in her eyes like she was spoiling for a fight, poked a bony finger at Jenny. 'Could have been my caravan, that could. Could have been when I was asleep, I'd have known nothing about it until I was smashed against them rocks . . .'

Jenny gritted her teeth. No matter how much she deserved it, she couldn't bring herself to tell an old woman to piss off. Had Karen always been this aggressive? Surely this was something that had bloomed in her over time. She remembered her being scary as a kid, though. Had Alex put up with this all along? She certainly seemed used to it. Alex was looking only mildly annoyed.

'You're the furthest one away, Mum. You're not about to go falling off the cliffs.'

Karen sniffed.

Seeing them both in profile like that, for the first time Jenny could really see the family resemblance. They both had the same line to their forehead and chin and, if you discounted the bump from an old break that Alex had once told her was a pirate attack, the same nose as well.

'Well, it obviously wasn't good enough for you, was it, Miss Princess? Moved out the second you turned eighteen, didn't you, not a single thought for your old mum, all alone at the top of a cliff, just left to fend for herself.'

Alex took a step closer, her lips raised in an almost-snarl, her face almost touching her mother's. Not two metres. Illegal. Jenny was noticing that with less and less urgency every time it happened. 'You told me to go, you stupid old bitch . . .'

And Jenny was glad, for a moment, to have a mother who'd pull her away from the edge of a cliff.

'Come on now,' Bill said. He hadn't said a word since Jenny had been back, not here nor at the funeral. He'd been there, though, his little tweed cap as familiar a part of the village as the brown cliffs. 'Language.'

Alex looked over to Jenny and for a moment they held each other's eye and Jenny could tell exactly what Alex was thinking. The amount of times they'd been working in the pub together and Bill had been propping up the bar and he'd said that to them, that exact same tone. And Alex would always tell him to fuck off and call him an old wanker, but not loud enough for him to hear, only Jenny, and the two of them would crease up with laughter and laugh even more to see him so indignant and not know what was funny. And Jenny smiled at her. It was like stepping back in time, just for a moment.

Then Jenny looked back down at the wreck of the caravan and the moment was over. It wouldn't really happen to Karen's caravan, would it? It couldn't.

'The tourists won't like it,' said Si.

Alex twisted her mouth, in a way that Ted always had when he had bad news to deliver.

'There won't be any this year, anyway. This is going to go on and on.'

Pete smiled. Not a nice smile.

'That's something, then.'

Jenny stepped carefully down the trail that wove from the caravan park to the old hotel. She breathed in a deep, cold lungful of air and felt her hangover finally start to recede. Her head had pounded all the way back down the cliff path with her mother, all the way through a cup of tea, her mother saying *could you believe it?* again and again, on a loop, all the way back up the cliff to check her messages. Jenny hadn't realised how accustomed she'd become to a life without meetings, without problems to be solved.

She'd better get used to it. They'd announced another three weeks of lockdown. That had been last night's snippet of news, overheard while pretending to do the washing-up. She was trying to pretend that she hadn't. Thinking about it wouldn't help.

There was an organic undernote to the air today. A hint of rotting fish and seaweed, of seagull shit and clay. It should have been unpleasant, this sweet tang of decay, but somehow it was comforting. There was life happening all around, here. There was comfort in the closeness of the land and the sea.

She looked over the edge, even though she knew she wouldn't be able to see the fallen caravan from here. She didn't want to see it anyway, innards spilling obscenely out, lying broken on the beach.

It was incredible that anyone still came to Pete's caravan park. When she was a child, the place was always full in summer, young families with their barbecues and their beach picnics and buckets and spades and ice cream. But looking at the caravans today, it seemed hard to believe that anyone would take a part of the brief, precious span of British summertime and spend it somewhere so exposed. You could fly to Spain in an hour. Why would you come to a place where even the seagulls looked pissed off with the cold?

Jenny looked at her phone. Finally, two bars. She tapped out a message to Ben and hit send. After checking the recipient, of course. There had been an incident, back in London, with a stray text message and her boss. Now she checked.

Big drama in little Ravenspurn! One of the caravans fell off the cliff last night x

She'd started washing her hands twice to make sure as well. But surely everyone was doing that, what with the pandemic?

Jenny pressed on. She had a spot that she thought of as hers now, where she went to check her messages and stare out to sea and not read the news on her phone. It had added a pleasing shape to her days, otherwise baggy and formless. There was news now though, intruding on the carefully constructed, boring little world she'd built herself these last few weeks. Would the caravan just lie there? It would have to until the end of lockdown, surely. What else was there to be done?

Jenny was almost at the edge of the cliff when she saw a figure sitting on a half-tumbled-down bench, with some kind of dog at their feet, both of them staring out to sea. Jenny felt herself bristling. That was her ruined bench. Her sea view.

Jenny's phone buzzed in her hand. A message from Ben.

Shit

She still hadn't been able to bring herself to put it back fully on silent, after Dad had died. It would mean finally admitting that she wasn't waiting for news about him, that there'd never be any news, not ever again. And the noise of the vibration made the figure look up.

On the bench, looking tiny against the sprawling backdrop of crumbled stone and marbled sky, was Alex. And for a moment she looked so much like she had as a child that Jenny was catapulted back in time. She could still feel the ghost of the urge to pull away, to make herself so small that Alex wouldn't be able to find her and make her smaller.

Another buzz.

Are you okay? Was anyone hurt? x

But at the same time ... Alex looked like a child again. It seemed stupid, now, to be afraid of a seven-year-old. And Alex was only a normal woman, with a work uniform that was too big for her on the top and too small on the bottom and a little dog that looked like it had arthritis in its hips and a flat and a job and a boyfriend that Jenny knew inside out. That had been Jenny's boyfriend first, after all.

'You going to answer that?'

And childhood was a world away, however close it felt

when she was back here. That creeping feeling of the past at her back, waiting to suck her back in, had kept her away for years. But it was just an illusion. Nothing more than a trick of the light.

'Yeah. That's why I'm here.'

No. They're abandoned. We had to have a village meeting though, very extreme! x

'Can you believe it about the caravan?' Jenny said, hearing her mother in her voice and hating herself for it. She stuffed the phone back into her pocket.

'Happens quite a bit. I'm always disappointed it's not Mum's one, to be honest.'

Jenny felt her mouth drop open in shock and Alex flashed her a smile and all at once she looked like another Alex that Jenny remembered. That summer when they'd been eighteen and for two, glorious, shining months, it was as if the awkwardness and rivalries of childhood had melted away and they'd been proper friends. Jenny had never felt, before or since, that same sense of belonging as when Alex and Si had both liked her. In a new place, where you'd built a new life, no one knew you that thoroughly, no one knew the absolute bones of you. It took the sting out of them rejecting you, but it meant you lost out on that feeling of having someone stare right into your soul and welcome you into their life anyway.

Alex gestured to the other end of the bench. Jenny eyeballed it. It looked like about two metres. More or less. She sat down.

'What you doing here?' she said, conversationally. It had

been a long time since she'd had a casual chat. But this was an accident. They hadn't planned to meet. So it was fine.

Alex jutted her chin up, sizing Jenny up. She must have passed, because Alex extended an arm to the hotel wall. At first, Jenny couldn't tell where she was gesturing. The butter-yellow brickwork was crumbled and worn, patchworked with cavities and shadows, hard to see anything beyond. And then she saw it. A hollow in a gap where some bricks had fallen away, and a little bird's head poking out. As she watched, another gull flew up, twigs in its beak, and squeezed into the hole alongside. She was close enough to see the black dot of the seagull's eye, and when they weren't swooping and grabbing at her chips, Jenny could see that they were kind of beautiful.

'Is that a nest?'

'Yes.'

Jenny's phone buzzed in her pocket and she took it out without thinking.

???

'I suppose they must like it around here. All the fish,' she said, absently.

Alex snorted, her eyes still on the gulls. 'Everyone thinks that. Round here, they're as likely to go for the fields, this time of year. Ploughed fields are perfect for them. Full of worms. And then they'll take what they need from us too.'

Jenny frowned at her. She hadn't expected Alex to be this contemplative. What had she expected? That she'd turned into her mother, perhaps, or that she hadn't changed at all.

Still holding court, hanging over a bar. Not up a cliff staring at gull nests.

'Is that why we're only meant to put the bins out for a ten-minute slot every day?'

Barney barked, a little yip of boredom, and Alex picked him up, her fingers working his wiry fur.

'It's fucking pathetic. All they want is our rubbish and we won't let them take it. Humans are dickheads.'

Jenny nodded. That seemed pretty unarguable.

'When will there be chicks?'

Alex scrunched her eyes up, but her mouth softened. 'I dunno. Depends when they lay. They're a month early on the nesting. It's hot, this year.'

What, in person?

Jenny sighed at her phone. It was so hard to talk in snatched messages and quick phone calls. A month ago, she'd have been sure he'd know what she meant without her having to go round and round about it, explaining every little thing. Now, there were times when it seemed so complicated, she sometimes wished she hadn't told him anything at all.

'Do you come and see them nest a lot?'

Alex didn't answer. She stared up at the wall, squinting in the thin April light.

'Do you know how long seagulls live for?'

Jenny stared up too. The two birds were still in their wall gap, fussing at their nest. Was it pathetic to be jealous of seagulls? Probably.

'No idea.'

Jenny swallowed and, without letting herself think about it too hard, typed,

No! On Zoom haha x

'More than twenty years. There are gulls up here that would have been chicks when we were kids. And you know what else? They'll remember you. Year after year. Hold grudges, too, if you deserve it.'

Jenny felt her mouth drop open. 'What?'

Alex looked pleased at her reaction.

'People round here give them no credit. Even in a village like this, with fuck all else to do, people won't pay attention to what's around them. They just keep their eyes on their phones and the floor. They want to look up once in a while. There's beauty, here, if you're looking for it.'

Jenny stared at her. She slid her own phone into her pocket.

'Holy shit.'

Alex nodded, like, holy shit indeed, then heaved a deep sigh.

'I'd best be off. Fuck loads to do. Can't all get furloughed.'

She stood up, and as she did, the bench tilted sharply to the side. For a second, Jenny felt sure that she'd fall to the ground and roll off the cliff and onto the beach below. This bench was designed to stand in the middle of the manicured lawns of a hotel, not perch on a cliff edge. The years of storms had dragged it closer and closer to the tumble and smash of the caravan, of the hotel, of everything that couldn't move away from the edge of the cliff.

Jenny imagined what it would be like. The weightlessness

of falling, the long moment before impact. A moment that might feel almost like flying.

If she was falling and she reached up a hand, would Alex save her?

Jenny stood up too. The atmosphere between them was awkward, again. They'd shed the selves that they were when they were eighteen and become two adults again – adults who'd spent more of their lives together than apart, but only just. Eighteen more months and the balance would tip. A seagull's lifetime since she left, or a little less.

'Hey. Cheers for sorting the payment stuff out for Si. Decent of you.'

Jenny shrugged, awkward. 'It was nothing.'

And it was, really. It wasn't like she'd been doing anything.

Alex lanced her with a look.

'Not to us. Difference between being all right and not, to us.'

Jenny swallowed. She should have done it sooner, though. She shouldn't have waited to be asked. But at least Alex didn't seem to be holding it against her, which was a pleasant surprise. Seagulls weren't the only ones who were good at holding grudges.

'You're welcome. Any time.'

Alex took a few steps away, and Jenny was sorry. She hadn't had a friendly chat with anyone for weeks. Her mum would only talk to her in clipped, tight little sentences about the house or give her orders for things to buy at the shop. Jenny shouldn't have even stayed this long.

Alex turned back.

'Hey. I heard. About the pub. I said he'd want you to have it.'

'Oh. Yeah. Cheers.'

Jenny hadn't let herself think about that yet. An email had come through. The pub was hers. She thought there'd be a meeting in a solicitor's office, like in a film, but no. That wasn't even a Covid thing. It just wasn't how it was done. She'd felt guilty about being snotty to Pete about it, when she'd found out. Not enough to apologise, though.

'Take care of it, yeah?'

'Yeah,' said Jenny, false-bright. She was going to sell it. Obviously. But maybe Pete would take it off her hands. Either way, there was nothing she could do until after lockdown, and so she was doing nothing. She was happy like this, suspended in time.

Some days she wasn't even sure she wanted to go back to London.

'Well. See you.'

And as Alex turned to go, she rolled up the sleeves of her oversized Co-op fleece and Jenny saw a glint on her wrist. And for a moment she assumed she was imagining it. She'd been thinking about Dad all the time, seeing him in the corner of her eye as she plodded to the Co-op, in the distance as she made her way up the cliff path. It was to be expected. She saw him in the house most of all, a flash of grey hair as she walked into the kitchen, slipper-clad feet on a footstool in front of the fire. He went away when she blinked. So when she saw her father's old watch on Alex's wrist, her first thought was that she was imagining it. But then Alex seemed to catch her staring, and pulled her sleeve back down protectively over her hand. So it must have been real.

And for a moment, all Jenny could do was stare, numb.

She waited and waited to feel angry, or shocked, or something, but all there was was a slow, heavy heart sink.

There was the necklace at the funeral as well.

And there was Alex. The fact of her. Jenny knew her inside out, didn't she? She knew the bones of her right back.

Alex turned and walked away. She didn't walk like a teenager anymore. Instead, she lumbered, like she was tired, like her bones ached, like adults always did. Jenny's bones ached too.

The sleeve didn't ride up again. Jenny watched until Alex was out of sight.

But she knew what she'd seen.

ABRASION

Summer 2004

Alex put her shoulder to the pub door and creaked it open. The wood was always swollen with the damp salt air, so you had to give it some heft. It wanted a good planing, really. She had told him.

She stepped into the bar of The Railway and breathed in the smell of spilt beer and stale fags and the sea – always in Ravenspurn, everywhere, you could smell the sea.

It wasn't that clean, the bar. Alex had been in charge of clean-up the night before, but if she was honest, she couldn't be arsed with upholding her normal standards. She could see patches of floor still furred up with fag ash, and streaks of beer wiped carelessly around the tabletops instead of off them. There was an empty pint glass sitting, reproving, on the mantlepiece of the old fire. But Ted had said nothing, and had let her go bang on 11.30, like he hardly ever did. Because she'd had the exam to get ready for, hadn't she?

'You're early.'

Ted was standing behind the bar, each hand gripping a beer tap, holding court to an empty room. The Railway wouldn't be complete without Ted around somewhere, behind the bar or in front of it. He was just as much a part of the fittings as the horse brasses and the red leatherette banquettes.

'Yeah?'

Ted checked his watch, ostentatiously. Alex had never

known a man to be as fond of his watch as Ted was of his. At the start and end of every shift, and whenever anyone wanted a fag break as well, he'd shake his wrist and rotate it towards himself, full attention on the time. He properly took pleasure in it, the way some people would with a cup of coffee and a fag.

'I reckon. The exam doesn't finish until half past, does it?'

Alex dropped her tattered old school bag on a bar seat and slumped down next to it. Trust fucking Jenny to tell her dad every moment of her day in advance. Did she fill in time sheets for him at home as well as in here?

'Is that right?'

He nodded, his eyes boring into her.

'I reckon.'

Alex opened up the frayed drawstring of her bag. She riffled through the contents, ostensibly for her baccy, actually to give her a couple of seconds to get her head together. What was it about Ted that always made her feel like she'd been told off? He ran the pub she worked in, and that was all. He was nothing else to her. Her hand closed around the tobacco pouch and she placed it on the bar.

'Right.'

She was kicking herself, if she was honest. She'd stayed out, skulking around the beach on her own and freezing her arse off for as long as she could stand it. Even in midsummer, the wind that came off the sea was biting cold, and the bleak emptiness of the beach on a random Tuesday in term time had got inside her head. She'd have stayed out a bit longer, though, if she knew she was going to get rumbled. The Railway was meant to be safe.

Ted pulled his own pack of fags down from where they lived on a shelf above the till.

'So why aren't you there, then?'

He knew, of course. Everybody would know. It was impossible to keep a secret in this little shithole village for more than five minutes. It was a miracle she'd made it to three days without anyone asking her yet.

Out loud, that was. She could see them thinking it, clear enough. But you couldn't help that.

'I've run out of filters, I reckon.'

He ignored her. 'Why aren't you there?'

He was going to make her say it.

Alex narrowed her eyes and pulled a tattered copy of *The Tempest* out of her bag. Ted asking felt a lot worse, somehow, then when the teachers had actually done it. She was so used to being told off at school. Every day since she was in reception, it felt like – *a bright girl, perfectly able, but naughty, so naughty* – she'd been in trouble for something – *just stop being so DISRUPTIVE, Alexandra, and we can find a way to get on* – and more than one of the teachers had said to her face they were surprised she was staying on for A levels at all.

Well, they could stick it up their bums, couldn't they? She did stay on for A levels, and she'd been doing bloody well at them too. She'd been well on track to get an A in Geography, like, a proper decent one, within grabbing distance of full marks, and Bs in English and Psychology. Not too bad at all. But, even so, she'd been in and out of the head's office – *there's a certain amount more freedom, Alexandra, but we do have boundaries here, this is still a school.* They just wouldn't let anything go – *now, come on, I will not tell you again* – but she was used to it. She didn't care.

But there was something about the way that Ted was looking at her that made her actually give a shit.

Alex shrugged, and carefully tore a corner off the front cover of the book. 'Not allowed.'

He looked at her, brown eyes steady and clear. 'No?'

Alex swallowed. She could still feel the sickening crunch of bone under her fist. She hadn't meant it. She'd lost her temper.

'Got kicked out.'

They told her she was lucky they hadn't pressed charges. Mrs Dennis, who was the only teacher Alex didn't reckon had it completely in for her, had said she'd better remember she was eighteen now. *I'm sorry, Alex. It's too far this time.* Not a minor. She could get into real trouble, these days.

'Right,' he said. 'So you're here, then.'

There was a long, long pause. Long enough for Alex to seriously consider picking up the empty pint glass and putting it in the dishwasher. Just consider, though. She wasn't on shift today. He couldn't get a free bit of tidying out of her, like she was some sort of mug. Instead, she said, 'I could still get a C overall. In Geography. Just.'

'Aye?'

'Yeah.' She rolled the rectangle of card tight between her fingers. 'If I got 100 per cent on the first exam. Just.'

'Aye,' he said.

Without asking, he clicked on the kettle behind the bar.

Alex sat and brooded. She'd done the numbers in her head over and over and over again. It had to be 100 per cent mind, not 97 or 98. That C wouldn't get her into Manchester, or Leeds, or even Hull, but it would get her into Manchester Met and out of here.

'I never got A levels,' Ted said. He spooned a generous heap of Nescafé into the giant Sports Direct mug that was generally acknowledged to be the best one they had. 'Not a single one. And I turned out all right.'

Ted was the first person she'd told about the exam maths, the first one she'd actually said the words to that she'd been kicked out, even. It was funny, but then they did spend a lot of time together. Work and that. It was weird to have one of your best mates be some bloke old enough to be your dad, but here they were.

'Did you now?' she said, and pulled a pack of Rizlas out of her bag. The packet was feeling alarmingly thin. She must have been smoking more than usual because of the stress of it all.

'Cheeky,' he said, and slid the coffee over to her.

Alex wrinkled her nose.

'Not got anything stronger for me?'

Ted frowned, cutting deep grooves down his forehead.

'Not your last exam day, though, is it?'

But he took the coffee back and held it up to the whisky bottle. The steam fogged the optic as he dropped in two shots.

'God. Rub it in.'

He handed her mug back and checked his watch again. And it occurred to Alex that, of course, it wasn't her that he'd been waiting for.

Whatever. Drinking whisky coffee with Ted while he

waited for Jenny was still better than being out on the flat grey beach on her own. Or at home, which was worse.

She wrapped her hands around the mug and her fingers barely touched on the other side.

'You did your best, pet,' he said. 'I know you will have done.'

Alex shrugged. What did it mean, to do your best? She'd tried really hard not to fuck it up. There were a lot of afternoons she'd spent before her shift, revision notes spread out on the sticky tables and only drinking halves so she could concentrate on them properly. Walking down the cliff every morning, her head full of Shakespeare and Beck's negative triad and the five different types of erosion. And she'd turned up, hadn't she? To pretty much every class.

But all it takes is one slip. Slip of the tongue, slip of the fist. And then it's done, just like that. The only place you get points for trying is at school, and she'd been kicked out of there.

'Well,' she said. 'Fuck it. It's not so bad here. I've got a job, anyway. That's what you get A levels for anyway, isn't it? To get a job?'

And to get to uni, she thought. To get out of the place you were made and have a chance at becoming something else.

'Aye,' he said. 'You'll always have a job with me here. You know that.'

Alex shrugged. She took her rolled-up bit of *The Tempest* and slotted it into the paper.

'You don't even want me to pass, do you, Ted? You'd have to pay me more if I was qualified.'

He sipped at his coffee. He took it with three sugars and no milk. No whisky either, today.

'Something like that.'

Alex sprinkled tobacco over the paper and started rolling. Ted winced and wordlessly slid his own pack of Lambert and Butler across the bar. Alex licked her cigarette shut and raised an eyebrow.

'I'm all right.'

'Just take one,' he said, and she did. She put her rollie back in the baccy pouch for later, though. It was nice of Ted and all, but she didn't actually care about her lungs. She'd told him a hundred times, if she did, she just wouldn't smoke in the first place.

Ted checked his watch again, and as he did, there was a bang of the door and a rush of salt air and Jenny burst into the room. As if she'd been waiting for her cue. And Ted's face lit up, like her coming into the room was the best thing that'd ever happened to him. Alex lit up the fag he'd given her. It must be nice. She couldn't say anyone was ever really that pleased to see her. But that's just what Jenny was like, wasn't it? Special.

Jenny and Alex were the only two girls in year thirteen from Ravenspurn, and all through primary school they'd been the only two girls in their year at all – just them and Si. When they were little, Alex had been the kind of girl who got cast as the angel Gabriel for the nativity plays – bossy, difficult to manage, but could be relied upon to speak loud enough to be heard at the back. Jenny, on the other hand, had been the Virgin Mary every year. She was blonde and slim and infuriatingly, maddeningly obedient. Alex had never liked her. But when you come from a village as small as theirs, liking each other doesn't really come into it.

'Hello, princess,' Ted said. 'How was the exam?'

Jenny perched on the bar stool, arms down and head flopped dramatically forward.

'It was such a nightmare.'

Alex rolled her eyes. It was only Physical Geography, the last one, which was ridiculously easy in that you could probably skate by most of it just by knowing some basic stuff about how the world works and adding some details got from looking out of the fucking window. Climate change makes the deserts get bigger. No fucking shit. Alex had got 85 per cent in the mock and she'd only tried a tiny little bit. Hardly at all.

Ted checked his watch once more. Extravagantly, of course. Like there wasn't a clock on the wall right behind him. He nodded approvingly.

'Seems to me like it's time for a drink,' he said and, instead of offering his daughter an instant coffee, pulled a bottle of fizzy wine out of the fridge under the bar. It was still dusty from the cellar – he must have put it in specially that morning. They didn't sell a lot of cava.

Ted pulled down three round wine glasses and handed Alex one, filled to the brim with glittering acid bubbles.

'Right, well,' he said, staring deep into his own glass. 'End of an era for you two, isn't it? I remember when you girls had just started school . . .'

Alex twisted her mouth and downed half her glass. She wasn't quite sure if it was nice of them or not, to include her. She remembered when they'd just started school as well. Ted had walked Jenny there every single day until they were old enough to catch the bus to the comp in Driffield. Alex used to walk behind them, trailing her bag like a dog on a lead, on her own. She used to wonder, even at ten, if anyone would notice if she just didn't turn up.

'You two and little Simon.' Ted was getting properly misty eyes now. 'Cute as buttons, you three were. Shame you had to grow up, really.'

Si had turned up with his mum every day as well, her pushing the double buggy with the twins in it and Chris, even at that age, forever running off into the road. But she'd been there. Alex's mum had walked her on the very first day, but that was it. There'd been a bit of a scene. Alex was glad they hadn't pushed it, to avoid more of that. It was just hard not to be sentimental about it.

Jenny was staring into her glass of cava. She'd barely touched it.

Ted reached out a hand to her. 'Only kidding, princess. I'm proud of you.'

Alex downed the rest of hers, and reached for the bottle.

'Thanks, Dad,' Jenny said. 'I'd best get home. Got to get ready for tonight.'

She took another sip of the wine, but her glass was still way more than half full. She leaned down and scooped up her school bag. Unlike Alex, Jenny got a new one every year. This year, it had the Powerpuff Girls on it. Last year had been *The Magic Roundabout*. Jenny liked kid stuff, which she always told anyone who'd listen was ironic, but Alex suspected she'd just never stopped liking it. Alex had had the same backpack since year seven, which she'd had no choice but to style out as a grunge statement. She'd swiped some safety pins from Textiles and made a decent fist of it. It looked okay.

'Hey,' Jenny said, turning suddenly to Alex. 'Do you want to come and get ready with me?'

Alex looked over to her, surprised. Jenny never asked Alex to get ready with her. In fact, Alex remembered the last time Jenny had invited her over to her house in great detail. They'd been six years old. Jenny had run up to her mother after school, chattering excitedly about fish fingers and baked beans and how Alex could come over and play now that she had two Barbies, because they could have one each. Alex still remembered the expression on Alison Fletcher's face. *No, darling,* she'd said. *I don't think so. Her mummy wouldn't like it.* Like Alex was contagious. Jenny had never asked again, and neither had Alex. She'd understood.

'Um. Really?' she said, and hated herself for it.

'Yeah. Why not?'

And Alex could tell herself all she wanted that it was because she didn't have anything better to do. Or even that she felt sorry for Jenny, for not being as popular as Alex at school, even though by rights she should have been, what with being prettier and less bright. She could remember that she always felt more generous to Jenny when there was no one around, and school was over now. It was a good idea to let her defences down a bit, so why not? But, really, the idea of standing in Jenny's bedroom, with its smell of her and all her clothes, was irresistible. Even if you didn't compare it with going home to see what state Mum had already got herself into.

'Okay. Cheers,' she said. She took a drag on her cigarette, for something to do, and tasted the burnt plastic of the filter.

See, straights were wasteful. Her rollie would have just gone out. She ground the cigarette out in one of the bar ashtrays.

'Right,' Jenny said. 'Cool.'

And a look flashed between her and Ted. And Alex understood, with a sickening thump, that it was Ted who'd wanted Jenny to invite her over. It had been his idea, because he felt sorry for her, because he knew about her mum and her getting expelled, and had done way before she told him, just like everyone knew everything about everyone in this tiny shithole village.

For a moment, Alex considered backing off. There was nothing worse than pity, and that included getting into a slanging match with an old drunk bitch in a caravan. But still. It was only Jenny. It's not like she'd tell anyone. Who was there even to tell, now that they'd left sixth form, and most of the years above them from Ravenspurn primary had fucked off to new lives in Hull or Leeds by now? And it would definitely piss Alison off. That was something. So she stayed silent.

Jenny faffed around, looking for something inside her bag, and Ted leaned over the bar towards Alex. He slid the rest of the packet of cigarettes towards her.

'Hey,' he said. 'It'll be all right. Don't worry.'

'I'm not worried,' Alex said. She opened the packet. It was still very nearly full. She turned one cigarette around, for luck, and threw the pack into her bag.

'There's worse things, anyway, than living your life around here.'

And he smiled. He looked so kind, and so sorry for her. Alex couldn't quite bring herself to smile back.

'Yeah,' she said. 'I know.'

The cava tasted of vinegar now, but she swallowed it anyway, and followed Jenny out of the pub.

In Jenny's house, it smelled of her. Overwhelmingly so – some mix of fabric conditioner and perfume and cooking that Alex couldn't quite name all the elements of but were nevertheless as completely and recognisably a part of Jenny as her face was.

'So ... This is it.'

Jenny was nervous, Alex could tell. She stood awkwardly on the thick beige carpet – as fluffy and uniform as if it had been brushed rather than hoovered – like she was waiting for Alex to say something. Alex picked up a little china dog from the windowsill. It was heavy and cold in her hand.

Jenny smiled, obviously relieved. Which pissed Alex off a bit. What did she think she was going to do, punch her too? It had been a mistake. She hadn't meant it.

'There's drinks in the kitchen, you can come on through ...'

Alex trailed after Jenny into the kitchen, which was pre-dictably as neat and deep-scrubbed as an empty fish counter. It was weird that Ted didn't smell like the house. He smelled of stale beer and cigarette smoke, the way that men should. Plus Old Spice for old men like Ted, and Lynx for young men like Si. It was the way of things. Comforting.

For a horrifying moment, Alex wondered what her cara-van, and by extension, she herself, smelled like. She tried hard not to smell the same as her mother, which was the mustiness of being in the same set of clothes for too long, overlaid with a squirt of whatever perfume her latest boyfriend had got cheap off the market. And booze of course. Which you'd think she'd hate because of the bad memories, but somehow Alex found reassuring. It was one of the things she most liked about working in the pub. Brains were weird. Alex had a shower and washed her hair every day, even if it meant she was so late she missed the bus and didn't make it to school. But the way the caravan smelled probably still clung to her. It was bound to.

Jenny opened the fridge.

'What do you want? There's Coke, orange juice . . .'

The fridge was groaning with food and drink. There were packets of ham and cheese, boxes of leftovers and wrapped-up meat and veg crammed into every square inch. Alex scanned the shelves.

'I'll have a beer, thanks.'

Jenny twisted a hank of hair around her fingers, in the same aggravating way she had since she was seven.

'There aren't any.'

There were four cans of Foster's shining, blue and inviting, at the back of the fridge. Alex rolled her eyes.

'Don't be daft. There they are. Behind the yoghurts.'

'Yeah. I mean . . .' The hair twisting intensified. She was going to snap a whole pigtail right off one of these days if she didn't watch it. 'I'm not allowed.'

Alex half laughed. 'What are you talking about? Your dad owns a pub. He gave you a glass of wine *this morning*.'

Ted didn't even like Foster's. He said it was over-marketed piss water. He said that at least once a month.

'He doesn't mind. Mum doesn't like it, though.'

Jenny darted her eyes around the kitchen, as if her mother was going to pop out at any moment. Alex restrained herself from another eye roll. Alison sounded like a right pain to live with, and Alex knew all about pain-in-the-arse mums.

'Will she really notice a can?'

Jenny's eyes were wide, almost scandalised.

'There's only four! Of course she will.'

Alex shrugged. As it happened, she agreed with Ted about Foster's, it tased of soap and jizz. She was only being polite, picking something she could see.

'Okay. I'll have a vodka Coke then.'

'They don't keep vodka in.'

Alex sighed deeply. This was ridiculous. She really wanted a drink, to do her make-up with. That was the best part of the night.

'You're joking.'

Jenny had the grace to at least look extremely apologetic.

'There's gin . . .'

Alex gave her a hard stare. How could this be taking so long? But she supposed it wasn't Jenny's fault if she was clueless and crap at problem-solving. She'd always been like that, since she was a kid – no initiative at all. That was what came of being spoilt.

'Okay.'

'Gin and lemonade?'

Alex nodded. She'd never had gin before. She'd never been in a house that didn't have a bottle of vodka knocking around somewhere before either.

As she poured the drinks – one for herself as well, Alex

noted – Jenny kept looking over her shoulder, as if her mother was going to appear at any moment. Alex felt it too. A giddy thrill of what might happen if Alison caught them. She'd be so furious at a little demonstration that her precious daughter wasn't so perfect after all. That maybe there was no point in keeping her away from bad influences for as long as she had.

But Alison didn't come.

Jenny carefully replaced the gin bottle in the dining room's mirrored sideboard and led them up to her room, padding up the squashily carpeted stairs with a glass in each hand as Alex followed behind. She followed Jenny through a door adorned by a Groovy Chick sticker announcing it to be Jenny's Room and gazed around. This was what she'd really wanted to see.

It was like a room from a magazine – if *J-17* had done a spread on 'how to make your bedroom as generic as possible'. There were a few outfits scattered around the place, a desk messy with make-up, a bed covered in bright cushions. There were some stuffed toys sitting on a shelf above the bed, like they were standing sentry for her. One of them Alex recognised – a fading brown stuffed koala. She picked it up and turned it over, light and soft in her hands. Jenny had gone through a phase of not going anywhere without this thing.

Jenny appeared at her elbow and pushed a glass into her hand, and Alex set the koala down on the bed. She thought she caught a flash of relief in Jenny's face. What, like Alex was going to rip apart the bear? For fuck's sake, what had Alex done to deserve that? She might have given Jenny a hard time at school sometimes, but she was here, wasn't she? Playing nice.

Jenny gave Alex a faltering smile.

'Cheers.'

Alex took a sip of the drink, which tasted like sugar and flowers and petrol. She said, all casual, 'How was the exam?'

Jenny sipped at her own drink.

'Oh, you know. Boring.'

Alex felt her fingers tighten on the glass. How could you think that the study of the land, of the sea and the sky and every single place in the world that you might ever visit was boring? Only if you had no imagination at all.

'Mmm. Yeah. What came up, though?'

Jenny opened a box, which started playing a tinkly little song. A tiny ballerina popped up and began spinning as Jenny riffled through the contents. There must have been more than twenty necklaces in there, all jumbled together and tangled.

'God, I don't know. I don't remember.'

Alex ducked her head and took another swallow of the gin, which she'd decided she really didn't like, to hide her annoyance. The exam had only finished a couple of hours ago. How could she possibly not remember?

'Don't you remember any of it?'

Jenny pulled out one of the necklaces and fastened it around her throat.

'I want to forget about it now. It was so hard!'

It wasn't fucking hard. What was hard about looking at a diagram and saying what was going on? Jenny was lazy, that was her problem, which was another thing that went along with being spoilt.

Alex pulled out the packet of cigarettes and lit one, drawing the smoke deep into her lungs. She had to admit, a Lambert and Butler was a lot nicer than a schoolbook rollie. Ted had never given her the whole pack before, but he'd almost always hand her one after she'd finished a late shift if she made out like she'd run out. The taste made her think of a sit-down and a cheeky pint after a long night on her feet. Relaxing.

Jenny's face was a mask of horror.

'You can't smoke in here.'

Alex took another puff. Jenny's lips tightened and Alex realised Jenny thought she was doing it on purpose, to take the piss. But Alex always wanted to smoke more when she was confused.

'But your dad smokes.'

These were his cigarettes. This was absurd.

'He only smokes in his study, though. If Mum smells it in here, she'll kill me.'

Alex rolled her eyes heavily.

'Okay. We'll open a window, yeah? Compromise.'

She could tell that Jenny didn't like it, but she at least shut up.

Alex overrode an impulse to stub the cigarette out on the pink-wallpapered wall and instead blew smoke out of the window in a narrow plume. Jenny still looked incredibly uncomfortable, but she could honestly fuck off. Alex was trying to be nice.

Jenny took a deep breath and let it out slowly. Alex was

sure she'd seen Alison do that before. She said, 'What are you wearing tonight?'

Alex shrugged. 'This.'

And she could tell that Jenny wanted to say something – that it was on the tip of her tongue. Alex felt a surge of anxiety in her throat, despite the calming effects of the drink and the fag. Strong enough to panic.

She said, quickly, 'I don't want to make too much of an effort, you know? Bit tragic.'

Jenny looked crestfallen.

'No. Totally.'

She took off the necklace, which glittered in the late-afternoon sun. It was a pretty thing – a golden heart on a delicate chain. Jenny tossed it down, where it fell on the counter, not even bothering to put it back in the jewellery box properly. She picked up an eyeshadow palette that had been lying on the desk. There was barely room for anything apart from the make-up and jewellery on there. She must do her homework on the bed, just like Alex did. Jenny dabbed some sparkly green onto her eyelids, then held it out to Alex.

'You want to use some of this?'

Alex's eyes widened. It was a massive palette, beautiful and barely touched.

'Yeah. You want some lipstick?'

She fished a tube out of her schoolbag. It was a decent one – a barely used Rimmel in a deep, rich red. Alex normally had stuff like lipsticks. They were a doddle to lift from Superdrug – you could slip them in your pocket easy-peasy. The only things easier then lipsticks were sweets, which were so simple they were barely worth bothering with.

'Thanks.'

Jenny took the lipstick and painted around her lips – a deep red O. With some satisfaction, Alex noted that the lipstick looked much better on her. Jenny was too fair for a colour like that, and she seemed to know it.

She looked at herself thoughtfully in the mirror and said, 'So . . . do you reckon Si's going to be out tonight?'

Alex chose a deep, iridescent purple. It was a shame Jenny was already wearing the green – it was easily the nicest colour in there.

'I would have thought so. Given that he's out every night, and he doesn't have anywhere better to go.'

Jenny pressed her mouth together a couple of times, spreading the lipstick around.

'Right.'

Alex took another drag on her cigarette.

'Why do you ask?'

'No reason.'

She blew a stream of smoke towards the window. Mostly towards the window.

'In the coastal question, did they ask about erosion? Or was it landslides?'

Jenny blinked a couple of times, her glittery eyeshadow catching the light.

'What?'

'In the exam.'

Jenny picked up a mascara.

'Oh. Right. Yeah, they definitely asked something about the coastline. There was an essay on that. I remember.'

Alex took another drag to try to calm down. Of course

there was an essay on fucking coastlines. That was like saying the question had words.

'Yeah, but what was it about?'

'God, I don't know.'

'Did they ask about climate change on the coastal bit? Or was that in glaciers?'

Jenny was painting her eyelashes, mouth hanging open as she carefully pulled the wand through them.

'Yeah? Yeah. I think so? I don't know. Does it matter?'

Alex sighed. The cigarette was nearly burned down to the end now. Alex drained the rest of her gin and took one more puff.

'No. I suppose not.'

There wasn't an ashtray, so Alex just threw the end out of the window. She heard Jenny huff out a sigh. Alex had obviously annoyed her enough to override the calming breathing.

'You definitely think Si will be there, then?' Jenny said, too casually. She took a big gulp of her gin. She didn't seem to think it tasted of petrol.

Alex looked at Jenny properly. Did she fancy Si? Alex wasn't sure how she felt about that. Jenny, with her cute little body and long, flicky hair. She wasn't sure at all.

'I dunno. It wasn't his last exam, was it?'

Jenny pouted, and Alex felt a tingle of alarm. She was definitely disappointed. She clearly fancied him. But that didn't mean anything, did it? Si had known Jenny for years, and he'd never said anything. He would have told Alex something like that, wouldn't he? Alex was, like, his best friend.

'It wasn't yours either.'

And somehow that was much more annoying than when Ted had said it. He'd seemed like he was teasing, just sharing a joke. There was something much more pointed about Jenny. Something mean glimmering just below the surface, like Jenny thought it made her cleverer that Alex, to have sat an exam when Alex hadn't. But it wasn't cleverness, it was just temper. That was the only thing. And anyway, she could still pass – *would* pass, surely, if there was any fairness at all. Alex couldn't possibly fail her A levels if this idiot passed them.

'We're going to be late,' Alex said, which wasn't true at all. They were going to be embarrassingly early.

But Jenny just nodded and picked up Alex's empty glass. The two girls walked silently down the stairs and into the kitchen, where Jenny rinsed out their glasses, much more thoroughly then she ever did at the pub.

Alex opened her bag and rummaged about in there.

'Hang on. Forgot my fags. You don't want your mum to find them . . .'

Jenny looked terrified at the idea of her mother having to see a packet of fags.

'Shit!'

Alex thumped her way back up to Jenny's bedroom, reached out and plucked the necklace from the table. She slid it into her pencil case. It wasn't like Jenny looked after any of her things. She just took it all for granted – her exam she couldn't even remember, her stupid parents who only had four beers in at a time and no bottle of vodka on the go, and her necklace she couldn't even be arsed to put away. There was no way she'd notice it was gone.

Alex clumped back down the stairs and into the hospital-clean kitchen.

'You got them?'

Alex dipped into her schoolbag, where the fags had been sitting all along, and showed the top of the packet to Jenny, who frowned.

'Huh. That's weird. Dad smokes Lambert and Butlers too.'

Alex smiled.

'Yeah?'

There was a sound from the hall. A door opening.

'Jennifer?'

Ridiculously, Alex felt herself tensing and shoved the pack of cigarettes back into her bag as fast as she could. As if she was afraid of Jenny's stupid mum. Which she hadn't been when she was five, and she sure as hell wasn't now.

'We're just off, Mum.'

And Jenny tried to hustle Alex towards the door. But Alison was very quick off the mark, Alex would give her that.

'Who's we, darling, do you have someone . . . oh.'

Alison came into her kitchen and stopped short when she saw Alex, a look on her face as if she'd just trodden in dog poo.

'We were just leaving.'

A look passed between Jenny and her mum, and Alex didn't know what it meant, but she could have a decent guess. She was surprised to find that it didn't bother her that much, though. They could think what they wanted about Alex not being good enough to be in their precious house. She didn't care. She'd be out of this village soon enough and it wouldn't matter what anyone thought of her, ever again.

Ted closed the cash register, slamming it shut with a defiant jingle even though they hadn't really made much that night. Alex rolled her shoulders, feeling the muscles in her neck twang in complaint.

'Right. That's that then. Another night done,' Ted said.

In a lot of ways, it was just another Tuesday. There'd been hardly anyone in, but old Bill had been propping up the bar half the night, and that wanker Pete had been in the other half. Alex had fantasies about being able to bar Pete, who was their landlord up at the caravan park. He'd been a prick to her since she was a tiny child. Still, he was Ted's brother, so it was unlikely she'd ever be able to. Disappointing.

Alex had stayed away from him as much as she could manage, but what with her being the only one working the bar, that wasn't a lot. Ted was on too tonight, but he didn't really pull pints anymore. He was always there – notebook out sometimes, stock-checking sometimes, with a smile and a chat for a regular always. But he didn't have a lot of interest in actually pouring the drinks. Back when Alex had started at the pub, just a few months ago, he was never out from behind the bar. Something had shifted.

'Are we going to chuck these two out then?' Alex said, and nodded towards Jenny and Si, the only other customers they'd had in that night. The two of them had spent the last hour huddled around the corner table. It was one of the best ones they had, right next to the fire and surrounded by windows. Chris sat in it, when he was out in Ravenspurn for the night, and Si did when he wasn't.

'Ha! Rather you than me, lass,' Ted said, all genial. He was still resting his arse on the bar stool. His back hurt, was what he said.

Alex winced and dug a thumb between her bra and the skin it was digging into on her ribcage. She hurt too. If Ted and Si weren't here, she'd just take the bloody thing off. Maybe even if Si was around, to be honest. There was no reason to be shy, she had nice enough tits. But not in front of her boss. She had a bit of respect.

'Oi, Jenny,' Si said. It was so quiet with the customers gone he didn't even have to raise his voice. 'These two are talking about us, I reckon.'

Jenny giggled in an irritating way. She'd obviously got herself all dolled up for the occasion of hanging around her dad's pub on a random Tuesday. She was thoroughly frosted with lip gloss, and wearing so much mascara that it was a wonder her eyes still opened at all. She had the look about her of a girl with something to prove, but Alex wasn't bothered. Si had shown almost no interest in Jenny, the night of their last exam. He'd barely looked at Jenny twice, though, to be fair, he'd barely looked at anyone. He'd got so pissed, he was already half asleep in a sand dune by the time Alex and Jenny had found him. Which was a little disappointing, as she was going to have a crack herself, but Alex was philosophical about it. If she had time to get something going with Si before the end of summer, then she had time. If she didn't, she didn't. She expected there were plenty of lads in Manchester.

Ted cleared his throat. He locked up the cash register and then held up the key, dangling them deliberately, letting them glint in the light. Very theatrical, but then Ted could be sometimes. He liked a bit of drama. Who didn't?

'Right, you three. What's everyone having?'

Alex raised an eyebrow and looked over to Si. It wasn't that Ted was particularly tight, especially not when you considered that he was a landlord, but it wasn't like him to be free with the drink. They got tipped in half-pints, printed receipts stuck into shot glasses on a shelf above the till, and that was their lot. Unless there was a barrel about to go off, of course, or maybe it was month end and he wanted to tidy up the stock.

Si drained his glass sharpish.

'I'll have a pint of premium. Cheers, Ted.'

Ted nodded and started pouring.

Si's eyes met Alex again and widened. This really wasn't like him.

'Cider. Cheers,' Alex said.

Ted nodded.

'Jenny?'

Alex shot a look at Jenny to check if she thought this was unusual too, but Jenny just blinked back, as placid and bovine as she ever was. Of course, if your dad was a landlord you could have as many drinks as you wanted, as long as your bitch mum wasn't around. It made sense she wouldn't go nuts for a free pint.

Alex swallowed down a sudden surge of something that felt a lot like jealousy. But it couldn't be. It's not like she wanted Jenny's life, she'd be bored to death. But it would be nice to have an unlimited supply of pints, she couldn't deny that.

'Yeah. Half a cider. Thanks, Dad.'

Alex still hadn't worn the necklace. She took it out of the shoebox under her bed sometimes, just for a quick look, but she always put it back again. She'd told herself that Jenny wouldn't notice, but obviously she would. Maybe she could wear it in Manchester.

As Ted pulled the drinks, Alex hitched herself up onto a bar stool. Her feet were killing her tonight, as well as her back and the flesh around her ribs. She'd been going through a phase of taking every extra shift that was on offer. If she didn't get out of that caravan, her mum was going to murder her, or the other way around. It had meant that since the exams were out of the way, she'd been doing six shifts a week, minimum. Not that that she was complaining – she needed the cash. But that didn't change the fact that the whole lower half of her throbbed. There'd been a few days she'd had to take a couple of paracetamol with her morning tea to take the edge off. No wonder Ted didn't want to pull pints any more, if this was what it felt like working the bar every night when you were eighteen, never mind as old as him. What would it feel like, being twenty-eight, thirty-eight, forty-eight and still working every day on your feet? As your bones got older and your hips went and you got pregnant or sick and had to push on anyway?

Alex shrugged off the idea. It didn't matter. She'd never find out. She was going to go to uni, and get the kind of job you could do sitting on your arse in a comfy swivel chair. Course she was.

The other two trailed over to join her and Ted lined up the drinks on the bar – a pint of special for Si, and two halves of cider for the girls.

Alex glared at the back of Ted's head. She hadn't said she'd wanted a half. Hadn't even implied it. She kept her mouth shut though, obviously, and raised her glass like the rest of them and took a deep swallow. The cold sweetness of it hit the back of her throat like sunshine breaking through clouds, or sinking into a warm bath, or drifting back off to sleep when you realise you only set your alarm by accident and you didn't actually have to get up.

She swallowed again and then made herself put the glass down. Three quarters of it was already gone. Halves might be enough for dainty little Jenny, but they weren't enough for her. Which was reasonable, wasn't it? She'd been working. She was thirsty.

Ted theatrically pulled a set of keys back out of his pocket and held them above the bar, just an inch or two. There were five keys on there: the till, the cellar, the safe and two for the front door. He always refused to have spares cut, so when Alex needed to go into the cellar, she'd have to go and ask him, like she was a five-year-old getting permission to go for a wee at school. Very annoying.

Ted deliberately dropped the keys onto the bar. They jingled, sounding out surprisingly loud in the empty pub as they hit the polished wood. As well as the keys, there was a key ring – a stress ball in the shape of a leprechaun. It was so worn and used now that the red of its hair was almost completely black.

Alex looked to her left and right. Si and Jenny were both

sipping their drinks, staring gormlessly at Ted. They clearly didn't have a clue what was going on. Both a bit pissed perhaps, or maybe they didn't care.

But not Alex. She knew exactly what was coming. She sat up straighter on the bar stool, despite the ache.

'Right, so,' said Ted, very formal. 'The three of you have done decent work here. Very decent.'

And he caught Alex's eye and flashed her a quick smile. Alex, trying to be humble, bit back the grin she wanted to shoot him. It didn't do to tip your hand. The fact was, Jenny and Si didn't do particularly good work. Not that good at all, in fact. Si, sweet as he was and as much as the regulars loved him, could never remember a round without being told it half a dozen times. And Jenny, who was competent enough when she wanted to be, didn't have the balls to simmer down a situation and tell someone when they were being a bit of a prick. That was important in a pub like this. When there was only one place to drink within walking distance, it mattered that people got on. Sometimes you had to be the one to step in, to put your foot down and take a bit of flack, so that an issue wouldn't escalate, tensions wouldn't build, and the community could keep itself just about running. Jenny didn't seem to understand that. To her, the pub was just a big house that sold booze. It was so much more than that to Alex, and, she reckoned, Ted too.

He drew in a breath.

'Aye, well. I've been thinking. I don't want to knacker my back quite as much as I have been doing. And you three are all out of school now, so it's time for a bit of a shake-up. So I was thinking we might have a little change of roles.'

Ted had Jenny's attention too now, though Si still looked as dopey as ever. Jenny was staring at her father with a little crinkle between her skinny brows. Alex realised with a thrill that Ted hadn't told Jenny in advance what he was going to do. Even though Jenny was his daughter, she didn't know any more than Alex did, and Alex was surprised at how much she liked that. Because it wasn't like she needed Ted's approval or anything. It's not like she had anything to prove to him, just because he'd known her since she was a tiny little girl. Everyone had, around here, so there was nothing special about him.

'Still,' Ted went on. 'Some of you might not stay in Ravenspurn, I know that, I know that. So we'll call it a trial. But, safe to say, for all three of you, if you ever need a job, then you'll have one here.'

Alex swallowed down her impatience, and wished again that she had a full pint. She could do with something to do with her hands.

'So I'm creating a new position,' Ted went on. 'Bar Manager, let's say. Trial Bar Manager. Just three months, you know? See how it goes.'

Alex would have liked to light up a fag. She'd been paid, so she had her own pack of straights now. Her little treat, since she was working so many hours. But she didn't want to do anything to break the moment. Or, like, count her chickens before they'd hatched, as it were. Not that she was superstitious. Of course not.

Ted nodded and, after another maddening theatrical pause, slid the keys across the bar. They ended up directly in front of Jenny. Alex had been so sure that, just for a moment, she wondered if she was hallucinating.

'How about it, lass?' he said.

And Jenny didn't even have the grace to look properly shocked. More like, mildly surprised. Even though it was fucking shocking, actually. It was so shocking, Alex couldn't feel her face properly. Jenny had been promoted over her? Asked-her-last-week-what-the-ingredients-to-a-shandy-were Jenny?

'Oh,' was all Jenny said.

Alex had really thought that Ted had more sense than this.

'You know I don't need you to take it on. It can go to Pete. When I'm gone, like. But I thought you might like a taste.'

And it was so obvious, in that moment, that it was all that Ted wanted. For his daughter to take on his business, to carry on in his footsteps. For her to stay. It was painful, it was so clear what he felt.

It must be nice, to have someone to want you to stay.

But Jenny didn't understand any of that. She just smiled, pleasant and pretty, like she always did. Like she was being offered a cup of tea and not a chunk of someone's world.

'Yeah. Right. I can do that. Yeah.'

Alex reached for her fags but remembered they were still in her hoodie pocket, hanging up behind the door in Ted's office. Without asking, she leaned across and took one of Si's. She didn't trust herself to leave her hands unoccupied. And as she lit up, she clocked Ted looking at her, in a way she hadn't been expecting. He looked really sorry. And she hadn't thought he'd look at her at all.

'Now,' he said, pretty clearly talking just to her. 'You've all done good work. Bloody good work. Because I don't want any of you to think that you haven't. And you'll always have a job here. You know that.'

'Aye,' Alex replied. 'You said.'

He looked almost nervous. Alex had no idea why.

'Well,' he continued. 'If there's anything else I can do, you'll let me know, won't you?'

Alex, whose philosophy was always that you might as well ask, drained the last of her cider and said, 'I'll have the rest of that pint.'

And she gave him a wink, to show him that she didn't mind. That he couldn't hurt her, however unfair things felt. She knew that he had to look after his daughter, even if she was a useless bitch. She'd do exactly the same thing if it was her. That's what family meant, wasn't it?

Much to her surprise, he took a pint glass and put it under the tap. And neither Ted nor Alex said much of anything for the rest of the night.

It was a quiet night. So quiet that Ted had only lit half the lamps in the pub – the old gas ones that were his favourites. He thought they lent the place a sense of atmosphere. Alex thought they lent the place a serious danger of going up in flames. There were puddles of light dotted around the pub – tables here and there, most of the bar. Alex had asked him what he was doing at the time, pointing out that this wasn't the friendliest setting for a drink, what with it being pitch bloody black around most of the room, but he wasn't interested. His response was pure Yorkshire – that he wasn't made of money. But that was a stupid thing to say because, as far as Alex was concerned, he was. Ted had more money than anyone in this village, and that included Pete with his caravan park and his clapped-out Mercedes and his £250 a month from her and her mum.

Either way, Ted had lit up his pub like it was the Addams family's local and gone out. The bar was empty, with no one in except for old Bill, who used to hire out sea kayaks on the beach before his back gave out, and Alex and Si. To be fair, it wasn't a bad way to spend a Monday night. You got paid the same whether there were people in the pub or not.

'Are you not thirsty?' Alex said to Si, and she was daring him with her eyes. This was a game they played a lot, but it was much higher risk than normal, because Ted and Bill were good mates. He would 100 per cent tell Ted what they were up to if he twigged. That made it more fun, though.

'A bit, I suppose,' said Si, so it was game on.

'Well get yourself a drink then,' she said, and smiled her best butter wouldn't melt. 'What do you want? Coke?'

She took down a glass from the top shelf and made a great play of putting it under the post-mix tap.

'It's not Coke, Alex,' he said, arse resting on the fridge and long legs sprawled out in front of him. 'Come on. It's a generic cola drink, you know that.'

'Yeah,' she agreed. 'Fair play.'

And she leaned right over to nudge him in the ribs, nice and friendly. And as she did, she shifted the glass out from under the sticky nozzles of the soft drinks and stuck it under the lager tap instead.

Bill rolled his eyes.

'Jesus. The amount you two chatter on.'

'Oh, sorry, Bill,' Si said. 'We putting you off your conversation, are we?'

Alex sniggered. She liked it when Si was cheeky. He'd always been a right handful when he was a kid, with his little round face and red hair sticking up in tufts all over his head and a mouth on him to rival hers, some days. He'd had the spark knocked out of him a bit when his dad died, and the red had pretty much faded to blond now, but with Bill, Si was still his old kid-self.

Bill was basically family to Si, same as Ted was and even that old bastard Pete. A lot of people were basically family to him – Si and his mum both seemed to bring that out in people. It was like they had this look about them – a kind of *come on, help us out*, lost kind of a look.

Alex had never mastered it, herself. She'd never even had

a dad in the first place – having one who died when she was fifteen, like Si, would have been a major upgrade to her. But people never seemed to think about her like they did Si. They just sort of assumed she'd be all right. Which, don't get her wrong, she was. It wasn't like she wanted pity. It was just strange.

'A bit of peace and quiet and a pint of mild. That's all I ask,' said Bill.

Alex leaned forward to give him an interested stare, like she was proper listening. As she did, she used the hand tucked under her bust to flick the lager on. It was a good strategy for this evening, because he was decent enough, Bill. He wouldn't look at her tits.

'Bill, mate. You live alone. What are you getting this peace and quiet instead of?'

'Cheeky little mare,' Bill muttered, staring deep into his pint.

And Si kicked Alex in the shin and she remembered too late that it was only just about a year since Bill's wife died now. She felt her cheeks start to burn and shot a *piss off, all right?* look at Si. She hadn't meant it that way, had she? And, anyway, it was still true.

The pint glass was three quarters full now, but Alex flipped the tap off anyway. The fun had gone out of the game. Bill wasn't looking, and now it was too easy.

'When do you get your results, then?' Si said, a bit too loud. He was obviously trying to move the conversation on, which was sweet, to be fair to him, even though he'd said bang on exactly the wrong thing. If it had been anyone else, Alex would have thought they were having a go at her – getting back at her for upsetting Bill, maybe, by bringing her A levels up, but Si wasn't like that.

'That dishwasher's done,' she said. She unlatched the machine door and bent over it, taking a face full of yeast and vinegar steam. As she did, she reached out and took a swig of illicit lager. Beer tasted of soap, especially the lager they had on here, but it was something to do. The cider tap was right in the line of the CCTV.

Alex stood up, bringing two hot glasses with her.

'Next month,' she said.

'Think you'll pass?' he asked, and repeated her manoeuvre, twisting the pint glass round so he was drinking from the opposite side to where she'd left her lip-gloss-frosted kiss. Instead of putting his pint glasses to cool on the shelf, Si stacked them up on top of each other and shoved them next to the ones Alex had placed there.

Alex rolled her eyes. She'd told him about that. You stack them while they're still hot, they get stuck, they shrink, they crack. But he wouldn't listen. It was like Si couldn't keep anything in his head. She opened her mouth to say something and then closed it again. Fuck it. She wasn't in charge, was she? Ted hadn't even bothered assigning a deputy for when he and Jenny were both out. The keys to the bar hung glinting under their gas lamp on a hook by the till. And every one of them assumed it'd be Alex, of course, who'd take them down and take the cash to the safe. Who'd lock the creaking doors, despite Ted knowing personally pretty much every bugger in this village. No one had asked, though. They just assumed that she'd know Si was too daft to be trusted with anything. It would have been nice to be asked.

'I dunno, Si,' she said.

And he gave her a look that made her think that it wasn't just for the sake of having something to talk about that he'd asked. That maybe, just maybe, he knew how much it meant.

'Really?' he said. 'No idea?'

Alex threw a quick look at Bill, but he wasn't listening. So maybe it would be okay to talk about it, for a little bit. It was only Si. She was one of those people who was almost like family to him too, when it came down to it. When there were so few people around you, they could become pretty much like blood, for better or worse.

'I mean, it'll be close,' she said. 'I'll need 100 per cent. On the one they let me take. But yeah, I reckon I'll get it.'

Si nodded and flashed her a smile. And the way that the light caught him, the stubble on his chin really didn't look so patchy as it normally did, but his eyes were as bright as they ever were, and that smile was as cheeky as it had been the day they'd met, when they were both four years old. And it was as if Alex caught a glimpse of the man he might turn into one day, if she stuck around to see.

'Of course you'll get it,' he said. 'You're the cleverest person I know.'

Alex treated herself to a little secret smile, and another sip of stolen lager.

'And there was me thinking you only liked me for my tits.'

'Aye, well,' Si said. 'Those too. Obviously.'

And he reached for the pint glass. This time, instead of drinking from the opposite side of the glass to her, he placed his mouth directly over the ghost of hers.

'Jesus fuck,' Bill said. And for a heart-drop moment, Alex

thought he'd caught them with the beer. But when she turned her gaze to meet him, all jutted chin and defiance, there was a smile in his eyes. 'Would you two get a room?'

And Si's eyes met Alex's, and there was a laugh building up inside him, she could tell. And, just for a moment, Alex was filled up with a kind of sticky longing for a life she wasn't going to have. Who would Si lock eyes with and smirk at, when she was gone?

'We've got a room, Bill,' he said. 'It's just that you're in it.'

It wasn't worth staying for though, was it? A boy who you knew better than anyone, whose smile was probably your favourite ever sight, sharing a joke with you. It wasn't better than Manchester.

'I'll tell Ted, mind,' Bill said. But he wouldn't.

Alex smiled and started stacking the pint glasses for real.

'What are you gonna do then?' she said, lining up warm pint glasses in neat rows on the shelf above their heads.

'What?' Si said. He still had his arse perched on the fridge, long legs stuck out over the channel of the bar. Ted was forever telling him not to sit like that. He said it was unhygienic, what with his bum being so close to the pickled eggs.

'What are you going to do? In September.'

'Christ, I dunno,' Si said. 'This, I guess? What's so special about September?'

Alex rolled her eyes. He could be a thick twat sometimes, no matter how nice his eyes were.

'No, I mean, like, you gonna move out, or what?'

He pulled his eyebrows together. It made him look like an ape. Not so attractive.

'What for?'

Alex puffed a lungful of air out. Christ, she was only making conversation.

'I dunno. You could move to Hull, Leeds maybe. Get a better job. Train up for something. What do you want to do?'

Si shrugged. 'I don't know. I'm happy.'

Alex frowned at him.

'Happy? In this shithole?'

'Yeah,' he said. 'Happy. You should try it. Most people are happy here, right, Bill?'

Alex looked at Bill, sitting on his own and nursing his one pint. Out in an empty bar on a rainy Monday night.

Bill met Alex's eyes and shrugged.

'Aye, lad,' he said, his voice kind. And something unspoken passed between Bill and Alex. Si needed to be protected. He was an innocent, which was a weird thing to think about a big lump of a bloke like him, but true nonetheless.

'There's a reason most people do it, you know,' Si said, and there was a bit of heat in his voice. Maybe he'd noticed them swapping looks behind his back. He leaned forward and took a pint glass from the dishwasher, tossing it from hand to hand. 'Get a job, get a girlfriend, have a couple of kids. Live your life by the sea and go drinking with your mates every weekend. It's not stupid to take the easy way. Not if it's what you want.'

He picked up another glass and jammed it onto the first.

'I didn't know you wanted kids,' she said.

Si shrugged and dipped back down to the dishwasher. There were no more glasses to stack. Instead, he crouched behind the bar and took a small sip of beer. The glass was very nearly empty. He left the last drop for her.

Alex rolled her eyes while pouring a pint, which was excellent multitasking and exactly why she should have got that promotion over Jenny, actually, not that she was bitter about it, or thinking about it at all in fact, no matter how useless Jenny was being tonight.

'It was five pints of lager, yeah, love, two bitters and a gin and tonic . . .'

And it was turning out to be a bad night to be useless. They were packed. Alex wasn't sure what was going on – some football match or something. It did happen sometimes. The whole place was heaving, not just with locals, but holidaymakers too. There was even a group of women with veils, who looked like they were out on a hen do – who had a hen do in Ravenspurn? – and a family sprawling across three generations, all of them pressing up against the bar. Jenny was beside her, dealing with the hen party (which was a piece of piss, as all they wanted were three bottles of white wine) and Alex was fighting her way through the family's order.

'Oi, Alex! Pint of mild, love, pint of mild.'

Alex ignored Pete, who was propping up the end of the bar, with some satisfaction. She'd never liked the old bastard, and this last five years of having him as her landlord hadn't improved her opinion of him at all. It wouldn't hurt him to wait a few minutes to get his pint. She was busy, wasn't she? Serving people who actually tipped sometimes. She racked up the bitters and gin on the bar and started working on the lagers.

'You deaf, love, or what?'

Alex rolled her eyes and found herself looking at her Auntie Jean. A look flashed between them. Auntie Jean always knew what she was thinking. She understood her better than anyone, and she could always tell when Alex was getting pissed off, before she could herself sometimes.

Jean widened her eyes at her and mouthed *Leave it*. One of her most-used phrases. Barney, the puppy, wriggled on her lap. It was way too busy for a dog in tonight, but she was obsessed with that little thing.

'I'm busy, Pete,' Alex said, and she flashed him one of her barmaid smiles. She had a few of them, from the hang-on-mate-I'll-only-be-a-minute to the go-on-babe-that-was-worth-a-tip-right? The one she gave Pete was the I-didn't-actually-say-fuck-off-so-you-can't-get-cross. He met it with a scowl. She didn't know what his fucking problem was. Half the people she was serving ahead of him were staying up at his shitty caravan park, paying way above the odds to stay in some damp little box by the sea. But Pete was the kind of person who was never happy. If you worried about him being in an arse, you'd never do anything else.

Alex raised her eyebrows at Auntie Jean and chucked a rum into a glass for her while the lagers ran. Alex found it particularly easy to stay calm at work. Whenever it got too much for her, she'd imagine barring whoever it was who'd wound her up. It was one of the very best things about being a barmaid – the ability to bar people. Just one word and they'd be out of your life for ever. Not that she could actually get rid of Pete like that, what with it being his brother's pub, and his dad's pub before that, but the idea cheered her up regardless.

Alex thumped three pints onto the bar.

Jenny turned to her. She was looking much less sleek than she usually was, her face red and her hair sticking up in a frizzy halo around her head.

'Fucking busy, isn't it?' she said, holding her glass by the lager tap. She'd finished the hen do order, and the gaggle of women had taken themselves off to the far corner. There was a cheer from over there, and then the sound of breaking glass.

'I'm doing five,' Alex said.

'It's all right, I could do with the breather. I doubt we'll get a break tonight.'

Alex rolled her eyes. She was right and all.

Jenny pulled the dustpan and brush out from under the bar and looked hopefully over to see if one of the hen do would come over and clean up after themselves. She'd be fucking lucky, though.

'What's got into everyone? Why's it so busy?'

Not that she should complain. Summer season had changed for Alex over the last few years. It used to be that she'd enjoy the ice-cream stand being open whether there were tourists around to buy them or not – the beach was just as good when she had it all to herself. But now she was old enough to work, she felt it the same way that everyone else did – a season of watchful waiting, of peering anxiously at the sky and at the roads, praying for sun, praying for cars. And when they came, the warmth and the tourists, you had to make hay while you could.

'Are you two girls going to stop gossiping and serve me my pint?' Pete said.

Alex turned to him and stared into his bloodshot eyes. Everyone else in the pub seemed to be having a decent time, but not Pete. He was sitting, one of the few people who'd managed to get himself a seat, taking up space on the bar with his elbows and wearing a face like a slapped arse. She gave him a sweet smile and thought about the possibility of barring him. It wouldn't stick, but she could chuck him out until Ted got back from the emergency crisp run he'd gone on, at least. It'd be worth it just to make a point, and to get him out of her face for a couple of hours.

'No, don't think so.'

She finished the last lager and didn't bother turning off the tap. Jenny handed the dustpan and brush across the bar – one of the hen party had miraculously arrived to take responsibility – and shoved a glass underneath it, while Alex took the note from the bloke who must be the grandad's outstretched hands, stabbing at buttons to ring it through the till as fast as she could. She shoved the change into his weather-worn palm and turned to scan the rest of the bar.

Obviously you wouldn't catch her saying this in front of Ted, but when it was busy like this was her favourite time to work in a pub. She'd like it even if it didn't mean she was less likely to get laid off when the weather turned sour. The bustle and the feeling of mastery made the time slip by almost as fast as it did when you were on the other side of the bar.

'Right, who's next?'

Six different blokes roared at her. It was exciting, having

this many new faces in the bar, and it almost never happened. Normally, there were only about five people in here, and Alex had known all of them since she was a kid. But tonight, there were tourists in, bringing their holiday spirit with them. Alex smiled at one of them – a bloke of about twenty-five, she reckoned. He looked like he was into the gym, his crisp white polo shirt stretched tight over wide shoulders. This was what it'd be like every night, in Manchester. People and noise. The feeling that something might happen.

'Yes, babe,' she said, as she topped off the rum with a dash of Coke and slid it over to Auntie Jean, who left the right change on the counter like Alex knew she would.

Shoulders smiled back at her. 'Three lagers, love. Cheers.'

Alex grabbed a few glasses to clear the bar a bit and tried to swing her bum around as she moved. That was what lads liked, wasn't it? Arses. Men were absolutely obsessed with big bums, in Alex's experience, even if *Cosmo* or whatever were always telling you how to slim yours down to practically nothing.

She was just reaching for another armful of empties when a hand shot out and grabbed her, closing tight around her wrist. Shocked, she let go of the glass she was holding and it dropped to the floor. It bounced once, twice, and then shattered to pieces next to her foot. It was so busy, she didn't think anyone even heard.

'Get the fuck off me,' she said, quietly, and she glared at Pete. As she looked at him, she realised that he wasn't the normal kind of drunk that she saw in the people who came to the bar – a kind of drunk that was cute, almost, in a stumbling and forgetting things kind of a way. The kind of drunk where they'd hand her a whole tenner and then walk off, leaving her with all the change. That was what was normal. But tonight Pete was drunk in a mutinous, furious way. She'd seen this kind of drunk before – trouble-drunk. Drinking-at-2 p.m.-on-a-weekday-and-lost-money-on-the-horses drunk. His hand was gripping her hard, completely enclosing her wrist. Alex looked down and was shocked at how small her arm looked in his hand – as if he could snap it right off if he wanted. Panic bubbled up in her throat. Alex wasn't used to being small and delicate. She'd always thought that it might be quite nice, but she was wrong. She hated it.

'I'll fucking let go when I want to let go, you cheeky little slag. You fucking pour me my pint or you'll be fucking sorry.'

His eyes were narrowed and his lips were wet – a disturbing, mirror-version of Ted. The same shape mouth, the same colour eyes, but so different in the way they arranged them that you wouldn't know they were related sometimes, when other times they looked like twins.

Alex could feel the blood pounding in her ears, making her dizzy, making everything seem like it was far away. But she kept her voice level and her eyes on him as she said, 'Let go of me right now, or you're barred.'

He didn't let go. Instead, he laughed.

'Barred from my own brother's pub? I don't think so, pet . . .'

Alex leaned back, tugging at her arm, but he was gripping on too tight for her to pull away. She scrabbled back, desperate, feet crunching on the broken pint glass beneath her.

'Let go of me. You're barred, you're fucking barred, you're fucking . . .'

Alex could see white dimples where his fingers were digging into the pudgy flesh of her wrist and wondered if it was possible that he could just break it. Just snap her like a twig. She looked up, desperate, scanning face after face. Auntie Jean and Jenny, both of them frozen, faces like masks, but not moving to help her. Barney yipped, little pink tongue flashing in his mouth, but held tight in Jean's grip. Shoulders looked worried, but he just stood with his pint, mouth half open, staring at them both. The breath caught in Alex's throat as her arm bone creaked.

'Let go of her, yer mad bastard!'

There was a roar and the pressure around her wrist released. Alex fell back, sagging against Jenny, who caught her and steadied her, stopping her from falling down to the broken glass and spilt beer of the bar floor.

Alex watched, stunned, as Ted Fletcher hauled his brother back by the collar of his shirt, his face red and furious. Alex felt her jaw fall open. Ted was normally so mild-mannered, and he'd never have a bad word said about his brother in front of him. The amount of times she'd got in trouble for slagging Pete when he was around was unbelievable. Now, arm muscles that Jenny hadn't known he had were bulging, and he looked like a warrior or something. His face was contorted with fury, but not in a way that made him look ugly. He looked powerful.

'You fucking heard her. You're barred, so get to fuck.'

Now that Ted had made the first move, the spell was broken. Auntie Jean pushed through to the bar, reaching for Alex's shaking hands, covering them in her own, and the men nearby all swarmed around Pete, pushing hands down on flailing limbs, propelling him towards the door. Forming a wall between him and Alex. Alex breathed out a long, juddering breath.

'I was only messing with the little slag, wasn't I? I din't mean ner harm, did I?'

Ted was still shoving him towards the door by his collar. The top button of Pete's shirt was pressing into his throat, strangling him (*good*), but he still managed to croak out, 'And, we all know why you're sticking up for the little slapper, don't we? We all know—'

His words were cut off with a sickening crunch as Ted's fist connected with his cheekbone. The whole pub was silent, staring at the two men, Pete slouching towards the floor and Ted standing over him, breathing heavily.

Alex stared in shock. Pete had said things like that to her loads of times, pretty much since she started secondary school: Alex would shag anyone who came near her, everyone wanted a go on her, she took after her mum, blah blah blah. Alex had got used to it, without even realising. But as she watched a thick gobbet of blood falling from his mouth onto the faded wood of the pub floor, Alex was filled up with fresh outrage, washing out all the tired pissed-offness that had been there before. She was glad Ted had hit him. She wished he'd hit him again. Why should Pete be allowed to talk to her like that?

'You're barred, Pete!' she shouted. She pulled herself up as tall as she could, pushing off Jenny to propel herself upright. 'You remember. Don't come back!'

And with one last firm shove from Shoulders, Pete was finally pushed out of the pub, Ted dragging him through the door and away, slamming the door behind them both.

There was a moment of silence then – even the hen do had shut up. And then there were a few shocked whispers, and then the odd nervous giggle, and before long the whole place was back to chatting at full volume as if nothing had happened at all.

'Um. You can have a fag break. You know. If you want.'

Jenny was looking shaken and pale, and honestly, why wouldn't she? Imagine having that as your uncle.

'Nah. Cheers, though,' she said. She didn't want to miss Ted coming back in.

When he did, five minutes later, his hand looked red and he rested it gingerly on the bar.

Alex pulled him a pint of bitter and plonked it down.

'On the house.'

He snorted. 'It's my house.'

'On me, I mean,' she said. She gritted her teeth. She could still feel the ghost of a hand gripping tight on her wrist. 'Cheers, Ted.'

He picked up the pint in his undamaged left hand.

'No need to thank me,' he said. 'We take care of our own around here.

Later that night, when Shoulders and the hen party had stumbled off back up the cliff path together and the pub doors had been locked up against the seagulls and the dark, Alex slumped even more gratefully onto the bar stool for her tip drinks than she usually did.

She tipped the last few drops of cider into her mouth, upending the pint glass. The taste of sugar filled her whole head, along with the tang of manure she'd spent the whole of the summer she was fifteen getting used to. Fermentation, that's what it was. It was easy to remember that all you were drinking was rotting apples. Especially after the third pint.

'Do you want another one? You've got loads left.'

Ted tapped the shot glass with Alex's name on it. It was still more than half full with the torn-off ends of receipts – by the look of it, she still had more than five pints left.

She shrugged. 'Go on.'

She hadn't really wanted a drink tonight, but then she hadn't wanted anything, so why not?

Ted nodded approvingly, fished two of her receipts out, and tore them in half.

'Anyone else?'

Jenny shook her head. Her half was barely touched as it was.

Si still had half his drink left. He downed it in one, smiled a big, dopey grin, and said, 'Yeah. Same again.'

He'd turned up for last orders, already four tins in after babysitting the twins. She was glad to see him. Alex always loved getting drunk with Si, because he was one person who never, ever got arsey. He wasn't an angry drunk, not even a little. He just got a bit more dozy and a bit more friendly then he already was. It was nice to have him around. It was an easy way to pretend that everything was fine.

Ted nodded again and stuck a pint glass under the tap.

'You're pushing us hard on the tip drinks tonight.'

Alex shifted her weight on the bar stool, only slightly wobblier than normal.

Ted gazed back at her, steady. He hadn't had any tip drinks. Just the one she'd bought him earlier, which she genuinely had, even though no one had checked.

'Aye, well. It's getting to month end.'

Alex gave him a shrewd look, the effect only slightly ruined by her hair falling over her eye. Had it been loose this whole time? Alex yanked out her collapsed ponytail impatiently.

'It's the fifteenth.'

Ted finished pouring Si's pint and started on Alex's. The drinks glowed amber in the low light of the bar.

'Well. Halfway's halfway, isn't it? I don't want you to lose them.'

Alex retied her hair, nice and tight. The ponytail pulled on her forehead, but the sensation wasn't unpleasant. It was almost refreshing. Having her hair up made her feel more awake.

'You don't usually care.'

Ted slid the pint of cider over the bar to her.

'This month I do.'

Alex sipped at her pint. The taste was overwhelming, almost making her gag on dead apples. She'd had way too much already. She sipped again.

'You made up that rule, though. About month end. If you cared, you could just let us have them whenever we wanted anyway.'

Jenny plonked her half-pint down on the bar. From anyone else, it would have been a slam. 'Oh for fuck's sake.'

Alex looked at her, surprised. Jenny didn't usually swear. Except at school, of course. Everyone swore at school, it would be weird not to. But, even there, she always sounded self-conscious about it. When Jenny said swear words, they seemed foreign somehow, like they didn't live in her mouth. Alex had always assumed that Jenny was one of those girls who never swore in front of her parents. But Ted didn't look surprised at all.

'Dad feels guilty about that prick Pete. It's obvious, isn't it? So he wants you to have a few pints and forget about it, so he'll feel better about his brother being such an arsehole. Like we always do.' Jenny heaved a deep sigh and stared into her drink, like she'd sunk a whole ocean rather than two and a half pints, tops. 'But we've already had a few pints. We've had loads.'

Alex scowled at her. Of course it was obvious, she wasn't an idiot. She'd wanted him to be the one that said it, that was all.

Si roused himself, dopey smile slipping off his face.

'That fucking wanker. I'll fucking deck him if he comes back in here again, you see if I don't.'

Alex looked at Ted, waiting for him to tell Si to calm

down, but he didn't. He just stood, hands resting on the bar, his mouth a grim, pressed-together line.

'You're all right, Si,' Alex said. 'I can take care of myself. Don't you worry about that.'

She wished she felt as confident as she sounded. Pete owned her house. But it wasn't for long. She tried to do the maths in her head – how many weeks, until she could leave? Not that many.

'Yeah, I know,' Si said. His eyes were glazed, his mouth wet with beer. Alex was surprised to notice that it almost looked sexy. 'Like, maybe I can take care of you as well as you. And then there'll be, like, two of us. Yeah?'

Alex took another sip of cider to hide a smile. She had to admit, that was pretty sweet.

Jenny rolled her eyes.

'Didn't you hear? She's fine. God, don't patronise her.'

'I can bar him,' Ted said quietly. 'Permanently, like. Your choice. You never have to see him again, if you don't want.'

For a moment, Alex let herself imagine what it might be like to never have to see Pete again. Never having to feel that angry prickle on the back of her neck, never having to feel four feet tall again.

'You can't bar your own brother.'

Ted smiled at her. He'd have been handsome, when he was younger. He had that look about him.

'My mum's not around anymore. It's not like I'll get in trouble.'

But that wasn't how villages like Ravenspurn worked. Even if she hadn't lived on his shitty caravan park, there was no getting away from anyone here. It was stupid to try.

He'd keep popping up, on the beach, in the Co-op, in the Cooplands, down the amusement arcade. She'd be seeing Pete every day until she died, and there was nothing she could do about it. Or he died, she supposed. That was a slightly more cheerful thought.

Until she got out, of course. That was the only way.

'What's wrong with you two?' Jenny's voice was shrill, bouncing around the empty room. 'She said she was fine.'

Well, well. Alex gave her a quick little grin, which wasn't returned. Jenny was full of surprises tonight. She wasn't sticking up for Alex. She was jealous of her.

Alex took a leisurely swig of sugar-manure-cider. She was almost sympathetic. It must be difficult having to live your whole life as Daddy's perfect princess, and then having to share the attention for two minutes. How was Jenny going to cope in the real world, when she left for uni? Alex would be all right, of course. She'd already been looking after herself for years.

She gave Ted a little shrug, and shook her head.

'Thanks, though,' she said.

And in those two words she tried to get across that she didn't just mean thanks for the offer, or thanks just for chucking Pete out earlier. But thanks for the distraction as well. Thanks for making them all drink a load of tip-pints, for creating a bit of a buffer between the blank panic of that horrible vice-like grip on her hand and the moment she had to walk up the cliff on her own in the dark, back towards him. That's what she'd meant. And that's why she'd wanted him to admit it, about the drinks. She'd wanted to say thanks.

Jenny sighed, flopping dramatically forwards to rest her head on the bar.

'Are we going home yet? It's nearly one.'

Ted shrugged, unhooked the towel from his shoulder and wiped at the bar where her head had rested.

'I'm knackered though,' said Jenny. There was a whiny note to her voice that set Alex's teeth on edge. Unbidden, her mother's voice floated into her head. *Kids what whine want punching.*

'You can go home if you like.'

Jenny looked shocked. 'It's dark out there.'

'What are you, five?' said Si. And as pissed as she was, Alex noticed a shift in the mood. Si was never snarky like that, not even when people deserved it, like Jenny did.

Ted sighed. 'All right, it is late. Drink up, kids.'

Alex shrugged. 'I'm done, anyway,' she said, and forced herself to drink the remaining half-pint of cider in one long swallow.

She hopped off her bar stool, and Si lumbered off his. Jenny was already on her feet, and she didn't even look pleased with herself for getting her way. Her face was totally neutral, with the sweet, slightly dozy look that it always fell into when she wasn't thinking anything in particular. Because it hadn't even been a question, for Jenny, that she'd get her way. Why would it be? This was how it always went.

The gas lamps were shut off with a little hiss, and Alex pulled on her hoodie and backpack by the glow of the beer pumps. As Ted faffed with the door, Alex pulled up her hood.

'Bye then.'

She didn't give them a chance to reply before she headed

off. There was no need to watch the three of them heading off to the posh bit of Ravenspurn inland, all chummy, while she made her way up the cliff alone.

Jenny was right about the outside – it was dark. Even darker than usual. On a good night, the moon seemed to hang in the sky, so close you could almost touch it, like a giant lampshade you could turn on or off. Even on moonless nights, for most of summer, you could see the stars spattered across the sky, their twinkle bounced back up by the sea. But tonight there was none of that. Just a couple of street lights and the threat of drizzle in the air. Over along the coast was the dirty glow of Bridlington, but it wasn't enough to be able to see by – only to spoil the dark.

Alex heard footsteps, running, pounding up behind her, and she felt her shoulders rise. But who was it going to be? There was no one in this village she didn't know. Of course, knowing someone didn't stop them from hurting you.

Alex forced herself to keep breathing, keep walking. It wouldn't be Pete. That wouldn't make sense. Why would he come down to the beach for her when he knew full well she was on her way up to her home, which he had a key for? The idea helped to slow her heart rate, even though it wasn't really that comforting when you stopped to think about it.

'Oi. Alex.'

She turned, already smiling. It was Si, jogging along the beach path. The fresh air seemed to have done wonders for him – he didn't look drunk at all now, and barely even staggered as he ran. He looked like he could run for miles like that – a gentle lope, exactly what he was made to do.

'What do you want?' she said. She tried to say it in a

friendly way, but he still looked kind of hurt. Alex chewed at her lip. Surely he knew her well enough to tell what she was thinking? He was pretty pissed, though.

'I just thought ... Maybe I could walk you home?'

Alex raised her eyebrows. In all the time she'd lived up in the caravan park, no one had ever offered to walk her home. No one had walked her home since primary school, when Auntie Jean would pick her up early on a Friday if she wasn't working a late.

'I'll be all right,' she said automatically, even though her heart was still beating hard from hearing the steps behind her, and the night was so dark she'd barely be able to see the cliff steps. But she'd be all right. Of course she would. She always was.

'I know you will. I just thought ... If Jenny gets walked home, you know? You should too.'

And Alex felt her face break into a proper smile – her first in what felt like months but was only a couple of hours. There was no harm in it, was there? She hadn't wanted the night to end anyway.

'Okay then.'

The two of them walked in companionable silence along the promenade and up the cliff path. Despite the darkness, Alex always liked it when the village felt like it was sleeping. The shops along the seafront all still had their boards out offering their various flavours of ice cream (though never her favourite – mint choc chip. They'd had it when she was a kid, but it had fallen from favour now. A shame.) and there were still big tubs of buckets and spades left out, ready for tomorrow's children to pick up and play with. But for now, a pause, and a village that was just hers, or maybe hers and Si's, if she wanted.

As they reached the top of the cliff, Si let out a big huff of air.

'Bloody hell. You do this every night?'

Alex shrugged. It was a pain in the arse, admittedly, but when she'd started, she'd been grateful enough to have anywhere to live. They'd been all squashed up in Auntie Jean's for a month; Jean and Karen sharing and Alex sleeping on the floor at the foot of the bed like a poodle. It had seemed worth the climb, to have her own room.

'It's where I live, mate.'

She'd liked living with Jean, mind. Alex remembered a lot of oven chips and *Coronation Street*.

Si shook his head and stared out to sea. She followed his gaze. There wasn't even enough light to pick out the point where the sea met the sky, tonight. Everything was inky black.

'You must be well fit. I mean, you are well fit. But, like, both meanings.'

He giggled to himself at his little joke, but Alex gave him a sharp stare and felt her heart rate pick up. Like she'd climbed a hundred cliffs.

'You think I'm fit?'

He turned to her and smiled, eyes a little out of focus and completely unguarded. That was the lovely thing about Si. Even when he wasn't drunk, there was no suggestion of him keeping a secret from you. He was a completely open book.

'Course I do. You know that.'

Alex played with the drawstring of her hood. She'd have

liked to unzip it a bit, but that was too obvious. Far too much like the kind of thing that Jenny would do. But boys did like Jenny. Alex tried to imagine what Jenny might say now, to be nice to a boy, to not scare him away.

'Why han't you ever done anything about it then?'

Coming out of her mouth, the words sounded angrier, more accusing then they had in her head. Not quite right, somehow.

But Si didn't seem to mind. He gave her a slow, sexy smile. He was only swaying a little bit.

'I dunno. Never seemed like the right time. You'll be off soon, anyway.'

Alex scowled out to the blank, black sea. 'If I get the grades.'

He reached out and touched her on the face. A very gentle stroke along her jawline. Alex's skin tingled all along where he'd touched it.

'Course you will. You can do anything.'

She looked up at him. It was a funny thing, watching the people you knew best grow up. His adult face still caught her by surprise, no matter how many times she saw it. Whenever she turned to look at Si, a part of her was still expecting to see a boy, but he was a proper man now. So different from the kid she'd grown up with, yet so completely, always himself.

'Can I?'

He leaned in so close she could taste the lager on his breath. So boozy it made her feel dizzy.

'Anything you want,' he said.

She took a deep breath and closed the gap.

'Eh up. What you up to tonight?'

Alex's mum appeared in the doorway of her bedroom. She was wearing Alex's pyjamas, a soft pink set with a teddy bear on the front. Alex glared at the teddy.

'Nothing.'

It was true. Si and Jenny were both working shifts at the bar. Alex had asked if she could work too, even though she knew that Ted had already given her more shifts than her share. But it was only a Wednesday. Two people was already overkill. And Katie and Sarah from the year above were long gone from Ravenspurn, and Kelly from the year below was pregnant, so she was no good to go out with. No one was meant to know yet, but obviously everybody did. Kelly had gone from smoking twenty Benson and Hedges a day and spending every weekend off her face on Archers and lemonade to only leaving the house to shoplift vitamins from Boots and have shouting matches with her boyfriend on the beach, always tantalisingly just out of earshot.

'You just going to mope around your room then?'

There was Chris, but ever since he scraped together the money for his knackered old Citroën, he'd been spending more and more time out of Ravenspurn, refusing to be drawn on exactly where he was. Tonight was no different. Alex had asked if she could tag along to whatever it was he was doing, but she'd been brushed off like an annoying kid.

Alex shrugged.

Her mum sighed, rolling her eyes up to the damp-patched ceiling. Alex followed her gaze. She'd need to paint over that again, if she could cadge some more paint off Pete, which would mean talking to him, but then she'd have to start that again sooner or later, so this might be a good excuse. She'd only put the last coat on the previous summer, but she supposed there'd been a lot of rain since then.

'Come and have a drink.'

Alex traced a line under one thumbnail with the other. A satisfying slither of dirt came out. You could wash your hands as often as you liked, but when you worked in a bar, the beer and grime would always find a way to stick to you.

'I'm all right.'

Alex's mum tilted her head in a way that was almost kind. 'Don't be daft. I'm not having you sulking in there all night.'

Alex shrugged again, but then she followed her mum into the living room.

'You want a drink?'

She was already on the sofa, wine bottle open in front of her and two of the glasses Alex had stolen for her from the pub lined up on the coffee table. Mum was all smiles now – she was never happier than when Alex agreed to hang around drinking with her. Like any proper alcoholic, Alex's mum hated drinking alone, but for some reason she'd never set foot in Ted's pub, which was the only one in the village. So it was only when she could convince her sister or daughter to have a drink with her that she could indulge in the fantasy that she was just a social drinker. Alex was sure that once upon a time there'd been friends that came over – men, mostly – but that seemed to have stopped long ago.

Alex shrugged. 'Just one.'

But both of them knew that was just talk. When was it ever just one? Alex would have loved to have just a couple of drinks with her mum. Just a friendly little buzz, three drinks and a chat and a laugh and then call it a night before everything went pear-shaped and they ended up screaming at each other again. But there was no point pretending. They'd be drinking right up until Alex passed out, waking up tomorrow still in these clothes and with her make-up on, and the best case scenario was that she wouldn't really remember the fight they'd had. She knew how it would go. But tonight she was out of options. She'd take it, over having no company at all.

The wine sloshed into the glasses and onto the table. Alex made a mental note to remember to wipe it down tomorrow morning. She hated a sticky table. But she didn't have the energy to do it tonight.

'Cheers!'

'Aye. Cheers.'

As the glasses struck each other, they sounded out like a dull bell in the cramped living room.

Alex took a sip of too-warm, too-sweet white wine and tucked her legs up under her bum. It was always cold in here. She turned to the TV, flashing bright in the corner. There was some kind of game show on. On screen, a woman with bright pink lipstick earnestly explained how she could really do with five hundred quid.

'What we watching?'

Alex felt like she could also really do with five hundred quid. Just for safety's sake, you know? Because, obviously, she was out of here. In two months' time, she'd have her student loan and be away. But, also, she'd looked it up, and that was pretty much what she'd need for a deposit and the first month's rent for her own place around here as well. Just in case. Because as bad as it would be to not go to uni, to get left behind, the idea of doing that and being stuck in this damp little box with her mother on top of her made her skin crawl. She'd sooner chuck herself off the cliffs.

And if she didn't need it, she could spend it at uni. Five hundred quid would buy you an awful lot of shots, even at city prices.

Alex allowed herself a small smile. Just two more months.

'Dunno. I'm not watching it. Here, do you want some of this?'

Alex's mum leaned over, a jar of salsa and a bag of Doritos in her hand, and some bright red sauce slopped out and onto her pyjama bottoms. Alex snatched the jar and banged it down on the coffee table, too annoyed to worry about the ring of salsa settling on the table like congealed blood.

'Oi! Watch it. Those are mine.'

Alex's mum swiped at the stain with the hem of the pyjama top, pushing the tomato deeper into the fabric, getting it everywhere.

'I had none clean.'

Fury bubbled up through Alex. What, like that was her fucking fault? When she was the one who worked for both of them, as well as doing all the cleaning, and the best part of the food shopping too. She was meant to haul double the stuff she needed to the launderette and back up the cliff again, on top of all that?

'That's because you never fucking wash anything.'

Alex's mum's whole face changed, like someone had turned a light out. Everything about her suddenly looked harder. In a way, it made her look a lot more like herself than the version of her that was sucking up.

'Cheeky bitch. After all the things I've done for you. All the things I've given up . . .'

Alex pulled a face and swallowed the rest of her wine in one gulp. She didn't want to go back over the list of things that her mum had given up in order to have her. Some career, never specified, some man, never specified, her body, her freedom. It didn't sound like she'd done much with any of those things while she'd had them. But they'd had this fight so many times before, and Alex really didn't have anywhere else she could go tonight, so she didn't push it.

Instead, she said, 'Did I tell you about Pete?'

It worked just like Alex had hoped. Her mum's eyes lit up with the dark spark they always got when she was settling down to have a good thorough hate of someone, and she topped up both their glasses, shaking the bottle to get the very last drops out.

'That wanker! What's he done now?'

'He was at the pub . . .'

Alex was trying to get into it, put on a decent show. She wouldn't get to tell this story a lot – her mum was just about the only person in the village who hadn't been there to see it for themselves. Except for Alison, of course. But her mum leaned back into the sofa cushions, waving a hand to cut her off.

'Well, that's not unusual. Always at the pub, that fucking alkie.'

Alex very, very nearly said that it was fucking rich coming from her, but she stopped herself in time. The whole point of telling her this in the first place was to head off a fight, wasn't it? She had to stay focused.

She nodded. 'Yeah, right, but then a few drinks in, he reaches over the bar and he fucking grabs me.'

Alex's mum's eyes were round as pound coins.

Alex took a sip of wine, which didn't even taste that sickly anymore, it seemed fine. Her mum was a decent audience, she'd say that much for her. So that was one good thing about staying in.

'He never.'

Alex nodded. 'Swear it. Right around the wrist. And I'm screaming, right, and pulling back, trying to get him off me . . .'

She held up an arm to demonstrate. As she closed a hand around her opposite wrist, she felt a cold jolt of disgust, like a kind of aftershock. But it was okay. It was only for a moment.

'That fucking twat. I'll fucking murder him. I always said to him, he ever put a hand on you again, a single finger, that'd be the end of him, I always fucking said . . .'

She was looking more and more upset. Alex was alarmed. She hadn't meant to stir anything up. It was just meant to be a distraction, just a bit of gossip, not a whole deep thing.

'No, but it was okay, right? Because Ted was there, and he

reaches over and pulls him back, by his fucking collar, like he's a kitten or something, and shouts at him. Proper shouts!'

Alex's mum downed the rest of her wine in one long swallow, like it was ice-cold squash on a hot day.

'Right. Well, I'm glad you're okay.'

She got up and went over to the bit of the caravan that was meant to be like a kitchen. Alex trailed after her as she opened the little under-counter fridge and pulled out another bottle of wine.

'And then, right, Ted chucks him out. And Pete's shouting about this and that, saying all sorts of stuff, but Ted says not to put a hand on me and to fuck off.'

Alex's mum untwisted the top of the wine and filled both glasses right up to the brim, all without looking at her.

'Right.'

Alex rolled her eyes. Why wasn't her mum getting it?

'And he does! He fucks off! Just like that.'

It was so frustrating. Normally, her mum loved any little bit of gossip Alex could scare up from the pub. Whenever Auntie Jean came over, the two of them would sit around cackling for hours, talking shit about everyone in the village, even though Alex's mum never saw any of them in person any more, if she could help it anyway. But now there was some proper, actual news, and she wasn't interested.

Alex tried again.

'And Ted said that he'd bar him for me, if I wanted. Even though that's his own brother, obviously, like, his blood. But he'd do it if I wanted. He'd do what I like.'

Alex's mum pursed her lips and screwed the lid back onto the wine.

'Hmm. Makes a change.'

Alex went and sat down, deflated. Her mum hadn't got the point of the story at all. Wasn't Pete the bad guy in this? Pretty obviously. Why had Ted somehow come off as the wanker, when he was the one who'd sorted it all out? Who'd shown that they actually had her back, unlike every other adult in this shithole village, and Driffield too. Not a single one of her teachers had stuck up for her about the exam. Not even Mrs Dennis, who Alex had always had a grudging respect for, which she had kind of hoped might cut both ways.

'You got some kind of problem with Ted?'

She handed Alex a glass, full almost to the brim with wine. It was a rich yellow colour where the light hit – a glass full of sunshine in the gloom of the caravan. If it wasn't for the smell, you could almost believe it was apple juice.

'I just don't like you licking his arse. That's all.'

Alex rolled her eyes. If her mum spent a bit more time licking arses and a bit less time off her tits, maybe they wouldn't be living in this dump.

'Why not?'

Alex leaned forward and slurped up a mouthful of wine to make it easier to carry. There was a sharp, acidic tang to it. Alex still remembered being young enough to wince at the taste of wine, but now she barely noticed.

'He's not all that. No fucking saint, that Ted Fletcher.'

Alex took another sip. If she was honest, she'd much rather have a Bacardi Breezer. She never drank stuff like that; they made her look too young. They were delicious, though.

'He treats me a fuck of a lot better than most people do.'

Her mum slammed her wine glass down on the coffee table. It didn't spill at all – it was half empty already.

'Well, I'd fucking think so!'

Alex narrowed her eyes at her mother. She took a deep swallow of wine, which she knew would prompt her mother to copy her. Something was up.

'What?'

Sure enough, Alex's mum swigged from her glass.

'I'd have thought you'd remember.'

Her eyes were out on stalks.

'Remember what?'

But her mum wouldn't meet Alex's eye.

'Never you mind.'

Alex narrowed her eyes. More than she wanted Simon Blower to fancy her, more than she wanted a spare five hundred quid to get out of this caravan, more even than she wanted to get her A levels and get out of Ravenspurn for good, she wanted to know what her mother was keeping from her. Alex's mum had never held out on her before. No one did, what with her being chatty and not afraid to ask questions and spending most of her time with people four drinks in at least. It gave her a horrible, crawling feeling, the idea of people knowing things she didn't.

'I'm eighteen now. I'm not a kid.'

She stood up and went over to the kitchen counter. She picked up the remains of the bottle of wine, and then, on reflection, another one from the fridge. There was hardly any left. The bottles were too small for them really, but there'd been a hell of a fight last time Alex had said they should just start getting their wine in boxes. Her mum had said that only alcoholics drank box wine, and Alex hadn't been able to bite her tongue at that, but she also hadn't mentioned it again.

'You already know, anyway. You were little, but you were told.'

Alex poured Chardonnay into her mother's glass, filling it all the way up to the top.

'Go on.'

Her mother stared into the glass, and then she sighed and drank deep, like she'd walked up the cliffs a hundred times. And then she looked at Alex. And Alex could tell that, whatever it was, she was desperate to tell someone. She had that look about her that so many of the regulars had when they came in before lunchtime and talked Alex's ear off about their long-ago divorces and disappointments and betrayals.

'You can keep a secret, can't you?'

Alex filled up her own glass too. She knew then that she had her. She knew this village and she knew the people in it and, for better or worse, she knew her own mother better than anyone.

'Have you ever tried to suck your own cock?'

Chris sat back on his cracked plastic garden chair, smug and regal as if it were a throne.

Alex laughed, narrowly avoiding Strongbow coming out of her nose, at Si's look of horror.

'Chris ...'

Chris shrugged and sparked his lighter – a heavy silver Zippo that Alex had coveted for years. Not that she'd ever nick anything from Chris. She got along with him pretty well, and besides, you'd need your head examining. Chris was the hardest person she knew by a country mile. He looked over the cliff and onto the village below, pretending like he wasn't bothered, pretending like he wasn't delighted to get the rise he was looking for.

'What, you're not going to tell us?'

The three of them were at the top off the cliffs, sitting out by the old hotel beyond the caravan park. The hotel had been grand once, back when the Victorians came here for their sea baths and their rest cures. But as the ground had given way beneath it, the hotel had crumbled bit by bit, and now all that was left was the front wall and a couple of ruined rooms. None of the children in Ravenspurn were ever allowed to play up here because it was far too dangerous, which, naturally, made it the most appealing place.

When Alex was a little kid, she'd come over here with

Si and Chris on the afternoons when they said they'd be walking out to the next beach along – the boys would even bring buckets and spades to make the lie more convincing. They'd abandon them on the scraggy grass and play thrilling games of tig, dizzy with the height and the view and the naughtiness and freedom of it. And once they had hit their teens, this had become the place they'd come to play truth or dare. There used to be more of them than this, but people moved out of Ravenspurn as soon as they could, as a rule. It wasn't as much fun, playing drinking games with just three rather than the gaggle that there used to be. But you took what you could get. It was better than another night in with her mum, at least.

Si's mouth was set in a hard line. Alex wasn't sure she'd ever seen him that pissed off before. She grinned, delighted at how uncomfortable he was. She always used to think that she'd like a sister, but the way these two carried on made her think she was best off out of it. It would be nice to have an ally against Mum, but, on the other hand, no one could throw you under the bus like your sibling could.

'Course I'm not going to tell you.'

Alex took another, more sedate, sip of cider.

Chris flicked the lighter again, a flare of yellow in the dull grey day. When it extinguished, it left the ghost of a flame behind, burned into their eyes.

'You'll have to do a dare.'

Si pouted, suddenly his seven-year-old self again. 'Fine. I'll do a fucking dare.'

Chris's eyes lit up, a proper evil glint. Chris was a right laugh, but he was scary too when he wanted to be.

'Go dancing in the ballroom.'

All three of them looked over to the hotel, and Alex tried and failed to suppress a shudder. Si scowled down into his cider.

'Oh fuck off.'

It was something they'd started saying to each other years ago – perhaps around the time they'd started playing truth or dare. Beyond the grand front door of the hotel was the entrance hall – technically dangerous, according to the grown-ups, but it seemed safe enough to them. The ceiling had already fallen in, but the walls were mainly intact. A huge staircase still climbed up one of them, leading to the open sky. Beyond the staircase, there was a door. You could tell that it would have been beautiful once, with its ornate carvings and dark wood. It kind of still was. The salt on the air got up even this high, leaving the whorls and cracks of the wood frosted a glittering white. Beyond the door was the ballroom, or what was left of it. There was about a foot of marble flooring still jutting grimly off the edge of the cliff, the rest of it long since crashed down to the beach below and taken away to be made into a new floor, or maybe a bar, or some other hotel or restaurant in one of the big cities. They looked like teeth, those marble slabs. Wobbly teeth that might snap off at a moment's notice. In the five years since they had started drinking up here, someone had offered dancing in the ballroom as a dare every single time. No one had ever taken it.

Chris shrugged. 'If you won't dance in the ballroom, then you'll have to tell us your truth. Won't you?'

Si flushed crimson, his eyes darting down to the side.

'Aye, well. Once or twice. I couldn't do it, though.'

Alex screamed with mirth, the sound echoing off the front of the old hotel and into the evening sky. It was still light despite being past ten, and while the light had already started to fade, it was doing the slow retreat of summer. And there were no clouds tonight, so even when the sun faded, there'd be stars, which looked amazing up here, Alex knew, a scatter of glitter on a deep dark sky. It was so pretty at the top of the cliff. Stood to reason that the best part of the village was outside it.

Si glowered. 'Your go, you wanker.'

Chris shrugged, leaning back in the chair. Every summer, they stole a new set of three clapped-out old patio chairs from the caravan park and dragged them over to the old hotel, and every winter they got blown over the cliff edge, presumably to be taken out to sea and washed back up on the shore at Bridlington or Scarborough. Maybe on a good year they'd make it to Whitby. Pete never seemed to notice. He wasn't the kind of man to count his chairs.

'Dare.'

Alex and Si locked eyes, a silent consult. They'd played this game so much together, they had a whole catalogue of dares. Different types, different strengths. Dares that were too outrageous to actually do, designed to push people into a truth, and dares that were for going really soft on somebody if you felt like they were about to storm off home. Chris could take their A-list dares, every single time. Apart from dancing in the ballroom, Chris had done everything they'd ever slung at him, over and over again.

'Streak?'

Alex nodded. 'Streak.'

Chris rolled his eyes, already undoing his belt. 'How far?'

Alex gave him a wide smile and took a sip of cider, for added drama.

'The caravan park gate.'

'FUCK off! That's miles.'

Si's smile was the mirror of hers.

'Well, if you're too chicken ...'

Alex knew that she was outgrowing all of this. Of course she did. There was no harm in enjoying her last summer, though.

Chris pulled off his top, just as she'd known he would, dropped his trousers and set off for the caravan park, pale arse jiggling behind him as he ran.

Si took a sip of cider and grinned. He'd perked up now his brother had his bum out.

'Dickhead! Look at him go.'

Alex turned her head to stare, making a big thing of it.

'Yeah, I will. That's the point of the dare, isn't it? To have a good look.'

Si knitted his eyebrows together. It took a lot of effort not to laugh at him when he looked all sulky like that.

'Fuck off.'

She finally let herself smile.

'Everyone's tried to suck their own cock, Si. Him and all.'

He still looked miserable. He wasn't even watching Chris run naked through the scrubby grass, closer and closer to the park and the distinct possibility of being seen. He was just staring out towards the grey sea. It was unlike him to be sulky. Si was usually a lolloping puppy of a man, into everything and never prone to too much reflection. It was weird seeing him in a strop.

'Yeah, right. Have you?'

She gave him a wink, and her best boy-eating grin.

'Han't got the equipment, have I? I'll need a lend of one.'

And he snorted a little laugh, at least. So that was something.

'I'm sure you can get someone to help you out with that.'

Alex watched Chris's buttocks receding into the distance. He'd been right – it was a bloody long way to the caravan park gate, which she'd known, of course. She'd wanted a little bit of space with Si.

'Cheers for the other night,' she said.

He drained his can and cracked open another cider, drinking from it like he'd just finished a marathon.

'Did I do something right for once? That's a first.'

Alex took a sip that she didn't want. It didn't do much to wash away the sudden tightening of her throat.

'You don't remember?'

Si wasn't looking at her – he was still staring at the sea – but Alex couldn't tell whether or not he was avoiding her eye. Sometimes the sea was just the sea, wasn't it?

'Nah, I was slaughtered. Why? What happened?'

Alex shrugged. Deep inside, a little part of her shrivelled, but on the outside, she just flashed him a quick smile.

'Nothing. You walked me home. That was all. Just wanted to say cheers.'

'Right.' He looked at her for a beat too long. But she just stared back, smooth and bland, like everything was normal. Everything *was* normal. 'Didn't make a knob of myself when we were still at the pub, did I?'

She took another drink and ran her tongue around her teeth. They were fuzzy and she felt like they itched, even though that was impossible, wasn't it? She imagined the cider acid eating into the enamel, working in moon-like craters, until they were brown and jagged like her mum's. But that wasn't going to happen. Alex never, ever, got so fucked up she fell asleep without brushing her teeth. She made it a matter of pride.

'Why do you care? You make a knob of yourself plenty.'

'I dunno. Just . . . I dunno.'

She stared at Si, a deep hollow of dread opening up in the pit of her stomach. So that was why he was being so moody today. Above her, gulls curled and screeched in the late-evening sun.

'You want to know if you were a dick in front of Jenny. That it?'

He shrugged, and a tiny little smile played around his lips. It made Alex want to kick his stupid face in. 'Maybe.'

She drank again, forcing herself to swallow. Then the can was empty, so she picked up her box of fags.

What was so special about Jenny? It had always been this way, and Alex had never been able to work it out. They were born just a few weeks apart, in exactly the same place. They went to the same school, had the same people around them every day, and went to the same places to do the same things. So how was it that Jenny always seemed to get whatever she wanted without even thinking about it, and Alex had to graft for every crumb?

But she was trying hard not to think about Jenny at the moment.

'You're safe,' she said.

The cigarette box rattled, unsettlingly empty in her hands. She opened it. There was only one fag left, the one she'd turned around and put back in when she had first opened the pack. The lucky one. She hesitated, then took it out and lit it. Fuck it.

Si looked at her, all earnest, slightly red-rimmed eyes.

'You think she likes me?'

'I doubt it, mate,' Chris said.

Alex nearly dropped the lit fag onto her lap, and Si wheeled round, panicked. Chris was standing behind them, one hand cupped casually around his dick and balls, totally naked except for his socks and trainers. Alex had forgotten all about him.

Si glared at Chris, who was cheerfully draining the last of his can. Si stood up, unfolding his tall frame from his seat on the grass like he was an umbrella.

'I'm off for a piss.'

Chris pulled up his jeans, buttoning them with one hand while the other still held a can.

'You better be quick. We'll know what you're trying if you're not.'

As Si skulked off, Chris chucked himself down on the ground and lit up a fag. He was still topless. He rolled over to grin at Alex, mock pouting.

'You didn't watch me come back. That's the best bit.'

Alex shrugged and took a deep drag on her cigarette, and then another one, so close together they made her feel dizzy.

'Yeah.'

Chris followed her gaze over to where Si was retreating

behind the side of the old hotel. It was ridiculous, him going out of sight. As if she hadn't seen him wee off the side of the cliff a hundred fucking times, shouting gleefully into the wind as he pissed into the void.

'Fucking ignore that one. He's a knob.'

She shrugged again. There was something about Chris that made her feel like she could tell the truth. Something about how unbothered he was about what other people thought of him was catching.

'Is he?'

Chris pulled two cans out of the Co-op bag and handed one to her. Alex noticed there were only two left after that. Someone would be going without.

He nodded emphatically. 'Anyone would be to take that stuck-up bitch over you.'

Alex couldn't hold back a little smirk at that. She cracked open the can, its sound like a tiny firework in the gathering gloom.

'I'm not bothered.'

Chris lay on his back, looking up at the sky. Just dimming now, but not dark, and it was getting on for eleven. Alex loved the summer for that. She never wanted the days to end.

'I know you're not. You'll be gone soon anyway, won't you?'

Alex ran her finger around the rim of the can. That was another thing she was trying not to think about. Not very successfully. Results were out in twenty days.

'Maybe.'

Chris smiled up at the sky.

'You will.'

Si came back from beside the hotel and sat down opposite Alex. He grinned and pointed a finger at her. 'Right. Your go.'

That was the nice thing about Si. He was never moody for long. Every twenty minutes or so, he seemed to reset himself to his default mode – cheerfully oblivious. He was like a goldfish like that.

It wasn't his fault that he fancied Jenny. There was no accounting for taste. Alex would just have to try hard not to care, and she'd be out of here before she knew it. She took a lungful of smoke and blew it into his face in a plume.

'Truth.'

Chris leaned forward, flashing her an evil grin. 'Who would you rather shag? Me, or Si?'

Alex rolled her eyes at Chris. He pulled an exaggeratedly innocent face, and she couldn't help but laugh at him. He could be such a knob. Would she find people at uni who'd be knobs to her like this? She hoped she would. Surely she was still young enough make these kinds of friends again. Alex shook the thought out of her head. She must be getting pissed, to be this sentimental. Maybe it was for the best that they'd nearly run out of booze.

'Fine. Dare.'

'All right! What do you reckon, Si, fancy seeing her arse?'

Chris grinned at Si, expectant, but Si didn't smile back. He didn't even look at his brother. His eyes were fixed on Alex as he said, 'Go dancing in the ballroom.'

Chris rolled his eyes and thumped his brother on the arm. 'Oi. Don't be a dick.'

Si didn't look away.

'She wanted a dare and I've said one. That's it.'

And the sea smashed and the seagulls shrieked and Alex held Si's gaze like it was a stone in her fist and said, 'Fine.'

She stood up and drained her can and took three quick, deep puffs on the cigarette, burning it right down to the filter. It was so low, she was only breathing in burnt plastic, but she couldn't taste it. She threw the butt on the floor and ground it into the mud. Si stood up too. He hadn't stopped staring at her since he came back.

Chris was still sprawled on the ground.

'Come on, give over. Of course she's not going to do it. Don't be daft.'

She threw her can on the ground and stomped on that too. The crunch of metal yielding beneath her trainer heel felt so satisfying. Clean, in a way. She'd had enough to drink tonight. Time for something new. She headed for the old hotel.

'Oi! What the fuck?'

Both boys were up now, trailing after Alex as she slipped through the gap between the front doors of the hotel and stalked her way into the entrance hall. They followed, skittering like puppies into the ruined hall. There was an abandoned check-in desk in the corner, and a once-grand staircase leading up to nothing. This lobby would have been beautiful once, with its carved dark wood and marble floors and high ceilings, conspicuously, thrillingly grand. Now, the mahogany was glazed grey with sea salt and there was no ceiling at all, but it was still impressive. With the doors to the ballroom shut, you could almost imagine the way it had been, stepping into this place back when it was somewhere to see and be seen, rather than to skulk and hide.

Chris jogged to catch up with her, the ghost of a grin still on his face.

'Alex, pet. Come on. He was just kidding. You don't have to.'

As Alex approached the ballroom door, the smell of the sea was getting stronger and stronger, and the salt, once a dusting, became a crust beneath her feet. She took step after step towards the cliff edge; she fancied she could feel the ground beneath her pitch and lurch. But that was only her imagination, of course. The hotel floor was perfectly solid. Of course it was.

Chris dropped back and punched Si on the arm. Hard, this time.

'Stop her, you prick. Why'd you want to know so much, anyway?'

Alex looked back at Si and he looked at her. And she'd thought she knew him better than anyone, but in that moment, she just couldn't tell. What was it that had made him push her like this? Had he picked up on something in her questions, something that he wanted to prod and probe at? Did he remember the other night after all? She hesitated, hand on the ballroom door, giving him the chance to say that it was okay, that he took it back, she didn't have to. He always did, didn't he? Didn't he always find a way of rescuing her in the end?

But he just stared, sheet-white and useless.

Alex pushed open the heavy, warped ballroom door. You needed to give it a good shove to unstick the hinges, no time to be timid. And then the door gave way with a crunch of shattered salt and Alex gawped out. Beyond it, all she saw was open sea, like a joke or a film or a dream. Before she could talk herself out of it, she stepped through the sea-frosted dark wood doorway and into the ballroom.

A rush of vertigo hit her, numbing her from the waist down. There was so much less floor here than she remembered. Last time, there had been a few marble lumps jutting out, with a bit of mud between. Not enough to be safe, but you'd have a fighting chance of scrambling back if you slipped, at least. But now the marble slabs were narrow, treacherous, and beneath them there was only air. They were so coated with salt, you couldn't tell what colour they used to be. Was salt slippery? Alex couldn't remember. She didn't want to move her feet to check. A seagull perched on the ruined wall, watching her with cold black eyes.

Chris stood, eyes wide and face drained of colour.

'Come back. Please.'

Alex only looked at Si. He looked just as scared as Chris did, his mouth pursed up into a tight, frightened knot. But he said nothing. Alex's legs tingled and her head was full of the waves crashing below. She took one tentative step out onto a marble slab, and then another. It held her weight, for now. She could feel the wind pushing at her side, snatching her hair, trying to topple her over, and just for a moment she wondered if it would really be so bad, to let the wind and the gravity take her. To submit. That was a way out, wasn't it, as sure as moving to Manchester?

She took a deep breath. She stared, defiant, into Si's stricken face. And with nothing but the music of the waves and the wind in her ears, she danced.

He first steps were awkward, heavy and lumpen and

self-conscious. Only a couple of years ago, Alex hadn't been above a dance routine over lunch hour, or a bit of arse swinging in Chemistry to see Mr Phillips squirm. Now she was a grown-up she only danced when she was drunk, just like everyone else. But a dare was a dare. So she shuffled her feet, arms above her head and bum wiggling defiantly.

'She's doing it! Si, look!'

Chris was gleeful, like he always was whenever anything actually happened around here, like they all were. When every day rolled in and out the fucking same as the last, you'd get excited about pretty much anything.

Si was quieter. She could feel his disapproval radiating over from the doorway, cold and wet as the sea.

'I'm looking.'

Let him look. Alex could taste cider and smell salt and the scream of the wind filled her ears and she couldn't look down, so she looked up. The gulls wheeled and circled above and something shifted inside her, and the self-consciousness faded and she was dancing, really dancing, and all that she cared about was the way her body felt as it moved, weight swung from side to side and up, arms flowed and flung through the air. That, and the wind and the pattern of her feet on the marble slabs. They looked like they should fall from below, like it was a mistake that they hadn't already, a chequerboard suspended in the sky and her along with them, held up by some enchantment, perhaps, or hope, which was the same thing.

'All right. Fair play. That's a dance.'

But Alex didn't stop. This moment of moving, of giving herself over, was the closest to an escape she'd come all summer. A shining minute of letting herself put the weight of her life down, of not having to feel the worry about her exams and her future and her mum and the endless cut of unfairness, of things being harder for her than for everyone else. She felt as if she'd shrugged them off like an old coat, leaving her finally free to move, much lighter than she had been. So light that it was difficult to believe that she could ever fall from here. She could see the drop and remember people going on and on about the danger, but it was hard to imagine it really happening. The wind whipped her hair like it was a pair of wings and surely, surely, all she needed to do was take a short step out, and she'd be able to fly.

'Come on,' Si said. 'That's enough. You've done it now.'

He sounded nervous, but there was no need. Because it was obvious, if you thought about it. She'd had a shit enough life, but she was brave and she was clever and she kept trying, so couldn't she just have this one thing? A step and a lift and she'd be gone. Flown away from this place. Please.

'Yeah, you've done it. Come back.'

And Alex was just turning, to tell them that it was fine, that they were worrying over nothing, that she knew what she was doing, and besides, it wasn't nearly as hard as they'd always said. And she placed a foot just a little too close to the edge. She felt herself tilt and, arms wheeling frantically, she stumbled towards the drop. For a moment, she was balanced, perfectly even, caught in a place exactly between falling and staying and she really really might go over and, honestly, she might as well. Because if she had to stay here for ever, what was even the difference?

The seagull looked her dead in the eyes and screamed at

her and she stared back. Wouldn't it be better to die, right here, right now, while there was still hope, while there still might be brightness? Because the only other thing that could happen was to let this place age her and dry her up and make her like her mum – with a kid to look after and no idea how, and either dead-end jobs or no job at all for her whole life and nothing in her life apart from TV and cheap wine and occasional fumbles with other people's husbands.

Fuck that. She might as well fall.

'Alex!'

And all at once there was a rush of warm body and Lynx and she was being pulled, dragged back, and she was lying on the marble, Si beside her, and he was shouting.

' . . .You were going to fall, you nearly fell, what the fuck do you think you're doing, you mad bitch, you scared the shit out of me . . .'

And Alex just lay beside him and looked up at the sky. White birds and dark clouds. Half an hour ago, she would have loved his. She'd wanted to be in his arms, and in his head – he wasn't thinking about Jenny now, was he? But now that she was back on solid ground, all she could think about was that moment when she almost fell. The nearly-sensation of flying.

Alex went into the pub, as early as she could without looking too desperate. Anything before twelve was a bit grim to go out boozing, but being there when the doors opened was even worse. She'd made herself wait until 11.45, and it was fine. There was no one else in.

Ted greeted her with a smile. 'In to drink your tips, are you?'

Alex scowled. 'Nah. I wanted to talk to you.'

He riffled through her tip glass, flicking through the stubby bits of paper with calloused fingers. 'You've still got a few left. It's the end of the month in five days.'

Alex tossed her head, impatient. She shouldn't be wasting her time like this. She should be being paid for this little chat really, if you were being technical about it. 'Whatever. Pint of cider.'

On the other hand, a pint was still a pint.

'Right you are.'

Alex reached in her bag for her fags, but then thought better of it. She was surprisingly nervous. Why was she nervous? It wasn't her who should be getting in trouble. But then, since when was life fair?

'You know I'm not a grass, right, Ted? You know that.'

She had his attention now.

'Aye. What's up?'

Alex glowered, and her fingers twitched to light up.

This was manager shit, this was, and she wasn't a manager, was she?

'She's shit, is what's up. Jenny's shit at her job. I've tried to put up with it, but she just fucks it all up. I can't fucking work like this!'

It was as if the words were pouring out without her even thinking them first, even hearing them on the way out of her. Perhaps her plan of not thinking about Jenny and the exams wasn't really working for her. It wasn't like she felt even the tiniest bit less wound up about everything.

Ted heaved a deep sigh. 'What's happened this time?'

Alex scowled deep into her pint. She was grassing, and she knew it.

'I've had to spend the whole of last night running my arse off trying to get everyone served, while she takes half an hour pouring one lager over and over. And now the till won't balance.'

Ted looked at her, slow, steady. Unnerving how steady he was.

'Right.'

Not giving her anything back.

Alex slapped a palm on the bar in frustration. The sound it made echoed satisfyingly around the pub.

'All she does is sneak off for fucking snogging breaks with Si and . . .'

She broke off, embarrassed to hear her voice cracking. She hadn't loved the last two weeks. Jenny and Si seemed to be officially going out now, not that they'd said anything about it. When she'd asked Si if he wanted to go up the cliffs with her, he'd been too busy every single time.

'Okay.'

But she wasn't upset about Si. That wasn't why she was here. He could do what he wanted, couldn't he? It's not like she'd ever been that bothered. It was only that in Ravenspurn there wasn't a lot of choice of lads. She'd surely never have looked at him twice if she already lived in Manchester. Surely.

'She's meant to be fucking managing me.'

And Ted still just stared.

'She is.'

And she stared back at him and the ghost of the conversation Alex had had with her mother echoed around her head. Another thing to not think about. She was going to burst, with the weight of them all.

'I shouldn't have even been in the till, except I don't trust her to do it right. That's a disciplinary on me, technically.'

'Is it now?'

Alex hissed a lungful of air out through her teeth. 'Are you going to fucking say something about this, or what?'

Ted wasn't rising. He was just standing there, looking steady, no drama, smiling at her. Fucking smiling.

'You know the story I always used to tell Jenny when she was a lass?' he said.

'What? No.'

Alex blinked, confused. She'd been trying to grass up his daughter. Shouldn't she be getting shouted at by now?

'It's about this girl, right. And she was fiery, a right temper on her. Not unlike some people I could mention.'

He twinkled at her, but Alex kept a straight face, because, fuck off.

'I'm not a fucking kid, Ted.'

He shrugged, unbothered. 'I didn't say you were. But this girl, even though she could throw a proper strop when she wanted to, she had a kind heart. So, one day, when she was walking in the forest, she found a witch who'd fallen off her broom. And she tried to help her back up, but the witch was too proud to take her help and the girl got offended that she wouldn't. And the two of them started arguing.'

Alex took a deep drink of cider. She was interested, despite herself. He knew how to tell a story, did Ted. Just like her.

'The girl's boyfriend heard all the shouting and he came through the forest to meet them, drawn by all the noise. But he didn't have anything to say that helped. All he did was stand there, being useless.'

Alex snorted despite herself and Ted gave her a grin.

'And the witch got angrier and angrier at these two, who'd come into her forest and done nothing but cause trouble. So she turned the girl into a seagull so that she could shout as much as she liked but no one would ever understand her. And she turned the boyfriend into a stone, because even a stone was more useful than he had been as a man.'

Alex gawped at him. 'What the fuck?'

He shrugged. 'Don't ask me. It's just a story. But anyway, the magic wasn't complete. The witch's heart wasn't totally in it, because she knew deep down that the girl was only trying to help her. So one day every year, when the day is as long and the night is as short as it's ever going to get, the two of them turn back into themselves. And they can talk together and laugh together and be humans again. But when the sun sets and the longest day is over, they turn back into a bird and a stone, and they have to wait for another year.'

And for a moment the pub was silent, except for the crackle of the fire and the drip of the bar sink tap and, as always in Ravenspurn, the soft distant roar of the sea. Alex looked at Ted and tried hard not to think about all the things she wasn't supposed to be thinking about.

'So what's that supposed to mean then?'

And there was another moment of almost-silence before he replied.

'It means that sometimes you can't be with someone as much as you want. Things happen. Life happens. It doesn't mean you don't love them.'

'Right.'

Ted sighed, and poured himself a pint of hand pull, which he almost never did while he was working. He said it wasn't respectable, to make a habit of it. Special occasions only.

He swallowed half of the pint in one deep gulp.

'What was it you really wanted to ask me about?'

Alex toyed with the necklace. Jenny's necklace. She'd put it on today, for a bit of a boost, but hidden it under a T-shirt for safety. Even though Jenny wasn't going to be in. But there was no point asking for trouble, was there?

'If Jenny goes to uni and I don't, can I have the manager job?'

Ted sighed even deeper, then swallowed the other half of the pint.

'I know it wasn't fair.'

Which wasn't answering the question, Alex noticed.

'Why do it then?'

He put his glass in the dishwasher, not looking at her.

'She needs it more than you.'

Alex felt a hot flash of rage and started talking before she could think, which she was meant to be getting better at not doing.

'Why's that then? Because of all the fucking disadvantages she's had? All those times she was told off for being late for school even though it was a fucking miracle she'd managed to drag herself in at all after she'd been kept up until gone two by her stupid fucking mum drinking cans with some dodgy pricks she met on the beach? Or when she got told there was no point in her even doing A levels because it wasn't going to bring any money in?'

Alex made herself stop. She hadn't realised she was so upset about it all. There was no point feeling sorry for herself. She'd done it anyway, hadn't she? Hopefully she'd done it.

'Anyone can tell that you're a hard worker. Bright as a tack. You don't need to prove that with some puff line on a CV. You can tell it a mile off.'

Alex scowled into her pint, still embarrassed. She wasn't even pissed. Fuck's sake.

'She doesn't need it, though. She's going to uni.'

'You're going to uni, Alex. Another one, yeah?'

And he poured her another pint without waiting for a reply. He didn't even take it from the tip jar. And he picked up his notebook and she lit up a fag and she thought that they were done talking, until he looked over to her and said:

'Are you all right? You can tell me.'

She chewed her lip and took a quick puff of her fag. The smoke billowed between them like sea mist.

'Mum told me something the other day.'

'Yeah?' he said. He started wiping down the bar. If she hadn't known him so well, she wouldn't have thought that it was because he was nervous. She wouldn't have thought anything at all.

'Yeah.'

The two of them looked at each other, Ted still running an old cloth along the bar. Probably making it dirtier than it already was.

'What's that then?'

She examined the end of her cigarette. It glowed an angry red.

'You know I've never asked her who my dad is? Not once.'

Alex always lit up if she had to walk home on her own. So that at least, if it came to it, she had a little bit of fire on her side. She imagined stabbing it into a hand, an eye, if she really had to. The idea of it was more comforting than the nicotine, sometimes.

'Is that right?'

But his voice was as steady as ever.

'Don't you think that's weird? Don't you think most kids would want to know?'

She made herself look up at him, and he was much closer than she thought. Looking at her. So steady. So calm. Exactly the same as he had been the last time she saw him, theoretically.

'I don't think you're weird, Alex.'

'No?'

'Nah. I think you're great. I thought you knew that.'

She took another lungful of smoke, and blew it out, a long plume into the empty pub.

'People seem to keep thinking that I know things. I don't know much.'

He smiled at her. And it was ridiculous, wasn't it? But it was a nicer smile than her mother ever had for her. Ted acted like he actually liked her, which was a lot more than Mum ever did.

That little bitch Jenny didn't even know she was born.

'You know more than all of us, pet. You've always been a little star.'

She looked up at him and she was furious at how much she wanted it. That little bit of approval. Furious, and scared.

'Always?'

He looked at her and shrugged. And this time she knew that he had nothing more to say.

'Yeah.'

And he turned away to the dishwasher, but he didn't unload it. He just stood there, still as a stone.

The moon was finally full again and Alex was staring at it, the way the sea bounced its light back to her, making more of it, filling the night with the glow of ice-white light. This light, third-hand, bounced from the sun off the moon and now the sea and transformed from the hot yellow of the day. Hard to remember that it was all just fire.

'Oh. Um. Hi.'

Alex wheeled around to see what for a glittering second seemed like a ghost, shining from within in a way that a ghost would only ever be when it had come to reprimand you for thinking something bad. But, of course, it was only Jenny, lit up by a street light. All light is borrowed. Almost nothing glows on its own.

'All right?' Alex said, and she turned back towards the sea. The beach was where she came when she wanted to be alone, but she was never sure why she bothered. There was no such thing as alone in Ravenspurn.

Jenny, without asking – which was *very* rude – plonked herself down next to Alex on the cold damp sand.

'What are you doing out here?'

'What are *you* doing out here?'

Jenny dipped her head and Alex looked at her more closely. She'd only meant to change the subject, but it was actually a good question. Jenny was hardly the type to sneak out for a crafty fag after lights-out. And as much of a bitch

as Alison obviously was, it was hard to imagine her drinking three bottles of wine and screaming and screaming and
screaming so much that Jenny had to get out of there, right
then, or go mad, which was why Alex herself was out on the
beach so late.

There was just enough light between the bounced-back
moon and the promenade street lamps to see Jenny blush.

'Oh. You know. Just out. Just seeing . . .'

'Yeah, yeah,' Alex said. 'I get it.'

She turned back to the shoreline, trying hard not to
imagine what Jenny and Si might have been getting up to on
their late-night visit. She was sick of seeing them together,
with their big cow eyes and grabby hands, and she was in a
shit enough mood as it was.

The two girls were quiet for a while, staring out to sea.
The constancy of the shush and roar of the waves was
soothing, humming its way through every day by day by
day. It was only when you stopped, when you let it into the
foreground, that you could really hear it, but once you did,
it was unavoidable. The sound of the sea was just like the
water itself. It would fill every gap you left it.

Jenny didn't leave it much of a gap at all.

'So what's up with you then? Can't sleep?'

Alex shrugged.

Jenny smiled at her conspiratorially. She was obviously in
a chatty mood.

'You worried about tomorrow?'

Alex shrugged again. Worried was an understatement.
Tomorrow's exam results were another water-thought – they
plugged every gap. Despite her best efforts, she was drowning

in the idea of the exam results tonight. No shift to work. No drinking games to play. No boy to flirt with. No wonder her mum had been drinking even more enthusiastically than usual – Alex must be a nightmare to be around today.

Jenny stretched out her giraffe-legs on the sand in front of them. She didn't flinch at the icy damp of the beach, despite her only wearing shorts, and pretty tiny ones at that. Alex wondered how much she'd been drinking at her little rendezvous with Si. It seemed like everyone was on the lash tonight apart from her.

'I know what you mean. I'm *so* nervous, oh my god. I don't know what I'll do if I don't get the grades.'

It was dark, so Jenny couldn't see Alex rolling her eyes. She knew exactly what Jenny could do. She'd have a plan B, wouldn't she? She'd stay with her parents for an extra year, and then she'd resit her exams and get in. That, or, she'd stay here and manage the bar, no matter how shit she was at it. She'd start earning a decent wage, making a bit of a career for herself, maybe get enough cash together to buy herself a house in a few years. And she'd knock about with Simon and have a laugh until she worked out the next thing she felt like doing. The thing about Jenny was, she never seemed to care. It was like she had so many options, she only had the brain space to give half a shit about each of them at a time. Alex wasn't like that. She had one option. One plan. And if it didn't work out, that was it.

And she could have said some of this. But looking at Jenny, she had to wonder if there was any point. There was no way she'd understand. And hopefully (hopefully hopefully) by this time tomorrow it wouldn't matter anyway. She'd have got her ticket out.

So she just smiled.

'Don't worry. You will do.'

Jenny smiled back, bright and unfocused. Definitely drunk.

'You want to come back to mine?'

God, she fucking wanted to go back to Jenny's. A warm dry house, no shouting, and, best, a little holiday from her life. A night of pretending that she always lived like this, that it wouldn't be such a big deal if she had to stay after all.

Alex shrugged. 'Yeah, okay.'

Even though Ted probably wouldn't even be up. So there was no point in thinking about how comforting it might be, if he told her there was nothing to worry about for tomorrow. She probably wouldn't even see him.

After a brief crunch-stomp along the promenade and up the high street, Alex followed Jenny into the kitchen. It looked quite different at night. If it were possible, it seemed even cleaner than before. Emptier, as well. Without the light, it had the look of a stage set waiting for the curtain to go up.

Jenny clicked on the light, killing the mood and revealing that the kitchen looked emptier because it was. All the fussy little knick-knacks – and even the toaster – had been spirited away somewhere, leaving behind them only bare surfaces, smelling faintly of bleach. Alex marvelled at the idea of being arsed to put your toaster away at the end of the day. She'd thought that she was fairly tidy, but Jesus. How much time would you have left to live your life?

'You want another gin?' Jenny said. 'They didn't notice last time.'

Her voice was deafening, bouncing around the too-clean

surfaces of the kitchen. She was definitely drunk. That boy was a bad influence on her.

'Aren't you worried about your mum waking up?' Alex asked, watching Jenny fling open the cupboards one after the other. It was like she didn't even know where the gin was kept in her own house.

'Hah. Not now. She'll have taken her pill hours ago.'

Jenny threw that little nugget of information out like it was nothing, but Alex filed it away. She wasn't the only one whose mum couldn't get to sleep without a bit of chemical help. It was good to know, comforting in a way that Alex couldn't quite put her finger on. Maybe it was just nice to feel a bit less alone.

Jenny sliced up a lemon and chucked ice into the glasses. Alex had to grudgingly admit that she was getting better at this. She wasn't picking up the basics of bar work as quickly as you might expect, true, and there was the fuck-up last week. But Jenny was undeniably becoming a less and less shit barmaid every day.

What would it be like if both of them stayed? Not as bad as being stuck here on her own, surely? But then, there was Si. Si. Ugh.

Jenny finished making the drinks and slid one over to Alex.

'So why were you really out, then?'

Jenny smiled at her blandly, like she was asking about the weather. Like there was no reason on earth she shouldn't be sitting with Alex in her kitchen, like the last fifteen years had never happened and there'd never been a time when Alex was too common to be allowed through the door. All Alex could do was raise an eyebrow.

'I told you.'

'You didn't,' Jenny said and took a deep swallow of gin and lemonade. Alex decided she liked Jenny a lot better when she was drunk. If she could restrain herself from shoving her tongue down Si's throat for five minutes, the two of them would get on fine.

Alex sipped her drink. The gin was heavy and perfumed with something sharp at the heart, like a hug from an elderly relative you didn't much like. She looked at Jenny, all bright-eyed and flushed from the gin and the sea air and almost certainly the sex, and for that moment Alex was so worn out with the worry of it all, she couldn't bring herself to feel jealous. She couldn't even be bothered to lie.

'My mum's pissed. She's been shouting at me.'

'Shouting at you?'

Jenny blinked. She clearly didn't get it. Imagine living a life where you just didn't understand what getting into a screaming match with your mum after three bottles of wine was like.

'Yeah. You know. Calling me a useless slag and that. Saying I fucked up her life. It made me want to go for a walk. So I did.'

Alex finished the rest of her drink in one burny swallow. She'd never said that out loud before. She always kept it just between her and her mum – even Auntie Jean didn't know the full story. When she was little, it was because Alex was scared of the social getting involved, because she'd still believed in a world where the authorities would give a crap about a seven-year-old getting called names from time to time. But lately – what? Habit? Or shame, perhaps. One of the two.

'Oh,' Jenny said.

Alex reached instinctively for her bag. She'd say she was going out for a fag, and just walk off. No need to stick around and get kicked out. That'd be even more embarrassing than this shitshow of a night already was.

'I wish my mum would shout at me sometimes.'

Jenny took a deep swallow and wiped down the kitchen counter where she'd cut the lemons. She was definitely getting better.

Alex blinked. 'What?'

Jenny squeezed the brand new sponge cloth, her hand a claw.

'I wish she'd do anything. She treats me like I'm a ghost, most of the time. Maybe a pet, if I've done everything right. So I try to do everything right. But she still feels cold. Like she's holding me away.'

Alex didn't know what to do, so she just stood in the clean, cold kitchen and thought about what it might be like to be Jenny. Properly, for once. Maybe it wasn't all plain sailing being a little princess. Maybe it didn't mean that you could do what you wanted – maybe it meant that you never could. It might be as hard for her to break out of her small, comfortable life as it was for Alex to escape her messier one.

Jenny downed the rest of her drink and smiled at Alex, only a little wobbly. 'You'd better stay here for tonight then, eh?'

'Um,' Alex said. She was touched, to be honest. This wasn't because Ted had told Jenny to be nice. This was just being mates. 'All right then.'

Alex obediently followed Jenny up the squashy stairs and

into her aggressively pink room. She stood there, suddenly shy. She didn't even have a toothbrush.

'Cheers. I'll sleep here,' she said, dropping her bag down on a cleanish patch of floor by Jenny's desk.

'Don't be stupid. Mine's a double.'

Alex looked doubtfully over at Jenny's bed. That seemed so intimate – weird somehow. She wasn't sure she'd ever shared a bed with anyone.

'It's all right.'

And it was all right. The carpet was so thick, it was probably softer than Alex's mattress from the caravan with the stains that freaked her out so much she put three bottom sheets on it so her skin would never touch them.

Jenny shook her head. 'I'll only forget you're here and tread on you in the night if you sleep on the floor, and then you'll kill me. This is better.' She rubbed her eyes and the make-up smudged. Like when they were little and they'd get the face painter who came down odd Saturdays for the tourists to do them first 'so we can be your advert'. Alex always wanted to be a tiger. Always.

'Um. Okay.'

She watched Jenny peel off her jeans and get into bed in her pants and vest top, still with her smudged tiger-make-up. She'd have to wash her pillowcase tomorrow. Annoying. Alex was glad she'd taken a night off with her own eyeliner. She hadn't thought she'd be seeing anyone.

Alex didn't take her jeans off. She just slid herself under the duvet, holding herself on the edge of the bed, as far away from Jenny as she could get without falling out. It was so soft you sank into it, this bed, and the duvet was soft and puffy, like it was full of candy floss. Alarming. And the whole place smelled sweet, like a bakery. Vanilla sugar. It smelled like Jenny.

Alex let herself take up maybe an inch more of the duvet. The smell wasn't that bad when you'd had a minute to get used to it. It was actually kind of comforting.

'Jenny?'

It felt right to whisper, somehow. There was something about the dark, and the quiet. Even the sound of the sea was quiet, here. It must be the double glazing.

'What?' Jenny whispered back. She sounded quiet, and young.

Alex swallowed down the lump in her throat.

'Thanks.'

And she meant it. After all this time, Jenny had shown herself to be a decent person. She didn't have to welcome Alex into her pink palace of a bedroom – it wasn't like Alex had ever been particularly nice to her. But she felt close to her now. Jenny felt like a person it was worth feeling close to.

'It's okay.'

Alex closed her eyes and tried hard not to think about the following day. If it all went her way, maybe she and Jenny could be proper friends after this. Maybe they'd meet up at Christmases and go to the pub together, or even get their old jobs back for a few weeks for a bit of pocket money, and it wouldn't even matter about Si – they'd both be leaving anyway, wouldn't they? So it'd be fine.

And they should be friends, shouldn't they? They should be close.

Alex felt the secret swell up between them. People who were as good as sisters shouldn't keep secrets.

'Jenny?'

Alex let herself fully relax onto the bed, feeling her arm flop down next to Jenny's. Her skin was smooth, and still cool from the beach and the night air.

'What?'

And Alex could tell from her voice that she was almost asleep. Tucked up in her soft, sweet-smelling bed, with all her pretty, perfect things around her, in her pretty, perfect-looking life that had a throb of sadness at the centre after all, just like everybody else. And Alex knew that she couldn't do it. She couldn't be the one to make it any worse. She didn't have the heart.

And after tomorrow, what would it even matter? She'd be out of here soon. She'd leave all this behind.

'Nothing.'

But Jenny didn't reply. She was already asleep.

Alex stumbled into the bar room at bang on eleven and she didn't even care how desperate that made her seem. Ted looked right at her. He was already standing there behind the bar, coffee in hand, like he was waiting for her. How early could she have come in and still had him welcome her?

'Well?'

Alex slammed the envelope down on the bar. It was still unopened. She couldn't stand it.

The two of them stared at it and it was like it stared back. Squatting there, waiting to pounce.

'Dunno yet.'

Ted jammed a shot of whisky into a glass and placed it on the bar next to her. He reached into his top pocket, pulled out a pack of fags and placed one next to the drink. He lit up one himself, which wasn't like him, smoking behind the bar. He always said it was unprofessional. Maybe he was nervous too.

'You gotta do it. Waiting doesn't change anything.'

Alex downed the drink and lit the fag.

'You won't let me enjoy one last minute of not knowing?'

'Hey. Look at me.'

And she did. His big warm eyes, brown like hers.

'You've got nothing to be scared of. Open it.'

Alex took a drag of her cigarette and held the smoke in her lungs. Without letting herself hesitate, she ripped open the envelope and stared down and felt the smoke puff its way out of her like she was a slashed tire, deflating all at once.

'Well?'

Alex swallowed. Her throat burned from the whisky and the smoke and the held-back tears.

'No.'

He took a deep drag and closed his eyes.

'Fuck.'

She pushed the glass back over the bar to him.

'Can I have another one?'

He poured it. She downed it. Another drop of fire. She'd have swallowed a razor blade if she could.

Fuck. Fuck fuck fuck.

'I'm sorry, pet,' he said.

Alex smoked mechanically, a drag with every breath, not tasting it, not feeling it at all.

'Look, it'll be all right. Here's what we'll do. We ...'

And just for a sliver of a second, before he stopped talking, she was beginning to feel less hopeless. Like he might have a plan, like it really might be okay. Then Alison stalked in and the feeling was washed away.

'Edward! Oh.'

When she saw Alex, she stopped in her tracks. There was a look on her face that suggested that Alex was something unwelcome and perhaps unpleasant, an inconvenience arrived to ruin her day.

'Oh. Hello, Alexandra.'

Alex took a deep drag on her fag and glared daggers at her. Alison fucking Fletcher was all she needed, on top of everything else.

Ted raised his eyebrows at his wife. 'How did she do?'

Ted had been going to tell Alex how everything was going to be okay. He wouldn't have been right, it would have been bullshit, but it might have made her feel a bit better.

'I'll let her tell you.'

The two of them smirked at each other. It was weird to see them on the same page. Weird to see Alison in the pub at all, in fact. Alex wasn't sure she ever had before.

'Not bad then?'

And he gave Alison a huge, warm smile. Like this was the best day ever, because of that. But this was not the best day ever.

Alex rolled the empty whisky glass from hand to hand, but no one got the hint. It remained empty.

Alison, obviously made uncomfortable by Alex scowling at the bar, offered her a fake little smile. 'How did you do in your exams, Alexandra?'

Alex tilted the empty whisky glass up to her lips. Just in case there was a drop left.

Ted pulled a sympathetic face. 'Alex didn't get into Manchester. It's a shame.'

'Oh.' Alison looked extremely uninterested in the conversation. 'What about your second choice?'

There was nothing left in the glass. Alex briefly considered poking her tongue in to lick, but that was proper alkie behaviour, even considering the circumstances. She slammed the glass down.

'Manchester was my second choice.'

Alex closed her eyes. Stupid bitch. Why didn't she pick somewhere really easy? Because Mrs Dennis had told her not to, that was why. Because she'd said that, the way Alex was going, as long as she sat the exams and wrote something half sensible, there was no way on earth she wouldn't get a B, never mind a C.

As long as she sat the exams.

'Oh. I'm sorry,' Alison said, although she clearly wasn't. 'You could try clearing?'

'And tell them why I didn't get the grade? Cos I got expelled?'

Alex's voice cracked as she said it. Flustered, she picked her fag up from the ashtray and took two deep pulls, one after the other. She needed the smoke more than air.

'Hmmm. I see.' It was obvious Alison was irritated that Alex would do something as inconsiderate as fail her A levels to take attention away from her daughter. Alex remembered what Jenny had said the night before. *Maybe a pet, if I've done everything right.* 'Well. I just came in to tell you Jenny's coming in in a sec. Time to get a bottle of something out, I think?'

Ted looked up at her. It was as if he was coming out of a trance.

'Oh. Right. Yes. I did . . .'

He pulled a bottle from the fridge under the counter. It was real champagne this time. Alex stared at it dully and ground her cigarette out.

'Right. Good. I want everything to be right.'

Alison was almost vibrating with anxious energy. But what had she got to worry about? Her daughter had passed, hadn't she? That was the thing Alex hated most about Alison. She never seemed happy, no matter how much she got. It was even worse than Jenny, who never appreciated any of it. At least that was just carelessness. Alison held up everything in her life and found it wanting. And what did that mean she thought about Alex, who had so much less?

'Daddy!!' The door to the bar burst open and Jenny strutted in, all smiles and vanilla musk body spray.

'Princess!'

Alex scowled at the counter. It wasn't like she was jealous of Jenny. Just because she had parents who seemed to give a shit about her, and she'd passed her exams. Not at all.

'I did it, an A and two Bs! I'm going to Warwick!'

Fuck. Alex closed her eyes. So that was it. Just like that. Jenny was leaving, and Alex was staying, and all her dreams, her careful plans, were gone. All the hours spent studying and working and hoping were for nothing. All any of it would mean is that she'd be able to name the plays she'd never see and the places she'd never go and the ways the cliffs were being washed away in front of her. Corrasion, abrasion, attrition, quarrying, solution. All fucking useless to her now.

'Ah, well done, love. Great stuff. I'm proud of you.'

And Jenny, sweet stupid Jenny, got into a really decent uni. Because she'd kept her nose clean, and frowned over her coursework, and because girls like her always did. And girls like Alex didn't.

Alex watched through a dull haze as Jenny fluttered and preened and Ted poured drinks and Alison smiled with all her teeth, triumphant.

'We're all proud of you! You've done so well.'

She shouldn't have even tried. It would have hurt less if she hadn't tried. She should have got a flat in Hull with Kelly when she'd asked last year. She could be halfway to being a hairdresser by now, if she wasn't such a stupid, stuck-up bitch. She should have left notions like that for the likes of Jenny, who at least knew how to be a snotty cow and pull it off.

'Watch your eyes, everyone . . .'

Ted popped the cork in a sound like gunfire, and poured. They didn't have champagne flutes in the pub, so they used the normal wine glasses, which at least were bigger. The champagne sparkled sharply in the glasses, wee-coloured and glittery.

He pushed a glass into her hand. 'Here you go, love.' His eyes were soft and, just for a moment, only on her. 'You're all right.'

But she wasn't. She wasn't all right at all. She felt like waves of sadness were crashing into her, forcing their way into the little cracks of herself, pushing her apart. Quarrying, was what that was called.

Jenny looked over to Alex, eyebrows up, questioning. Alex shook her head, just a tiny fraction, but it cost her. She couldn't do any more. Jenny opened her mouth, but Alison got out a fork and started dinging on her glass. She angled her body so her back was to Alex and her voice sounded high and bright as she said, 'A toast. To new beginnings!'

Alex had never tasted champagne before and she still hadn't. As she drank it, all she could taste was ash.

ATTRITION

Summer 2020

In London, it was a fucking hot summer in a way that surprised Ben every single time. Every year, he and his mother would throw open all the windows of their top-floor attic and tell each other the different ways the heat was hitting. Stifling. Strangling. Boiling, roasting, frying hot. Each year, they'd both agree that it seemed hotter than the last, but surely that couldn't always be true? It would trend upwards, yes, what with us burning up our planet from the inside, but surely there'd be some variation, or, to put it another way, respite.

Ben's mother bustled in, a stack of three hoodies in her hands, washed and folded.

'I washed these.'

They looked suspiciously like they might have been ironed as well.

'I told you, Mum, you don't have to do my laundry.'

She spiked him on a raised eyebrow.

'That's a funny way of saying thank you.'

He sighed and reached out for the jumpers. It was so hot. The hoodies hadn't been in the laundry basket, or even on the chair for wearing again – she'd gone into his wardrobe for them and rewashed them. They'd talked before about this, but today wasn't the day. He got it. Weren't they all a bit funny about cleaning, these days?

'Thank you.'

He set the jumpers on the bed, and his mum looked pointedly at the weekend bag on the floor.

'You take them. It's cold by the sea. And so far north.'

'It's Yorkshire. Not the Arctic.'

She gave him a look so as to suggest that it was pretty much the same thing as far as she was concerned.

'You make sure you pack them. Don't be cocky.'

Ben stared down at the jumpers. One of them was even fleece-lined. This was ridiculous. This was a summer when even a T-shirt felt like way too much to walk around in, when he'd lay naked in bed at night, body spread wide on top of his covers and the windows thrown open as far as they'd go, trying desperately to catch a bit of breeze.

It was good he was going to Yorkshire. Maybe it really would be like the Arctic, and he could have a break from the oven-life of almost never leaving the flat. At the very least, he'd be able to swim in the sea.

'You'll remember your sandwiches for the train?'

'Yes, Mum,' Ben said, and thought about M&S and Percy Pigs and cans of beer in the afternoon and watching through the window as the countryside unspooled itself for him.

'I don't want you eating anything else, you understand? Especially things that aren't wrapped.'

He'd promised her, no train picnic. They'd been through it again and again. It was one of the things she was most worried about. Which was stupid, of course, but he didn't feel like putting her through a blow-by-blow account of exactly why. She was worried enough about him leaving as it was.

'I'm not going to get Covid off an apple,' he said, and he

tried hard to make his voice gentle, reassuring, but a little flint of sharpness still got through.

She twisted her hands together, rubbing at the darker patches on them from too much washing and scrubbing and hand sanitising.

'Not if you don't eat one, you won't.'

She still washed all the shopping when he brought it in. He told her again and again that she didn't need to, that no one caught it like that, and how do you wash a loaf of bread anyway? But in the end it was quicker not to argue. His world had shrunk down so much that his mother took up most of it now, so who wanted to start a fight over something so small? And the job went faster when both of them did it, and he was furloughed, anyway. He didn't really have many better things to do than helping wash tins of kidney beans.

'Are you sure you don't want me to nip out again? One last trip. I've got time.'

She shrugged.

'I'm fine,' she said, which wasn't true. Since she'd been told she was shielding, she'd been behaving a little bit less fine with every passing week. She needed work to keep her together, even more than Ben did himself, it turned out. She pined for her patients, her hospital, felt so guilty not to be there when everyone knew how short-staffed the NHS was. He'd had to stop her from watching the news.

'Nothing else you fancy?'

She flapped her hands at him. She hated it, not being able to shop for herself. He tried to make her say, every time he went out, what little extra treats she'd like. She only ever asked for plain food for them both.

'I wish you'd let me sort out your hair.'

He brought home things he thought she might like anyway. Punnets of strawberries, boxes of dates, packets of KitKats – all her favourites. She didn't touch any of it.

'It wouldn't take long. Just a quick buzz before you go. You look nice with it short.'

Ben rubbed the back of his head. A generous puff of hair he'd never thought he'd be able to try out, what with working in law and the fact his boss was an arsehole and a racist.

'I like it like this.'

What if he just went back with little dreads? He'd have enough time, the way this fucking pandemic was going. What would they do? Surely they wouldn't fire him. They couldn't, could they?

'Makes you look like your dad.'

Ben sighed, and said nothing, which was his policy when Dad was mentioned.

They'd think of something more subtle than a straight-up firing. But it wouldn't go well. The hair had to go. Maybe he would let her cut it like she used to, clippers buzzing on his scalp, neck stretching back over the bath, counting tiles on the bathroom ceiling. If the firm opened up before the barbers did he was going to have to.

His mother sat on the bed next to him, a conciliatory gesture.

'Don't forget the sandwiches. And come and kiss me goodbye before you leave, okay?'

She hadn't always been like this. When she was still working, she was so easy-going. He never had to tell her when he was in, out; once he'd stayed at Jen's for four nights straight, when they were brand new, and didn't even text her.

'Of course.'

She squeezed his hand in hers, scaly as well as darker from the soaps.

'Benjamin?' she said and she didn't let go.

'What's up, Mum?'

He tried his best to sound normal. Light-hearted, even. Like it was all okay, although he knew it wasn't. Of course it wasn't. He'd barely left her alone this past three months.

'You're going straight to the station, yes?'

'Yes.'

'You're not going to another one of them protests first?'

Ben closed his eyes. He never lied to his mother, not ever, but he wished he'd lied to her about that.

'No. Just to the station.'

It was the only thing he'd broken lockdown for. He'd really thought she'd understood why he had to.

'Because I've seen the videos. I've seen the videos of the police. And you'll get all pressed together, you won't be able to keep to the two metres, I've seen the news . . .'

He stroked her knuckles absent-mindedly. It was what she used to do to him when he was a little boy and he woke up in the night, stroke stroke stroke until the nightmare shadows receded.

'There's a lot that goes on that's not on the news.'

She snatched her hands away and he felt their absence in his.

'But you know it's asking for trouble. They're looking for any excuse . . .'

'Mum.' Ben turned to face her and did something he'd never done, before the pandemic. He smiled and said, 'I'm a lawyer, aren't I? I know what I'm doing. I'll be fine, don't worry. They aren't going to arrest me.'

He should just tell her he was never going to go to one of them again. It was the right thing to do, to put her mind at rest. But there was still a part of him that couldn't stand to tell an outright lie.

'You won't be able to talk yourself out of getting sick though, will you? There's still that. Standing next to who knows who. I've seen them on the news. All jostled together. I couldn't believe it.'

She wasn't looking at him properly anymore, more like through him.

Ben stared at his weekend bag and thought about Jen and their stilted little phone calls.

'Mum. Are you going to be okay?'

She smiled, an autopilot smile, he could tell, but still somehow reassuring.

'What? Of course I am. I'm fine.'

She was rubbing at her hands again.

'I don't have to go.'

And he could tell, for a moment, that she was considering it. He'd laid in enough food, and Jonny, who'd been coming round their flat since he and Ben were in reception together, was on standby to drop round anything else she needed. But there was nothing he could do about the company. That wasn't something you could lay in stocks of.

But then her gaze snapped back to him and she said, 'Of course you should go. A bit of sea air'll be good for you.'

In a firm, no-nonsense voice that sounded suddenly like herself again.

'Honest,' he said. 'I'll stay if you want.'

And he would. Of course he would. As much as it would mean to see his girlfriend again and to swim in the sea, his mum was worth more. To see his girlfriend and swim in the sea and get out of this flat and have a chance to catch a decent breath. But he would stay, if she wanted him to.

She took his hand back and stroked his knuckles this time, and Ben felt his shoulders start to loosen.

'No. I want you to go. Just don't touch anything on the train.'

Ben stared out of the window and up at the hotel. Staring was unavoidable – it was the first thing you saw, visible from miles away, hanging over the skyline, dominating the view. Grey and imposing and sticking out of a tumbling stretch of cliffs like it had been dropped there by a giant with such force, the ground around it had been shaken to bits, and so had the structure itself. Because it wasn't really fair to call it a hotel, not anymore. What it was was a frontispiece, with nothing behind it. Ben thought of an unsuspecting tourist being welcomed in, an empty smile of a receptionist and a key to a room with no floor. They unlock it and they plunge down, down, down . . .

Which was silly, of course. The place would have been closed for years. How many years, for the ground to crumble beneath it like that?

The cab was blasting out metal, which had been weird at first, incongruous against the grey little clusters of houses they drove past as they left the station, but now seemed like a decent soundtrack to the ride. The hotel soared and the guitars screamed and Ben wondered how far they were from Whitby here, because with a view like this, you could almost believe in vampires.

'Wow,' he said, and the cabbie said nothing.

Ben had rolled his way through the Yorkshire countryside for what felt like hours. Miles and miles of fields stretching out and away, flat and dull green and the same as he'd seen on the train. But he couldn't pretend that when they started getting close, he hadn't felt a childish leap in his chest. He could see the sea!

And it was such a day for it, as well. Unlike in London, the air here was clean and fresh and salt-kissed, even what he could smell through the filters of the car air con and his mask. It wasn't oppressively hot, here. It wasn't baking, or roasting, or sweltering. It was just sunny.

They pulled up outside a big, boxy semi with a fussy front garden full of rose trees and gravel. Ben raised an eyebrow. The way you heard Jen talk about it, her parents lived in a poky little two-up, two-down and half the village still worked down the mines. This looked like a spacious three-bed semi a five-minute walk from the beach.

The driver turned down the stereo.

'That's thirteen pounds.'

Ben raised his eyebrows. He'd been in this taxi more than half an hour.

The taxi driver sat there, inscrutable behind his mask, his nose poking over the top like a beak.

'Okay,' Ben said.

He fished around in the pocket of his jeans and held out his bank card, offering it to the driver. He didn't reach for it. The two men just sat there, staring at the bright blue Co-op card held in the air between them.

'Thirteen pounds,' he said again, and Ben gawped at him. Was this some kind of pass-agg racism, some way of making him feel unwelcome, or what? Was he going to pretend that Ben couldn't pay and drag him to some shitty rural police station to shop him for the crime of not paying for a surprisingly affordable cab ride?

Then he understood.

'Do you not take cards?'

The driver rumpled his forehead. 'Ner. Cash only.'

Ben tried not to think uncharitable thoughts about nothing working outside of London. It was such a cliché, and mean besides. This was just one cab driver being an arse. It didn't mean anything about anyone else. He made himself smile, then remembered his mouth was hidden behind a mask and felt stupid.

'Can we swing by a cashpoint then?'

There was a long, pregnant pause, and Ben watched the cabbie's eyes narrow, taking him in.

'There isn't one.'

Ben struggled hard not to roll his eyes.

'So where do people get their money from?'

He pulled out his phone. Jen would have cash, if that was his only option. But there was no reception. Ben raised his eyebrows. He'd assumed that was an excuse for only messaging him for about half an hour a day. He didn't realise it was literally true.

'There's a cashpoint in the Co-op.'

This was like being in a riddle. Was there a password or something he was meant to say?

'Can we go to the Co-op?'

Another pause, this one longer than the last.

'I don't know you.'

Ben allowed himself a quiet sigh. He should never have left London. You could be as understanding as you wanted, but some stereotypes were true for a reason, and this guy was almost every reason Ben hadn't come up north with Jen before.

'Can I get out to ring the doorbell, at least?'

That and, if he was honest, he just hadn't felt like she'd wanted him to. When he'd offered, every time she came up with a reason that this wasn't a good year for him to come for Christmas, or Easter, or whatever, he'd always agreed without much of a fight. His mum would be on her own. He did have a big case at work. The train would be expensive and rammed. It was all true, technically, but really not the reason at all. He'd pushed a bit harder for her dad's funeral. It had felt like the kind of thing a shit-head would do, to miss that. But there were only so many times he could offer before it was stalking.

'I don't know you,' the man said again.

Ben briefly closed his eyes. Brilliant.

He'd been surprised when she'd invited him this time. He'd really thought he was just never going to meet her family. He'd been promising himself he'd think about why when the pandemic was over. It wasn't the kind of conversation you could have over the phone.

Ben forced himself to smile. Even though he was wearing a mask, it made your voice sound more friendly, everyone who'd done a phone job knew that. He said, in the most reasonable tone he could manage, 'What are we going to do, then?'

The cabbie looked at him, eyes flat and calculating, and for the first time, Ben was really worried. Not so much about the police station – this wasn't a film – but he wouldn't put it past this guy to take him back to that arse-end-of-nowhere town the train had stopped at and leave him there. He'd tried three different numbers to get this cab, and none of them went as far as Ravenspurn. His return ticket wasn't for another two days. With him looking at redundancy and Mum not working, he couldn't afford a day rate.

Ben kept up the forced smile. If this guy thought he looked aggressive, he was fucked.

There was a sharp tap on the side of the car, and Ben felt his muscles tense, which was annoying. What new wicker-man shit was going to happen now?

The cabbie rolled his window down, his eyes not leaving Ben's.

'Eh up.'

'All right, Chris.'

The man outside was tall and thin. He had long, gangly arms and he held himself in the self-conscious way teenagers do when their bodies are still new and unfamiliar to them, even though this guy must have been thirty at least. There was something around the eyes that made him look a little like the driver. Maybe they were brothers, or maybe everyone out here just looked the same.

Another uncharitable thought, but this time Ben couldn't find it within himself to be sorry.

The tall man peered in at him with interest.

'All right?'

Ben didn't really want to get into it, so he just nodded. Like this random guy was going to lend him twenty quid? There was no point.

'Mum wants sitting with,' the tall man said. 'You off yet? It's gone three.'

Ben felt vindicated. He wasn't being a prick. They really were brothers.

The driver jerked his head back, indicating Ben. 'He's not got the fare.'

The tall man tilted his head to the side, like he was genuinely curious. 'Why not?'

'He won't let me out to get money,' Ben said, and internally cringed. He sounded like he was trying to dob in the driver. Like this guy could make him change his mind.

'Well, he doesn't know you, does he?' the man said. Ben had to concentrate very hard on not screaming. 'What you here for anyway?'

'I'm visiting my girlfriend.'

The man stared between Ben and the semi with the rose garden that was apparently Jen's scruffy, deprived family home. His eyebrows furrowed.

'Are you Ben?'

'Yeah,' Ben said, and the two brothers exchanged a look. The driver's eyebrows worked their way up into his receding hairline, and the tall one, whose face was on show, looked even more surprised.

'You know Jen then?' Ben said, but it was just to break the awkwardness of the moment. Bloody obviously they did. And obviously he didn't look like what they'd had in mind for her boyfriend.

'Course we do,' the driver said. He was openly staring now.

Ben had never really got what Jen meant about it being claustrophobic – there was so much sky, wasn't there? He understood now.

The driver heaved a deep sigh, his mask puffing out with the force of it. 'All right. You can pay on the way back then.'

The driver reached over and clicked the central locking off.

Ben sat in the back, hand on his seatbelt buckle, immobile.

'I can go in the Co-op and get cash now. It's fine,' he said.

'Nah, you go on. You're all right. Make sure you carry cash up here though, yeah?' The driver looked almost friendly now. 'It's not London.'

'Right,' said Ben. 'Cheers.'

He got out of the car and pulled his bag from the boot.

The tall man nodded towards the house they were standing outside. 'That one's hers. Red door.'

Ben pulled a deliberately friendly face, and nodded, waiting for them to leave. They didn't. He went over to the door and they carried on watching him, their eyes tracing his progress up the garden path. When he got to the red door, he turned and took his mask off. He smiled, awkwardly.

'I'll be seeing you, then.'

They didn't return the smile.

It was the tall one who eventually spoke.

'Yeah. I expect so. Not a lot else to see, round here. Chris, give us a lift.'

And he got into the car and the two men drove away.

Ben took a deep breath, and tried to shake off the weirdness of the encounter. Two annoying guys didn't mean anything about a whole village, did they? It wasn't like there weren't weirdos in London. He blew the breath out and put a smile on his face again and leaned forward and rang the bell.

Ben sat in the living room, same settee but not touching Jen, which was weird. Back in London, they'd intertwine, sitting on and under each other, arms reaching out of the tangle of them for wine or coffee. But here it was different. She'd given him one chaste kiss and the far end of the sofa.

'More tea, Ben?'

He smiled at Alison and she smiled back. They were both trying really hard.

'No thanks, I'm fine.'

Of course, that was the difference. In London, his mum was around, but she gave them space and Jen knew her so well, it was no different really to having a flatmate around. Alison was clearly not like a flatmate at all.

'A biscuit, then?'

Their fake smiles at each other intensified.

'I'm okay, really.'

He hadn't really thought about it. The meeting the parents bit. It was weird they hadn't done it a couple of years ago. He would at least have liked to have met her dad. But when this was done, hopefully he'd get her on her own. Beer on the beach, and some time with her, in real life, at last.

'Go on, we've got chocolate ones ... oh!' Alison looked mortified. 'Sorry! I didn't mean ... I don't think that you like chocolate biscuits. I mean. Not any more than anyone does. I mean ...'

Ben flicked his eye over to Jen, who'd turned a deep beetroot red. He stifled a grin.

'Thanks. I like chocolate biscuits.'

And he tried to catch Jen's eye, but she wouldn't look. She was staring fixedly at the floor. Was she really that embarrassed? If Alison hadn't been there, he'd have reached over. But she was.

'Jenny? Can you help me get the dinner on?'

'Um. Yes?' she said, and stood up. She finally turned and met his eye. 'Make yourself at home, yeah?'

And the two of them went off through the kitchen door and left him alone.

Ben looked around. The problem was, this didn't feel remotely like home – his, or Jen's. He went over to the mantlepiece and picked up a little framed photo of a wide-eyed blonde child. He glanced over the rest, but there were none of her as an adult. The most recent of the photos was teenage Jen, gawky and thin, wearing blue eyeshadow and smiling awkwardly. Ben smiled back at her. He was glad he'd come. There'd be time for a snog on the beach soon enough, surely.

A strangled whisper came through the kitchen door.

'You didn't say that he was black!'

Ben froze, then put down the picture, making sure not to make a sound. He felt his eyebrows knitting together.

'Yes I did.'

Ben hovered in the middle of the living room.

'Of course you didn't! I'd have remembered!'

He didn't want to go any closer to the kitchen – of course he didn't, he didn't want to listen to them on purpose – but at the same time, he wanted to give Jen the benefit of the doubt. Surely there was a reasonable explanation. Alison must be mistaken.

'Okay, what if I didn't? What difference does it make?'

Ben stared out of the window, gazing at Alison's patch of obedient roses.

'I can't believe you never showed me a photograph of you two together. In all this time. You can't have, or I'd have known. It's been over a year.'

Ben swallowed. It had been three years.

'Okay. Maybe I didn't show you a photo. But he's here now.'

When Alison responded, her voice was choked, as if she was going to cry. Ben couldn't imagine that. He'd only just met Alison, but she really didn't seem the type.

'I don't know anything about you. I don't know how you live your life. I've been imagining you wrong, all this time.'

There was a tense, throbbing silence.

'You imagine me?'

And Ben became suddenly and acutely aware that he was eavesdropping. And he was nearly out of the door, nearly on his way to the loo to wait out their chat and let them have a bit of privacy, when he heard, 'What will he eat?'

Ben puffed his cheeks full of air and breathed it out, slowly.

'Mum! Don't say things like that.'

And Jen sounded mortified, to be fair. Which wasn't helpful, obviously, but he could maybe understand.

'Don't you start on me, this is all your fault in the first place.'

Their hissy little whispers were escalating in volume. It was getting harder and harder to pretend not to be listening.

'What do you mean, my fault? All I've done is bring a

boyfriend home. You're the one that's making a massive drama out of it.'

'Don't you speak to me like that!'

And Ben just couldn't stand it. He pushed open the kitchen door and stepped in.

'Can I help?'

Both women stared at him like they'd been caught stealing sweets. Ben thought longingly of other holidays he'd had with Jen. They'd have already had a shag and two beers, if this had been anywhere else. Even considering the pandemic, it would have been nice to have booked a hotel. There was no way, though – they'd have had to have pretended that they were travelling on business just to get different rooms in the same shit Travelodge. Depressing.

'What would you like for dinner, Ben?'

Ben gave Alison a proper smile, this time. He'd been waiting for someone to ask that.

'Fish and chips?'

Jen and Alison shared a look with each other, for a moment in total agreement.

'It's okay, Ben, we don't have to just get chips.'

Alison nodded. 'I'll cook for you. It's no bother.'

And, suddenly, it really felt like a home. Being fussed over, having your favourite food cooked . . . it'd been a long time since he'd been a guest.

'It's just . . . It's what you have at the seaside, isn't it?'

And Jen looked at him like he'd said something amazing. The way she'd looked at him that very first night. She said, 'Yes. It is. Of course we can.'

'Well. You're lucky it's summer,' Alison said. He hoped

she was more charmed than she was put out by the rejection of her cooking. 'You won't be able to get nice fresh fish in London, I suppose.'

Jen rolled her eyes, but Ben smiled.

'No. That's what my mum always says.'

Alison sniffed her approval. Ben imagined her meeting his mum. She'd be okay again, one day, leaving the flat and getting on the train. She adored Jen. Surely she'd be able to do that again soon.

'Well, she's right. We'll get you your fish and chips, Ben, don't you worry. If that's what you want to try.'

She was clearly under the impression Ben had never actually eaten chips before.

He smiled at her. Best behaviour for a girlfriend's mum.

Jen raised an eyebrow. She clearly wasn't on her best behaviour.

'Do they use oil for the chips now, or is it still dripping?'

And Ben had assumed that was a joke, or at least a dig, but Alison pulled a shut-up-and-don't-make-a-scene face at her and said, 'Don't be silly, Jenny. That's settled then. Fish and chips!'

'Great,' Ben said, and meant it. It was Jen who was vegetarian, not him. 'Can't wait.'

And Alison gave Jen a raised-eyebrow look that clearly said, *Fancy that! Being black, and wanting to eat fish and chips!*

Jen met it with a frown.

'We'll go out and get them,' she said.

He flashed her thanks with his eyes and she widened hers back, and just like that, they were on the same team again and everything was okay.

Ben breathed in the smell of the sea and smiled up at the big wide blue of the place. It was very, very nice to be out of Jen's mother's house.

'Still light.'

Jen, sitting next to him, smiled back, open as the sky.

'What's that?'

She cracked open another bottle and handed it to him. Ben accepted it, cold and comforting in his hands. A beach. A beer. The sound of seagulls and waves. He hadn't thought he'd be getting a holiday this year.

'I said, it's still light.'

She looked up, nose wrinkled in that way she only ever did when she wasn't at work.

'Oh. Of course. Yeah, long nights up here.'

For a moment, the two of them just sat together and drank and listened to the waves as they rolled in and out. Like the village was being rocked to sleep.

'So, what do you think?' she said.

Ben looked around. The wide expanse of grey sand and the jut of the brown cliffs and the shadow of the old hotel and the endless roll of the sea. The little shops along the promenade, faded but pretty, and Jen's house, which smelled very strongly of air freshener and had a kitchen as big as some of his favourite bars. He thought of the taxi driver and his brother and the awkward, whispered conversation Jen had snuck off to have with her mother just after he'd arrived. He thought of the fish and chips, the best he'd had since he was a kid, sandy and exhausted on the train home from Kent whenever his mum could swing a summer day off. It had been years since he'd been to the seaside.

'It's not what I thought,' he said.

Jen's face fell like a stone and Ben felt like an absolute dick.

'God, I'm sorry, I know . . .'

'No! No. Don't be sorry. I like it.'

And he really did. He looked up. A perfect sky, perfectly fading into the navy of a night time blue. It was beautiful here.

'You don't have to pretend,' she said.

He grimaced to himself. He really hadn't meant to upset her. Maybe the days spent just him and his mum had made him weirder, made him more closed up and awkward and further away from the rest of the world. From her.

'I'm not pretending. It's not quite how you described, though.'

She tilted her head at him, like she didn't know what he meant. 'How so?'

Ben rolled his eyes. She'd basically lied about living in a hovel, and pretty obviously hadn't told anyone here the first thing about him, that was how so. Her mum had asked if he could eat fish and chips, for fuck's sake. What did she think? That he was going to turn his nose up at anything that wasn't plantain or jollof rice?

'From what you said, it didn't sound that great,' he said, using his measured, lawyer voice.

It had sounded like a total shithole, was what he meant. That's what she'd painted – closed shops and brown cliffs and grey seas and unemployment. She hadn't mentioned the ruin of a hotel, poised dramatically as if it was going to jump into the sea. She hadn't mentioned the sweep and scale of a village on two levels: one so high it looked like every house was going to teeter into the sea, the other clustered around a coastline, arranged like a child had lined up their toys. She hadn't told him about the roar of the waves and the way it filled up the space around all the other sounds so it was like your whole head could breathe. Or the way that when you sat and let yourself take in the vast expanse of water in front of you it made anything you were worrying about seem small and insignificant.

'It's not that great. It's okay.'

Ben made a decision. He pulled her towards him and took a deep inhale of her hair and decided to let it go.

'It's better than okay.'

And she smiled up at him like a light had come on inside of her and he decided that maybe he'd leave it for another day to call her out on not telling her friends and family about him. He was here now, wasn't he? They were both here now, and the last three months were already fading away, washed, perhaps, by the endless waves.

'Actually, that reminds me . . .'

Ben held up his phone and snapped a photo of the way the last rays of sun hit the waves and made them sparkle. He admired it for a moment. When Ben was a little boy, he'd wanted to film nature documentaries. He thought it'd be so cool, lying patiently in a hide on a savannah, massive zoom camera poised on his shoulder, waiting for a rare leopard to wander by. He thought he'd be good at it, too. He was very patient. But that wasn't a proper, sensible job, like being a lawyer was. It was like being an astronaut. He still liked to take snaps on his phone, though.

'Pretty,' Jen said, from under his arm.

'Told you,' Ben said, and laughed as she swiped at him. He opened WhatsApp and frowned. 'There's no signal.'

Jen shook her head and her blonde hair gleamed in the last of the light.

'Nah, not down here.'

He frowned at his phone.

'There wasn't back at your house, either.'

'Nope. Who are you sending the sunset to?'

'Mum. We have this thing. If we ever go on holiday without each other, we take a picture of the first sunset and send it home. Dad used to do it with us, back in the nineties. Obviously it was postcards then. But it's a way of saying goodnight, you know? Sunset.'

She was smiling in a way that made him glad he'd explained.

'Oh. I didn't know that.'

There was a moment's pause. They drank their beers. They stared at the sea. The gulls shrieked a chorus above them, and the air was fresh and didn't taste of other people's breath at all.

'I've been on holiday with you, though,' she said.

'What?'

The light had faded even more now. Her skin and hair seemed to glow in the dusk.

'We've been on holiday before,' she said. 'So how come I didn't already know about this? I would have remembered.'

He shrugged. 'I dunno. I must have done it while you were getting ready.'

But that wasn't it, and he knew it. He'd always hidden it on purpose. No matter how long he'd been with Jen, there was always a little boundary there, like he couldn't quite shake that she'd been a colleague first. Because how much could he really trust this girl, who always made some reason up why they couldn't move in together, and still didn't want to tell anyone at work they were going out? She was properly herself when they were alone, like this or at home, but at work, and even out, there was always something cagey about the way she treated him. Like she never quite relaxed. He couldn't shake the idea that there was something he could do, something he could say, that would unlock her. He hadn't found it yet, though.

'Well, I think it's lovely,' she said.

'I haven't sent it yet. There Wi-Fi back at yours you can get me on?'

She pulled a sympathetic face. 'Nah, sorry. Just plug-in internet.'

'What?' he said, and he hated the note of alarm he could hear in his voice. He didn't want to be some cliché knob of a Londoner visiting, making a fuss about being forced to be more than a twenty-minute Uber from home. Still, though. No internet?

'I know! Mum never uses it, though. There was Wi-Fi in the pub, but . . .'

She turned and looked over her shoulder at the mention of the pub. He tried to look too, but he couldn't pick out a building that might be a pub in this light.

'So when you messaged me, you went to the pub?'

'No! It's been shut off since lockdown. I've been going up the cliff to catch a couple of bars. It's the only place there's any signal at all round here.'

'Up the cliff?'

Now she mentioned it, there was a path winding up to the top from the beach. It was steep and treacherous looking. If he'd been on holiday, it was the kind of climb that Ben would tell himself he'd definitely do before he came home, for a bit of a challenge and a nice view, and then accidentally on purpose never get round to actually climbing it.

'You've climbed up there every day just to message me?'

It might have just been the light, but he thought he saw her blush a little bit. She looked different here. Less polished somehow, her hair and nails not so done. She wasn't wearing make-up, or at least, not as much. He could imagine her as a teenager now, something he wasn't sure had been possible before. He liked her like this, with her freckles uncovered and her accent broadened out.

'Yeah, well. Don't flatter yourself. I wanted to look at my Insta as well.'

But she was grinning.

And despite the stress of the journey, and that weird little scene with her mum earlier, he was suddenly, overwhelmingly glad he'd come. It was good to be with her, and good to be away from the heat and the closeness and the tensions of London – to be somewhere he could breathe.

He slung an arm over her, knocking her beer over so it fizzed out onto the sand. She shrieked and reached for his.

'Come on, you're sharing now.'

And she giggled and he tickled her lightly on the side and leaned in for a kiss and, honestly, it could have been Spain or Thailand or anywhere. Beer and a beach and a girl. That was all.

But something made him look up.

Standing there, between him and Jen and the sea, there was a woman. Her age was hard to tell – she could have been anywhere between twenty-five and forty-five. She was wearing a scowl and a tight ponytail right on the top of her head. Her hair was dyed a bright, determined red, shocking against the navy and grey of the night.

For a few moments, it seemed that Jen hadn't noticed. She kept kissing a line along Ben's collarbone, little flutters. He stared up at the woman and she stared back, cold and clear.

'Ben, is it?'

Jen finally stopped and looked up at the woman as well. There was a beat where they just stared at each other. The chill of the evening lifted the little hairs on Ben's arms. Who knew that he'd feel cold? It had seemed impossible, yesterday, in London. His mum had been right.

Jen didn't say anything, so, eventually, he did.

'That's right. Um. Nice to meet you . . .'

'Alex.'

And she held out a hand and smiled.

Without thinking about it, without considering it at all, Ben jumped to his feet and took her hand. Her fingers closed around his, warm and slightly rough, her skin catching very slightly against his. She was so close, he could smell the cigarette smoke and sandalwood of her.

Remembering himself, Ben took a step back. How long

had it been since he'd touched someone he didn't know like that, since he'd been close enough to smell them? It must be the sea, he decided. It was filling his head up with shushing, making him feel like he was on any other holiday, rather than a seaside trip in the middle of a pandemic.

He fought the impulse to wipe his hands against his trousers. That would be unforgivably rude, wouldn't it? What were the rules these days? Ben told himself firmly it would be fine, but he was still imagining germs dancing over his hands, wriggling their way into the tiny creases of his skin.

Neither of the two women looked at all bothered by what he'd done. Was everyone still shaking hands out here?

Jen jumped to her feet.

'Hiya, Alex.'

There was something in her tone that Ben couldn't place. Not unfriendly exactly, but not friendly either. A kind of easy familiarity there, but not a lot of warmth. Looking at Jen and Alex staring at each other, Ben got the impression the two women must know each other very well. Another person she hadn't mentioned.

Alex stared over at Jen, not smiling anymore. Her face was hard and flat again.

'I came down to ask about tomorrow.'

It was reassuring in a way, to know that Jen hadn't just not told the people here anything about him – she'd been keeping both parts of her life separate. Like she had one life that was about London and work and him in one box, and then in another box, this, which Ben had barely known existed.

'Right. Tomorrow. Of course.'

He'd introduced her to his mum when they were only a few

dates in. It hadn't occurred to him to do anything else. But then, he found it easy to be around his mum. He didn't get all scrunched up and miserable whenever he was in her house.

Maybe he shouldn't have told Jen not to come back to London.

'What's happening tomorrow?' Ben said.

Jen gave Ben the kind of tight smile she normally used when a case was going south, or her workload was getting ridiculous, even by their standards. Her extremely stressed smile. It looked out of place on a beach.

'We're opening up my dad's pub again.'

Alex gave her a cool stare and pursed her lips.

'It's your pub.'

Jen looked uncomfortable suddenly, even though Alex was clearly right. It was her pub.

'Well . . .'

Alex's scowl deepened. 'The deeds are in your name. You're meant to be the lawyer, aren't you?'

Jen turned to Ben, her jaw a hard line.

'Alex has worked there for a long time.'

And Ben felt like maybe he got it. That look the two women had exchanged – maybe he didn't know what it was like to grow up in some tiny village that looked like it was halfway to falling into the sea, but he knew what it was like to have people in your life that you'd rather avoid, and couldn't. These two were clearly cousins – not literally, perhaps, but as good as. They'd spent too many family functions over the years simmering at each other and now they had to work together and it had tipped them both over the edge. He could get that.

'What time did you want me? You never said.'

Ben stared at Jen, aghast.

'You're opening a pub? In a pandemic?'

'I told you on the phone.'

She stared back at him, eyebrows knitted together like he was a mild annoyance, if anything at all.

'I thought you said it was just a takeaway night,' he said, which wasn't true. He thought he'd talked her out of it, if he was honest.

'It is! We're not even opening the bar. Table by the door. It's all perfectly legal.'

Ben frowned at her. Not illegal, no. Not technically.

'Yeah,' Alex said. She was smiling at him, just a shade too sweetly. Ben got a fairly clear impression that this was someone who liked causing trouble. 'I mean, they'll stay to drink their pints, though. Obviously.'

Jen rolled her eyes and tossed her hair over one shoulder. It shone bright in the gloom. 'Alex! No they won't. They're not allowed.'

Alex smirked. 'We'll see.'

And Jen shot Alex a look, a hard one that made Ben think of all the times they'd laughed over how many ways a lawyer has to tell you to fuck off without saying it. He'd always loved watching her work. He didn't even care that they kept their relationship quiet in the office – it was worth it to get to see her in work mode every day. He missed it.

'They're not going to stay. We're just selling takeaways. That's it.'

The two women turned away from Ben, as if he was no longer a part of the conversation. Which was true, he supposed. But harsh.

Alex tilted her sleeve and checked a chunky silver watch.

'We'll want to be getting there at eleven, latest, me and Si.'

Jen shook her head briskly. 'You can't have that many hours on set-up. That's ridiculous.'

Alex's face was a mask of dislike. No wonder Jen hadn't mentioned her before.

'It's ridiculous to need a six-hour set-up after a full four months closed?'

'It's a table by the door.' Jen's eyes flicked towards Ben. Guiltily, he thought, but he might have misread her. 'Because it's not a full open. It's just a takeaway night.'

'It's not enough time any way up. There's cleaning to do, sorting, inventory, it doesn't matter where the bar is. And we haven't had a wage since spring.'

As well as the anger, there was a pleading note to Alex's voice that made Ben uncomfortable. How often had Jen complained about Derek being a dick to work for? Surely that wasn't just all talk, now that she was the one in charge.

'I'm sorry, but the hours are what they are. And I sorted out the furlough for you.'

'Yes, and we're very very grateful.'

Alex's voice was dripping with sarcasm. Ben could feel Jen bristling beside him.

'I'll see you tomorrow then,' she said, in the voice she only used when someone had really fucked her off. Jen didn't crack it out often, but Ben had seen her work miracles with that voice.

Alex remained unfazed.

'You don't own the beach, yeah? This is public property, you can't kick me out of here.'

There was a long moment where the two of them stared at each other and the tension built and Ben sat silently.

'Fine. We'll go then. Come on, Ben.'

And they gathered up their things, Alex staring at them, and all three silent.

As Jen rolled up the picnic blanket with an air of barely disguised fury, Ben realised that it was completely dark now. The stars had come out, little pinpricks hanging in the sky. He hadn't noticed. The photo of the sunset sat on his phone, unsent.

'This box needs washing as well, Jenny.'

Jen swiped a palm across her forehead and, even from the far end of the bar, Ben could see it came away slick with sweat. It wasn't that it was so hot today – nothing like as hot as London, when they were out with the sea and the wind and the sky. It was cold in fact, a harsh wind blowing in and promising a storm, but as soon as they'd stepped inside, it was sweltering again. The only windows in the place were tiny, and Jen had only been able to lever them open a couple of inches before they stuck.

Si was standing in front of Jen, proffering a clear plastic storage box that was theoretically meant to be full of crisps to sell but was currently empty, a suspicious amber liquid pooling in one of its corners. Beer, hopefully.

Jen blew a stray lock of hair away from her face and it immediately fell back, sticking to her forehead.

'Okay. Put it in the washer then.'

Ben reached down and pulled another two cans out of the crate at his feet, setting them neatly on the table above him. It was surprisingly hard work, even doing this simple task. Everything was filthy, everything had to be washed, moved, washed again. And not just a quick wipe, but a scrub. It was as if the grime didn't want to be washed off. Dust stuck down with salt.

'It's already full,' Si said. He had apparently worked here

since he was a teenager but acted like he had less experience than Ben did. Seemed nice enough, but a nightmare to manage. Jen clearly agreed.

'Could you figure it out, Si? I don't know either. Haven't worked here for a while.'

Ben stooped and picked up another couple of cans. Sweat stung his eyes. It had been ridiculous to think that this pub could be cleaned in just a few hours. Ben had never worked in bars regularly, just the odd shift to help mates out here and there, but even he could see that they should have assigned even more time than Alex had suggested.

'That's hardly our fault,' Alex said, carrying over a ridiculously high tower of grubby pint glasses.

Jen glowered at her, but said nothing.

Alex was doing easily as much work as the other three of them combined. She clunked the glasses down on the bar in six neat stacks and started pulling them apart for washing. 'I thought being a lawyer was meant to be a tough gig. Harder than lugging a load of glasses about and pulling the odd pint.'

Ben stood up and wiped his brow. His back ached, and his throat felt dry and grubby. Perhaps Alex was right, and he was too soft for this kind of work. But Si had stopped too. They both just stood, staring at Jen and Alex.

'I never said working in a bar isn't hard,' Jen said, and Ben could tell that she was deliberately trying to make herself sound steady and reasonable, the way she did when she was really pissed off. 'They're different jobs. Mine's not harder than yours.'

Alex smirked at her, unpleasantly. 'Yeah? Why are you paid so much more than me then?'

Ben raised his eyebrows. He couldn't help but respect her for saying it. She was kind of like the cliffs. Intimidating, but the drama was compelling.

Not that that made it any easier for Jen. Her lips were pressed together, as if she was trying to stop herself from saying something. She failed.

'Why can't you just keep your mouth shut and help me for once? And, Si, can't you just try to use your brain and put a bit of effort in? It's the least you could do after ...'

She managed to choke herself to a halt. But it was too late, Alex's eyes had already lit up.

'What do you mean, the least he could do?'

Jen leaned down and fiddled with the dishwasher. Ben wondered whose eye she was avoiding.

'Nothing. Forget it.'

Alex was still standing, hands on the bar like she owned the place. But she didn't. It was still weird to Ben that his girlfriend owned a pub. It didn't fit with the woman he knew in London, who didn't even like queuing at the bar and always handed him her card when it was her turn to get a round in.

'Nah, come on. The least he can do after what? What did you do?'

Jen was staring at the dishwashing machine as if it held the secret to something. How to get out of this conversation, perhaps. Why was she being so shifty?

'What's she talking about, Jen?' Ben said, and she met his eye for a second and her mouth was pressed tight into a line and he barely recognised her.

She pressed three buttons at, what looked to Ben like

might have been, random. One of them must have been right, because the machine sprang into life. She turned to Si.

'I got you furloughed, didn't I? I made sure you still got paid.'

Alex glared at Jen over the bar.

'You act like you paid that to him out of your own pocket, but you didn't. That was free money from the government. You really think he should be grateful because you did the bare minimum to make sure he didn't starve? I had to tell you to do that, and I didn't get a pat on the back, did I? Meanwhile, I've got nothing because it's a second job, because no one in this shithole village will pay me enough to live on.'

Jen reddened and cast an imploring look to Ben.

Ben swallowed. They'd talked about employment rights and responsibilities, loads. She'd said she thought it was cool that he'd only become a lawyer because he wanted to work with trade unions. She'd said that, in London.

'I did include you! I put his hours up!'

Alex snorted. 'Only to what he was actually working before your dad went into the hospital. He only ever put down 75 per cent of our wages, he topped us up cash in hand. We couldn't make it work on the tax rate.'

There was a silence, which is to say, the gust of the wind and the crash of the sea took over from words for a while.

'I didn't know that.'

Her mouth looked normal again now. Soft. Ben took a deep breath of dust and salt air. He wouldn't know how to run a pub either, to be fair, and he wouldn't want to.

'Well, you didn't ask, did you? You didn't care. You just

leave us mouldering on whittled-down wages for months, and when you do bring us back, when you do chuck us a crumb of work, you cut the hours so tight, we're running around like blue-arsed flies, with barely enough time to do the most basic set-up.'

Jen looked around the pub as if she'd never seen one before. 'I didn't know . . .'

Alex's lip curled. She looked like she was really enjoying this fight. Like she'd been waiting to have it for a long time. Jen really would have been better cooped up with Priya and Adam over lockdown. This atmosphere wasn't worth the beach.

'You didn't know, you didn't know. I did though, didn't I? And I told you, but would you listen? No. Why not? Because you think you're better than me.'

'I don't think I'm better than you,' Jen said, fast, like it was an instinct.

'Bullshit,' Alex said. And it was so obvious that she was right. And Ben realised that it was easy to imagine what Jen had been like as a teenager, but it wasn't the carefree, magnetic version he'd had in mind. Maybe teenage Jen had been flushed and flustered, caught out having not done her homework and trying to bluster her way out of it, convincing no one. It wasn't a comfortable thing to be thinking about her, but he couldn't pretend he wasn't.

'I don't think I'm better than you. I just did better at school.'

Alex scoffed, like Jen had said something ridiculous.

'What? I did.'

'I always did better at school than you. You struggled with the easiest little things.'

Jen's mouth dropped open, fish-like.

'You failed your A levels!'

This had the feel of an argument they'd had before. Not out loud, perhaps. But many, many times.

'But not because I didn't know it, though! Not because I wasn't clever. They didn't let me take them.'

Jen slapped her hands down on the top of the bar. There was an ugly twist of triumph to her mouth. 'Oh, and that proves that you're great, does it? One of us got slung out of school for half killing a girl and the other one didn't. I don't think it's fucking controversial to say that one of us did better than the other one there. Do you?'

And for a long time, Alex didn't say anything. And even though Ben had met Alex less than a day ago, he knew her enough to know that this was unusual.

Eventually, she slammed the last of the pint glasses down and jerked her head at Si.

'Come on. We're off on a fag break, and we'll be twenty minutes. And before you think about kicking off, this shift's going to be longer than six hours, so I'm legally entitled. I might not know enough to get into uni, but I know that. Come on, Si.'

And she stalked outside. Si offered an apologetic smile, but trailed out after her without a word.

Jen turned to Ben. It seemed that she'd finally remembered he was there, now everyone else had left. She puffed her cheeks out.

'God, sorry about that. I told you Dad had the patience of a saint.'

And she smiled, but he couldn't.

'You didn't furlough your staff straight away?'

'They weren't my staff! And I did get them furloughed, as soon as they asked.'

Ben frowned down at the beer cans.

'But she had to come to you and ask for it? You didn't reach out?'

All the conversations they'd had about workers' rights. When he'd told her how gutted he'd been not to get the union training contract he'd gone for at Thompsons three years running. Was she just nodding along?

'I wasn't their boss. Pete was interim manager, not me. I didn't know I was going to get the place.'

And she looked at him, eyes big, and appealing, and he knew that she wanted him to drop it, and he did too. This wasn't his business, was it? This was meant to be a break. But it would pick away at him. He knew it would.

'But it was either going to be you or him. And you didn't check what had happened to the staff?'

'I was fucking busy, Ben! I was bereaved, it was lockdown . . .'

Ben took a deep breath in, and then out again. He didn't want to be having this fight with her. He didn't want to slip into work mode – letting Derek spin himself out, give himself enough rope to hang himself with before he stepped in to make his point. He always knew exactly how long to wait. He always knew how to win the argument. He didn't want it to be about winning, with her.

'Okay,' he said.

But it was as if she hadn't heard him.

'You don't know her. Her asking for something's no

indication of anything. She'll ask for anything, that one, and if she doesn't get it, she'll just take it. Didn't you see the watch on her wrist? She's bold as fucking brass!'

She stopped, breathing heavily.

Ben felt his eyebrows ruffle. A watch? She'd mentioned a watch before, in messages. He'd never understood, but there always seemed like there were other things he wanted to say to her, other questions he wanted to ask. Why had she never mentioned Alex to him, if she was so consumed with her? 'What are you talking about? What's your problem with her?'

'What's *your* problem?'

Ben closed his eyes, briefly, and felt the full weight of the months they'd been apart, the distance between them widening, from nothing more than a trickle of water to a stream to a river.

'My mum'll have kittens when I tell her about this, you know? She's been shielding all this time, and I spend a day and a night opening up a pub.'

He'd thought that seeing her in person would fix the distance. Close the gap. He'd wanted it to, enough to leave his mum, to get on a train, even though he knew it meant she wouldn't sleep for five days for worrying about him. He'd thought that it was worth it.

'Don't tell her then.'

Ben raised his eyebrows at her, incredulous, and she flushed.

'Or don't do it at all! You can go for a walk, read your book on the beach or something. It's a nice enough day.'

He pushed the table away, harder than he'd meant to,

sending all the dusty cans juddering. One of them rolled off the edge of the table and bounced on the floor, once, twice, and then rolled away into a corner. Ben absently thought about the customer who'd buy it. Drenched in a fine spray of lager and sea salt. How long did a can keep shaken up for?

'And then I stay in your room and if you've got it, I've got it anyway! Or should I not do that either?'

He wasn't sure that she'd ever really seen him angry before. She'd seen him pissed off, and irritated, and passionate about something. But not angry.

'Look, I'm sorry. I don't know what you want from me?'

And suddenly, he wasn't angry anymore. Just very tired.

'I want to spend a bit of time with you. I want to not be bickering over a bar, I want to be seeing you for the first time in a third of a year.'

Jen swallowed. He wondered if she could also taste the dust.

'I'm sorry. They need the work. It's just this one night, right? This is just bad timing. I want to be together too.'

And he knew that it was true they needed the work. And he knew that she was trying, that it'd been hard, that this hadn't been an easy place to live. But he didn't – couldn't – believe her on the last part. Why had she arranged this for one of the few, precious nights that he was here? Wasn't he worth a bit of consideration? Wasn't he worth showing your mother a photo of, just one time in three years?

Ben could feel anger bubbling up in him, hot and sour. He grabbed the hoodie he'd been regretting bringing with him for this whole, sweltering afternoon and headed to the door.

Jen just stood there. She didn't move a single muscle to stop him.

'Where are you going?'

'On a break. Alex was right, you know. I'm entitled to twenty minutes.'

And he stalked out of the pub, leaving her alone, surrounded by empty glasses and salt and dirt. And he hoped that he was wrong, but he couldn't help feeling that something had shifted between them. The river's worth of space between them had become a sea, and now they were standing on different shores.

Ben climbed and climbed and climbed and finally stopped. He leaned on a bench for support. Surely he should be fitter than this. Why hadn't he spent the last three months getting really into running, or yoga, or just chucking about the kettlebells he'd bought a bit more? He'd done nothing over lockdown except for keeping himself and his mum alive. That had felt like all he could possibly do. He hadn't even been able to read. He'd just watched all the Marvel films in order, taking deep comfort from the fact that he knew what he'd be doing, night after night after night. He'd be watching a film. He'd never seen *Antman* before, and it was fairly good. But he could at least have done a bit of cardio, so that he could drag himself up a cliff in a huff without half dying in the process.

It was beautiful up here as well, to be fair.

He checked his phone, but there was still no reception. He remembered, the old hotel. That was where the signal was here. Like a fucking treasure hunt.

He wandered through the caravan park, trying to resist the impulse to stare in through the windows and failing. They were all empty anyway, just cheap upholstery and dust. No sign of human life.

Unlike the hotel. In front of the ruined front, there was a figure hunched on a bench, far too close to the edge for comfort. The wind was getting stronger. Ben frowned, and the figure looked up.

'She here too?'

It was Alex, of course. How many people even lived here? A hundred? A thousand? How many of the houses down in the bay were as empty as the caravans?

'No,' he said. 'Just me.'

She pulled a packet of rolling tobacco and some papers out of her bag.

'Why's that then? She getting on your tits as much as she is mine?'

Ben stared out to the sea, jaw set.

'Maybe.'

Alex grinned, taking out a paper and a filter.

'Well, at least you're honest. Wouldn't have expected that, from a lawyer.'

She laid a line of baccy onto the paper and the wind snatched it away.

'Ah, fuck,' she said.

Without thinking, Ben stepped close to her, blocking the wind. Closer than two metres.

She pinched out more tobacco and this time, it held. 'Cheers. I did quit, but . . . you know. Apocalypse and that.'

He shrugged.

'What have you got against lawyers?'

She smirked and span the wheel of a lighter. Ben thought of Saturday afternoons hanging around Brockwell Park with his mates. Every time someone left a lighter unattended, they'd jack up the gas gauge again and again, wiggling it around to get a massive plume of a flame the next time someone used it. Jonny had burned half an eyebrow off like that and Ben had laughed so much he'd only narrowly avoided pissing himself in front of Michelle, who'd been his big crush in year ten.

'She's the only one I know.'

The cigarette caught, and Ben stepped back.

'Did you two keep in touch, before this year?'

'No. Not at all.' Alex stared out to sea. She looked a lot older when she was frowning. Maybe everyone did, when times were bad. 'I still know her, though. They get into your skin, don't they? The people you grow up with.'

Ben thought of Jonny, still the person he'd trust to leave his mum with, and the rest of the lads. They used to go for drinks together twice a week, and now it was twice a year. But it was still twice a year. And Michelle, who he followed on Instagram. She was running some kind of business doing nail art now. She was doing okay. She had been doing okay, at least.

'I suppose so.'

Alex smiled at him indulgently. Like, patronising.

'Did she ever tell you that we were the only three kids in our primary class?'

Ben blinked. 'No.'

Alex took a deep drag on her rollie, cheekbones popped with the effort. Even he could tell she'd rolled it too tight, and he hadn't smoked in years.

'Did she ever tell you anything about us?'

Ben thought about it.

'No.'

She smiled. Almost wistful.

With only three of you in a class, that wasn't even a cousin, was it? That was more like a sister.

'No. We knew fuck all about you as well.'

He frowned, narrowing his eyes against the puzzle of it and the gathering wind. The weather was getting wilder. Maybe it was just because he was up high. No one had ever been blown off these cliffs though, had they? No. That was ridiculous.

'Yeah. That was obvious.'

She frowned and took another drag.

'Did Si give you hassle?'

Ben shook his head. 'No.'

'Chris?'

He shrugged.

She wrinkled up her nose.

'He's a good lad. Deep down, you know? He's got a lot on. His mum's not well.'

Ben offered her a tight smile. He'd heard that before.

'Mine neither.'

And she looked over to the caravans, which he'd thought were all empty. Maybe not.

'No. There's a lot of it about.'

He followed her gaze, and for a moment they were quiet. Ben pulled out his phone and finally sent the sunset.

Sorry, no signal anywhere here. Better late than never! xxx

When he looked up, Alex had her eyes trained firmly on his face.

'So, what did she tell you? Anything at all? Or did she pretend that she was living here on her own, nesting with the seagulls?'

His phone lit up immediately.

You take care xxx

Mum must have been practically sitting on her phone. Ben thought of her, carrying it about, waiting for his text. She'd have spent the night with it next to her head, volume all the way up, and still checking the screen every five minutes, just in case. The idea gave him a twist that was maybe guilt and maybe anger and maybe both.

He couldn't be bothered to lie. 'She said it was poor. Made out she pretty much lived in a hovel, growing up. Really chippy about it, to be honest.'

Alex laughed. A humourless kind of a laugh.

'Yeah. She didn't grow up in a hovel.'

She looked back to the caravans, and he followed her gaze.

'No. I know.'

'Anything else?'

His eyes went to her wrist, but it was covered. Fuck it.

'Something about a watch.'

She pulled back her sleeve and showed a man's watch, clunky and incongruous on her wrist. 'This watch?'

It was such an ordinary-looking thing.

'Was it Ted's?'

Alex shook her sleeve back down.

'Yep.'

'How did you get it?'

She looked at him, and maybe it was because they were up so high, but he was struck by how birdlike she was. The tilt of her head and the shine of her eyes.

'Will you tell her, if I say?'

Ben sighed and looked out at the waves. It pulled your focus back again and again, the sea. He wasn't used to it, the constant shift and swell, hypnotic and huge.

'I dunno. Probably.'

Did there come a point where you could tune it out, the huge, roiling presence of the ocean? Or did you learn to live with it, half your attention always on the sea.

'At least you're honest.'

His phone buzzed again.

Promise?? Xxx

And he sighed, guilt souring to annoyance in an instant, which was what it was like to have a mother, of course.

I promise xxx

He put the phone back in his pocket. When he looked up, Alex was eyeing him, like she was trying to decide something.

'They really do nest up here, you know.'

Ben blinked. 'What?'

The wind whipped at her ponytail and she smiled at him, wide and wild.

'The seagulls. Want to see?'

She gestured over to a gap in the crumbling front of the hotel.

Ben leaned in to see four fluffy little heads, spotted grey and black. They all looked back at him with bright reptilian eyes.

'Fucking hell.'

She leaned her head in to look too. Very close to his own.

'I know.'

She held up a hand for a second, as if she was going to touch one, gazing at the little birds with fierce joy. Just a second. Then she dropped her hand and stepped away.

'There's a storm coming.'

Now he was up close, the angle of the bench made him even more uncomfortable. There wasn't enough cliff left to support any kind of a structure, and you couldn't even scramble back, if you were sitting. That bench's days were numbered, as surely as the front of the hotel. Both of them, so obviously, waiting to drop.

'I've heard.'

Almost as if she knew what he was thinking, Alex rolled her neck and stretched back. Her whole torso over the edge. Ben tried not to wince.

'I've heard you don't really get storms in London.'

'Of course we do.'

She smiled and looked over at the beach below.

'Houses down? Power down? Trees blocking the road for days?'

He followed her gaze and stared down to the beach below.

'Okay. We don't.'

Below them, there was some kind of wreck. It took him a moment to work out what – at first all he could take in was the jagged edges of broken wood, plasterboard, the odd spoke of twisted metal reaching up like robot fingers. As he looked, it resolved itself and he saw an old electric cooker, dented but intact, and a swirl of patterned upholstery that must be a sofa. It was a caravan, smashed to pieces and partly obscured by the green slime of the sea, but unmistakeable once he realised. He remembered now – a scrambled couple of texts in early lockdown. The caravan had fallen. He looked to the not-empty caravan park, and back down.

He was silent for a while. Then, 'What's it like?'

She shrugged. 'I don't know. It's home. What's London like?'

He thought of lights, of shops and streets and always music or traffic or shouting or something, and of the idea of walking off the edge of a cliff being ridiculous, when it wasn't. Not really.

'Yeah. Home. I suppose we'd have to ask Jen, to know the difference.'

Alex raised an eyebrow.

'Yep.'

But neither of them made a move. A seagull wheeled and Alex smoked and he stood and they both stared out to sea.

The forecourt of the pub thrummed with laughter and chatter in the glow of the evening sun, and Ben was uneasy. It seemed like there were more people here tonight than a village this size could possibly hold, as if people had come from miles around to stand by the sea and drink bottles of San Miguel in a car park and pretend for an evening that life was normal again.

'Next please.'

Ben had ended up working behind the bar, of course, along with Alex and Si, and Jen too. As much as Jen had absolutely insisted that she'd booked enough staff to work, that he was just there to enjoy the night, have a beer on the beach and a stare up at the stars, that she herself would only be popping in for the odd five minutes to check and make sure things were going smoothly, he had known that it was inevitable. If your girlfriend runs a pub, you're going to find yourself behind the bar of it before too long, that was just the way of things, and it was fine – he wasn't above the odd bar shift. But he couldn't help but find it annoying how she hadn't even asked him directly. For that or for helping with the cleaning today. She just seemed to assume that if there was slack, he'd step in to fill it. It had felt slippery, these last two days of spending time with her, like he wasn't getting the full picture. He'd always liked that she was so straightforward.

The cab driver was next in line. Chris, his name was,

and the brother had turned out to be Si, and the whole lot of them had known each other since they were foetuses apparently.

'Three bottles of lager, mate, cheers.'

On instinct, Ben took a step back, and the cabbie looked affronted. Ben had felt the guy's breath on his face. While he wasn't too good for bar work, surely they all agreed that no one should be doing it in the middle of a pandemic. But no one seemed bothered. Another thing Jen had assumed would be fine.

'Here you go,' Ben said, making his arm stretch as long as possible to hand over the drinks and forcing a smile that Chris did not return. Jen had promised that all of this would be socially distanced. Beyond the fact that there was a table with a cash box on it between him and the customers, it was hard to know what that meant.

'Cheers,' Chris said, with an air of deep menace. He took his beers and went to stand with a knot of his friends, a couple of feet away from the table.

'Oi, lads, can you go down to the beach please?' Ben forced his face into its least threatening smile. 'It's takeaway only.'

Jen came back up through the pub, arms full of bottles of beer. They kept selling out. The little cash box on the table was overflowing. They'd been really good before all this, him and Jen. Surely she'd snap out of it soon.

Chris nodded towards Jen. 'It's her pub, mate,' he said, from his station three feet away. His voice dripped with sarcasm on the word mate. 'Let her run it however she wants to, yeah?'

Ben let himself scowl and pulled a few tepid bottles out

of the box Jen had brought and lined them up on the table. They'd run out of cold ones within half an hour of opening, and now they were emptying the cellar. Ben had been studiously avoiding looking at the best-before dates on them so he didn't feel duty-bound to moan about something else as well.

'Yeah, well, apparently I'm working at it. So I get some kind of say about the way it's run while I'm on shift, don't I? Mate.'

Chris twisted his torso around to display his full width to Ben, which was a transparent and pathetic attempt to intimidate him, even if it did make Ben wish he'd bothered with his YouTube kettlebell routines a few more times before he'd shoved them under the bed two weeks into lockdown.

'All right, chill out. You should be glad of the work. The rest of us are from here, we've been part of this community for years, yeah?'

Ben bristled at the mention of community. He was surprised it'd taken this long for someone to tell him flatly he wasn't from around here, if he was honest.

'Glad of the work? I'm a fucking solicitor.'

'Well, why don't you fuck back off to London and solicit something, then?' said Si, and Ben looked at him, surprised. He hadn't picked up that Si had a problem with him. They'd been behind the cash box elbow to elbow for more than an hour now and he'd seemed pretty amiable so far.

'Leave it, Si,' said Jen.

But he carried on, red-faced and belligerent, looking like any arsehole causing trouble on the tube for no reason. 'Fucking turning up and taking our work away and then saying you don't even want it when you get here, what the fuck?' He turned to his brother, as if appealing to him. 'He's a cheeky fucking prick.'

Alex popped open a beer, but she didn't hand it to the old man who stood in front of her, far too frail and unmasked for it to be a good idea for him to turn up to the pub. Ben felt a lurch of nausea deep within him. It might have been legal to open up tonight. That didn't make it the right thing to do.

'What's up, Si, you jealous?'

A look of horror flashed across Jen's face. Ben wouldn't have thought anything of it, if it wasn't for that.

'What?'

But Alex just shrugged and handed over the bottle. The old man pressed the exact change into her hand and she threw it into the cashbox.

Ben frowned. 'Why would he be jealous?'

'Didn't she even tell you?'

'Leave it, Alex,' Jen said. Her jaw was hard and tight and she was glaring daggers at Alex.

Alex turned to Ben, eyes wide, clearly having so much fun.

'She's got very snakey since she's moved back here, hasn't she? She used to be a lot more straightforward.'

Ben privately agreed.

'Why would Si be jealous?' he said.

'Oh, he's her ex. I'm surprised she didn't mention it.'

'Alex!' Jen said.

'Yeah, they were proper high-school sweethearts. Stayed together ages through uni, too. Sad it didn't work out, really. Because I had to go out with him instead.' Alex flashed around a malicious little smile. 'I really don't see why she wouldn't have said anything. Unless . . .'

She left the sentence hanging in the air. In a detached kind of way, Ben was impressed. She was good at what she did, Alex. That was a fine performance. And he wouldn't have been taken in by any of it, if it hadn't been for the fact that Jen looked like Alex had just slapped her.

The old bloke tottered off and a man in his thirties swaggered up to the table. He nodded around the group.

'All right, Chris? Nice to see you again after all this bullshit. Didn't catch you at the beach party last month?'

Chris looked uncomfortable. It wasn't an expression that sat easily on his face. 'Nah. My mum, yeah . . .'

Ben appealed to Jen again. 'Come on, this is ridiculous now.' He turned back to the man in front of him, who wasn't smiling any more. He looked decidedly unfriendly. 'Everyone will have to move along before we can serve you. It's packed round here, it's meant to be takeaway only.'

And he felt a warning hand, heavy on his shoulder. Ben tried to shrug it off, but Si was taller than him and kept hold tight.

'Oi, mate. You might be a fucking solicitor or whatever, but this is my job. My livelihood. So don't fuck it up for us, yeah?'

Again, he could feel someone else's breath on his face. It was a sensation he hadn't missed. Fuck, he might have to stay in a hotel for a few days when he got back, to make sure Mum didn't get it. Which he couldn't afford, despite the illegal, and no doubt, unpaid bar shift. Fuck.

Chris leaned in, grinning. 'Remember me, yeah? You still got my number? For any time you want to just fuck off and leave us. You just give me a bell.'

His breath, on Ben's face, too. So many people, all pressed together, and breaking the rules, and endangering everyone, him, them, his mum, that random old man . . . And for what? To get intimidated in a car park.

Fuck that.

'Right. I'm out,' he said. He reached up to his shoulder and took Si's hand off. He was so surprised, he let him easily.

'What?' Jen said. She looked panicked. Ben felt a private, petty thrill. At least he had her attention. 'Don't go.'

Ben stepped out from behind the table and headed to the beach.

He took lungful after lungful of breath as soon as he wasn't packed in with other people and felt immediately calmer.

Jen ran after him and fell into step beside him, but he didn't slow down. He wanted to be somewhere where people weren't for a bit.

'Ben! Come on. What am I meant to do?' she said.

'You're meant to manage the situation, Jen. You're meant to clear them out of that car park, and if they won't leave, you shut it all down.'

She looked genuinely faint at the suggestion.

'I can't.'

Ben shrugged. It was liberating, the feeling of not caring. Everything felt easier when you didn't care that much anymore, and something had shifted, and he found that he didn't. Maybe it was the pandemic, or this place, or her dad's death, but something seemed to have changed for Jen. She wasn't who he thought she was. He wondered if he'd ever really known her at all.

'Right, well, I can't either. I'm off for a walk.'

He was on the beach now, sand shifting beneath his feet. Why would everyone want to stay so close to the pub, when this was right here, and deserted? Idiots.

'Ben!' Jen said. She was looking teary now, but Ben found himself oddly unmoved by it.

'Catch you later, Jen.'

'Why are you being such a prick?' she said.

Ben wheeled round.

'I took a risk coming here, you know? I've barely left the house these last four months, except to look after Mum. But I thought it was worth it, to see you.'

She sniffed and then rolled her eyes.

'Oh, come on.'

He made a conscious effort to unclench his fists. Everyone was so aggressive round here, he'd had to watch out for it rubbing off on him.

'What's that supposed to mean?'

She delicately dabbed underneath her eyes with a tissue. It came away stained brown, He'd thought she wasn't wearing make-up this week, It was upsetting that he couldn't tell.

'I know you've been going to the protests.'

He stared at her, mouth open.

'That's different.'

'How is it different?'

And she didn't even seem embarrassed, to be saying this. To be comparing asserting a moral right to illegally selling booze from a trestle table.

'Because that's a fucking human rights issue, that's why it's different.'

She rolled her eyes again. Rolled her fucking eyes, at him mentioning human rights.

'Look, I get that it's important, but this is important too. There's nothing keeping this community together apart from this. This isn't London. There's nothing to do here, nothing. No practical support, no mental health support. Community's everything here.'

Community, community, like a Tory running for local councillor. Ben realised with a jolt that he didn't know how Jen voted. Not 100 per cent. She always seemed like she agreed with him, when he talked about politics. He'd just assumed.

'Everyone needs that,' he said. 'That's not about here.'

'It is. This place has been marginalised for decades, there's no work, it's hard to live.'

Hard to live? Harder to live than if people in power kept murdering people who looked like you?

'It's not getting killed by the police, though, is it?'

She winced when he said that. Like it was a really low blow. Like it wasn't the absolute heart of the argument.

'It doesn't have to be. It's still important.'

'Oh what, because all lives matter, is that it?'

At that, she looked genuinely hurt. Was that because she really felt like she'd been misunderstood? Or because she thought that being accused of racism was worse than having someone perpetrate racism against you?

'Fuck off. I didn't say that. Fuck off.'

Ben took a deep breath. And another one. The wind was picking up, and he was glad of it.

'What are you saying, then?'

'I'm saying it's different here. This isn't London. We really need this.'

We. She'd lived here three months, after spending half a lifetime putting as much distance between herself and the north as possible, losing her accent, barely mentioning it, and now it was we.

'You think we don't want to have a pint in London?'

She tossed her head. Some strands of hair had worked their way out of the bun and were being pulled off her face by the wind. He'd normally think she looked lovely.

'In London, if an entire fucking borough fell into the sea, the news might mention it. The government might do something. Here, we're invisible, and there's nowhere else. It's just a harmless bit of release, that's all.'

But he was already too angry to hear her properly.

'There's nothing in London either! There's even less there! Here, you've got the sea, you've got the cliffs, you've got a hundred people you know all living within five minutes' walk of you. You think there's, what, people strolling down the South Bank arm in arm in London? Cosy picnics in Hyde Park? The only time I've been into central London was to come here. I've not left Peckham for months. You've got no idea how easy you lot have got it. Every house with a garden and walking distance from the sea, are you shitting me?'

Ben was breathing hard, his heart thumping. He'd been putting a brave face on things for a long time. For his mum, for his friends, for himself. But being cooped up in a little flat with nothing to do apart from read the news on his phone and wash tins of chickpeas had taken its toll on him.

'All right,' she said, holding her hands up in mock surrender. 'Jesus. I get the point. You're always so aggressive.'

'I'm not aggressive,' he said, making his voice quiet and smooth, as non-aggressive as possible. It was easy. He did it a lot. A reasonable voice, for unreasonable people. 'I'm just sick of this. I don't know why you're kissing up to these people so much.'

She frowned at him. Like he was the unreasonable one.

'It's my dad's pub, Ben. I need to do him proud.'

'Where's that come from, though?'

She blinked and plucked a strand of hair off her face. The wind was even stronger now. It whipped the waves into foamed peaks, like underdone meringues.

'What do you mean?'

Like she didn't understand. But was it real? Or was it just to get out of the argument, or buy herself a bit of time? Because he'd noticed her doing that, once or twice. No decent feminist pretends to be stupid so people go easy on her.

'You never seemed to care that much about the pub when he was alive.'

She stared him down, face hard as flint.

'I don't know what you're talking about.'

Had she ever even said she was a feminist?

'Jen, until the pandemic I didn't even know your dad had a pub.'

She chewed at her lip.

'You must have done. I must have told you.'

He laughed at that, a mirthless bark of a laugh that was immediately snatched away by the wind.

'Just like you told your mum that I was black?'

Big, wounded eyes again. Like all of this was his fault.

'You said you were fine with that.'

He hadn't.

'Tell me you can't see why this worries me,' he said. 'It's like you have these two selves, and they've got nothing to do with each other. You have to know how weird that is. It's like there's a whole side of you that I've never seen before.'

And she looked back at him, straight. No doe eyes, no fake misunderstanding. Just her.

'Well, you're seeing it now.'

She looked so beautiful. It was a shame he'd probably never touch her again.

'Yeah. I am.'

Neither of them said anything else. The wind raged on above the roar of the sea and the people chatting and laughing in the distance. They sounded so far away.

The first fat drops of rain fell and Ben watched them splat dark circles onto the pavement. He shivered and pulled his hood up. His mum had been right – it was freezing up here. He was looking forward to telling her that. He was looking forward to seeing her, to being home, to being out of this place.

'Do you have your ticket, Ben?'

He smiled at Alison. She wasn't that bad. It was obvious how lonely she was.

'Yes, Mrs Fletcher. Thanks.'

Ben clocked an old lady walking across the street. She was limping hastily by, casting scared, darting looks in his direction. Ben sighed and pulled the hood back down. A raindrop landed squarely in the middle of his forehead.

Jen scowled at her mother and, because it seemed like it was catching, letting your inner teenager out, Ben had to stop himself squirming with embarrassment, because she was going to get a right bollocking if she carried on like that.

'They don't have tickets anymore, Mum.'

But they were adults really. All that happened was that Alison looked hurt, and a little more frail then she had before.

'Don't be silly, Jenny.'

Ben took off his glasses and rubbed them on his T-shirt, trying to pretend the conversation wasn't happening.

'I'm not being silly. It's just a fact. He won't have the ticket, it'll be on his phone.'

'How can you get on the train without a ticket? That's nonsense.'

Ben put his glasses back on, and they were immediately speckled with rain again. It was picking up. Getting worse.

'When was the last time you were on a train, Mum?'

And Alison looked alarmed, as if she hadn't really thought about it and the answer was upsetting, and Ben couldn't stand it anymore.

'You can get them to print out tickets for you if you go to the counter, Mrs Fletcher.'

Alison grinned triumphantly at Jen, who shot him a glare. Let her. He wasn't actually a teenager, no matter what it felt like in this weird little village. He would be back in London in time for the ten o'clock news with a cup of tea and a list of excuses for his mum about why she didn't really need to worry as much as everyone said.

'There's a storm coming,' Alison said, as the rain fell with more urgency, audibly thumping onto the ground around them. Ben looked over to the clouds swarming on the horizon, a heavy tarmac grey. Where had the sunny little seaside village he'd come to gone? It felt like a lot more than a couple of days he'd been in Ravenspurn. It felt like an entire season.

Alison was looking at him, as if she was expecting a response.

Ben shrugged obligingly, and she nodded, satisfied at his response.

'You don't get storms like this in London. Not real ones. It's only out in the country that you get real weather.'

'Oh, what do you know about it, Mum? Of course they get real weather in London.'

The two women glared at each other and Ben willed the taxi to turn up.

Alison smiled at him, sweet as candy floss. 'What do you think, Ben? Are there more storms here? Does it rain less in London?'

He offered a tight little smile back. The best he could do. 'I don't know.'

Jen glared at him, and he wondered, not for the first time since last night, if he'd been wrong about her this whole time. Maybe she was another spoilt little princess like all the other girls at the firm, just with some slightly flattened vowels.

'What do you mean, you don't know? You have to know. Make a decision.'

And he wasn't planning on telling her until he got home. He'd ring her, which would be more respectful than doing it by text, and think about some good times he could mention, maybe lay it on thick about needing more time to look after his mum. But he reckoned he'd made his decision.

'No, I don't know. I don't have to. It's just totally different, isn't it? London's got more places to shelter. It's not just about the storms.'

The rain got heavier and Jen shot him a look that made it fairly obvious that she thought he was a pretentious twat. Well, Jen could think what she liked.

Chris rolled up in his cab, windows open despite the rain and nu metal blasting out, booming around the street. Was there anything in this village that wasn't stuck some time in the mid-noughties?

'Right. Thought it'd be you. You off back to London then?'

Chris was wearing sunglasses. It took a special kind of twat to wear sunglasses in the middle of a rainstorm, no matter how hungover you were. And he would be hungover. He'd already been three drinks deep when Ben had left the pub, and that was early. Jen hadn't come home for another four hours. The two of them had curled up, carefully separate, clinging tight to opposite sides of the bed.

'Yep,' Ben said. Screw it. There weren't that many cars around for Chris to crash into, and he'd rather take his chances than stay here any longer.

Chris opened the boot and made to pick up Ben's weekend bag. Ben was suddenly embarrassed by it. Si and Chris wouldn't have spotless little wheeled suitcases. They'd have knackered, grubby old camping backpacks that might look like they were falling apart but could hold their own body-weight again for them to climb up a mountain with, easy. Well, Jen was welcome to these men, with their ruggedness. Men who didn't have to put their hoods up, and didn't have to pull them down again. Who knew how to face down a storm. They were welcome to her.

'I can do it,' Ben said, ridiculously, and Chris shrugged and stood aside.

Ben lifted his little suitcase and stashed it in the boot before turning reluctantly to Jen and her mum. The three of them stood there, awkward and unmoving on the pavement. Jen clearly wanted to say something to him.

'Okay. Well. Text me when you're home.'

He nodded and offered her half a smile. Was she going to apologise, maybe?

'I will.'

Because maybe it was all a misunderstanding. People

did say things in anger. Stupid, stupid things. If she could convince him that she didn't mean them, that she wasn't really that person, that he'd been right all along about her, then maybe it would all be fine. It would be great if it could all be fine.

She walked over to him. Was she going for a hug after all? A last time, to hold her and smell her hair and pretend. He might like that. But, instead, she leaned over to Chris.

'You seen Alex today?'

Ben would have punched the car if he'd been that sort of guy. But he was being stupid. He knew the drill. People didn't change.

Chris was still and indifferent behind his sunglasses.

'Nah. Not yet. Why?'

Jen let out a sigh and straightened up.

'It's just . . . Nah. Forget it.'

'What's there to forget?' Chris said.

Ben had seen blokes like Chris before. It was funny how the men that fancied themselves as the hardest ones loved gossip with a passion. It was all about people, toughness and tittle-tattle. The same thing, if you thought about it. Jen seemed to think it was only people in small villages who were interested in each other's lives, rather than that being the foundation of human society.

'I think she's got something of mine. I can ask her later.'

He never had told her about the watch. He didn't feel guilty. It's not like it would make her feel better. When things got in your head that way, the only thing you could do was work out a way to let them go. Knowing more never helped. Ben pulled open the cab door.

'My train's at ten. Cheers, mate,' Ben said.

Jen started, as if she'd forgotten he was even there. An inconvenient other slice of life already receding, slotting back where it had come from.

He was glad they'd never moved in together. He wouldn't have seen his mum for months otherwise. He'd never have forgiven Jen for that.

Alison seemed unfazed by his rudeness. She offered him a sunny smile. 'It's been lovely meeting you, Ben. I hope to see you again.'

He held up a hand from the back seat in a kind of wave-salute. Very awkward. Not something he'd try again.

'Absolutely, Mrs Fletcher.' He was pretty sure he would never see this woman again for as long as he lived.

'Call me Alison!' she said, beaming.

Ben noted with relief that the moment had passed. He couldn't have hugged Jen now even if he'd wanted to. He didn't want to. Maybe it would be awkward for them, when they went back to work, but the idea of going back to work seemed very distant now. Very difficult to worry about when there was so much right there in front of him to think about.

Ben waved at the women and got into the back of the taxi.

'Oh, and good luck!' Alison said.

Ben stuck his head out of the window, a moment's relief from the smell of stale lager and the sound of Limp Bizkit.

'What was that?'

'Good luck! You know. With the Black Lives Matter.'

Jen went beetroot red and Ben allowed himself a smile.

'Thanks, Alison,' he said. And Chris pulled away and Ben

turned his head to get one last glimpse of the sea. He never had managed to go swimming. He would have liked to, even though he knew it would have been cold.

Jenny creaked the door of the pub open and sighed. It was worse than she remembered. When they'd finally finished serving, going way past eleven as it seemed such a shame to deny her dad's old regulars *just one more drink*, *just one more*, *go on*, *pet*, *just one more*, it had seemed perfectly reasonable to do the clean-up herself the next morning. It hadn't looked so bad, and besides, she hadn't booked Si and Alex to help with it and she didn't want to admit that she'd fucked up again.

'Good grief.'

She hadn't expected her mum to want to come along. Alison normally made up any excuse not to come into the pub – apart from the wake, as far as Jenny was aware, she hadn't set foot in the place in years. But as awkward as having Ben over had been, as much of a disaster as it was, his absence had really left a hole in the house. Her mother seemed like she didn't want to be left alone, and Jenny could feel it too – after the brief return of a third person, the house felt emptier than ever.

It was nice to be wanted, at least. Even if it was just as a replacement for your own boyfriend.

'It's just a few bottles,' Jenny said, trying to inject an air of authority into her voice.

It wasn't. There was rubbish overflowing on the floor, which was tacky with beer leaking from bin bags full of empties and mud and sand that the four of them had trailed in. Cleaning materials lay haphazardly around the place, and the whole space had the same air of being abandoned that it had before they'd started.

'How many people came last night? You must have taken a fortune.'

'I haven't counted up yet,' Jenny said, and she could tell she sounded defensive. But Si and Alex had both commented on it, angling for a bonus, no doubt, and Pete had slurred something on his way out as well, about her certainly making the best of the hand that life had given her and didn't she always, and Ben had been silently judging her, of course, just like he always was. Like he thought that it was immoral to make money somehow, even though she knew what he earned and it was more than her, if they were going to split hairs.

'It must have been a fortune,' Alison said again.

Jenny shrugged. 'I have to pay wages. Stock. There are overheads I'm behind on that weren't paused . . .'

It was true that she hadn't counted up, but it was a decent amount. It had been obvious.

'You sound just like him,' Alison said, lips thin and tight.

Jenny heaved a deep sigh, and picked up a bag, spinning it shut. Maybe on balance she'd prefer her mother's usual silence to this.

'You asked me about his pub.'

'More than that. You've got that same air about you that he did with this place. Like it's got under your skin.'

Under her skin. What a silly thing to say. What was the point of building a place up, of giving it your time, your energy, your life, if you were going to hold yourself separate from it?

'It was his livelihood. He built it up for forty years. Of course it was under his skin.'

Her mother wrinkled up her nose like Jenny had said something unpleasant.

'Yes, that's what he said too. Funny, how you've turned out to be so like him.'

Alison said that like it was an insult. Jenny wondered, not for the first time, why she'd stayed married for so long to a man she obviously disliked.

'Why's it funny? You mean because I wasn't here?'

Jenny was hurt, waiting to start a fight, but her mother didn't rise to it. Of course she didn't. She only blinked.

'That's not what I mean.'

Jenny heaved up a bin bag and dropped it just outside the door. The car park was even worse. She tried hard not to look too closely at what a gull was pecking beside the wall. Perhaps she would get Si and Alex back. She'd have to eat her words a bit, but they'd be glad of the work.

'I'm here now.'

Alison stared out at the scene and sniffed. 'I hope all this mess was worth the money.'

Jenny shut the door and went back to the cleaning-supplies cupboard. She was sure she'd seen some spray cleaner in there, in among the dusty rags and bottles of Brasso that looked like they were as old as she was.

'It wasn't about the money.'

Alison pursed her mouth. She'd done that so often, over so many years, that the puckers it created around her lips seemed to be permanent now. Your face is a map of all the expressions you've ever formed, and there's no way to cheat it. Not really.

'What was it about, then?'

Jenny sighed and plucked out an almost empty bottle of Flash.

'The community.'

'That's what Ted used to say as well. The community, acting like he was doing the village some great favour, abandoning his family to sell booze to a load of pissheads.'

Jenny frowned. That was angry, for Alison. Much, much more than she ever usually showed. But her father had been around all the time when Jenny was a child. He'd walked her to school every morning before he opened the pub up, and got Pete to cover the day shift for him most weekends when she was small.

'He didn't abandon us.'

Unexpected as snowfall, her mother reached out and stroked Jenny's hair.

'No. He didn't abandon you.'

For a moment, Jenny enjoyed the touch. Then she moved her head back, and bent down to pick up another bag.

'This shouldn't take too long. We could watch that Olivia Colman thing you liked the look of later . . .'

The rubbish bag split, sending empty bottles skittering across the floor. A wedge of kitchen roll, sodden with old beer, flopped out onto the floor after them. The air reeked of stale yeast.

'Oh, Jenny,' her mother said, in a tone of voice that catapulted Jenny right back in time to being five years old. As if she'd done it on purpose. Her mother had always done that – Jenny had never meant to forget her PE kit or get a B on a test. Who did? But Alison had always behaved as if Jenny did these things as deliberate personal slights against her.

'What, you think I meant to drop it?'

Jenny sighed and rummaged for more bin bags and kitchen roll.

'You should be more careful.'

She pulled off a bag and started stuffing bottles into it. She made sure to put the rest of the roll within easy reach of her mother, who ignored it.

'At least I'm doing something. Why come with me if you were only ever going to stand around bitching about it?'

Jenny tore off a wad of paper and left the rest next to the bin bags.

'Jenny, language,' her mother said, and did not reach for the paper towels or the bin bags. She just stood, watching, projecting an aura of faint disapproval.

'What happened to Dad's old watch?'

The words slipped out before Jenny even realised she was going to say them. Alison looked shocked.

'Jenny!'

The two women glared at each other, but Jenny held her gaze firm. It was only a question.

'What? I'm just asking. Where did it go?'

Alison sighed and glared down at an empty crisp box. It was as openly pissed off as Jenny had ever seen her look – normally, she used a lot of snippy words and wounded silences. Under the surface and unsaid, always. Not like Ben or Alex or Si, who said what they were thinking and trusted themselves to fight and then move on, rather than carrying around every tiny grudge with them for ever.

Alison raised her glare to meet Jenny's eye and it was funny – she'd always used the threat of getting cross, when Jenny was a child. *Don't do that or I'll get cross*, and *Put it back or we'll fall out, you and I*, and it had worked – Jenny had spent her whole childhood walking on eggshells. And then, as a teenager, when she'd started noticing that it was weird to have a mum who never, ever shouted, but never swept you up in a big hug either, or laughed with you, or ever, ever cried, she'd craved it: a loss of control – thrilling and enticing, and validating. But now she was seeing it, as an adult, it wasn't so scary at all. It also didn't make her feel any more noticed than she had before.

'Haven't you got enough?' Alison said.

Jenny felt a deep punch to her gut.

'What?'

Alison was leaning on the bar, and Jenny noticed that her knuckles were white. As if she was clinging on.

'You got everything. All the money he had, and this place, and you know you'll get the house too when I'm gone. Isn't that enough for you? You want an old watch too? Every little corner of him?'

Jenny's mind was racing.

'You've still got it, then? You kept it.'

Alison's jaw was set and hard.

'That London has made you very . . . grasping, you know.'

Jenny dropped the clump of kitchen roll she was holding.

'I don't want it for myself. I just want to know where it is. If you've got it, that's fine.'

Grasping? What was that supposed to mean? Just because she sold beer for one night and wanted to know what happened to an old watch?

'I can't talk to you when you're like this. I'll see you at home.'

Alison slapped the bar and stalked out of the pub. That same old threat of anger that she'd always used on Jenny, simmering with promise and unsaid things. But Jenny wasn't afraid of the things left untold any more.

'It's only a question. Why can't I ask a simple fucking question?'

But Jenny was shouting at ghosts in a dusty pub, which seemed all the bigger now she was left alone in it again.

Jenny had missed the view and the air and even the climb, to her surprise. She hadn't done it when Ben was here, and she'd felt restless. Her legs were used to it now. They needed the stretch and push and burn of the cliff.

Or maybe it was him, that had her restless. Difficult to say.

She sucked in a deep breath of seaweed and ozone, but the twitchy, crawling feeling that had been building ever since she'd left London didn't lessen at all. She kept thinking about what people were doing in London without her. Her house-mates Adam and Priya, who, in normal times, she would go for an awkward glass of wine with if someone had a birthday or a new job, but otherwise would pass in the mornings, wrapped in dressing gowns and silent as if they were commuters on the tube, walking through their careful choreography so that no one had to queue for the shower or the kettle or the toaster. Adam and Priya would be proper friends now – they'd have had no choice. Jenny thought of them and their cosy little chats and their nights in and the favourite takeaway that they'd have now, and their shared favourite films that were stupid but that they loved anyway because they were theirs.

Should she have stayed? She couldn't go back. They'd sublet the room to one of Adam's posho mates, and besides, it would be much worse if she was there and being left out. At least while she was here she could pretend that it was distance, and not simply preference.

And Ben, of course. She'd missed him so much, she'd given in on a visit. But she should have known it was a bad idea. She should have known that she shouldn't show this part of herself to people, the part that was left out, that people said was spoilt, stuck up. The part that felt invisible half of the time, irrelevant. She should have kept it hidden.

She checked her phone. Two bars, which would do. She scrolled through a long list of names of people she never, ever got in touch with, looking for Si. There was no way she'd be able to clean up the pub on her own, and no way she was going to ask Alex for help.

It would have been quicker to go round. But it seemed less embarrassing, less personal, somehow, to call. It was weird, to be his boss, but it would be weirder to be his friend.

Just as she found the number, her phone rang, glowing and vibrating in her hand like something alive and angry. Jenny jumped. Her phone never rang, not now she lived with her mother. It was unnatural. She pressed the button to pick up.

'Hello?'

'Hi, Jen.'

It was Ben, and he was using his work voice. Smooth and non-aggressive and very obviously braced for a difficult conversation. Jenny felt her spine prickle.

'Oh, hey. Did you get home okay?'

'Yes.'

There was a long pause. Jenny reached for something to say to him, something normal. She desperately wanted this conversation to be normal.

'How was the train?'

'Weird,' he said, sounding like himself again. 'Being on a train is still weird.'

Another long pause.

Jenny swallowed down a tight, swollen feeling in her throat and stared out to the horizon, smudged with clouds and dark with the threat of more rain. It was rare that you could pick out the horizon, out here. It blurred into the sea.

'What did you think of Ravenspurn?' she said, and immediately regretted it. Now he could say anything to her, and it would be almost impossible to pretend that she didn't care what his answer was. Stupid, stupid.

She'd thought that she'd grown out of this feeling. The itch of paranoia, the feeling that everyone was talking about you behind your back, whispering poison from ear to ear. Was it this place? Was there something about a village that meant that people could see you more clearly to pick you apart? Or that made them want to? Maybe it was that there had been this impulse all along and everywhere, and it was only now that she had more time, she noticed. Either way, Jenny had grown tired of the constant thrum of unease that came with a certainty that she wasn't liked, that she didn't belong.

When Ben replied, he used his diplomatic voice.

'It was interesting. It was nice to see where you come from.'

Jenny couldn't help letting out a tiny snort.

'Did you like anything about it?'

Another pause. Everywhere and always, a pause.

'I liked the view.'

Jenny tilted her face to the sky and felt the bite of wind on her cheeks.

'Anything else?'

'Alex.' Jenny felt her eyes pop open in surprise. He wasn't being so diplomatic now. 'I know you don't, though.'

A piece of honesty, at least. But the problem with that is that it can leave you with little left to say. So you have to go back to your scripts. Like, 'Well. It was nice to have you. Thank you for coming.'

But that just made you feel all the more disconnected. Talking to someone and saying nothing was worse, in a way, than not speaking at all. But who could get by without speaking at all?

'Thank you for having me.'

She decided to risk a joke, or maybe to pick a scab. It was hard to tell the difference sometimes.

'You're not calling me to break up with me then?'

Another silence, that stretched and stretched and stretched.

'Look. Jenny . . .'

'Yes?'

And she knew, of course, what he was going to say. They'd started another script. But she wasn't about to spare him the unpleasantness.

'It's just a really hard time at the moment. My mum's really not well and she needs—'

'My dad's fucking dead, Ben. You're not the only one who's had it hard.'

A pause, and she could almost see him doing that thing where he pressed his temples as if he could physically push a headache away. She was the headache. She was the thing that he wanted to push away.

'I know that, Jen. It's not a competition.'

'Why bring it up then?'

A childish strategy. A filibuster, of sorts. If he was arguing with her, then he had to stay on the phone. As long as he was still talking, she still existed.

'All right. Forget that.'

She didn't speak. She made him finish the thought.

'I can't have you talking to me like that. I can't have you talking about my politics like that. It's too important.'

'What?'

Her voice sounded very small and sad when it came out.

'I think you heard.'

Jenny remembered. The beach, and the fight. He'd seemed so smug, so sure of his rightness. He was the one who wasn't listening to her, wasn't he?

'What did I say about your politics?'

A tired sigh from the other end of the line.

'Look, Jen, I'm not running over the same fight again. Let's not make things hard for ourselves.'

She let out a laugh. High and hard. Like a seagull.

'Hard for you, you mean.'

And there was another little sigh and even the sound of the air leaving his throat was painfully familiar. He was her longest ever relationship. She'd never told him that.

'Why are you fighting for this so hard?'

Jenny squeezed her eyes shut. *Because I love you because I love you because I love you.*

'I don't know.'

He cleared his throat, in a way that was achingly familiar. It's the end of the meeting, time to wrap up, get your coat.

'Look. Take care, okay?'

And he left a pause. A beat. Two. And he hung up.

Jenny stared at the handset, numb. It would have been nice to get the last word. Some kind of small comfort.

She sat on the bench and stared out at the sea and tried to hold back a tide of humiliation and loneliness and a scuttering little worm of fear.

This feeling was so familiar. A hollow ache, a sense of deep wrongness. The same feeling as a Saturday afternoon with nothing to do, the feeling of no one to sit with on the bus, of whispers at lunch, of conversations falling silent when you enter a room. A teenage palette of feelings that the brights of her early twenties had painted over, but the streaks were showing, stronger and stronger.

She assumed she'd grown out of it.

You don't grow out of anything. Not really.

But what can you do? You can't force people to like you. You can only force them to notice you. The irresistible urge to niggle and pick, to make yourself feel visible again. Alex, aged thirteen, pretending she didn't exist. Ben, aged thirty-seven, pretending she didn't exist. Inescapable.

She did fucking exist.

Jenny sniffed deeply and swiped angrily at her face. She didn't have time for any of this. She stabbed at her phone and counted the rings. He'd have it on silent, of course, like everyone else who didn't have a relative who might need them at a moment's notice. To her surprise, Si picked up on the second one.

'Hey.'

She hated the sound of her own voice. So high, and forced,

and southern now. She wished she'd kept her accent. Loads of people did. It was so tempting, to let it soften and round out, when you moved, to let your edges get rubbed away so that you didn't stand out. But you could let yourself get rubbed as smooth as a sea pebble, and you'd never really fit in. All you were left with was a voice, a face, a life, that didn't fit in either place anymore.

'Hiya.'

He sounded like he'd been asleep when she called. And why not? What else was there to do, these days? They all had to find something, or they'd go mad. Banana bread wasn't cutting it anymore, for anyone.

'Will you come in and help with clean-up?' Then, on impulse, 'I'll pay you double.'

There was a pause.

'What? Really?'

The note of hope in his voice made her feel like a real prick. She fucking hated being someone's boss. The responsibility, the judgement. She'd never asked for it. She could have had it, back when she was eighteen, and she'd said no. People always seemed to forget that. This wasn't what she'd wanted.

'Yeah. Cash, obviously.'

'All right.'

She could hear a smile in his voice, and she felt her shoulders drop, just a little. You could count on Si, to be available, and friendly. To make you feel real.

'See you later?'

'Yeah. When?'

Jenny stared down at the guts of the caravan below. They were blurred around the edges now with seaweed and mud.

'When can you get there?'

'I dunno. Tomorrow lunchtime?'

And it might have been her imagination, but she was sure she could hear him smiling. That same old smile.

'See you then.'

This time, it really was a nightmare. Jenny was locked in the pub, her father's pub, her pub, and she needed to get out. She had to call Ben, to tell him, to explain, that she knew what she'd said now, that she was sorry that she hadn't been paying attention, that she was sorry. But every time she opened a door, thinking that this time it would be the way out, all that happened was that she ended up in another room, the same as the one she'd left in almost every way, except for a little smaller, every time. So the more she tried to escape, the smaller the pub became around her, and the bigger she became in comparison, until she could barely squeeze herself through each door. But she still kept going. She had to get out. She had to talk to Ben.

She woke up with a jolt, and for a horrible second, she couldn't breathe. There was something on her face, resting lightly on the skin beneath her nose. Then the thing on her face twitched a little and with a sick sense of falling, Jenny realised that it was alive. Warm and yielding and fleshy.

For a moment, she considered biting. But what might she be biting into? What monster might have come for her to press itself against her, smothering her with soft warmth.

'Noooooooo!'

Jenny choked out the word, half scream, half sob, shoving herself away from the thing, the thing away from her.

Her hands connected with the warm loose skin of the thing and she pushed and shouted and scrambled. To be met, not with some roar or hiss or eldritch rattle, but a small, disappointed sigh.

'Jenny, really.'

Her breath came hard, like it was being ripped from her.

'Mum?'

'Honestly, there's no need to make a fuss. It's only me.'

Jenny sat, hands clawing into her bed sheets, feeling her heart thump, trying to calm down.

'What the fuck are you doing?'

There was a reproachful little pause.

'I was making sure you were okay.'

She rubbed her eyes. They were gritty with tiredness – what time was it? It was fully, properly dark, so it must be well after midnight.

'Why would I not be okay?'

'I don't know.'

Alison sounded small. Old. Perhaps the pause hadn't been reproachful. Perhaps it had been guilty, or something else.

Jenny forced herself to take a deep breath, and a reasonable tone.

'You're in my room. I was asleep.'

There was a long pause, but Jenny could still hear her mother breathing, still closer than she'd like, even though she was pressed up against the bedroom wall now.

'I'm your mother,' Alison said.

Jenny squeezed her eyes shut. She felt as if she was going mad.

'You can't come and touch me when I'm asleep.'

Another pause.

'Don't be ridiculous.'

'I mean it,' Jenny hissed. Ridiculous? She was being ridiculous? 'What the fuck were you playing at?'

Alison didn't hesitate at all this time.

'I wanted to make sure you were still breathing,' Alison snapped out and then made a little gulping noise that might have been a sob.

'What?'

Was this about Ted? Had she cared more than she'd let on, all this time? It'd been months now, though. And Alison hadn't seemed upset since the day of the funeral – though she wouldn't have shown Jenny if she was, she supposed.

'Nothing. Go back to sleep.'

Jenny rubbed her eyes. Her dad hadn't died at home. He'd been in hospital. There was never a moment when Alison would have found him not breathing, and cold, and . . . Jenny forced herself to end the thought there.

'Breathing? Why?'

Alison sniffed. 'Never mind.'

Jenny sat there as the silence stretched. After this year, what did she expect? They'd lived together for three months now and they still barely spoke. There'd never be a time when they'd speak clearly to each other. But Jenny could try, at least. She could try to tell the truth.

'You can't come into my room and touch me in the middle of the night.'

Alison patted the bed, authoritative, and stood up.

'Don't be silly, Jenny. I'll see you in the morning.'

Jenny watched, arms hugged around her ribs, as her

mother retreated from the room. As Alison closed the door, Jenny shouted out, 'This isn't reasonable!'

And she sat alone in the deep dark. Breathing. Still breathing.

Jenny opened the door and let Si in with a gust of sea air and a smattering of raindrops. It had started raining again. It always started raining again. She'd heard stories of heatwaves in London, but it seemed like, for them, summer was over before it had even begun.

Si looked around the pub, lips pursed, taking in all the mess.

'You know you didn't have to pay me double? You know I would have come anyway.'

He pulled a bin bag off a roll.

'Yeah. I know.'

Jenny felt her shoulders lift a little.

'What's going on then?'

He threw bottles into the bag steadily, mechanically. He wasn't like this when Alex was around. With her in the room, he had to be told to do everything.

'We did all right.'

He rolled his eyes. 'Well yeah, course you did. Don't matter, though, does it? You don't pay on commission.'

She shrugged and pulled her own bin bag off the roll. It seemed like a much more manageable task, now he was here. Trivial, almost. It was going to take them under an hour. She wasn't sure what she'd been so worried about.

'Can't I just do something nice?'

He chucked two bottles into the bag and grinned up at her.

'Can I have a bottle to work with then? If you're so into doing nice things.'

She sighed. 'Go on.'

He reached under the bar and pulled out two bottles of San Miguel. Jenny was absolutely sure they'd run out of them. They'd been the first to go. But she said nothing. He cracked them both open and handed one over. She drank, warm lager slipping down her throat, comfortingly disgusting.

'Decent night, the other night.'

She nodded and swept a couple of cans off the bar and into her bin bag. The place was looking better already.

'Yep. Not a bad take.'

He laughed and scooped up four beer bottles with one hand. They made a happy clatter as they hit the others in the bag.

'You sound like him.'

She knitted her eyebrows together.

'Thanks?'

He gave her a smirk, and suddenly it was 2004. Nothing to do but clean up a pub and flirt with Simon Blower and life was simple and good.

'Can I have a fag break?'

Jenny shrugged. He'd been here five minutes. He'd cleared about half the rubbish already. 'Yeah, go on.'

'Cheers.' He leaned his bum against the bar. He was all limbs, a little heavier than he was back in his teens, but still unmistakeably the same old Si. 'There's another storm on the way,' he said, and pulled a rollie from his top pocket.

'Mmm,' Jenny agreed. She dropped her bag of rubbish, embarrassingly empty next to Si's, and perched awkwardly on a bar stool next to him. They were the same height, with her up there. 'You think it'll be a bad one?'

He lit the cigarette. The pub seemed even more itself with the smell of tobacco in the air. Polished wood and spilt beer and tobacco, that was what this pub smelled of. It can't have, though, not for the last fifteen years. Had she even been in here since the smoking ban? She remembered the morning of Ted's funeral. The scent of fresh Lambert and Butler.

'Hard to say, hard to say.' He was looking distracted, tugging at the short hairs at the back of his neck and staring intently at the end of his fag, as if he suspected it of going out.

'Any storm's bad, I suppose,' Jenny said. She thought of London. That wasn't true, there. In London, storms meant cancelled barbecues and gritting your teeth through a wet ten minutes home if you'd forgotten your umbrella (Jenny always forgot her umbrella). Here, a storm was a different beast. Something to be truly afraid of.

'There's bad and bad.' And his eyebrows were wrinkled, meeting in the middle. It was weird to see him worried. It really didn't suit his face. 'Summer is normally just bad. But you get to autumn, you get bad bad.'

She worried at the edge of the beer bottle label with a thumbnail.

'What happens when it gets bad bad?'

He gave her a tight little smile and tipped some lager down his throat. For a moment, he looked so like Chris.

'You know what happens, pet. The fucking hotel falls off the cliff.'

She'd worked enough of the label loose to pull a strip of it off. They always used to say that it meant you were horny, if you were ripping up beer bottle labels. Or maybe that was beer mats? She could never keep track, even when she was a teenager.

'It must have been hard, watching it go like that.'

His face softened into a real smile and he shook his head. 'I'm lucky. My flat's at sea level, isn't it? Mum too.'

She tore another strip from the bottle and slipped off the bar stool, shoving the label into the bag of rubbish at her feet.

'No, I mean . . . You love this place.'

'Yeah. I do.'

He stared out of the window and so did she. The sea was an angry grey, throwing itself again and again at the shore.

'So it must be hard,' she said. 'Watching it go.'

He looked back round, his eyes the same grey as the sea, the same grey they'd always been. Everything about him was so familiar.

'Everything you love dies. That's part of the deal. You have to enjoy stuff while you have it, don't you?'

And he took a step towards her. The broadness of his shoulders and his smell of smoke and sweat. Like sweat, but delicious.

'I suppose so.'

She took a step away and swallowed a mouthful of beer that she didn't enjoy and didn't want. She wasn't sure how much she'd wanted to step away, either. It was what you did though, wasn't it?

'I hope you do. Enjoy stuff, I mean. I hope you've been happy.'

He took a drag of his cigarette and Jenny listened to the crackle of the tobacco and the whisper of the wind and the shush of the waves and the nothing else. Not a word from either of them. Until:

'I hope you've been happy too. Your fancy boyfriend and your job and that,' he said.

She smiled, tightly, and took another drink of beer. She almost wished she smoked. It'd be nice to have something to do with her hands.

'He's not my boyfriend any more. And that won't be my job for much longer. I'm just Jenny again.'

And as she said it, she realised that it was true. Just Jenny. Whatever that meant.

Si stepped back towards her, closing the gap.

'Is that right?'

He grinned. She was so close to him, she could barely see his mouth, but his eyes crinkled at the corners in a way that she remembered so well, it brought a lump to her throat.

'Don't you worry about that. I'll protect you from the big bad storm.'

'Oh fuck off.'

And for a perfect, shining second, Jenny remembered. What it was like to be young, and besotted with someone, and to be 90 per cent sure that they were just about to kiss you. That 10 per cent of doubt adding a thrill to the experience, that little chink of uncertainty that made the kiss all the sweeter when it came.

He leaned forward, or maybe she did. There was so little space between them that it could have been either one of them, or perhaps one of them just taking a breath. Their lips were together, softly at first, barely touching, just brushing themselves together, and then firmly, pressing into each

other. And it was just exactly the same as Jenny remembered. She felt her own body respond, arch against him and
his mouth, in exactly the same way that it always did. Just
for a moment, the kiss was like stepping back in time.

Then Jenny started noticing things. A roughness to the
stubble on his chin that was never there before. An under-
tone to the taste of his lips, an acridness that she didn't
remember. He pushed his tongue into her mouth and it lay
there, flicking listlessly like a whale washed up on the beach.

It wasn't 2004 any more.

'No.'

Jenny pushed him away and stood, heart pounding, staring
at him. Not the Si he'd been at seventeen, not her boyfriend,
not the boy she'd been making eyes at from over a bar for a
long, hot summer. Just a man. That was all.

He stared at her, wide-eyed, saying nothing.

'Look, I . . .' She trailed off. What was there to say?

She really missed Ben.

'Fuck.'

And he stood there, tugging at the hair at the back of his
head the same way he had since he was a kid.

'Yeah. Look, I think you should . . .' Jenny gestured awkwardly towards the door.

'Yeah. Yeah. Sorry.'

He drained the last of his bottle and threw it into a rubbish
bag. He looked like he wanted to climb in along with it.

'I'll still pay. For today, I mean . . .'

And he met her eye, a flash of anger there.

'Don't.'

And Jenny understood then that this wasn't a whim,

for him. This was something he'd been planning. She felt a cold drop down her spine. She should have pushed him away sooner.

'I . . . Sorry. I can't . . .'

The anger mellowed to panic.

'Don't tell her.'

'I . . .'

She couldn't bring herself to say she wouldn't. She couldn't bring herself to say anything. She just walked over to the door and held it open to him. She wanted, the most and least of anything, to be alone.

QUARRYING

Autumn 2020

There's going to be a storm. – Alex Bainton

And that was all the post said.

Jenny frowned. She clicked refresh. And again. She scrolled through the last seven days' worth of posts in the Ravenspurn Online! Facebook group. Nothing. Nothing about the storm, nothing about the new lockdown. Just lost cats and bitching about litter on the beach and the local bus service.

She pressed refresh again. Still nothing.

Jenny rolled her eyes. It was typical of Alex to drop something like that and then say nothing more. What a drama queen. Breaking the news, but not offering any helpful advice. How bad a storm? As bad as two weeks ago? Worse? How would it affect the Co-op's opening hours? Was there anything people could do to prepare, should they be checking on elderly neighbours?

Jenny clicked refresh and an emoji appeared on Alex's post. A laughing reaction, from Chris. Chris was entirely silent on Facebook except for adding laughing reactions to seemingly random posts, regardless of content. The one exception to this had been when his little sister, Chelsea, had announced that she was pregnant a few weeks ago – he'd put a heart on her scan photo instead. But that was it.

Maybe the post wasn't even from Alex. Si and Alex shared a laptop, and they rarely bothered to log out of each other's accounts, which struck Jenny as ridiculously, suffocatingly close, but then what would she know? She had been avoiding Si for three long months now. From him, it was still an infuriating status, but in a very different way. Si wouldn't be expressing himself like this for the drama of it. It would simply be because he had nothing else to say, nothing more to add to the situation. That was the way his brain worked – as if someone had turned a light switch on, and then, abruptly, off. Was he happy, living like that? She'd always assumed so.

She was trying not to think about him. That was part of the avoiding.

She clicked refresh again, to find a like from Dave and no comment from anyone. She hissed air out from between her teeth. Did she have to do everything? She typed:

Should we do anything?

Almost immediately, there was a reply.

What, like put up a really big brolly? – Alex Bainton

Jenny bit her lip. Definitely Alex, then.

I'll go up and look at the caravans. – Chris Blower

Jenny raised her eyebrows. The first time she'd ever seen him comment on something, and he was even offering to help.

What, so you can watch them fall off the cliff? – Alex Bainton

Fuck off – Chris Blower

Aren't you meant to be working? Those old ladies aren't going to rip themselves off for £20 to get to their hospital appointments. – Alex Bainton

Cheeky cow – Chris Blower

Jenny closed the laptop. She'd go mad if she had to keep watching this play out. Instead she wandered out to the hallway. Her mother was still in the process of sorting through the boxes in the loft. She kept bringing them down, again and again, and unpacking them and making the three piles and putting them back in the boxes and then back in the loft. Saying she was going to find things to donate to charity, which she never did. She did this every week.

'They say there's going to be a storm,' Jenny said.

'There is,' Alison replied. The two of them had an agreement to keep their communication mainly factual these days. 'Who's they?'

'On the Facebook group.'

As a strategy, it was working fairly well for them. They had managed to bury back down the things they fought about. Now it was just a background hum of enmity. No different from how it had ever been.

'Oh yes,' Alison said, holding up a worn camel-coloured jumper and carefully folding it back into a square and placing it on the bed. Jenny leaned against the doorjamb. She didn't feel comfortable setting foot in her mother's room. The doorway was fine.

'No one's saying what we should do, though.'

Alison flicked out and then folded another jumper.

'What do you want them to say?'

'What we should do. Something. Something about the new lockdown.'

Alison rolled her eyes and held up a bottle-green cardigan to the light. There were visible holes on the elbows and armpits. Alison carefully folded it and placed it on the bed.

'Oh, Jenny. Who's got time to worry about the new lockdown?'

Jenny felt the familiar surge of panic wash over her. It was okay, though. Breathe in for four and out for four. Only read the news when you're ready. They weren't really panic attacks. They were manageable. She was managing. She could manage another lockdown. She'd managed the last one.

'It starts tomorrow.'

Even though it hadn't worked. They were here, again, not controlling the *germs germs germs*, again, locked down again. How many more times would it be?

'Well, worrying won't make it happen any later. You shouldn't go on the Facebook if it's just going to upset you.'

Jenny scuffed a toe on the carpet. She'd always hated the carpet – so soft that you couldn't trust it to bear your weight. She thought sometimes about a place of her own, and hardwood floors. She'd always thought that was something she'd like when she finally moved in with Ben. If she'd found a replacement for her flat six months ago, she might have had a shot at getting the whole amount covered and she'd be edging closer to a deposit on her own place. She wouldn't even need the second person, if she'd done that. But everything was too late, of course.

'I haven't got anything else to do.'

Jenny scowled deeper. It had only been three weeks since she'd been made officially redundant from her company. She didn't know if they'd let everyone go, or most of them, or just one or two people they'd been waiting for a chance to get rid of. She wasn't talking to anyone from London, these days. What was the point? Even looking at them on social media made her feel worse, though, of course, she still did.

She had sent Ben a message. He'd been made redundant too. Derek had always hated him. It was nice to have an excuse to get in touch. He'd been quite polite, considering.

'You've got a pub to run.'

Jenny squeezed her eyes shut. The fucking pub.

'It's illegal, Mum. It's lockdown again tomorrow. There's a pandemic on.'

And, what was more, Jenny had started to hate it. The novelty of seeing the whole village crowding around smiling, glazed and bored and angry and desperate for something, anything, to happen had worn paper-thin. She didn't know how her dad could have stood it. But then he'd loved people, Ted, loved them with a passion. Jenny wasn't sure, when it came down to it, that she really did.

There was the cash, of course. But what for? It just got eaten up by the stock and the wages and the upkeep and the amount that was left was barely enough for a decent dinner or a cheap mini break, neither of which were really on the cards for her. So what was the point?

'That didn't stop you in the summer.'

And then there was Si. As much as she tried to only book Alex on, there were nights she couldn't do, and nights when she just couldn't pretend she didn't need the extra pair of hands. So she'd stand next to him, doling out bottles of lager and bags of crisps with him, pretending not to feel humiliated and guilty about the whole thing. She could barely look at Alex.

'Well, I don't want to.'

Jenny stared at the yellow box. It was brought down every time her mother did this, and not opened, and returned silently to its place in the loft again at the end of the day.

'We can't always have what we want, love. You know that.'

Jenny closed her eyes briefly. Of course she knew.

'Mum.'

'Yes,' Alison said. She wasn't folding anymore. She was just watching. Outside, the wind was picking up. Alex was right, of course. There was going to be another storm.

'Were you and Dad happy?'

Alison laughed, or something that sounded a bit like it. Her eyes darted nervously over to the yellow box.

'Jenny! What a question.'

Jenny looked at her, properly, which she usually avoided. She'd been away so long that her mother's face was blurred with time – an unfamiliar quality, if she let herself notice. It was unsettling – almost like not recognising herself.

'Were you, though?'

Her mother shrugged, tight-lipped. They weren't really the kind of family to make any meaningful confessions. Not without Ted.

'At times. No one can be happy all the time. It's just not possible.'

There was a pause. Alison had left the clothes alone now. Jenny had her full attention. She shrank under it, just as she always had. It was always too much, or never enough, with Alison. Or maybe with herself. It was hard to tell sometimes.

'Your dad would have liked it. The pub being open again. You back here.'

Jenny huffed a breath out, sharply.

'Don't.'

'He would, though.'

Jenny squeezed her eyes shut. There was another reason she'd stopped the nights. That pub was full of ghosts. Ghosts of Si, all cheeky smiles and curtains as his boy-self, and Alex, fierce and funny and before the spark had been knocked out of her. And her dad. Leaning his elbows on the bar, reaching down to hand her a pack of crisps when she was tiny, and then later, a half of shandy and a wink, *Don't tell your mum.* The first time she'd pulled him a pint.

'This isn't for ever. It's just this next lockdown. As soon as the city opens up again, I'm going to find another job and go back.'

Alison was twisting her wedding ring round and round her finger. She always did that when she was nervous.

'I'm sorry.'

Jenny blinked. 'What?'

Alison rolled her eyes and everything was normal again.

'Jenny. Don't say what, say pardon.'

Jenny restrained herself from rolling hers. She wanted to hear this.

'Pardon?'

Alison was looking down, her hands buried in an old

navy jumper in her lap. Moth-eaten, but cashmere. Moths love cashmere.

'I'm sorry. I know I was never ... Well. I wish things could have been different sometimes.'

Jenny said nothing. As if it was a spell she was trying not to break.

'You could stay here for longer. If you wanted to.'

Jenny forced a casual shrug. 'You said the pub was a trap. That I'd be better off in London.'

The two women looked at each other. Jenny owed her the eye contact, at least.

'I know what I said.'

There was a silence. Jenny couldn't think of anything to say. The vertigo of suddenly having something you'd wanted for so long thrust into your lap. Of not being able to trust it.

'You don't like me being here.'

'I never said that.'

You didn't have to.

Jenny stepped into her mother's room and patted her awkwardly on the arm. It was thin, birdlike, to her touch.

'I'm going for a walk.'

Her mother looked up, her eyes wet and old.

'There's going to be a storm.'

Jenny backed the two steps out of the room. She itched to run, to swim, even. She wouldn't, of course. She'd always had so much self-control.

'I know.'

Alex sat on the edge of the bath and stared at the little plastic strip and waited to feel something about it.

No one ever just had a neutral reaction to a pregnancy test, did they? There was the TV reaction, which was all shouting and whooping and hugging each other and crying happy tears, and then there was the real reaction, which was a raised eyebrow and a smug little wink to your partner if you were lucky, and if you weren't was swearing and gritting your teeth and crying a few little tears of humiliation because you were such a twat you couldn't even work out how to use a condom right.

But Alex didn't feel any of that. She didn't feel anything.

She sighed in a deep breath and then let it out, little by little, trying to think. Trying to feel. She just didn't know.

He'd been so distant recently. And she knew it was mug's thinking to imagine that a baby might fix anything, might bring them together. She knew that didn't work. But, on the other hand, how could it hurt, at this stage?

He'd always said that he wanted kids. Ever since they were at school, he'd said that.

She pulled out her phone. No signal, of course. But this wasn't meant to be a phone thing anyway, was it? This was meant to be an in-person thing, where you told him and you hugged. You were definitely meant to do those things, whether it was good news or bad news, so she could start there at least, couldn't she?

But she couldn't deny that there was a deep part of her that simply didn't want to. As soon as she told Si, her thoughts would have to crystallise and she'd have to take a side. It would have to be either good news or bad news, and it would have to be dealt with, and either way, she was going to be the one who'd have to do it, because Si had never made a decision or taken responsibility for anything, ever, in his entire life.

She thought about taking another test. A more expensive one, maybe, one of the ones that light up. But she'd googled it, and she knew they weren't better, they just cost more.

She had to face facts.

There were two versions of future Si dancing behind her eyes. One, throwing a kid up in the air, the way he did with his nephews, higher and higher, shouting with laughter, face wide open with the joy of making a tiny person laugh. The other, hunched over a phone with the football on in the background, sitting on his arse for hours at a time and then having the fucking cheek to ask her when lunch was going to be.

But why couldn't it be both? Both those Si's existed at the moment, the one who drove her nuts with his stupid lumpen refusal to take initiative, to do the smallest thing to help himself, and the other who she couldn't believe had chosen her, whose every smile was a personal triumph. The funniest, fittest, sweetest boy she'd ever met. Didn't that count for something?

But that was the thing about life, wasn't it? Different versions could, and would, exist all at the same time. There was no rule that said that a person had to be good or bad – they just were, and they always would be, and you couldn't change people, and you couldn't change yourself, and you couldn't escape, no matter how much they told you you had a choice.

She hadn't chosen this, but then, what had she ever chosen? And had it worked out that badly, in the end? Did she have regrets?

Well, yes. But she was still here.

There was a knock at the door and Barney skidded into the living room, yipping. Alex twitched upright. It was Si, just as she wanted him, turning up for her. Because he had, hadn't he? Ever since she was little. He'd turned up for her.

She dropped the test on the side of the sink and swished her fingers under the tap before heading to the front door. The dozy twat must have forgotten his keys again. But it was a sign, wasn't it? That she got to do a proper announcement to him, a proper little drama, and show him the pee stick, and they could cry and hug, and maybe she was wrong and he might take the lead, just this once. Because Si had always wanted kids. And if he took the lead on this, if he properly went for it, really enthusiastic, then he could win her over. He'd always been able to win her over. That was one of his skills. And he was here right now, even though he was meant to be up at the old caravan park.

She didn't believe in signs.

Maybe it was a sign.

She reached the door, and even though she hadn't officially decided how she felt about it all yet, she noticed that she was smiling. But when she unlatched it and looked out, it wasn't Si standing on the doorstep, looking all sheepish and like he had when he was ten and he'd forgotten his PE kit and was going to have to play rounders in his pants again. It was Pete. The smile dropped off her face like a stone.

'I want a word with you.'

He didn't wait to be invited into the flat. Scowling, he pushed the door open, hard enough to make the handle bounce off the plaster of the hallway that was already cracked, like she was still in the caravan and he was still her landlord. Her real landlord wasn't going to let them see any of their deposit back, at this rate. If they could even afford to fucking move. She supposed they'd have to, now. If she kept it. If she made up her mind.

The little dog growled.

'Barney. Back to bed,' she said, but she gave his ears a scratch. He wasn't daft, that dog. She met Pete's glare with one of her own. 'What do you want?'

Fucking Pete, of course, haunting this village like a bad smell. Over the years, her relationship with Pete had thawed a little bit. She couldn't stay seventeen for ever, and besides, he was an old man now, and not a threat. But she was still entitled to think that the man was an arsehole, and she did.

'It's your mother.'

Alex rolled her eyes. At least this'd be over quickly. It'd better cost under two hundred quid. That was all there was in her emergency account that no one knew about, not Si and particularly not her mum. It'd taken fucking ages to save it up, but it made her feel better to know that there were a few things she could buy her way out of. She'd assumed it would be some cock up of Si's that would drain it this time round though. Nice to be surprised.

'What's she done now? I'm not paying. I've got nowt.'

He looked around the room, rudely. She could feel him taking in the damp patches on the wall, the parts where the plaster was crumbling away. Alex felt her face settle into a scowl. He could fuck off. She worked hard to afford this damp shithole flat, and it was a fuck of a lot better than his manky caravans.

'It's not that.'

He lifted a stray piece of wallpaper and peered at the bare plaster underneath. Alex narrowed her eyes but said nothing. She wanted him out, not to fight.

'What is it then?'

He pressed his lips together, a hard line across his face.

'She won't budge.'

Alex shook her head. 'Nah, that's not my problem either. You want rid of her, you need to get the bailiffs in or something, I'm not getting into it if she's behind on rent.'

He laughed, in a not-very-Pete kind of a way. Like it was actually funny. A little bit like Ted used to laugh.

'Like I've taken any rent off that old bitch since she first moved in.'

Alex blinked. Fair play to him, he'd properly surprised her.

'What?'

He shrugged, and said nothing.

'She told me—'

'Reliable, is she, your mum? Always straight with you 'bout money?'

Alex sighed and rubbed at her eyes. She didn't have the time for any of this shit.

'What do you want, Pete?'

He sat down on her sofa, making himself far too comfortable for her liking.

'Her caravan's too close to the cliff edge. She won't get her shit out so I can move it. She won't move into one of the other ones.'

Alex frowned. She hadn't been up to the cliffs for a while. She'd been busy, and the weather had been shit for what felt like months, and anyway, all the seagulls had already fledged.

'She's not the closest to the edge, though, is she?'

She refused to offer him a cuppa. He could die of fucking thirst for all she cared.

'Did your Si not tell you what it was I've been having him doing this past week?'

She blinked. She hadn't asked. She was grateful enough that Si was working at all.

'No.'

He sighed, and again, for a moment he didn't seem like himself. For a second, he was Ted.

'She's the closest to the edge now.'

Alex swallowed.

'Right.'

'There's storms blowing in. It's November. Winter already, time to stop sitting about. And they get worse every year, you know that.'

She rubbed her eyes harder. So hard she saw dark stars.

'Yeah, right, I get it.'

The two of them stared at each other, silent for a moment.

'Why won't she move?'

'Stubborn, in't she? Just like you.'

Alex dug her nails into her palms to distract herself from the idea of chucking a cushion right into his stupid old face.

'You can fuck off coming in my house with that kind of shit.'

But he didn't rise to it. He just stared at her, so long and hard that, despite herself, she looked away.

'We're on the same side today, yeah?'

She sighed, deeply. Whatever.

'I'll have a word with her.'

Of course she would. She was always going to, wasn't she? As long as they were both alive and in this village, her mum would be her problem. And they were never going to leave this village.

'I'm having a piss before I go back up the hill, right?'

'Charming.'

Pete stood up, slowly and by degrees, pulling himself up first to the edge of the seat, and then a folded-over lean, and finally upright. She watched him walking slowly over to the bathroom. She could never quite get used to how different he was from the Pete that lived in her memories. He closed the door, but then quickly, far too quickly for him to have had his piss, it banged open again.

'Alex, what the fuck?'

Her stomach lurched in horror. He held the pregnancy test in his hand.

'What the fuck do you think you're doing, snooping around my stuff?'

He looked at her like she was being ridiculous, which, to be fair, she knew she was.

'You left it right out on the side, you daft mare. Does he know?'

He chucked it down on the coffee table and wiped his hand on his trousers, face screwed up, presumably remembering that it was covered in her wee.

'None of your fucking business.'

He jutted his chin out at her, as bullish as he always had been despite the grey hairs.

'Why the fuck doesn't he know?'

Alex rolled her eyes. This fucking place! You could never get five minutes to yourself to think.

'I only did it ten minutes ago. He's out, isn't he? Patching up your piece-of-shit caravans.'

He pointed one of his bony old fingers at her. 'So you'll let him know as soon as he gets home then, will you? You'll tell him tonight?'

Alex glared at him. Everyone was always getting at her. Opinions, opinions everywhere, you couldn't get away from them. She didn't expect that would get better when she had the baby.

If she had the baby, she meant.

'You mind your business, you daft old cunt.'

His face flashed, and all at once he was the Pete Fletcher of her childhood – someone to be minded. Dangerous.

'You want to tell him,' he said, and he wasn't shouting. He was worse than shouting, he was speaking in the quiet hiss of a man who expects to be obeyed. 'That lad's been like a son to me. He's a right to know.'

But Alex had enough experience of Pete's bullshit to know how to handle him when he was like this.

'You tell him, and you know what I'll tell Jenny. Yeah? I will. You want all that dragged up again?'

She tilted up her chin and speared him with a gaze, and put every little bit of authority she could muster into it.

She was the grown-up now.

'Well, do you?'

He sighed deeply, and all of a sudden he was an old man again.

'I won't tell him, all right? Not if you're going to be a nightmare about it.'

She nodded decisively. 'I am.'

'You should, though.'

Alex went over to the door and held it pointedly open.

'You got any more advice for me, or are you going to fuck off out of my flat?'

He heaved a deep sigh, and for a moment, he looked as knackered as she felt. It had been a tough year for everyone, she supposed.

'You'll talk to your mum, yeah? I've tried. It's your problem now.'

'I don't know why you even give a shit, Pete Fletcher.'

She could have sworn he looked over to the pregnancy test before he said, 'No. Me neither.'

And he finally left.

Jenny did not always walk up the cliff path now there was no need for daily reception. Instead she let herself wander, tracing routes around her past adventures in Ravenspurn. The bench where she'd smoked her first cigarette, egged on by Alex, tears streaming from her eyes, humiliated that at eighteen years old she still hadn't learned to do this. That sheltered part of the cove where she'd first had sex – the same. Not humiliated, thanks to Si and his big warm eyes and lighthouse smile, but still not sure what to do. She'd always seemed to be lagging behind Alex and Si, the baby, always playing catch up.

But then she'd left. She'd changed the rules. What else could she have possibly done? There was no way to win with those two, though.

She looped around the outside of the pub, the car park clear and empty now except for a few tab ends. They collected there every day – people liked to come there for a fag and a stare at the sea where once they'd have had a pint. Returning like migratory birds to the places they'd been to before, again and again. Is that what she was doing here? Is that why she hadn't moved back to London?

It was too late now. Lockdown was tomorrow, and there was a storm coming in. She was stuck again.

She carried on walking and found herself in front of the house she still thought of as Si's. It was a neat little semi, just like the one that her own mum lived in, except that this one wasn't as close to the sea, and four kids had grown up here instead of one. Only Si's mum here now, though. Her husband had left when Si was still at school, and all her kids had grown up now. And it was just as she was thinking that, that Jenny saw the unmistakeable outline of Si's head pass behind the net curtain.

A tall figure loomed behind the door, blocking out the hallway light, and the curtain twitched.

Jenny took a step back, hesitant. But she was only walking. What was there to do except for walking, if there was another lockdown coming? She could go where she wanted.

Si wouldn't see it like that, though. He'd see it as some kind of sign.

She took another hesitant step back, and another, and just as she was about to turn and walk away, the door banged open and she met Chris's eyes.

'What do you want?' asked Chris. He scowled, his eyebrows heavy in his face. It was like his features were designed to make him look angry. When Jenny had been younger, there was a time when she was genuinely afraid of Chris. The bulk and glower of him had seemed to fill their school some days. Now, he looked different. His body was softer – the days of him playing football after school and labouring for pocket money were long gone, now he had a sitting-down job just like hers. Not quite like hers, maybe.

Chris was still a big man, still a solid presence in the narrow hallway, but somehow not as intimidating as he'd once been. His menace had been diluted by the years so that the hulking twenty-something he'd once been had faded into something a bit pathetic – or maybe it was Jenny. Maybe it was fifteen years of late-night journeys on the tube, of clutching her handbag close to herself on the bus and pretending not to see the street drinkers that gathered in clumps by the corner near her flat. It was hard to be frightened of a man you'd known as a seven-year-old boy, next to that.

'What do you want?' he said again.

'Nothing,' she replied. She could hear the nervous squeak to her voice. 'I was just passing.'

His glower intensified and Jenny found herself wondering how much Chris knew about the ins and outs of his brother's life. Did they still tell each other everything? Had they, even, when they were younger? Jenny used to stay up at night wishing she had a sister. She'd always thought that was the whole point – to share secrets with each other. Now, she wasn't sure.

'Fucking likely story.'

Jenny pulled her hoodie around herself. The wind was picking up, but she hadn't brought a coat with her. It was spring, when she'd first packed. A whole half-year ago.

'I didn't knock, Chris. You opened the door to me, remember?'

His scowl intensified.

'Don't flatter yourself. I wouldn't have bothered if I'd known.'

Jenny rolled her eyes. At least she wouldn't be seeing him so much, with no more takeaway nights or taxi trips.

'Fine. See you then.'

But then a frail old lady peered out from the living-room doorway.

'Christopher?' she said. 'Who's that at the door? Is it the twins?'

Chris squeezed his eyes shut and looked miserable.

She tottered up behind him, craning over his shoulder.

For a moment, Jenny didn't recognise her. The woman was stooped, almost bent double, and she was wearing a faded red dressing gown that swamped her.

'Ner, Mum. It's no one,' Chris replied, scowling into the corner. And, of course, that's who it was. Who else would it be? But in her memory, Si's mum, who was much younger than hers, was like a fantasy mum, the kind of mum you might see on TV or in a magazine. All flippy ponytail held up with a scrunchy, and jeans that looked like they were bought this year rather than back in 1982, and cute little trainers that were always bright white. Jenny had often thought that she'd prefer to have Si's mum rather than her own, feeling a thrill of disloyalty every time but unable to take it back. Debbie was the kind of mum who'd let you have chicken nuggets for tea, and you'd be allowed to eat them in front of the TV, rather than having to have pork chops sitting bolt upright at a table and not be allowed to get down until you'd finished everything, even the broccoli. Especially the broccoli. Jenny never ate it, as an adult, not ever.

'Don't be silly, Christopher. It's Jenny, isn't it? So lovely to see you, Jenny! I'd heard you were back. Come in, come in . . .'

Jenny was ushered into the living room, where Si was slumped on the sofa, cradling a can of beer. When he saw Jenny, he lifted his head and frowned.

'Uh. Hi.'

Debbie bustled around, painfully slowly, offering biscuits

and tea. Jenny accepted a cup of coffee and a chocolate digestive and Chris gave her a furious glare and then followed his mother into the kitchen. Jenny hovered awkwardly in the middle of the room, and she and Si looked at each other, her nervous, him just mildly confused.

'Well, sit down then ... Nah, on the other sofa. That's Mum's chair.'

The armchair Jenny had been about to sit down on had an oxygen tank beside it and was draped with a heated blanket. Jenny leaped up and perched on the other sofa. She wanted to ask him what was wrong with his mum, and what had happened, and why he hadn't told her. Instead, she said, 'How are the twins?'

He scowled, and for a second he looked exactly like his big brother.

'What are you doing here, Jenny?'

Jenny pulled the sleeves of her hoodie over her hands. She used to do that all the time when she was a teenager. Why had she stopped? It was so comforting.

'I dunno. I just walked.'

He slammed down his beer can on a coaster decorated with the picture of a fat, smiling baby. Jenny stared at it. She really had wanted to know how the twins were doing.

'What, you want to come here and gloat over your perfect life? With your job and your pub, and your mum and that?'

She rubbed her eyes. He'd been her second favourite person, for years. That felt a very long time ago now.

'No, Si. Come on.'

He looked up at her, less defensive, more like his child-self. 'Are you getting back with whatshisface?'

Jenny thought of Ben. They'd been texting back and forth, since she'd messaged him about the redundancies. Nothing heavy. Just little things they thought each other might like, every few days. Links to viral videos they always pretended they hadn't already seen.

'I dunno. Maybe.'

His gaze was almost pleading now.

'So what are you doing here?'

And Jenny suddenly knew the answer.

'Do you know where she got my dad's watch from?'

For a second, Si looked confused, like she'd asked him a riddle. Then his forehead cleared. It had obviously clicked what she meant.

'Fucking hell! Not you as well. You two are obsessed with that fucking watch! The pair of you go on and on about it, like there aren't problems to fix, like there aren't bigger things to worry about. It's just a fucking watch. Why can't people just leave things alone?'

Jenny stared at him, her heart pounding in her chest. Alex too?

'What does she say about it?'

Si cast a quick look over his shoulder, towards the kitchen.

'I think you should go.'

But, just then, his mother came back in. A mug of coffee clinked precariously against the side plate as her hands shook. Jenny leaped up to take it from her, and Si and Chris glared identically at them both as Debbie got settled back into her chair.

'Oh, it is lovely to see you, Jenny, lovely to see you. I was so sorry to hear about your dad.'

She was breathing heavily, her head resting against the wings of the chair. Jenny immediately regretted accepting the drink.

'Mmm,' Jenny said. She took a mouthful of scalding coffee and forced herself to swallow as fast as she could.

'I'd have liked to come to the funeral, pet. I was sorry not to pay my respects.'

'It weren't your fault, Mum. You weren't well,' said Chris, glaring hard at Jenny.

'How are the twins doing?' Jenny asked again. The twins were two girls, much younger than Si and Chris. The whole family doted on them. They were normally a pretty safe bet for something to talk about.

A look passed between Si and Chris, but their mother only smiled.

'Ah, well they moved out to Leeds. They can't get over as much as they used to be able to. I don't mind. It's a long way.'

'It's not that long,' muttered Chris, glaring down at the carpet.

Debbie couldn't seem to catch her breath. Jenny took another scalding sip of coffee. There was a deep, animal part of her that wanted to be away.

'They were supposed to come on Sunday, but—'

'Ah, of course. But now they won't be able to come over for a few weeks,' Jenny said, pushing half a biscuit into her mouth.

Both Chris and Si snapped their heads around to Jenny, giving her identical blood-curdling glares.

'What? Why not? What do you mean?' said Debbie. Her breathing still hadn't gone back to normal, and there was a reedy rasp to her voice, making her sound querulous and, again, so much older than she was. How old could she be – maybe in her late fifties? She looked at least eighty. Jenny felt a stab of sympathy for Si and Chris. At least with her dad it was quick.

'Well, I just mean with the new lockdown. It'll be a few weeks before they can come.'

'What? What new lockdown? No! Why's that? Is it coming back? Chris, is the virus coming back?'

And with a slow thump of horror, Jenny realised what she'd done.

'No, Mum. It's not coming back,' Chris said.

Jenny took another burning gulp of tea. Half penance, half escape.

'But then why . . .'

The anxiety in the room was palpable, a tense throb. Jenny looked from one man to the other, and forced a smile.

'It's just precautionary, Mrs Blower. It's nothing to worry about. Just precautionary. You know, because of winter,' Jenny said.

'Oh, okay,' Debbie said. 'That's all right, then.'

She looked exhausted – even more so than when she'd come to the door. There was a greyish tinge to her face and her eyes were drooping closed.

The men were both looking murderously at Jenny, and something deep within her twisted miserably. But how the fuck was she supposed to know?

'I'd . . . best be off,' Jenny said, forcing another swallow of coffee and leaving the cup half empty on the side table.

'I'll walk you out,' Chris said and, before his mum could

object, he had Jenny by the elbow and pushed her into the hallway. The front door was already open. 'You stupid cow,' he hissed, his voice quiet and humming with threat. 'What did you say that for?'

Jenny rubbed her eyes. This place was so tiring.

'I didn't know it was a secret, did I? I'm sorry!'

His jaw was set into a hard square.

'You think it helps her? Knowing that the hospitals are full. Knowing that there might be no one coming if she needs? No ambulance, no doctor? You think she needs to be worrying about that on top of everything else?'

'I'm sorry,' Jenny said again. Tears pricked at the back of her eyes, and the two of them stared at each other, Chris breathing hard. Jenny felt vaguely ashamed of herself. She wasn't quite sure for what. For not knowing how hard things had been, perhaps. For being able to get away with not knowing. 'I didn't know you'd been lying about the news to her, did I?'

He threw a fist at the wall, hard, but pulled it at the last second so it didn't connect, didn't make a noise. The gesture had the feel of something he did a lot.

'You and fucking Alex! So fucking judgemental, *tell the truth, tell the truth*. Well, she's our mum, okay! You two can take a fucking walk off the cliff if you don't like it.'

Jenny fought to keep her face neutral. So hard, when she wanted to talk about it so much, when she wanted to pry, to ask, to pull apart the pieces of Alex's brain and peer inside.

Where did you get it why do you have it why why . . .

'What does Alex say about it?'

Chris's face contorted with fury and he choked out a strangled whisper.

'Fuck off!'

And Jenny took two hurried steps out of the hall and into the street, and the door banged closed in her face.

Si came in with a gust of sea and wind and took his hat off like it had done him a personal wrong.

'Bloody blowy up there, you know? Nearly got chucked off't cliff.'

Alex was curled up on the sofa. This whole afternoon, every twinge, every time she needed a piss or even stood up, she'd fretted and worried over. Was this what it felt like? Surely she should be able to feel a change in herself, something special or magical or even straightforwardly uncomfortable. But there was nothing. She was exactly the same as ever.

'Yeah?'

He unzipped his coat, which looked not warm enough for the weather, even by northern standards. It was just a track top, no more than a jumper really. That would never last him the winter. It was fucking freezing already, and only set to get worse.

Barney hopped down from where he'd been lying, nestled into the side of Alex's waist, tottered over to Si and offered his chin up for a scratch. Alex's lap felt empty and cold without him.

'Yeah. Never seen it this bad. Not in all my years of going up there. This is something different. We really might lose the main road this time.'

Alex frowned. Was that an ache, deep down at the centre

of her? A quick throb of nausea, maybe? She couldn't say. It was actually incredibly easy to make yourself feel sick.

'Right.'

He shrugged off his jacket and dropped it on the floor and she found that she didn't have the energy to want to have a go at him about it, so something must be different.

'You want to have a word with your mum. She wants to be moving to a caravan further in, but she keeps telling Pete to fuck off when he goes round.'

She frowned over at him. This was chatty, even by Si's standards. There was a fizzy, nervous energy about him that almost crackled between them in the small flat. She hadn't seen him like this since he went through his speed phase, but he hadn't touched that since he was twenty-five, and besides, where would he get it? It must be the storm, filling the air up with electricity. Lightning is just another type of energy, after all.

'I know.'

That stopped him. He gawped at her,

'How do you know?'

She pulled herself tighter into a ball. It was bloody nippy in here. She could do with her dog back, but he was still off, trotting after Si. Disloyal.

'Pete came round.'

Si raised his eyebrows. Unlike the entirety of the rest of the village, Si didn't have a problem with Pete. Probably because he'd always treated Si and Chris like they were some kind of miniature, honorary mates of his. It was just because he'd promised Kevin he'd look after them after he was gone, that was the only reason he wasn't a twat to them like he was to everyone else, just duty and pity and guilt. But Si didn't think like that. And he was probably the happier for it, honestly, but what can you do? You can't turn your brain off, and you can't unknow what you know.

'Pete? Did you tell him to fuck off?'

She shrugged. 'Eventually.'

'Right. Well. You'll know then, that she won't get her shit out. Crazy. She's going to get blown right off there, you need to tell her. She'll listen to you.'

Alex rolled her eyes. 'She won't.'

He came and sat down next to her. Properly, not like the way he usually chucked himself down onto any horizontal surface he happened to be passing. Gently. Intentionally. Beside her, like always. And Barney jumped up too, but he sat on the wrong bit of her. The balance was all off now and she wasn't as comfy as she'd been before.

'Aye, maybe she won't. You've got to try, though, don't you?'

Alex looked at him. This boy she'd watched grow up, she'd spent her whole life with. There was no one else she wanted to bring another life into this world with, was there? There'd only ever been him.

She'd known since she saw the line, really. Or further back, since she pocketed the test at the end of her shift. She'd just been trying to justify it to herself. Because it wasn't the sensible decision. Alex knew what it meant, to bring a kid into this world that you couldn't look after, that you couldn't even easily afford a fucking pregnancy test to find out about for sure.

But she knew what she felt. And it had been fifteen long

years since the last time she truly wanted something. It would be silly to let it go now, surely. When she'd just found something else.

'I've got something to tell you.'

'I wanted to say summat.'

They both spoke at once, and stared at each other, awkward, like two people who were on their first date rather than had known each other for ever and ever.

'You go first,' she said, because who ever wanted to go first? What if it was something horrible, and then you'd laid yourself open to them, just waiting to get stabbed in your soft, open belly.

But she was being stupid, of course. It was Si. It wouldn't be anything awful. It'd be something annoying, like Pete had fired him for the millionth time, or he wanted to borrow a few quid to get baccy until payday. If she couldn't trust him, then who could she trust?

'Umm. Right.'

And he just looked at her. A bit less hair and a bit more belly than he'd had as a teenager, but still absolutely and perfectly himself.

She wanted to tell him. He was going to be excited.

'Come on, spit it out.'

And he still didn't say anything. And it was as she was rolling her eyes and just about to open her mouth to tell him that she'd go first then, since he wasn't getting round to it, and she bet that her one was more important anyway, when he said, 'I kissed Jenny.'

And he just looked at her. Same stupid face as he'd always had.

'What?'

He kept swallowing like he was going to be sick, and he said nothing.

Alex pulled her feet up under her bum. She was suddenly colder. Freezing, in fact.

'You fucking WHAT?'

Surely the things you worry about this much don't happen. Surely the worrying is protective. Why else would everyone do it?

'Don't be angry with me,' he said. He had a pathetic little child voice, like he was still six years old.

'When?' she asked. No idea why. She didn't really want to know. But it's what you said, wasn't it? She was in another script now, a different and ugly one.

'Summer,' he said.

Alex closed her eyes. She'd known she didn't want to know.

'You've been sneaking out to see her all this time?'

This was what you did, wasn't it? You asked the questions, got the answers, rumbled on with the whole sorry business.

'No! No. It was just the once. That time when I went over to help clear up.'

A little spark of hope. Not as bad as she'd thought. But then, straight after, a fresh wave of humiliation. She shouldn't be begging for scraps of him like this. There'd been a time when it seemed like she could have everything, she could beat the odds and not just get what was expected of her, but get what she wanted. Which wasn't fucking much, was it? And less now that she'd been whittled down by the years, hopes dwindling, horizon dwindling, wants getting smaller and smaller.

'Just once?'

But it hurt just as much to have a small hope dashed as a big one. Maybe it hurt more.

'Just once. Only for a second. She pushed me away.'

Alex felt a flare of rage. Jenny was the one who'd stopped it? Swanning around the place, benevolently letting Alex keep her own fucking boyfriend. Keeping the moral high ground, and ruining it all anyway. Absolutely fucking typical.

'That doesn't make it all right, you know, you cheating fucking prick.'

And it was infuriating, the way he was looking at her. Like a puppy waiting to see if it'd get a treat or a kick. Like she was the one who was in charge of this situation that she hadn't planned and didn't want.

'I'm sorry. That's why I told you.'

The problem was, she couldn't help having her small wants. They sprang back up like mushrooms, popping back to fill the gaps left by the ones that had already been plucked.

'You told me because you thought she'd tell me.'

He looked up, big eyes. A child, or even a puppy. Not a proper person.

'I kept thinking she'd just go back.'

Alex gritted her teeth, but that was all. The fact was that she needed him. If she was to have this one small want glowing inside her, she needed him to stay. She thought about finding money for rent and food and tiny little baby clothes, and the time to look after the kid, to take them to the park and teach them to read early rather than just letting them wait until they hit school and felt like the thickest person in the world for the first couple of years until they caught up.

It would be tough enough with two of them. With just one, it would surely be impossible.

'Right. So I'd never have known, if she had.'

Because she did want this baby. It was inconvenient, but undeniable.

'Do you want me to go to my mum's?'

She closed her eyes again. She needed time to think about this. Space.

'You make the decision, Si. Make a choice for once in your fucking life, yeah?'

He turned the puppy dog eyes back onto her. If she was going to take on a real kid, there'd have to be a bit less of this in the future. He'd have to grow up. Could he?

He said, 'I don't want to leave.'

And all she could think to say was, 'Okay.'

And that's all she said to him for the rest of the night.

Jenny stood at the top of the cliff, breathing heavy and thighs burning, but triumphant. She could still do something. She could still do this.

She walked over to the edge and peered down at the ruins of the caravan on the second bay. She was getting cocky with the cliffs again, the way she had been as a teenager. It seemed so unlikely that the cliff would crumble when you were up here. You thought about how impossible it was even as you stared down at where it had happened before, again and again. But whoever thinks that the ground beneath them will suddenly cease to hold them up? Nobody. Until it does.

The ruins of the caravan were sun-bleached now after the whole of autumn and summer of it never quite being the right time to get them taken away. In the end, few of the tourists had noticed, and the ones that did seemed to think of the wreckage as almost a curiosity – like fossils or the Berlin Wall. Not relevant to their reality.

'Oi.' There was a croak behind her. For a moment, Jenny thought it was just the wind, but then, 'Oi!'

Jenny turned, and smoothed back her hair as the wind tried to snatch it out of her low ponytail. Karen was tottering towards her, wearing skinny jeans that sagged on her skinnier legs, and a pale pink T-shirt. It wasn't nearly enough clothes for the chill wind of November on a cliff top and Jenny shivered at the sight of her.

'You want to get away from there,' Karen said.

'Why?' Jenny knew that she sounded like a teenager and she didn't care. 'Will the cliff crumble, and I'll fall off and die?'

Karen twisted her inaccurately lipsticked mouth.

'I'd be glad if you did.'

Karen must only be about the same age as Alison, but just like Debbie, she looked so much older – not just comfortably into late middle age, all pastel jumpers and extra padding, like Jenny's own mother – but properly old. She looked wizened and beaten down, not by cancer but by life, like the years were a sea that had been, bit by bit, chipping away at her, and now there was nothing left. But she was still alive, for now.

'Charming,' Jenny said. She stared pointedly away, back down to the ruins of the caravan. The sharp edges and splatter of detritus had been mostly worn away and washed by the sea, leaving the remains softened somehow. There was already seaweed draped along them, and it didn't take much to imagine plants sprouting from the filling of the sofa cushions, perhaps a crab moving into the busted-open oven. The wreck of the caravan had started to look organic, almost like it was meant to be there. It's amazing how quickly something can be taken back by the sea.

'What are you even still doing here?

Karen fumbled at a tin and pulled out a tiny, rumpled rollie from it. She hunched over even more and flicked a lighter once, twice, three times, until a flame sparked. It was immediately blown out by the wind.

'There's a lockdown.'

'You had a chance to get back. You've had months.'

Jenny watched as she fussed with the lighter. She finally got the cigarette to catch and blew a long plume of smoke to get immediately vanished by the wind.

'I dunno. I live here now.'

Karen seemed satisfied at that.

'Well, don't you let yourself get too comfy. We don't settle for incomers round here.'

Jenny rolled her eyes. 'I'm not an incomer. I was born here.'

'I know that. But you gave us up.'

Jenny heaved a deep sigh. The air tasted of rotted seaweed and tobacco smoke and salt.

'If you say so.'

Karen stared at her, a glint of cunning in her eyes, or maybe something else.

'I know you gave her the money. I'm no fool.'

Jenny shrugged. She wasn't afraid of some mad old woman in a caravan. She wasn't a kid, and she didn't care what people thought of her anymore. Well, not what Karen thought, anyway.

'I dunno what you're talking about.'

Karen started making her way over to Jenny, slightly unsteady.

Jenny's first thought was to run, but she squashed it. She was in her thirties, for fuck's sake. This was an old lady. Everything was fine.

'The deposit! I know you gave it to her. She needed five hundred quid to move out, and I know where it came from, you vicious little—'

As she came closer to Jenny, Karen slipped. On instinct,

Jenny reached out and caught each of her bony forearms. The cigarette dropped to the ground and rolled off the side of the cliff.

'Fuck!'

Jenny hauled the woman to her feet, but when she let go of her arm, Karen tipped to the side alarmingly. Jenny grabbed her again, holding her skinny arm tight in her hands.

'Is that a twist? Can you put weight on it?'

'None of your fucking business.'

Jenny rolled her eyes and, for a glorious moment, imagined dropping her arm, letting Karen crumple to the floor, and walking away. Wouldn't it serve her right? After all the bitching and the bad feeling, wouldn't there be some justice to it, to leave her shivering alone on the cold ground? But, of course, Jenny held on to her. She was still a frail old lady, even if she was a bitch.

'Come on. Let's get you back.'

Jenny walked Alex's mum – as she could not now or ever shake the habit of thinking of her – back to her caravan. Karen walked meekly alongside. She smelled so strongly of alcohol that it was overpowering and vaguely medicinal, like antiseptic.

'I don't need help, you know. Not from the likes of you.'

The caravan was alarmingly close to where they were standing, alarmingly close to the edge of the cliff. There were only a few metres between the little terrace at the end of the caravan and the steep, stark drop down to the angry sea.

'Shouldn't you move to one of the other ones?'

This seemed like incredibly shoddy maintenance, even by Pete's standards. But all the thanks she got from Karen was a glower.

'You mind your fucking business.'

Jenny pushed the door open and tried not to wince. Inside, it was a maze of piled-up newspapers and a quantity of furniture you'd never think would fit in such a small space. Empty bottles, batted by the opening door, rolled and skittered across the floor like rats. Jenny guided the other woman through a labyrinthine tunnel towards her chair. She tipped her down unceremoniously.

'You okay?'

Karen looked around the room. She seemed surprised and vaguely horrified, as if she was seeing the place for the first time.

'It wasn't this bad before she left. When she was a kiddie, it was fine here.'

Jenny shrugged. She was trying not to breathe in.

'If I had her to help, it'd be all right still. She was the one what left.'

Jenny stared down at Karen, curled in her chair. She'd only seen her a handful of times when they were growing up, and even as a tiny child, Jenny had sensed the air of chaos, but there was also an undeniable whiff of fun. Bright red lipstick and high heels and Alex had always claimed she didn't even have a bedtime and Jenny had believed her. It seemed so much less fun, now.

'I didn't give her the money. I didn't have five hundred quid going spare. I was just a kid.'

Karen pawed weakly at her pockets, digging out a pouch of tobacco.

'Who did then?'

She fumbled at the papers, but it seemed like her hands

weren't steady enough to pull one out. Jenny resisted the impulse to offer to help. She shouldn't even be in here. She shouldn't have touched her. It was lockdown.

It was hard to care.

'I don't know! She wouldn't have told me that.'

Karen gave up, stuffing the papers back into the tobacco pouch and the pouch back into her packet. She looked up at Jenny accusingly.

'You were her best friend.'

Jenny frowned. 'I wasn't.'

Karen was clasping her hands together in her lap. Even with the pressure of her clutching them, they were still shaking.

'You were. She's never been great with friends. Same as me.'

It was lockdown. She should go. But ...

'Why's Alex got my dad's watch?'

For a moment, the two women stared at each other in silence.

Then Karen started to laugh. It was an unhealthy, rattly wheeze of a laugh, and it went on and on and on and on. She was curling in on herself in her chair, as if she was cramping up with mirth.

Jenny stood, humiliated, and waited for her to speak.

Eventually, she said, 'Oh dear, oh dear. Do you really not know? You've been away a long time, haven't you, lovey?'

Jenny swallowed. And again. And again. Her mouth kept filling up with saliva.

'What do you mean?'

Karen's smile lit up her face like she was a jack-o'-lantern.

'I suppose that's my answer about the money, though, isn't

it? He always was a gent, your dad. And he always fucking hated me. Well, almost always.'

Jenny felt a deep flush starting in her neck and working its way up her face. She pushed away any ideas of what that might mean, and focused on making her way out of the caravan, staggering and picking her way back to the brisk grey air.

'I'll not be the one to tell you, though! Not outright. That's for her to do, not me. She always was a tricky little minx . . .'

Jenny knocked her shoulder against a tower of newspapers. They fell and exploded on the floor, slithering over each other. Jenny made her way to the door and wrenched it open. She slammed it shut behind her, on the mess, and the smell, and the cackling that followed her out. She leaned back against the door and pulled in a deep lungful of cool sea air, but she still couldn't quite seem to catch her breath.

Summer 1994

Alex was standing on her mummy's bed and looking at herself in the mirror. It wasn't easy to look at herself in this mirror, but it was the only one they had left. There used to be a big mirror in the bathroom, very easy to see into, but one of Mummy's friends had taken it and laid it flat on the coffee table and then Mummy had broken it by jumping up and dancing on top of it. When Alex had asked where it was, Mummy had got cross and said that she was only having fun, actually, and it wasn't a big deal, but now Alex didn't have anything to look at while she brushed her teeth in the morning. She used to do staring competitions with herself while she brushed her teeth – Alex was absolutely brilliant at staring competitions. She could beat everybody in the whole school, even Chris Blower in year six, and he was enormous and fierce when he didn't get his own way, but he still couldn't beat her. If she couldn't practise, would that mean that Chris would start winning? Alex didn't like it when other people won.

Alex tightened the scarf around her waist and started staring hard into her own eyes, to get a quick bit of practice in now. It was only another half-term until Chris was going to leave primary and go off to the big school in Driffield anyway. When you went to big school, you had to get on a bus at eight o'clock every morning and if you missed it, you'd be stuffed because it was more than seven miles away and it would take you two hours to walk that AT LEAST and you might get run over on the road or killed even, so you better not miss it. Alex would not walk for two hours and nearly get killed just to go to school. It wasn't worth that. She'd just get an ice cream from the stand on the promenade and go down to the beach instead, which would be way better. Maybe when she went to big school she'd miss the bus on purpose sometimes, and do that.

Alex's eyes were watering now, but she didn't blink. She wasn't old enough for big school yet anyway. She'd only be in year four next year, which was good because it meant she wouldn't be the littlest of the juniors anymore. Alex didn't like being the littlest, but there were only three of them in her year and the other two were way taller than her, so there we were. There was Si, who was all right and funny even though he was a boy, and there was Jenny. Jenny was three inches taller than Alex, even though they were almost exactly the same age, but Alex always got better marks on the tests then Jenny did. The teachers always said that there was more to school than being good at tests, but everyone knew that they only said that to make the stupid kids feel better. What was the point of the tests if they didn't matter? Alex could tell that Jenny cared about them by the pathetic way that she looked up at the teacher when they were giving them back, like she was hoping that this one time she might have beaten Alex, but she never had. The best she could ever do was to get the same, but it was like Alex had won even then, because she never tried as hard as Jenny, so it was like her mark counted for more.

Si did worse on the tests than either one of them, but he really didn't care, so that was fine.

Eyes burning, Alex finally blinked.

She adjusted the pirate hat she'd got at Si's birthday the year before. She was doing dressing up today, but she didn't have very many clothes so she had to use her imagination. Jenny had an entire big box of hats and scarves and dresses and things at home that her mum had got from the charity shop for her to play with. She'd told Alex about it in class one day. And Alex had got a funny feeling in her chest and told Jenny that dressing up was for babies, and that it was gross to wear other people's hats from charity shops, with all their head grease and nits in them, and she'd catch the plague from doing something as dirty as that. And Jenny had gone bright red and not said anything else for the rest of the lesson.

Secretly, Alex would have loved to go over to Jenny's house after school and have a go with her dressing-up box and also eat a mint Club, which Jenny always had in her lunch box and were Alex's favourite. Alex's mummy didn't buy food like that or, at least, not reliably. Sometimes at Alex's house there were loads of sweets and cake, so much that you'd be sick after eating it all, but still, you did. Because if you didn't eat all of it straight away, then it would be gone and there'd be no telling when you'd get some again. But having a pack of biscuits in the cupboard and having one every single day for lunch – Alex's mummy didn't do things like that. So she'd like to go over to Jenny's actually, for the biscuits and the hats. But Jenny had only ever invited her over one single time, two years ago. And Alex had been standing right there in the playground and Jenny's mummy had pulled a face, all scrumpled up like she could smell something disgusting and said oh no, dear, I don't think so, her mummy wouldn't like it, and even though Alex had said that it would definitely be fine with her mummy, 100 per cent, her mummy didn't care what she did, Jenny's mummy wouldn't budge and Alex had to walk home alone that day with no mint Club and she still remembered how that felt after all this time. So it was safer to say that she just didn't want to.

Who needed lots of dead strangers' hats anyway, when you could be a pirate? That was the very best thing to dress up as, so why would you ever want to be anything else? The scarf that Alex had tied around her waist was one that Mummy wore for parties sometimes. It wasn't a woolly scarf, but a pretty, floaty one that smelled of the perfume Mummy always wore for special nights – spicy and sweet. It made Alex want to sneeze, but kind of in a good way.

'You have to walk the plank!'

She wished she had a sword to swish around while she said it. That would be what a real pirate would do, and they'd stab anyone who didn't agree with them or interrupted while they were talking. She could go and get a knife from the kitchen, she supposed. That would be a bit like a sword.

Alex tilted her head and regarded her reflection. Peter Pan had a knife rather than a sword. Maybe it would be good to have a knife. She should get one now. Mummy and Auntie Jean were in the living room smoking fags and drinking cans, but that was okay. They'd be in there for a while yet, and they wouldn't pay her any mind as long as she was quiet about it.

Alex gave herself one last ferocious glare in the mirror, and headed to the kitchen to find herself a dagger.

'Eh up!' Uncle Pete said. Alex froze. 'You didn't say the little 'un was in, did you? All right there, little 'un?'

The pirate hat slipped down over Alex's eye, but she didn't care about that. Now she knew that Uncle Pete was here, she didn't care about anything apart from getting as far away from him as she possibly could.

Unlike Auntie Jean, Uncle Pete was not Alex's real uncle. He wasn't her anything, except for some man who came over to hang around with Mummy. He wasn't as fun as Bill and Kevin, who were silly and sprawled over the sofas and were a bit annoying sometimes, but also made Alex laugh and made Mummy laugh too. Or even as good as Ted, who was Jenny's dad and came over once in a while, and wasn't silly and just sat there talking in a low voice to Mummy and then when he left, there'd be more food around for a week or two. And none of these men ever, ever wanted Alex to call them her uncle. Pete did, which made Alex uncomfortable in a way she couldn't put her finger on but felt deep all the way to her bones.

'She's meant to be out playing,' Auntie Jean said. Her eyes were big and dark, and the words were like something she'd say when she was cross, but she didn't sound cross to Alex. 'Alex, you go play. Leave the grown-ups alone.'

'She's all right, she's all right,' Uncle Pete said, and he drained the last of a can and then threw it onto the floor, where Mummy and Auntie Jean and Alex all looked at it. None of them said anything about it and the can just sat there, leaking its last few drops onto the deep pile of the beige rug. The rug was pretty dirty anyway. Somehow that didn't make it better.

'Come here, little 'un. You come sit in my lap. Give your Uncle Pete a kiss.'

Alex wrinkled her nose up. She did not want to sit on

Uncle Pete's lap and give him a kiss. She'd rather give him a kick in the shins, to be honest. She looked over to Auntie Jean, who could usually be relied on to be a bit more with it than Mummy.

'I don't want to,' she said, and Auntie Jean sniggered and earned herself a glare from Pete, who reached over and scooped Alex up and towards him, like she was a kitten.

'Now then. Are you going to give your Uncle Pete a kiss?'

Alex tried to turn her head away from him, but he had her face gripped tight tight tight in his hands. She thought about pirates, and Peter Pan. What would Peter Pan do, if he didn't have his knife? But even Peter Pan was bigger than Alex. What would Tinkerbell do, then? She'd never kiss anyone she didn't want to, that was for sure. Tinkerbell would never do anything she didn't want.

'You're not my uncle!' Alex said, desperate to make him stop, to distract him. A fight would be better than this, or getting told off for being cheeky, even getting sent to her room with a smacked bottom. She'd take it happily.

But Uncle Pete didn't look angry. Instead, he laughed.

'I am, actually, little 'un. Did you know that?'

Alex looked up to Mummy and Auntie Jean, unsure. Was this some kind of a joke? Sometimes grown-ups did teasing, and she didn't quite get it, which made her very angry. But Mummy and Auntie Jean didn't look like they thought it was funny, at all.

'Don't stir, Pete,' said Auntie Jean, but she didn't sound convincing.

Uncle Pete smiled like a shark. His hands were still tight around her face.

'No one ever talks about anything that matters in this village, just chatter chatter chatter about nothing, but we all shut up when it comes to anything unpleasant about little Teddy.'

'I said that's enough, are you deaf?' Auntie Jean said, but it didn't seem like Uncle Pete had heard her. Alex didn't think he really was her uncle, though. She thought he was just pretending.

'The golden boy. But he's not that perfect, you know?'

Mummy looked like she'd swallowed something horrible, but she didn't say anything.

Pete kept talking. 'Because even though he pretends he has the perfect marriage, the perfect family, it's just not true. Because he wasn't only fucking Jenny's mummy when they were getting ready to have a baby. He had to have his little bit on the side as well, didn't he?'

Alex didn't know what that word meant, *fucking*, but it was clear it meant something big, something powerful, from the way the women flinched when he said it. She filed it away for future use. Fucking.

'So I am your uncle, actually. Gettit?'

He smiled at her triumphantly, like he'd won an argument.

'Liar!'

And she leaned forward and bit him, hard, on the hand. He let go with a yell and Alex ran out of the door, not looking back and not listening to any of the shouting, except for Jean's voice,

'Leave her, Pete!'

But Alex didn't slow down to see if he'd paid attention to that. She just kept running, all the way to the edge of the cliff where she wasn't meant to play, where everyone said it was dangerous, but it felt dangerous inside as well, and at least out here she could breathe.

'I meant it, kid.'

She whipped round, back to the cliffs, and tried her very hardest to show that she wasn't scared of him, not at all at all at all.

'I don't believe you.'

They were very, very close to the cliff edge. Closer than Alex had meant to go, but she was panicking. Pete didn't look bothered, though. He raised an eyebrow and smirked.

'You don't have to.'

Alex gave him her very worst stare. The one that she saved up for when Chris was trying to throw his weight around and saying she couldn't play with him because she was a girl, or for whenever she saw Jenny's mum.

'You're a liar.'

But he just stood there, smiling at her, not listening, so she reached forwards and beat at his chest with tiny fists.

He looked down, smiling, watching her tap away at him, like she was just a tiny bird, like she was nothing. Then he hoisted her up in wiry, muscled arms, and held her out. Alex's feet scrabbled away, but they didn't find purchase on the ground beneath – all there was was air. She wheeled them frantically around, panic gripping her hard. He was holding her out, over the edge of the cliff.

'I'm not a liar.'

She couldn't breathe, and she could barely think. The only thing that fit in her head was the cliff and the drop and these arms, holding her up, just for now, surely, not for long at all. He could drop her any time he wanted, and in that moment, she was absolutely convinced that he would. That he wouldn't even hesitate for a moment.

'Mummyyyy!'

But her mum didn't come. All there was were the arms holding her and the air beneath her, nothing there to stop her dropping and falling and crunching down onto the beach below.

'Say it.'

Alex felt a warm trickle down her legs as she flailed in mid-air. With a hot rush of humiliation, she realised that she'd wet herself.

'Auntie Jeanie,' she gasped out, and warm strong arms came and scooped her up and away from Pete and onto blessedly solid ground. Alex sobbed and clung to Jean and she hugged her back, not minding about the wee and the snot and the shaking.

'What the fuck, Pete?' Auntie Jean said, glaring daggers at him.

Pete reached up a hand to his head and tugged at his hair.

'I was only messing. Wasn't I?'

And even Alex could tell that there was a pleading quality to his voice. Like he knew that he'd gone too far, and he wanted to say sorry, but he couldn't quite let himself.

'She's soaked,' Jean said.

'She had an accident.'

Auntie Jean cuddled Alex close, stroking her hair back from her face.

'She's scared.'

'I'm not,' Alex said, and twisted her face away from the

stroking, even though she liked it, to try and prove that she wasn't afraid.

Pete gave her a small smile.

'That's right. Good girl.'

And Alex glared at him, and then buried her face in her auntie's neck. She would never be his good girl, not ever. He was a liar and a baddie and she would never forget that until the day she died.

Autumn 2020

Jenny marched straight into her mother's room. Alison didn't ask permission before she came into Jenny's room at all hours of the night, waking her up and scaring the shit out of her, so Jenny wouldn't ask either. She'd just take what she wanted. Everybody else did.

She found the box immediately. It was sitting, sleek and yellow, on the top shelf of the wardrobe. And, on some level, didn't that mean that her mother wanted her to look in there? Why wouldn't you hide something properly, if you didn't want it to be found?

Jenny pulled the box down and set it on the bed. It was light, with only a few flimsy papers rattling around within it. If Jenny was right, that was exactly what she'd expect.

She closed her eyes and sat for a moment. A last moment, of not knowing. But, of course, she did know. What else could it possibly be?

She pulled the lid off, carefully, and stared inside. Exactly as she'd thought. A handful of baby photos, a tiny teddy bear, and a blurry, monochrome scan. She'd even been right about the lock of hair – a bright curl of blonde, tied up in a blue ribbon.

She bit her lip and picked up the scan. A tiny scrap of a thing, a curled-up ghost. It was hard to hate a baby. No matter what.

She was still sitting, holding the scan in her hand like it was something alive, when her mother walked in. Alison didn't say anything, but Jenny could sense her. She could quite often, now. You didn't really need to get on with someone to know them better than anyone else in the world.

'This isn't Alex,' she said. She'd read the date of the scan again, and then again. The third of February 1985.

Alison sat on the bed and seemed to sink down much more than normal, like she was heavier than she'd been the day before.

'It's not Alex, no.'

The box was between them now, sitting on the bed, so neat, so messy.

'It's not me either. It's not 1986. For both of us, it should be 1986.'

Alison reached into the box and picked up the little teddy bear. She stroked its white fur with one finger and placed it carefully back.

'No. It's not you.'

Jenny followed her lead and replaced the scan. She placed it on top of a photo of her mother holding a tiny baby and beaming out at the camera as if she was about to burst.

'What happened?'

Alison took a deep, juddering breath, and met Jenny's eyes. She didn't do that a lot. Jenny was always surprised to remember they were exactly the same shade of blue as her own.

'He was ten weeks old. His name was Timothy. Your big brother. We loved him so, so much.'

Jenny blinked. She looked back into the box. Just a few brittle fragments. So little, not enough to even come close to filling the box.

She'd been so sure of what she'd find.

'Timothy?' she said.

Her mother nodded, and placed her hand on the side of the box.

'We tried to get by. Get back to normal. I was pregnant with you again quite quickly. I thought that would fix things. I thought . . .'

She trailed off, and squeezed her eyes shut.

Without thinking, Jenny reached for her mother's hand, and she squeezed back. As if they'd always done that.

'It didn't fix things. Me and your dad, we just drifted further and further apart. I just kept to myself, didn't talk, didn't cry, tried not to feel anything. And he started going out more. All hours at the pub, longer than he needed to, never home . . .'

Jenny realised that she was chewing her lip. She let herself.

'Is that why you come in at night?'

Alison was still clinging on to her hand. So tight it was starting to hurt, but Jenny said nothing. It was like a deer had stepped into a clearing – she didn't want to do anything that might scare her mother away, or break the spell.

'I thought he'd slept through for the first time,' Alison said. Her eyes were unfocused, as if she was looking at something far, far away. 'I was so happy. I hadn't had more than a couple of hours' sleep in months. I was happy, before I went to check on him. Stupid, stupid . . .'

She took another suck of breath and went on.

'It was never the same after that. I was never the same. I didn't used to be like this, I swear. But that kind of loss, it just breaks you. Crumbles you. You have to rebuild yourself, and you sometimes build yourself back up wrong.'

1985. Alison would have been younger than Jenny was now, when this happened. Jenny let herself imagine it for a moment. The disbelief of it, the blank horror. Everyone's worst fear, made real.

'Oh, Mum.'

And it didn't erase it, but it did make it better, somehow, to know that there was a reason. It wasn't just that she was unloveable. It wasn't her fault. And as if her mother knew what she was thinking, she focused on Jenny and gave her a sad little smile.

'I'm sorry, love.'

And it was enough.

'Me too,' she said.

And Jenny put her arm around her mother and neither of them flinched away. They just sat, leaning against each other, comfortably quiet at last.

Alex breathed in the smell of the sea and looked out along the horizon. There was another storm rolling in – clouds like bruises were advancing on the village. It wasn't quite raining yet, the sky pregnant with the promise of the water yet to fall. The air tasted of ozone and threat.

Barney nosed at her ankle and Alex scooped him onto her lap, grateful for the excuse. She had never, and would never, let on that she was afraid of thunderstorms. When she and her mother had first moved to the caravan park, every time there'd been a storm, Alex had hidden under her bed sheets, trembling and feeling tiny and powerless against the relentless swell and howl and smash of the weather. And it seemed as if the storms came all the time. By then, she was six, and already more than old enough to know not to go to her mother with these fears. The summer they'd moved out of their flat down in the village centre and up to the caravan had been the summer that Alex's mum had been always, always angry. She'd flipped overnight from being a quiet, mousey little woman who Alex always felt she had to protect to being someone who was constantly looking for a fight. Alex tried to be good, but she didn't seem to have the knack for it, so most of the time she just tried to be out of the way.

But, one night, Alex's mum came to check on her during a storm. She'd been drinking, and she must have been feeling sentimental. Perhaps she wanted to watch her sleep. She'd found her, instead, huddling under the covers, shaking and blocking the sound of the wind from her ears. Alex's mum had asked her what she was worried about and when Alex had choked out something about falling off the cliff and into the sea, her mum had just laughed. She'd said that was never going to happen to them, not ever. That their caravan was too far away from the edge, that it was safe. And Alex hadn't wanted to push the point, because already that day they'd had a fight about biscuits and another one about telly and Alex didn't want to add on a fight about falling into the sea. But she knew deep down in her heart that it wasn't true – that the caravans did fall sometimes. She'd seen them, spilling open like bin bags pecked apart by gulls, showing their insides up to you on the edge of the cliffs above. But she said nothing and told no one that she hated the storms. She just let them batter her, year on year. You can't fight with a storm. You could just fight with people. And she did.

She'd been fighting for a way out of this place since she was a little child, but she hadn't managed it yet. Maybe it was time to face up to the idea that she wasn't as smart as she thought she was – if even Jenny Fletcher could find a way out, it couldn't possibly be that hard.

The wind picked up. Alex's hair, a faded, rootsy red now, was down for once, and it whipped around her face. It was getting dangerous, up here. She should go home. She didn't. Instead, she buried her fingers into her dog's fur, feeling the warmth of him, the thud of his tiny heart against her finger-tips, every one of his delicate ribs.

Jenny was back, though. Back for lockdown, and then the whole summer, and now it was lockdown again, and if she wasn't careful, she'd never leave. Despite her degree and her job, Jenny wasn't that bright, and she didn't seem to realise that this place seeped its way into you, day by day. Reasons to stay crept up on you, like ivy or brambles, so slowly you didn't notice, but then one day you tried to stand up and you were pinned in place – as much a part of the landscape as the cliffs. She could see it happening already, to Jenny. It had happened to Alex herself fast enough.

Alex turned to look at one of her reasons. Karen's old caravan was closer to the edge than it ever had been, now. Pete and Si had been right – of course they had. Back in the nineties, it really had been a silly, childish thing to worry about. A fanciful thing to think of – it was miles away. Now it was only about three metres, and four could go in a night, if a storm was bad enough. But how could she find the time to worry about it? Even though her mother never left the place almost ever these days, relying on Alex to get her groceries. The only thing Alex wouldn't get her was the booze. So if the caravan went, her mother would be inside it.

Alex stared at the caravan, glassy-eyed. She'd told herself she'd come up here to try to convince the old woman to move. She knew she wouldn't be able to. And there was part of her that thought – so what? Let the bitch fall. She didn't care.

Karen shouldn't even be here. It wasn't residential, this park – Ted had drilled that into them often enough, all through her teens. Back then, she'd been arrogant enough not to question why he was doing them the favour – him or that bastard Pete. Was it just a part of having siblings, to fight with them for ever? She didn't see how else you could go about it. That was what family meant, wasn't it?

There was a flicker over to her left and Alex pulled Barney towards her in a tight hug. But it wasn't the start of lightning, it was just a flash of movement over on the cliff path. The dog yipped out a protest, but Alex didn't put him down. She walked over to see, even though she knew who it was. The thing about a village like Ravenspurn was that everyone knew you and you knew everyone – the village itself breathed to a rhythm that you knew so well you could predict it. You knew before it had even happened who'd say what to who, who'd have an issue, who'd have a go and who'd stew about it for months. And people knew you right back. They knew where to find you.

There was another gust of wind, heavy with the promise of rain. And Alex turned to face it, because being scared didn't get you anywhere. Emotions were only useful if something good came out of them, and it never had. Anger, you could use as fuel, but fear was a pathetic emotion – weak and useless. It was lucky it was close enough to anger that you could convert them. Energy can't be created or destroyed, can it? But you can change it, and you should.

She'd been watching the storms, all these years. Watching them getting worse, watching the sea claim the land, watching the changes speeding up. And, in the future she'd planned for herself, she wasn't just watching. She should have learned about this stuff properly, what it meant and how to help, not just been exiled to this tiny piece of land, falling into the sea in agonising slow motion. Crumbling in every way it could. The pub standing cold and empty, and the caravan park closing for longer and longer every winter, and

Ted dead. Jean, dead. Her mum shrinking in on herself so much there was barely anything left. And now she was faced with another tie to the village. She'd have to start talking to Si again, she'd have to take him back, if she wanted to keep the baby. She really wanted to keep the baby. Fuck.

It wasn't supposed to be like this.

The figure came closer. Alex stared back out to the sea. She could pretend that she hadn't been waiting for her, at least.

She looked down at Ted's old watch. It was quarter past seven. If she was honest, Alex had been expecting her sooner.

There was a shifting in the sky, something that Alex couldn't quite describe, but a feeling as familiar as her own face, or Si's. There was a subtle change in energy and the storm wasn't coming any more, it was here. It finally started to rain.

Jenny clambered her way up to the top of the cliff path, lungs on fire, and the rain lashing down on her hard and soaking. The promised storm was finally here, and the wind caught the falling water and slung it into her face. Jenny thought of London, with its tubes and Ubers and escalators. Had that ever really been her? Her life there had taken on the quality of a dream.

Alex was standing at the edge of the cliff, pretending to stare out at the clouds. She could pretend all she liked. Jenny had caught her giving her sly little looks, watching her come over in spite of herself, fussing over the dog to pretend she wasn't watching. But she was fooling no one. The idea gave Jenny a sharp spark of satisfaction. At least she could get under Alex's skin, the same as Alex could get under hers. If she couldn't build herself back up, at least she could drag someone else down.

There didn't seem a lot of point in messing about.

'Where did you get the watch?'

Alex stared placidly out to sea. She didn't seem to be reacting at all. Jenny wanted to shake her, to punch her – anything to get a reaction. Why was she so calm? Was Jenny the only one who was aware that things were worth getting fucking upset about yet?

'I don't know what you're talking about.'

Jenny felt her face get hot despite the icy, pelting rain. The absolute cheek of her. And Alex had always been like this. Always pretending that she was unshockable, that she was somehow above whatever anyone else was feeling, like she was too cool to care. Well, Jenny was sick of it. She'd find a way to make her care, whether she wanted to or not.

Jenny took a step towards her, as threatening as she could manage. As she did, she stumbled slightly on the waterlogged ground. She heard her mother's voice ringing clearly in her head. *Get back from that edge, you'll fall, it's more dangerous when it's been raining.* Yeah, yeah.

She fixed Alex with a hard stare. After all this time, Alex still thought she could just fuck with her, whenever she wanted. Well, she couldn't. Jenny wouldn't let her.

Jenny stood, mouth open, staring down at her. The rain lashed at them, so thick that you could barely see the village below, could barely see the crumbling front of the old hotel, could certainly not see the bottom of the cliff. All she could see was Alex.

'Did you steal it? Is that it? Like you stole my necklace?'

Alex looked surprised for a second, as if she hadn't expected Jenny to notice, or remember. But, of course, Alex had always thought that Jenny was stupid.

'I didn't steal the watch,' she said.

'Fucking tell me.'

Alex smiled at her, a grim little smile. She wrapped her arms tight around herself. An armour. A hug. 'Are you sure?'

And the two of them looked at each other, and for a moment Jenny really wasn't sure. Alex didn't look malicious, or angry. She wasn't full of that glee she always had as a teenager when she saw something and she knew just the way to bust it open, to cause a scene. She looked thoughtful. And sad.

'I want to know the truth.'

Alex laughed into the wind. 'Do you? Because I fucking didn't.'

And Jenny felt as if she wasn't sure where the conversation was going any more. As if a piece of the ground beneath her had fallen away.

'What do you mean?'

And Alex stared at her, steady. Seemingly calm. But you couldn't trust Alex to stay calm. That was one of the first things Jenny had learned about her.

'I didn't want to know. About you and Si.'

Jenny felt a drop in the pit of her stomach. Not that she should have been surprised. Everyone knows everything about everyone in this village, don't they? Or they come to, sooner or later.

'I . . .'

But Jenny let the sentence trail off. She wasn't sure what to say.

Alex didn't seem to mind. She seemed happier to be talking.

'You what? You couldn't stand for me to have something of my own? You had to take it?'

Jenny felt her cheeks blaze.

'I didn't! I pushed him away!'

Alex took a deep breath and put the dog down. He whimpered, wanting to be back with her.

'That doesn't make it better, it makes it worse!'

Jenny shoved a handful of wind-whipped hair out of her face and went closer. She still had to almost shout to be heard.

'Look, I'm sorry, okay?'

Alex looked away from her and scowled back out over the sea. The waves looked angry too. Like Alex, they often were.

'You're not. Don't lie.'

Jenny took in a deep breath. It was hard to argue against someone who knew you almost as well as you knew yourself.

'I'm sorry I didn't just tell you.'

Alex barked out a laugh. It was almost immediately snatched away again by the wind.

'Don't fucking apologise for that. I told you. I'd have been happier not knowing. So think about it. Do you want to know?'

Jenny looked at her, rain-lashed and wild-eyed, and she knew that Alex was right. But she had to know anyway.

'Where did you get the fucking watch?'

'Well, you're meant to be the clever one. What do you think?'

Jenny had half expected her to lie about it. To try to, at least. But as she glared up at Alex, she looked for all the world like she was the one who'd been wronged, like she was the one who was owed answers. There wasn't a hint of deceit anywhere in her face.

And Jenny's mouth dropped open. She tasted rain, with a hint of sea. Suddenly, all the certainty had drained out of her. She didn't really think that Alex and her dad had been sleeping with each other. She knew that, deep in her bones. He wouldn't.

'I don't know.'

Alex was still pulling that face, like she was the one who was owed the confrontation, like she was the one who was putting something to rest. No matter what was going on, Alex had always thought that she was the main character in whatever story was going on around her.

'Don't you think it's weird that I never tried to find out who my dad was, when I was a kid?'

Jenny pushed her hair and a fistful of rain out of her face. For a moment, all she could do was blink at Alex.

'What?'

But she knew what she meant. Of course. She wasn't as dim as Alex thought. She never had been.

Alex gestured over the edge of the cliff, to the village below. The drop looked even higher in the gloom of the storm. 'It's a small enough village, Jenny. And you know my mum never leaves. So who do you think my dad is then? Huh? Is it Bill? Is it Kev? Is it that old fucking pervert Pete? Who do you think? There's only so many people it could be.'

She took a kick at a stone and Jenny watched as it plunged into nothingness below; she felt a swirl of vertigo shifting inside her stomach. It was more dangerous when it had been raining. It was more dangerous when you were close to the edge.

'I don't know what you're talking about,' Jenny said, lying, trying hard to make it true.

Alex had to shout to make herself heard over the sound of the wind.

'I think most people would have asked a few more questions. Had a bit of a nose around. But I thought I was too clever for all of that. I thought I already had the answer, and I didn't like it. I really did think it was Pete.'

'Stop it,' Jenny said, and her voice sounded small and tight even to her own ears. 'Just stop it.'

Alex's eyes glimmered with triumph and hate. Her face glistened with rain, and in the half-light of the storm, she almost seemed to shine.

'But it was obvious, wasn't it? The only person in this shithole who ever really looked out for me. How could it possibly have been anyone else?'

Jenny thought of her mum. No one can be happy all the time. And you don't have to keep hold of the scans, do you? It's not compulsory.

A dull thunk of realisation settled within her. Alex was right. It felt as if it had dislodged some other part of her. Some part she might need. Jenny stared out at where she knew the sea would be, if it wasn't cloaked in the rain.

'How long have you known?'

Alex stared out across the cut of the cliff, the roaring waves, the heavy mass of grey above them both.

'Mum told me when I was eighteen.'

Jenny couldn't help, despite everything she knew, feeling betrayed again.

'What, the summer you and me were friends?'

And up until that moment, Alex had been eerily calm. Just them and the rain and the waves, but at that question, she flared up, like a siren clicking on. Her fists clenched and her jaw jutted and her mouth was pinched into a tight white line. She'd always been like that. Volatile, is what they'd say at school. It was easy enough to learn to live with – you just left her for ten minutes and she'd always simmer down in the end. Jenny wasn't like that, herself. She got angry like she was boiling a cauldron of water. Nothing seemed to happen for ages and ages, but then, all at once, there was a huge boiling pot and no way to cool it down fast. Alex clicked on and off like a light switch – everybody knew about it. No one really thought of Jenny as getting angry, because they'd only ever seen her at a simmer and they just hadn't looked hard enough to see the bubbles break. But it was still there.

Alex got up from the bench and faced her, scowling, nose to nose.

'Were we friends that summer, though, Jenny? After all that time, all those years of hating each other. I thought we were friends. That's why I didn't tell you. I didn't want to fuck everything up for you. But then you left and you never got in touch again, so were we friends?'

So close now that Jenny could smell her. Cheap perfume and chewing gum. Same as ever.

'I never hated you.'

Alex shot her a contemptuous look.

'Fuck off.'

'I never.'

And she meant it.

Alex kicked at a clod of earth, which tumbled off the cliff, taking more mud with it as it went. Jenny hadn't noticed before, but Alex still wore clunky black low heels – exactly the same type of shoes she'd worn at school. Maybe even the same shoes. She'd been too out of it to notice at the time, but she was almost sure that she'd worn her old school skirt for her dad's funeral.

Jenny tried to swallow, but it was as if her throat didn't work properly.

'You're lying.'

Alex tossed her head. Her hair, caught by the wind, flew out like a flag behind her.

'Come on. You know me, Jenny Fletcher, whether you like it or not. You know you can tell when I'm lying. And like I said. It's obvious.'

Jenny stared blankly out at the waves, climbing higher and higher, throwing themselves against the side of the cliff.

She really could tell when Alex was lying. She knew her better than anyone.

Alex went on. 'It wasn't just biology, though. Ted loved me more than he loved you. He came to, in the end. I was the one who stayed.'

The wind howled and the rain pelted and Jenny almost wished for lightning to strike the skeleton of the old hotel beside them.

'Shut up,' she said. Her fists were clenched and her blood was pounding in her ears and she couldn't think. Couldn't think.

'And, after all, I was his daughter. I was his, just as much as you were. And he was mine.'

And at that, something inside Jenny snapped. A little ping, and she was somewhere else – someone else. The part of her that kept control, the reasonable part – it was as if it had dropped away.

'He's not yours! He was never yours!'

It was as if she didn't have control of her own arms. As if some other force had taken her over and all she could do was watch as she reached out and shoved.

It was only a little stumble. Barely any distance at all. But as Alex stepped back and the rain lashed down on her and on Jenny as well, her weight hit the fudge-cake clay of the edge of the cliff and it was as if the ground was swallowing her up.

Jenny watched as Alex stepped back again, trying to get her balance, and more and more of the cliff face fell. Jenny scampered back, horrified, scrabbling her feet along the ground and landing hard on the wet mud of the ground. As she watched Alex teeter on the edge, she could see, as clear as anything, her broken body lying on the beach below, smashed open, insides on display, like a caravan.

It could happen. No one would ever know why. And didn't people say that it was going to happen, all the time?

It would be easy, to just let her fall.

'No!'

Jenny flung herself forward, arms grabbing for Alex's, fingers digging in, scrabble of nails and scream of muscles as she clutched and pulled and Alex's fall was stopped.

The two women lay in the mud, hearts beating and breaths heavy in a puddle of limbs, until one of them, or both of them, started the crawl back to solid ground. Barney whined above them, darting his tongue out to lick Alex's face, the sharp animal scent of him mixing with the ozone in the air.

When they were safe, it was Alex who spoke first.

'You've got to get out of here.'

Jenny heaved a deep sigh. Of course she did. That had been true for months and months. This place was no good for her. But where would be? Wherever she was, she'd have to take herself with her, and the scratch and itch of the thoughts she always carried, circling around and around and around.

'Sure. You too.'

Alex shrugged and pulled a face. Jenny wondered if there ever would be, or every had been, a time when Alex wasn't hiding something from her. But Jenny didn't push it. Maybe not every secret needs to be shared.

Alex said, 'I didn't think you were going to pull me back up.'

And Jenny wrapped her soaking arms around her sodden knees.

'No. Neither did I.'

Alex took a shaky breath, and then another.

'You should book a train. You need to get out by tomorrow.'

Jenny looked at her. It was as if something bad and tight had fallen of the cliff, or perhaps been blown away.

'What will you do?'

She'd always liked storms. The way they washed everything clean.

'I'll manage.'

And in the end, Jenny barely thought about it. She slung an arm around Alex's shoulders and didn't look at her face and didn't let herself be put off. She squeezed tight.

'Let me know if you need anything. We look after our own.'

Alex took off her coat and wrapped it around Barney. He was shaking, his little limbs trembling. The wind whipped her arms, but Alex didn't care. The cold helped with the nausea anyway. It had suddenly kicked in, and for the last two days it had been like she was battling through the fug of a hangover, but it never lifted.

'You got a fag?' Jenny asked.

Alex raised her eyebrows at her. 'Jenny Fletcher. I'm surprised at you.'

Jenny rolled her eyes and Alex grinned. The simple pleasure of taking the piss out of a friend. How long had it been, since she'd felt like she'd had a friend.

'Have you, though?'

Alex tried not to wince at the idea. That was one difference between what was going on and a hangover. When she was hungover, a fag was always part of the cure, along with a banana and a can of full-fat Coke. But the idea of a fag was disgusting now. She wouldn't want to smoke even if it wasn't for the little life inside of her, the idea of its pink, innocent little lungs.

'Nah. I quit.'

Which was stupid, she knew. They weren't proper lungs yet. But there was more to them than she'd thought. At ten weeks, the little tadpole thing inside her already felt like a person, to her.

'You started again over summer, though. I saw you smoking up here yesterday.'

'It was three days ago,' she said, and she could almost feel the prickle of interest coming off Jenny. It was like Barney when he sensed a squirrel.

'Alex?'

She was a terrier too, of course. Because that was Jenny's secret. Alex had always thought that she was a bit thick, and maybe that was true, but probably it wasn't, and it didn't matter. The reason Jenny got what she wanted was that she never, ever gave up.

Alex sighed. 'I'm pregnant.'

Jenny stared at her, smirk frozen to her face like it had forgotten what it was meant to be doing.

'Fuck.'

Alex flashed her a quick, tight smile and then stared out to the sea. The sea was always there, at least, and always the same. Stormy or calm, it's all the same water.

'Yeah.'

Jenny bit her lip. It made her look very young, doing that. Like nothing had changed.

'What are you going to do?'

Alex shrugged. There didn't seem like a lot of point in lying. She'd made up her mind, after all. Despite what she'd always thought, she'd known ever since she saw the second line.

'Keep it.'

Jenny nodded, big-eyed and solemn.

'What about Si?'

Alex thought of Si. That treacherous bastard. Her sweet, funny boy.

'Dunno.'

Jenny's eyebrow rocketed up.

'No?'

Alex shot her a quick glower. No need to look so shocked. What the fuck did she know about it?

'I need him,' Alex said, as if she was explaining things to a little kid. It wasn't like she wanted him back. She'd absolutely love to tell him where to stick it, at least for a couple of months to get her head together. But she was barely managing with him, never mind without him.

Jenny smiled, placid, like it was all simple.

'I don't think you do.'

Alex would normally have argued, but a wave of fatigue and nausea rolled over her. She sat down, heavy, on the bench, and swallowed, her throat slow and uncooperative. It really was like a hangover, this – you thought it was lessening, and then it slammed you again. Relentless.

'Hey. You okay?'

Jenny was beside her, Barney in her arms, and Alex gave her arm a grateful squeeze.

She swallowed again, and said, 'We'd best get down.'

Jenny nodded.

'You want a hand?'

Alex stroked Barney's greying muzzle.

'Yeah.'

And together they went, Jenny holding the dog, Alex slightly staggering, both of them staring down at their feet. With the rain, it was properly slippery now. It really was dangerous. Time to pay attention.

And it was just as she was thinking that that Alex heard a rumble – so faint at first that she could barely hear it above the wind, and then louder. And then, a high, sharp shriek of a seagull, and the flap of wings in her face.

'Hey ...'

The bird flew past her again, right by her head, forcing her to stop. She waved her hand in front of her face and the bird circled her and Jenny. And as it did, a waterlogged clump of earth a few feet ahead of them detached and rolled off the side of the cliff. Where they would be standing now, if it wasn't for the gull.

Alex felt a pulse of fear. She grabbed Jenny's arm.

'Get back, get away. Come on!'

The two women struggled their way inland, scrambling up the scrubby grass, hurrying from the edge. Alex kept going, pulling Jenny behind her. Ten metres. That was what they needed to be safe.

She let herself shudder to a stop at the top of a grassy little hillock and turned back. It seemed like that was all that the storm had taken – that one clump. Alex rested a hand on her abdomen, fighting not to scream or cry or vomit or collapse.

There was another shriek from the gull and another rumble from the ground and a sickening, groaning creak of wood, and Alex turned to stare in horror at her mother's caravan. It was the only one near the edge now, the rest arranged in a tight grid towards the other end of the field. As Alex watched, a clump, and then another, fell from under the far end of the caravan, leaving the last foot of it sticking out into the sky.

'Mum,' Alex wailed, and took two heavy, running steps forward, before Jenny reached out her wiry arms. Shockingly strong.

'No. Not you. Let me.'

And Alex felt a wriggle deep within her, although she must be imagining it, it was early, far too early, and Jenny thrust the bundle of coat and dog at Alex and set off at a sprint towards the caravan, towards the cliff that was disintegrating, nightmarish.

'Help her!' Alex called, and she watched, helpless and still, as Jenny ran.

The rumbling got louder as another chunk, and then another, and then what looked like a whole boulder, fell out from beneath the caravan's flimsy wooden base.

'Mum. Mummy. Mum . . .'

But all Alex could do was whimper, and stand, as if she was pinned in place, arms full of old dog and a new life flickering inside her, and dizzy with the adrenaline and fear.

The rumbling deepened even further and she was sure that she saw the caravan starting to tilt.

'Jenny!'

And Alex wasn't sure what she was going to say. Whether it was an encouragement or if she was warning her off. But it didn't seem to matter. As Jenny ran towards the door of the caravan, the tilting became unmistakeable, and then pronounced, and then the caravan seemed to hover at an impossible angle before it slid, slowly at first and then faster and faster, over the edge.

'No!'

Alex watched as her mother's caravan, with her mother in it, surely – she was always in it – finally lost its purchase completely and tumbled to the rocks below. And Jenny, brave Jenny, screamed and threw herself at the caravan, reaching out, as if she could grasp an edge of it perhaps, as if she could pull it back. But no one could and nothing could and there was nothing, absolutely nothing, to be done.

Alex felt herself sinking to the floor and she and the seagull screamed and screamed and screamed.

For what seemed like a hundred years, Jenny stood, staring down at the wreck of the caravan and Alex slumped, staring at her, and it was as if time was frozen.

Eventually, Jenny turned and ran back over, head bent against the rain.

When she got to Alex, Jenny was gasping and crying, the kind of panicked air gulps that kids do.

'I'm sorry, I'm sorry I couldn't, I'm so sorry . . .'

But Alex couldn't speak. Clinging to the dog, she forced herself to stand, and to walk over to the edge, and look down.

She wasn't sure what she'd been expecting, but she could see the smashed-up wreck of the caravan, twisted metal and fractured wood, something no one could ever hope to survive. And she could see, caught on a jutting rock halfway down the cliff, a scrap of pink fabric. Her mother's pyjamas, or rather Alex's old pyjamas, taken over by Karen many years ago. Her favourites. She couldn't see her mother.

Alex gasped out a sob and let Jenny pull her back from the edge. In her other hand, she had her phone. Alex thought, ridiculously, that she was lucky. It was the only place in Ravenspurn where a mobile would work.

'We should call . . . I'll call an ambulance. I'll . . . Hello?'

But Alex let herself sink back down to the wet and muddy but, for now, solid ground. She stroked the dog and stared out to sea as Jenny cried and gasped out instructions and the rain lessened and the storm rolled its way over them and out to sea.

Alex already knew that it was too late.

SOLUTION

Summer 2021

The vicar finally rustled his papers and stopped speaking and baby Edie wriggled, sweaty against Alex's chest in the carrier, but quiet – thank you, baby – and Alex closed her eyes and kissed her daughter on her soft downy head and finally, finally, it was done.

No coffin, of course. It'd been nine months. Just a ceremony from a religion Karen hadn't and Alex didn't believe in, and a party, which they both understood, at least.

She'd done what she could.

'You okay?' Jenny said, and Alex nodded, and all things considered it was even true. 'All right. Time to go.'

Jenny and Ben were with her at the front of the church, which was what Alex had asked for. There'd been a bit of a WhatsApp stand-off, Alex sending her snatched voice notes when Edie was in her bouncer, Jenny replying, always after 8 p.m., with long, considered paragraphs. But there was no need for the fuss. Jenny was the closest thing to family that Alex had left. Yes, Karen had hated her. She'd hated everyone, though.

The four of them filed along the pew and went to stand by the door. This was the bit Jenny was most bothered about. She'd said it was weird, Ben being on the receiving line, what with him never having actually met Karen. But if someone's living with your sister, especially if they moved out of London for the first time ever to do it, then that's a big deal and it basically makes them family, as far as Alex was concerned.

'Here?'

Jenny had been pretty flippant about Ben moving to York, but Alex was sympathetic. She knew what it was like to live in one place for your whole life and finally move out in your thirties. It was scary to start again.

'Here.'

Trust Jenny to end up in the poshest place in Yorkshire, though.

'All right,' said Si. There were only a handful of people, but he'd obviously rushed up to be first. Si was still trying hard, texting about the baby, driving over to her new place in Hull twice a week to see her, taking Barney for those first six impossible weeks. He was always well chuffed when Edie did a poo so he could show how cool he was with changing it.

'You want me to take Edie while you do this?'

And it was nice, and he was welcome. Si'd always wanted kids. And he was doing better than she'd have thought.

'Nah. She's asleep. Cheers, though.'

Si nodded, and reached out a hand to stroke their baby, gently, on the face. Alex swallowed down a lump in her throat. She'd made the right choice. She knew she had.

'Sorry about your mum, Alex.'

Chris was there as well, of course. People were hard on Chris, but she'd known he'd come. He was good at showing a bit of respect, strange as it seemed. And up until Si finally learned to drive, Chris had taken her to all her hospital appointments and sat in the cab waiting for her and never taken any money for it, even though it was a good three hours of lost wages for him.

'Cheers, mate.'

But not Debbie. She'd died during lockdown too. She'd got to see the twins again at Christmas, but she hadn't made it to meet Edie. She'd known, though. Alex had gone over for Christmas too, to tell her in person. The only day it'd been allowed. She'd been absolutely made up about the idea, like Alex knew she would be.

'All right, Jenny. Ben.'

And Chris shuffled away. Ridiculous, these receiving lines. Like he wasn't going to see her again for months, when they both knew they'd be drinking pints together within half an hour at the wake.

Well. Half-pints. She was still breastfeeding.

'Nice to say goodbye to her,' Pete said. He was next in line. 'Finally. Bloody pandemic.'

Alex nodded in an approximation of politeness. At least he'd bothered putting on a suit this time, unlike for his own brother. Alex had had to accept a plain black dress off Jenny's credit card this time around – her school skirt didn't have a hope of doing up now.

'Look, lass, I'm sorry. I'm really sorry. All right?'

And he looked devastated.

And maybe it was the hormones, but Alex felt like letting him off. Just this once.

'It wasn't your fault, Pete. She wouldn't move. I know you tried.'

He stared right into her eyes and she looked back and, like he always did when he wasn't sneering or shouting, he looked just like Ted. For a moment, it felt like having him back.

Pete leaned forward, voice low and eyes soft and brown like hers.

'Sorry for all of it, yeah? I should have looked out for you better. I was trying. I just kept fucking it up.'

Alex swallowed and held on to the soft, tiny feet of her daughter, and found it within herself to say, 'Right.'

And that was all he got. And that was more than fair.

It didn't take long to see the rest of the guests. The village was slightly smaller, again, than it was before, and getting smaller all the time. Because who'd move to a place like this, that was out to kill you and all there was was gulls and sea and the people who'd known you for ever?

Jenny took a deep breath in and gazed around the church.

'Are we going, then?'

Alex looked around as well. It was empty, back to its default state of abandonment between funerals. There weren't marriages or christenings in Ravenspurn any more.

'Yep. That's it.'

The four of them walked over to the pub in silence. Alex glanced down at her chest, wanting to show Edie the sea, at least, point out the cliffs, *your Mummy used to live way up there, look,* but she was miraculously still asleep, her mouth pressed into a perfect rosebud pout. Alex leaned down for a kiss, breathing in her smell. White chocolate and Sudocrem. The best smell ever.

When she got to the pub door, she hesitated.

'Will you go in for a bit, Ben? Check if Alison needs any help with any extras. Make sure the food's all done.'

Ben snorted. 'There's no way Alison won't have done all the food. What are you talking about?'

He was right, obviously. It had been a shock that Alison had wanted to help with the funeral, but now she had there was no way she'd half arse it. It wasn't her style.

'Ben ...'

Alex glared at him, and Ben wasn't thick.

He held his hands up, mock surrender. Ben and Alison liked each other, anyway. No one really understood why. He probably liked her more than anyone who lived in the village. But then, he hadn't known her before Ted's death. She'd softened, in the last year and a bit. She always asked about the baby. She'd sent a little pink cardigan when she was born.

'Fine.'

And he walked in. It was still Jenny's pub, technically. It had been on the market for six months. It turned out that no one wanted a salt-soaked old boozer in a dying village on the edge of the world. And it was a good job, too. The caravan park had finally shut for good and there was nowhere else they could have gone.

Alex stroked the baby on the head and took a deep breath. This kind of stuff didn't come easy to her.

'I wanted to say thanks. Seriously.'

Jenny waved her hand like she was swatting a fly. 'It was no bother.'

'Bullshit,' Alex said. She knew what went into making a funeral, she remembered from Jean. Endless forms and questions and booking things and phone calls. Like having a second job, but one that made you cry every time you had to do anything. There's no way at all she'd have been able to do all of that and look after a newborn. She'd only just stopped bleeding.

Jenny shrugged. 'All right. It was. Happy to do it, though.'

It had felt important to do the funeral as soon as the restrictions lifted enough to do what Karen would have wanted. Alex needed to say goodbye. To close the chapter. It was time for something new.

'I've got something for you.'

Jenny tilted her head, eyes bright as the waves. 'Yeah?'

The sea was calm now, the wind just a gentle breeze. You'd barely know that they ever got storms, round here. But change comes, again and again. It's the only thing you can count on.

Alex reached up, arms awkward under the weight of the baby carrier, and unclipped her favourite necklace from around her neck. It was childish, perhaps, but she'd wanted to wear it for her mum's funeral. It was the nicest thing she owned. She held it out, the fat heart locket glinting on her palm in the afternoon sun.

'The watch is mine. But I shouldn't have taken this.'

Jenny reached out and took the necklace out of her hand and held it up. For a moment, Alex thought she was about to give it back, as a gift, and she couldn't stand the idea. She'd had to take so much off Jenny already. She needed her to take this.

And as if Jenny could read it on her face, she plucked up the necklace and said, 'Thanks.'

And she hung it around her own neck. It sat there, glinting in the hollow of her throat.

Alex nodded at her. Even at last.

Except they weren't. But they were uneven in such a way, tangled into and around each other, that there was no way to separate themselves any more. So they might as well accept it, and grow stronger around each other, holding each other up rather than tearing each other down.

'No bother.'

And with a yawn and a kitten-wail, Edie woke up, and Alex felt exactly the same way she did any time she woke up – annoyed her time to think, to breathe on her own was over, and like her favourite person in the world was home again. She smiled down at her and held her chubby little baby hands and walked into the pub to see the people that knew her best in the world, that she'd finally left behind.

She was where she belonged.

Acknowledgements

This is a book that was written through storms. I wish you the best in weathering yours.

Firstly my thanks go to everyone in Beverley. I wrote the first draft of this book when my dad was ill – my mornings were spent in the library he used to take me to every week as an 8 year old. I'd bash out a first draft, spend my afternoons visiting him, and then I'd read the work back over on the train home to Oxford. So many people made sure Mum and I were okay. Thank you so much. I still feel like I have a home there after nearly 20 years away.

Most especially, to Frances Moxon, Laura Minnikin, Sam Keating, Victoria Hill and Scott Wigglesworth, who've been there for the ciders and A levels and births and marriages and deaths. Thank you, my friends. The Railway is Nellies, of course. I'll try and put Spiders in the next one.

Other friends who've helped are – Daisy Johnson for keeping me steady through so many freakouts, whether literary, pregnancy, pandemic, sleep or life related. Tiffany and Richard Johnson for letting me write half the second draft in their beautiful house, while drinking their rosé (and everyone who was on that magical trip). George Lewkowicz for some crucial early plot advice and approaching 20 years of creative help, and Nikki Lewkowicz as well for feeling my triumphs and disasters with me. Kiran Milwood Hargrave and Tom de Freston for the same, and for advice and ideas bouncing. Richard Pickard for his joy and enthusiastic support. Laura Parrack for her kindness and solidarity. Jess Oliver, for answering so many messages with kindness and enthusiasm. Sam Novak-Mitchell for the writing help and for celebrating me and celebrating with me. Issy Riddy, Anna Borlase and Suzie Jackson, for making my transition from newborn life to working again much less painful and for support and friendship at the time when I needed it the most. And thank you to all the students I've taught over the last 5 years – at LCCM, Crisis and the University of Oxford. Your spark and application, creativity and talent inspired me more than I think you know.

My massive thanks to my publisher Sharmaine Lovegrove, for her belief in the book, and in me, and her honesty. It made the book much, much better. And to my agent Laetitia Rutherford as well, for her belief too, and her tenacity.

This book took a LONG time to write and went through three different editors. As well as to Sharmaine, my thanks go to Maisie Lawrence and Amy Baxter. Each of you brought a clear, compassionate and insightful perspective to the book, and I'm so grateful for the time and attention you gave to helping it grow.

To Mum and Dad, of course, of course! Thank you for being nothing like any of the fictional parents I write, and for your unwavering love and support and engagement with the subjects I write about.

To Paul, who was there through all of it. My deepest thanks for accepting me for who I was, who I am, and who I will become, and for the hours and hours of practical help so that I could write, and for being a truly equal parent with me. I wouldn't be able to write if you didn't truly share the work and the joy with me.

And lastly and always, to my lovely Rowan Edie. The later drafts were written in the haze of life with a young baby, tapping quietly at the keys while you slept on my chest, working on my phone during the night feeds. I found out I was pregnant two weeks before lockdown, which was bloody rough, but throughout a horrible, lonely and frightening time, I always had something to look forward to. You.

Bringing a book from manuscript to what you are reading is
a team effort.

Renegade Books would like to thank everyone who helped
to publish *Things We Lose in Waves* in the UK.

Editorial
Amy Mae Baxter
Alexa Allen-Batifoulier

Contracts
Anniina Vuori
Imogen Plouviez
Amy Patrick
Jemima Coley

Sales
Caitriona Row
Dominic Smith
Frances Doyle
Ginny Mašinović
Rachael Jones
Georgina Cutler
Toluwalope Ayo-Ajala

Design
Ben Prior

Production
Narges Nojoumi

Publicity
Millie Seaward

Marketing
Mia Oakley

Operations
Kellie Barnfield
Millie Gibson
Sameera Patel
Sanjeev Braich

Finance
Andrew Smith
Ellie Barry

Copy-Editor
Jade Craddock

Proofreader
David Bamford